KNIGHT IN CHARLOTTE

KNIGHT IN CHARLOTTE

EDWARD MCKEOWN

AD ASTRA BOOKS

to Laura Jean Stroupe, a dear friend, editor of this work, writer, and quite a character

CONTENTS

INTRODUCTION

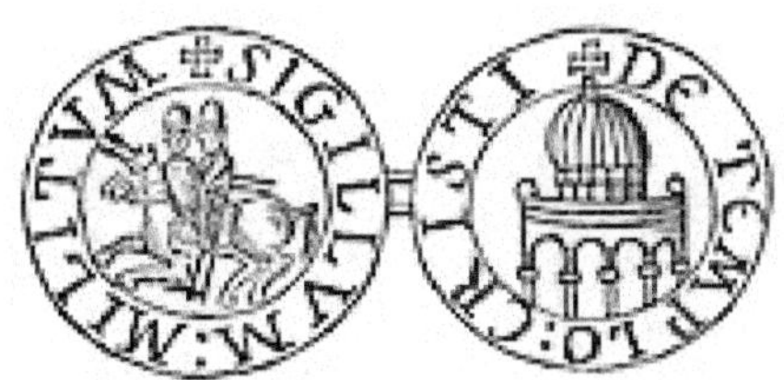

The Poor Fellow-Soldiers of Christ and of the Temple of Solomon, or as the world knows them, the Knights Templar, were the foremost of the Western Christian military orders. Endorsed by the Catholic Church around 1129, the Order became a favored charity throughout Christendom and grew rapidly. The Templar Knights formed the most skilled fighting units of the Crusades. Their white coats and red crosses struck fear in many a foe.

When the Holy Land was lost, support for the Templars faded and resentment of their financial success grew. King Philip IV of France, deeply in debt to the Order, decided to murder his bankers to avoid his debtors. He caused rumors to be spread about the Templars' secret initiation ceremonies. In 1307, Templars in France were tortured into giving false confessions and condemned to be burned at the stake.

Pope Clement V, conspired with Phillip IV and disbanded the Order in 1312. The Order disappeared, taking with it much of their wealth. Phillip and Clement died under mysterious circumstances not long after their moves against the Order. Rumors and legend persist that the Knights Templar still fight evil in the shadows.

FOREWORD

EDWARD MCKEOWN

Forewords are usually of interest to the writer's family, friends, and professional writing acquaintances. If you enjoy the book though, you may come back and want to know a bit more of what was in my mind. So here it is, and I will keep this one short. Jeremy Leclerc was my first foray into fantasy and specifically the genre of urban fiction. The inspiration for this character struck me when I was listening to Greenday's song, "Boulevard of Broken Dreams." As is so often the case for me while listening to the music, I found a movie playing in my head, just a series of images. The first image was of a young man in a long, black leather coat wandering down a darkened street. I knew somehow that under that coat was a magic sword. I knew that he walked a lonely road and that there was supernatural danger on it.

When the line "my shadow's the only one who walks beside me" came, I knew that Jeremy, as I later named him, did not walk entirely alone. It struck me then that of all the characters in fantasy, the hardest one to believe in and to write, is an angel. Why is that, I wondered? We think of them as either insipid or as all powerful, or we find the religious trappings of an "angel" troubling or confining. What's worse for a writer, how could my character then have doubts about the universe or the meaning of everything when he had a direct pipeline to God? I'm not religious, nor did I feel like trying to answer those "big questions" about "the meaning of it all." I certainly didn't think I would do as well as Kant and others in any event.

I found the answer to this writing problem easier than I expected. My angelic character, Shadowheart, does not give you answers, nor does she solve your problems for you. She's a friend, an annoying kid-sister, a deadly warrior princess, an obscure oracle, bound not to interfere with human free will. Humans are and will always be the balance between good and evil. Neither side can win us over by force majeure; it always falls to us to choose to be good or evil. Otherwise, we are mere meat-puppets, and who needs those? They probably smell bad after a few days. At the end of the day, the creatures of evil are of and in our space-time and subject to at least some of its rules. Shadowheart is not, but is bound by law to help Jeremy only so much. Only when the forces of evil cheat and break the barriers between the worlds can Shadowheart bring her full force to bear. And while she may disapprove of his taste in girlfriends, that too she just has to put up with....

All of these stories have been published and/or podcast in a variety or magazines and anthologies with one exception and are gathered here to be offered together for the first time. The new story is "Let's Go to Hell"; this story was originally intended for Janet Morris's "In Hell" series where I have had stories in *Lawyers in Hell*, *Rogues in Hell*, and the upcoming *Visionaries in Hell*. This one didn't quite fit the "In Hell" series, as it was a bit too optimistic and cheerful, I mean what the hell?

Update: Since the first edition, we have added the brand-new Jeremy Leclerc and the Chicken of Doom and one of my favorite ghost stories, "In the Mourning," written while at Orson Scott Card's Intergalactic Medicine Show. While not a Jeremy story, it did influence my thinking for the upcoming Jeremy Leclerc novel. Oni-chan.

Cheers

Edward McKeown

1

THE WHITE PASS

Jeremy Leclerc, Knight Templar, ducked behind a pillar to get away from the cold drizzle blowing into Charlotte's SouthPark Mall's parking deck. He shivered under his black leather duster but could not close it for fear of slowing the draw of his bloodsword. Nor did he want to stand in the shadows with a thirty-inch blade drawn. Security at the mall wasn't good, but the weapon reflected any glimmer of light.

"Swords, yet another way in which we have failed to enter the twenty-first century," he whispered, brushing dark-brown hair out of his eyes.

From the large, gold-encircled crystal that hung under his shirt, a sprightly female voice issued. "Complaining again? Some hardy warrior. It's just water."

"Cold water," he said. "Keep your voice down."

"Son of Adam," she said, "only you can hear me unless I will it."

"Right, and I'm the one who doesn't need to be hearing you. I'm watching for a hideous human-eating beast from the underworld. Quit distracting me."

"Distracting? More like keeping your sorry-self alive. Not all monsters are ugly bunches of muscles. This one might be gorgeous.

And we don't know that this one eats the women. They just disappear. We know nothing about what we're up against."

"My guardian angel," he muttered, "is a know-it-all pain in the ass."

"I sense something," she said, "a hint of pain and terror in the wind. I fear we are too late."

"Damn it. Which way?"

"North, by the cell phone tower."

Jeremy ran down the ramp, avoiding the video cameras that he'd earlier noted. Then he was out in the December mist, his feet splashing through shallow puddles as he raced out past the high-end restaurants, ducking behind SUVs and monstrous pickups to avoid the eyes of the miserable valets by McCormick and Schmick's. The rain and mist grew worse, curtaining him off from the mall and late holiday shoppers.

"So much for America's sunny South," he muttered, putting his right hand on the bloodsword's grip.

The darkness next to him wavered, and Shadowheart appeared. Her blond hair and blue shift did not cling, as she'd only manifested as an image. Incarnation was tricky for her in the earthly realm.

"This is no natural storm," she said. "Look, there, where the streetlights have failed."

Jeremy moved out, staring into a darkness that was more than the absence of light. Then he saw it.

It drifted forward, one with the mist, towering over the nearby cars. The creature was a pale image of a woman, with colorless hair draped down its back, wearing a flowing dress. The rags of its dress and hair tossed in the wind. A grief-ravaged face of haunting beauty seemed to focus on the horizon. It was as if the rain and mist had taken their own mournful form.

In one hand it held what looked like a bunch of blood-soaked rags. In the other, hanging loose-limbed as only the dead can was the body of a woman, well-dressed with a handbag dangling from her shoulder. Her wide, staring eyes and open mouth were stretched in horror.

"A Bain Sidhe," Jeremy snarled.

A sound reached him, a high painful sound that might have been the wind sighing but wasn't. The Bain Sidhe sang its awful song. It raised the hand holding the corpse over its head, easily fifteen feet in the air. The long bony hand opened, and the corpse flew up into the sky and vanished.

Jeremy's sword slid from its sheath as if eager. Its silver shone bravely in the low light. Jeremy rushed forward, weapon held high.

"Jeremy, you fool. No!" Shadowheart called.

The Bain Sidhe's mournful face lowered to regard him. Its eyes were huge dark pools that drew him in.

Despair shattered Jeremy. A howl of grief and pain burst from him as he stumbled to the ground, sword falling from nerveless fingers. Every loss he had ever experienced welled up fresh and painful as a new cut. The rain felt colder than the pit of Hell, and his body shivered with ague.

He managed to look up at the looming Bain Sidhe with its soulless eyes and ravaged beauty. Its wind-like song filled his ears:

> Fall to the cold ground
> Never rise again; there is no point, no hope
> Fall to the cold ground.
> Rot and be food for worms.

Jeremy could only barely draw a breath.

"Back, hellspawn," a voice cracked.

Suddenly Shadowheart stood between him and the Bain Sidhe, but she was not the slender blond teen. This Shadowheart towered over Jeremy in her black armor. Her green eyes, set in a face of heartless beauty, framed with midnight hair, blazed down at him. She turned to face the Bain Sidhe, her great black and red wings spread between him and the apparition.

"Back," Shadowheart shouted. "You will not have him."

Energy surged between angel and Bain Sidhe, causing a flickering, roiling disturbance of the soul and the very air. They extended hands toward each other, and the space between them shimmered.

But across the link that bound him to Shadowheart, Jeremy instantly knew his guardian was overmatched and losing. While her wings shielded him from the worst of the Bain Sidhe's influence, he struggled to his feet, dragging the sword up with him, its point scratching the asphalt. He staggered away, somehow managing to keep his feet under him.

Shadowheart, he sent, *run.*

Jeremy's strength returned with every yard he gained away from the creature. He paused between two cars and looked back. The Bain Sidhe was nearly invisible through its protective mist of fog and rain. It passed a streetlight, which dimmed and went out, then the creature was gone.

Jeremy heard the sound of wings over his head, and Shadowheart dropped from the sky to crouch alongside him. By the time she landed, the wings and black hair were gone and she was her smaller blond self. This time she wore a fur-trimmed leather jacket and the usual paraphernalia of a Charlotte mallrat. But when she stood, it was slowly and her speech was halting. "Jeremy, are you hurt?"

"No." Free from the Bain Sidhe's baleful presence, only his knees and hands, scraped from falling to the pavement, troubled him. "Are you all right?"

"No," she said as rain dripped off her jacket. "I am badly damaged. Jeremy, let us go into the mall and rest."

"You don't look hurt," he said, suddenly frightened.

"I had to fully manifest in this universe to fight the Bain Sidhe in this plane, and I do not feel pain as you mean it," she said, starting forward. "But I have taken injury from the beast. It is ancient and powerful, and I am limited when in the Realm of Earth."

Jeremy followed her, sliding his sword into a hidden sheath in his coat. "It will not pursue us?"

"No," she said. "Your life-energy does not interest it. This one consumes only the female."

"It doesn't want you?" he said.

She gave him a slight smile and brushed rain off her face. "My animus is female, but I am not of the race of Eve. My energy is hostile to the creature."

He walked alongside her, concerned by the unsteady gait. After a few more steps, she leaned on him. She did not feel human. Her body was light and generated no warmth, but at least no one would walk through her.

"I'm sorry," he said. "I thought…well, I guess I didn't think."

"Something new about that?" she snapped.

They reached the side door to the mall. Passersby likely took them for a couple on a date. The light of the doorway was welcome, but the tinkling Christmas music made Jeremy want to scream. Scream warnings to those walking out into the night. Shouts of his failure and his defeat.

"I am too hard on you," Shadowheart said, her voice gone gentle. "Too hard because I am afraid and hurt and because you're young and reckless. You flung yourself at a monster that even I dread, and I rebuked you. Forgive me. It's only my wounds speaking."

"What can I do?" he whispered. "How can I help?"

She pointed to an alcove in the food court. "A quiet spot, some hot chocolate from the Caribou would be nice too. It's outrageous what they charge, but what can you do?"

Jeremy left her in an alcove and hurried to buy two hot chocolates. His frantic looks back at Shadowheart seemed to charm the staff. As he grabbed the cups and headed off, he heard one girl say, "Lucky bee-yotch, I want a guy who is so eager to look after me. And he has such a cute French accent."

Shadowheart leaned back in her seat, eyes half-closed. But the sight of the chocolate made her sit up. "Ah. You know, God gave us chocolate."

Jeremy strove for lightness. "Benjamin Franklin said he gave us beer."

She rolled her eyes and lifted the chocolate. Before Jeremy could warn her of the heat, she took a healthy swig. Shadowheart quickly finished hers and gave a sigh of contentment. At her casual glance at his untouched cup, he quickly pushed it across to her. She sipped the second cup more slowly.

"Better?" he asked.

"Yes," she said. "Even talking with you is restorative. I am, after all, your guardian angel. But I am going to need to retreat to my crystal soon and for an extended period."

"My guardian angel," he repeated.

Shadowheart sighed. "This again? You have your own angel and still you do not believe. Doubting Thomas has nothing on you."

"You say you're an angel. Clearly you're supernatural, but beyond that, who knows? It's not like you'll answer my questions about God and the universe."

She sipped her chocolate. "I keep telling you that it's forbidden."

"And I keep telling you that makes no sense. What are we, God's ant farm? Is there nothing good on TV in Heaven? Why do we suffer? Why is there evil? What use am I supposed to have for a God who makes ridiculous rules?"

"I'll be sure to tell him you said so."

"Please do."

She frowned. "What is it with you and rules? Who ever heard of a Taoist Templar? Not to mention what you did with the oath of celibacy."

"I had my fingers crossed on that one, and obviously, so did my father."

"Do you forget how we met and were sealed to each other?"

"No," he said. "It was very impressive. The Templar master took me to a door in the deepest part of Roslyn Castle one morning. Yet it opened to a field under stars. What did you call it?"

"The place between the worlds."

"So how does an angel lose to a Bain Sidhe? Your power comes from beyond space-time."

"I am not here to fight your battles for you, Jeremy. If you do not have free will then you are merely a puppet. No, in the Realm of Earth, I am severely limited by design, allowed to intervene only when there is a breach of order of the universe. The Bain Sidhe is of the space-time that man was meant to inhabit. My interference by directly confronting it made me vulnerable as I was the one in violation."

He looked at her calm, gentle face. "Thank you. I'm grateful you don't always follow the rules."

"You must be rubbing off on me. I, for one, would be grateful if you could follow at least some of the rules." Suddenly she swayed and looked faint.

Jeremy grabbed her by the shoulders. "You're not going to…going to die? Are you?"

Shadowheart steadied, then looked out over the throngs of holiday shoppers with their noise and packages, the running children busily ignoring the hapless adults trying to negotiate with them about their behavior.

"I am not alive, Jeremy, and cannot die. But in this earthly realm I can dissipate to where we are parted and I am no longer me. I would pass to the hollow place where I have no purpose, no function, and no reason for being. When I am not a guardian angel, I am nothing."

Jeremy struggled to comprehend as he tore at his shirt, trying to pull out the crystal. "Then go now."

She put a calming hand on his arm, a light touch, like a bird settling. "Soon," she said. "But you must promise me not to fight the Bain Sidhe until I return."

Jeremy pressed his lips together. "That was the third woman murdered in two weeks. When will it strike again?"

Shadowheart shrugged. "It's not a natural creature. It doesn't need to eat every day. It might not kill again for a thousand years or it might kill a thousand times tonight."

"Is there something we could give it?" he asked. "Could we bargain with it?"

"No, Jeremy. It is not a personality. It has no intelligence, no self-awareness. A Bain Sidhe is more like an animated wish to kill. It's a fragment of matter from the beginning of time that has taken on this form. It exists on the borderline between life and unlife. Perhaps that is why it seems to hate and destroy the living."

"Am I to leave that horror to kill God knows how many while you recover?"

She frowned. "The Bain Sidhe is an enemy beyond us. You cannot get close enough to strike with the bloodsword. I cannot stand against it again."

He slammed a fist to the table. A group of teens at another table turned around. They met his glare and returned to their iPhones and Droids.

"What harms the thing?" he demanded.

"Iron," she said, her voice gone dull. "All things of ancient Faerie fear iron and steel." Her head nodded and then snapped up. "Jeremy, I must go. Do nothing until I return."

Suddenly he was alone in the food court.

Jeremy spent the day recovering at his apartment. Shadowheart could be felt only by her complete absence. Worry about her "health" conflicted with a relief at being free of her badgering to explain about who he was about to turn to for help.

Hell, he thought, *if she was mad about my breaking the rules before...*

He drew the bloodsword from its scabbard and knelt on the rag rug in his living room. He pressed the cold gemstone to his forehead and concentrated. After a few minutes of strain, an image resolved: a bright red mouth, sex, sharp teeth piercing flesh, blood flowing.

Near midnight Jeremy left for Charlotte's north side in his Mini Cooper, heading for the rundown Montezuma apartments. He drove into the rundown complex of 1980s-era slapped-up apartments. No one was out in the shadows of the aged buildings. Jeremy parked the small red car and waited.

She exited from a second-story apartment, presumably her latest victim's, and walked toward the outside staircase. Piled masses of dyed blond hair caught the streetlights. She wore a denim jacket over a sweater that looked like it might explode under the pressure of her bustline. Rhinestone-studded jeans and cowboy boots completed the picture.

Jeremy got out of the car and walked over to face her at the bottom of the stairs. She paused briefly on seeing him, then sauntered on, the heels of her cowboy boots tapping on the stairs.

He placed a hand on the haft of the bloodsword and looked up at her. Her pale face and luminous blue eyes regarded him over generous, bright red lips.

"Why, Jeremy Leclerc," she said in a high, country twang. "I haven't seen you since I tied you to my four-poster and had my way with you two or three times."

"Three," he said.

She smiled. "It was a good night."

"How's your latest victim, Debbie?"

"Oh, he's fine, honey. Got his feet propped up, lots of blankets. I made him drink a pint of Gatorade with some vitamins then left him on what remains of his bed with a smile on his face. I told you before. I don't have time to bury hundreds of corpses a year. I sip 'em and leave 'em happy."

"That's what I'll find if I check?"

"Knock yourself out, sweets, but I did give you my word. Speaking of which, is our truce still holding? You at least owe a girl a fair fight."

Jeremy grimaced. He'd gone hunting Debbie alone, just after arriving in Charlotte and after a major tiff with Shadowheart. He'd ambushed Debbie in her lair only to hesitate to strike the petite vampire. But Debbie hadn't hesitated, and with a strength that he hadn't anticipated in the small body, she'd wrenched the weapon from his hand and flung him on her bed. What started out as a desperate fight turned into foreplay as she played his body like she owned it. Hundreds of years had given her knowledge of anatomy that could make anyone into her bed toy.

"I promised that so long as you did not kill or turn humans, you were safe from me," he said.

"Yep, 'course I was sitting on your chest and threatening to drink you dry if you didn't."

He shrugged. "A Templar may not claim duress. His word is inviolable."

She smiled and came down the remaining stairs to take his arm. "What brings you out looking for me? If it's a party you want, it will have to be another night, I'm beat."

Jeremy couldn't help but smile at the buxom vampire. "No party. I need your help. There's a—"

"Is this a long story?" she said. "I mean, I love listening to that European accent of yours and all but..."

"Kind of."

"Good. There's an all-night diner on Central. I love their food and the chocolate shakes."

"Didn't you just eat?"

"I nourished my vampiric essence," she protested. "It hasn't done anything for my tight little tummy. And being the undead, I can eat any damn thing I want and not gain an ounce."

Jeremy drove them to the Lodestar Diner on Central. To his surprise, the old Indian gentleman on the door knew Debbie and gave her a wink. He took them to a quiet corner booth. Debbie slid in and rested her formidable breasts on the tabletop.

"Oh," she sighed. "Try carrying these things around for a couple of hundred years."

"Uh, yeah," he said, trying to keep his eyes on hers.

The waitress, a slim, pretty girl with a ponytail, walked up. "Do y'all know what you want?"

"You betcha." Debbie smiled. "A big thick steak with a pile of onion rings and a chocolate shake."

"How do you want that steak?" the waitress laughed.

"Rare," Debbie said, rolling the R's.

"Now how can you eat like that and have such a tiny waist?" the waitress asked.

Debbie batted her big blue eyes at her. "I'm on a liquid diet most of the time. But better watch out, cutie, I may take a bite out of you."

The waitress giggled and blushed.

"Coffee and a Danish," Jeremy grumbled.

The waitress walked off, with Debbie giving her a speculative look.

"Do you mind?" Jeremy said.

"Come on, Jeremy." Debbie smiled. "A girl always has to be thinking about where her next meal is coming from. I sensed her interest."

He started to speak, but she raised a hand. "No business until after dinner."

The meal came out quick and good. Jeremy watched in astonishment as Debbie ate enough dinner for two men, washing it down with chocolate shakes. Meanwhile she chatted amiably. Debbie was a good small talker, a necessary skill to lure victims.

"So," she said with a sweet smile, "now that you've given a girl her propers, what can I do for you?"

"You've heard about those women disappearing from the malls?"

"Now, Jeremy, I had nothing to do—"

"I know, I know," he interrupted. "It was a Bain Sidhe."

"A what?" She raised an eyebrow along with her shake.

"Bain Sidhe," he repeated.

She sipped and shrugged.

"An ancient spirit of death and doom that appears as the ghostly image of a woman holding bloody rags. This one was over twelve feet tall."

"You're funnin' me."

"What kind of vampire are you?" He threw up his hands.

"You think we get some sort of handbook for the undead when we turn? I mislaid my copy of *Evil for Dummies*."

"An Irish spirit of doom," he grated. "It kills women for their life force, using despair as a weapon. It almost killed me last night. My guardian angel saved me, but she was badly hurt in the process and is recovering in the overworld."

"Good." Debbie shuddered, tossing her blond hair. "Angels scare the crap out of me. Wait a minute, how does an angel lose against anything?"

"Shadowheart can only intervene with her true power if some rule, which only she seems to know, is broken. When she saved me, she broke the rules and became vulnerable. She was nearly destroyed."

"Too bad, so sad," Debbie said.

"Be serious for a minute." Jeremy leaned forward. "I need someone to act as bait for me while I find a way to kill it. You're the only powerful supernatural creature around here not likely to try and kill me. So, I've come to you."

"And I do this, why?" she said, resting her chin in her hands.

"Money?" he asked.

She shook her head.

"Because it's the right thing to do?"

It took a full minute for her to stop laughing. "Jeremy, you kill me, sweetie. Oh, that was a good one."

"What do you want, Debbie?"

"I've got truce with you," she said. "I figured it would be useful to have a good guy who owed me a favor. But I can't screw every Templar or other good guy into submission… Well, I could, but it would take a lot of time, and I might get unlucky and run into a gay one."

"There are no gay Templars," he said, "or so they try to tell me."

"Yeah, right. Don't ask, don't tell. Sure. Anyway, what I want is the same deal with all the forces of light. I don't kill or turn humans and no one hunts me."

"A *White Pass*," Jeremy murmured. "There have only been three of those given in the last five-hundred years."

"Start a trend," she said.

Jeremy considered. Having spared Debbie, or truth be told, been spared by her, he'd studied all he could find on her. There was no record of Debbie killing anyone, besides a serial rapist in the 1960s, since the Civil War.

"There are dead that you slew after you first turned," he said slowly.

She nodded. "I had a few bad years with that bastard, Ben Carrier, after he turned me. Don't expect you to understand, or forgive, but I was dying of yellow fever in a Charleston whorehouse when Ben took me. I wanted revenge on the world for a while. Realized after a bit that all I was doing was making more of the same misery. I stopped."

"What happened to Carrier?"

"I cut off his head and shat down his neck."

"I thought the expression was 'ripped off his head.'"

"He was strong." For a second, Debbie's facade of youth and good humor cracked. Jeremy was looking at something older and more dangerous. It was his turn to shudder.

Perhaps, he thought, *Debbie was as much sinned against as sinning.* She was nothing like the vampires he'd trained to fight, being a creature more of dark sex than of death. His choice was to insist on retribution for ancient past sins or prevent present and future deaths.

Debbie got coffee and had the waitress drop the bill on him while he thought. She looked out the window as traffic whipped by on Central Avenue. A horn sang in the distance.

"Very well," he said. "As a Templar, I can speak for the Master. He speaks for all forces of light. Do you understand Latin?"

"My best foreign languages are Spanish, Japanese, and Yankee."

"I'll translate the ritual. We'll have to go to a church."

"Save your ritual, Jeremy, and I can't set foot in a church. Do we have a deal?"

"I so bind the order and all forces of light," he said, "on pain of death and excommunication. I extend the White Pass to Debbie Middleton on behalf of the Knights Templar. The pass will be recorded in every database, in the stone tablets of Joseph, and you will receive the traditional sheepskin and the ring of peace. The ring's aura will warn any soldier of light that you are protected."

"Great," she said, twinkling her fingers. "I love bling."

"Right," he said. "Here's the plan. We'll meet at eleven tonight by the Symphony Bandshell. The mall is open late again..."

Jeremy and Debbie sat in a truck cabin in the outskirts of SouthPark Mall where the bloodsword had told him to expect the Bain Sidhe.

"You didn't mention anything about a stolen truck," she said.

"You didn't steal it; I did." He shifted in discomfort. Mindful of what Shadowheart had said about the Bain Sidhe fearing iron, he wore a chainmail coat under his Kevlar.

"And a leaf-sucking truck at that? What are we going to do, clean up Myers Park lawns?"

"Shut up and duck," he said, grabbing her and pressing her down in the seat. A CMPD cruiser went by, its searchlight playing briefly over their truck as it scanned the distant reaches of the parking lots.

Debbie turned from where her head lay in his lap. "Did you want me to do something as long as I'm down here?"

Jeremy sighed. "The bloodsword has never been wrong before."

"It's been hours, Jeremy."

The windshield began to glisten with mist, then a fine rain started.

"Good sign," he said, starting the truck's motor.

"Says you." Debbie peered out the side window.

"Time for you to get out there."

Debbie opened the door and climbed down, then looked back at him. "Now, Jeremy, honey, you are going to back me up? Right?"

"Jesus Fucking Christ," he said. "How many oaths do I have to make to you?"

She grimaced. "Vampire whores have trust issues. And don't swear."

"I will be there. My word to God."

"Didn't I hear something about you being a Taoist?"

"Debbie!"

"All right. Keep your shorts on." She strode off into the gloom and mist, which thickened by the second. He could barely see the glimmer of her blond hair.

Jeremy got out the other side, drawing his bloodsword and adjusting the controls on the side of the vacuum truck. Then he slid under the huge metal drum of the dieseling truck as far back as he could and tried to be invisible. He couldn't see Debbie anymore but comforted himself with the knowledge that she had better night vision than he did.

A shriek split the air. Debbie came flying out of the darkness, her cowboy boots clacking like mad on the asphalt. For a busty woman, she was really making speed. "Jeremmmmeeeeeee!!!!!"

On her heels came the Bain Sidhe. It wailed its wordless song of misery and death. But Debbie wasn't listening. She plunged past Jeremy, still screaming. Behind her, the Bain Sidhe, perhaps puzzled by Debbie's failure to succumb to its song, reached out a long bony hand.

As it strode past Jeremy, he plunged out from under the truck, striking a backhand cut. The enchanted sword cut through the Bain Sidhe's mist-like body without resistance, but its effect was immediate. The Bain Sidhe howled in pain and bent double. Before Jeremy could cut again, its ghostly claws struck him. His Kevlar split under the Bain Sidhe's attack, but its hands rebounded from the chainmail beneath. Still its mad eyes bore into him, chilling his soul, emptying his mind of purpose and his body of warmth. With his last fading rags of energy and will, he stabbed with the bloodsword in his right hand and thrust the nozzle of the leaf-sucker with his left, pulling its pistol grip trigger. He heard the roar of the engine, then fell into darkness.

The world came back slowly, first with the sense of water falling on him and penetrating his clothes, then the sound of the truck and its roaring vacuum. He opened his eyes to look up into Debbie's luminous ones. He lay in her arms, his head pillowed on her large, very soft breasts.

Right, he thought muzzily, they're real.

"Did I get it?" he asked.

"Yeah," she said. "It disappeared up the nozzle and into the truck, but I don't think it's dead. I can still hear it." She shivered.

He painfully craned his head around to look at the truck. The huge steel drum had evidently contained enough of the property of iron to keep the Bain Sidhe contained.

Jeremy groaned as she helped him to his feet. He felt a little woozy and reached up to his neck, finding some waterproof Band-Aids. He glared at her. "Debbie!"

"Oh, come on," she pouted. "It was just a nip and a sip. You lose more when you cut yourself shaving."

"Take my car," he said, handing her the keys. "Follow me."

They pulled out of SouthPark and headed up Sharon Road to Independence Boulevard then East on Highway 74. A half-hour and a countryside road took them behind Bubba's Auto Salvage yard. Jeremy cut the chain on the fence and they both drove in, heading for the auto crusher.

As he pulled up and got out of the truck, Debbie parked next to them. Jeremy hopped out and looked up at the huge machine. *Impact Five*, it said on the side. It was an orange metal box with enormous pistons, used to flatten cars.

Growls sounded behind him. Jeremy spun, his hand reaching for the sword. Three huge Rottweilers and a Doberman faced him. As they started to rush, Debbie jumped in front of Jeremy and drew herself up to her full five-foot, three-inches and hissed. The dogs stopped so fast that one somersaulted. Then all four fled yelping into the darkness.

Debbie gave him a smug look. "Dogs are terrified of the undead. It's in *Evil for Dummies*, Chapter Four. You oughta get yourself a copy."

Jeremy hopped back into the truck and maneuvered it into the massive crusher. The whole machine wouldn't fit, so he backed the metal cylinder in. He leaned out to call to her. "Debbie, start her up."

"Oh hell," she said. "Now he thinks I'm a damn mechanic. Let me throw some switches."

As Jeremy turned off the truck, a gray mist emerged from the dashboard vents, manifesting as ghostly claws. Somehow the Bain Sidhe had found at least a partial outlet.

"Debbie," he shouted, as the claws struck. There wasn't enough room to pull his sword, but even half drawn, it cut the ghostly hands reaching for his throat.

"No use yelling at me," she shouted back. "I'm going as fast as I can."

"Now!" he yelled again. The claws struck, and his arm went numb. He switched hands and whipped the sword around in its sheath. One claw dissipated. The other struck, and his left leg went numb.

With a sound like an old Star Trek phaser, the *Impact 5* came to life. Massive jaws pinched down on the back of the truck, drawing it in and crushing it. The Bain Sidhe gave a dreadful howl from its imprisoning cylinder as metal was driven into it. Its final shriek of agony and despair almost made Jeremy pity it. The machine cycled, dragging more of the truck into it, with Jeremy still in the cab. The roof over his head started to buckle. Jeremy struggled, but his half-frozen body betrayed him. The door hung in its bent casing, holding him in.

"Debbie," he screamed. He let the sword slip back into its sheath and threw his shoulder at the door.

Debbie leapt to the truck's runner, wrenching the door off the frame with inhuman strength. Grabbing his arm in a way that made him glad it was numb, she yanked him out of the cab. They thumped onto the oil-soaked ground. Diesel fuel spilled out of the ruptured tanks, and the truck burst into flames. Debbie threw him up on her shoulders, and they sprinted for his Mini.

By the time they reached the car, Jeremy's body again responded to his demands, though his arm felt like it had been pulled from its socket. They jumped into the Mini and roared out of Bubba's.

An hour later, Jeremy let Debbie out by her pink VW Bug.

She smiled. "You sure know how to show a girl a good time."

"Thanks," he managed.

"Just let me know when my White Pass is ready. I'm looking forward to getting my new ring."

"I'll call the Grandmaster and have it FedExed." Jeremy drew a breath. "I owe you."

She looked at him, her smile fading. "Jeremy, honey, I like you, so I'll tell you a couple of things. Don't get too fond of me. I ain't good for you, or anyone living. You are a little too trusting and way too naïve. Try not to get killed."

"Deal. Sunrise soon. Better get underground."

She shook her head and sashayed off toward her car.

Jeremy drove home, staggering up the thirty-six steps to his top floor apartment. He gratefully made it to his bedroom, collapsing across the bedspread, fully dressed, too hurt and miserable to draw the curtains. He stared at the rising sun.

Suddenly Shadowheart stood in the room. Sunshine streamed through her simple blue shift and her golden hair made banners on the wall. She vibrated with health and energy. "I'm back," she sang, spreading her arms, "restored and returned." She danced her little joyous dance to greet the sunrise, smiling beatifically at all God's creation. Then she turned to Jeremy, who lay unmoving on the bed, glaring at her from one open eye and stinking of oil and smoke.

"You look like crap," she said.

The End

2

KUDZU JESUS

Samantha Jean Pelton looked up at the telephone pole in disbelief, brushing golden brown hair out of her face with a frown. "Rub, you dumb ass. You dragged me out here at nine in the evening to see this?" She folded her arms and glared up at the lean, cigarette-wasted man in his fifties, his faded blue shirt tucked into worn jeans. In the distance a car drove by; its lights briefly illuminated the empty parking lot and the woods beyond. Crickets chirped. Overhead, a few bats swooped past the lone sodium light hanging off the abandoned factory building.

Ronald "Rub" Finger shook his head. "'There are none so blind as those who will not see.' Open your heathen eyes, girl, and see our Lord."

"Oh, for crying out loud, Rub. It's a bunch of foliage hung on a pole and some wires."

"In the shape," Rub said with some heat, "of our Lord on his cross. Look girl, look." He gestured upward. "See the head, the spread of the arms and the feet, as if nailed. It's a sign. A manifestation of the divine, right here in Dallas, North Carolina."

"Oh, Rub," Samantha laughed. "Jesus come to Dallas, population 3,200, as a plant? Please."

"It's a sign, Samantha," Rub said sternly. "We are living in the final days: wars and rumors of war. If Jesus decided to come to Dallas and use the humble kudzu for his body, who are we to question?"

Samantha flashed a rueful smile. "I hate to rain on your apocalypse, while I grant it kinda does look like a man on a cross, that ain't kudzu, looks more like poison ivy."

"Not the point, girl. We are entering the end times and we have been given a sign. It's time to get right with Jesus."

Samantha cocked her head and gave Rub a warning glare. "Am I in trouble with Jesus and no one told me?"

"Do I need to quote Leviticus to you?" Rub said, drawing himself up.

"Only if you want me to stomp on your toe," Samantha shot back.

"You're a good girl, Samantha. I know that," Rub said in a more placating tone. "Heaven knows you're pretty enough to get a proper man if you just said yes to one. But you've fallen onto the sinner's path."

Samantha sighed. "Rub, if you hadn't been so nice to my dad when his truck broke down, I would put my delicate and attractive foot up your behind. I don't think Jesus worries about my dating preferences, and neither should you. But you have given me a great idea. When I finally do open a bar in this pesthole, I'll name it *The Sinner's Path*. Now, it's late, I'm tired, and I'm going home."

Rub shook his head. "I will pray for you, Samantha Jean."

"You do that, Rub," Samantha said as she got in her silver Subaru. Seconds later, she sped off.

Rub turned back to the foliage figure that seemed to gaze down on him. The head, sunk on the mighty chest, looked as if it were crowned with a halo of faint stars. Rub composed himself for prayer, bowing his head and dropping to one knee.

From the center of the foliage, two long ropy vines snapped down. One looped around Rub's throat, stifling the startled cry. Another seized his arm. Instantly, Rub's face and arm swelled and discolored. Rub clawed at his throat, but it was already too late. With the inexorable power of a tree root cracking a rock, the vine tightened and his neck snapped.

The vines drew the limp form up into the center of the mass, which rustled and crackled for hours. Eventually, in the early morning hours, torn clothing tumbled loose from the poisonous embrace. A pair of shoes was spat out, tangling in the phone wires to twist like hanged men. Before dawn, the mass of vegetation slid loose of its perch, thinned out, and traveled atop the phone and power lines strung over Dallas. A few cars were out, and each time their lights touched the plant, it froze, waiting for them to pass before reaching a shady area on the back roof of a tumbled-down barn.

Jeremy looked up as the buzzer to his studio sounded. As usual, he was surrounded by the paraphernalia of his cover as a photographer and graphic designer. He made a decent living at his cover. Which was good, as the Poor Knights too often lived up to that name, fighting supernatural evil on a shoestring.

A girl walked into the studio looking about for, and failing to spot, him behind the reflecting panel.

Cute, he thought. About 5'4", athletic with golden brown hair wearing the traditional clothes of the South—jeans and a T-shirt. Her glasses complemented an attractive, intelligent face.

"The day looks up," he murmured.

Easy boy, the voice of his guardian angel sounded in his mind. *She's older than she looks.*

"Vampire old?" he asked, his hand unconsciously covering the gold and crystal pendant that housed his guardian's essence.

No, Mrs. Robinson old, you snorting, pawing miserable excuse for a warrior-monk.

"Celibacy is just institutionalized misogyny," he said. "Besides, there are whole books devoted to the virtues of older women. Now be quiet."

"Can I help you?" he called.

She spotted him. "Jeremy Leclerc?"

"Yes." He walked up and shook her hand. She had a firm grip. She looked up at him with a puzzled, dubious expression.

"Something wrong?" he asked.

"Umm. I was expecting someone older and kinda different looking. What are you, about twenty-three?"

Jeremy smiled. "Well, I haven't been in Charlotte long, but I have a list of clients and references—"

"Debbie said to say hello."

Jeremy concealed his surprise and casually put a table between them. His bloodsword rested under the table where he could reach it in a second. Next to it hung a 7.65MM Walther PPK. "So," he said, "you know Debbie?"

"Not really," Samantha said. "But I went looking for help. Very specialized help. I put the word out in some special circles, and the word came back. It led me to her. But she wouldn't help me. Said that sort of thing was more up your alley."

Jeremy studied Samantha. She looked to be human. He checked her neck. Debbie either hadn't bit her or had chosen some other spot. The vampire's truce with Jeremy and the forces of light relied on her not killing or turning humans. Debbie had even aided Jeremy several months ago against a demon preying off the Nordstrom's crowd at SouthPark Mall.

"I had...had questions," Samantha began, "about some disappearances in my hometown, Dallas."

"Texas?" Jeremy said.

Samantha sighed the sigh of a woman who had heard this way too many times. "North Carolina, out beyond Gastonia. I asked Debbie to come out and help me solve the disappearance of a friend of my father's. He's seen a vision of Jesus in a giant mass of kudzu or something atop a pole. It kinda looked like a man, I'll grant. In the morning, they found a pile of his clothing torn to shreds, and the thing was gone from where I saw it."

"And she said?"

"She said, 'Debbie doesn't do Dallas,' and that I needed you."

"What else did she tell you?"

"That you're a Knight Templar. You fight monsters. You have your own guardian angel." Suddenly Samantha was shaking her head. "This is nuts. Nuts. Look," she backed away, "I am really sorry to bother you. This was a mistake."

Shadowheart popped into existence in front of Samantha, who jumped a foot in the air. The angel wore her usual guise, a girl of about Samantha's size, blond and blue-eyed, barefoot, clad in a simple blue shift, belted in gold at the waist.

"I figured it would save time earning your belief if I just appeared," she snapped. "Yes, he's actually a Templar. I'm a guardian angel. Demons and monsters are real, yadda, yadda."

Samantha stared wide-eyed at Shadowheart, then reached out a hand toward her; it went through, and Samantha jumped again.

"She usually doesn't manifest in solid form," Jeremy said.

"You're an angel," Samantha said. "An actual, made by God, freaking angel?"

"Yep."

"Good," Samantha said, breathing hard and pushing her glasses back on her nose. "I want to talk to your boss. I got a lot to say to him. I want some damn answers."

Shadowheart gave Jeremy a disgusted look. "Crap, another one like you. I'm for my crystal. Call me when you know what sort of boojum we are hunting. Bye." She was gone. No flash, no sound, just gone.

"Don't bother," Jeremy said gently. "I've tried to ask her about Life, the Universe, and Everything. She either can't, or won't, tell me much. I'm afraid I'm something of a disappointment to her."

Samantha gave him an uncertain look. "So, will you help me? I've got some money."

Jeremy smiled and said in his best Bogart accent, "Fifty dollars a day plus expenses." Then he shook his head. "No, I'm not Sam Spade. My help is free."

Jeremy followed Samantha in his red and white Mini back to the place where the man she'd called "Rub" had disappeared. They parked and crunched over the gravel to the spot where the sheriff had found the torn clothes. He stood next to Samantha, staring up at the bare poles lit by the afternoon sun.

"It was there," Samantha insisted.

"Don't doubt you," Jeremy said. "Shadowheart, do you sense anything?" He turned slowly about looking at the rundown sections of the town's edge.

Shadowheart popped in, looked about at the town. "Ignorance and provincialism," she said and popped out again.

"That cannot possibly be an angel," Samantha said.

"That's what they told me when I was issued her," Jeremy said. "She's really not so bad. She's kind of snarky just now since I ran off for a weekend with an incredibly attractive Asian physical therapist. She gets jealous when I am with other women."

An irate Shadowheart reappeared. "Before this gig I was the heart of a flaming star. I have never been a human soul and have no interest in your sweaty gropings and lusts."

"Glad you're back," Jeremy said. "Now that you are, riffle through your angelic memory for man-eating plants."

"Nothing comes to mind," she said, her feet making no sound as she moved over the gravel. "But as you should know by now, there are many ancients from the other side that manifest differently when they break through to Earth. This may be one of those as opposed to a vampire, zombie, or such."

"Vampires," Samantha said with a laugh.

"What do you think Debbie was?" Shadowheart asked.

Samantha's laugh was cut short, and she turned pale. She looked at Jeremy, who nodded. Samantha wrapped her arms around herself, shaking her head.

The sound of engines made them turn, and Jeremy saw an odd procession heading their way. A motorcycle with sidecar rolled toward them, followed by a police car with Dallas markings and a van that said "State Police Forensics" on it.

"Hey, Samantha." The motorcycle rider was revealed as a sprightly older woman as she pulled off her helmet.

"Mayor Crossley," Samantha returned.

"Still looking for Rub?"

"Yep."

"See you got yourself a handsome youngster." She winked at Jeremy. "About time."

"Ah, yeah." Samantha smiled weakly. "This is Jeremy, my… ummm…friend. I thought he might help me look. What are you doing here?"

"We got another missing person report," she frowned. "Seems that young Rita Mackey went missing after leaving her job at the M&M Superette. Only her clothes have been found. We were on our way when I saw you at this crime scene. Thought you might have learned something."

"Nothing yet," Samantha said.

"Come on, you crazy kids," Mayor Crossley said. "Jeremy, you can ride shotgun. Been a while since I had a handsome young man's arms around me. Samantha, you get the sidecar. Hop on, sonny. We're off to fight crime."

Seconds later Jeremy wished he'd insisted on getting in one of their cars as the mayor roared off with the cruiser and van in trail. The bike went briefly airborne over a curb and across the centerline, causing a Hummer to screech its brakes.

Jeremy found himself tightening his grip on the aged mayor, which she seemed to like as she sped up even more.

"Isn't there a helmet law in this state?" Jeremy shouted.

"Sure." The mayor cackled, gunning the engine. "Good thing I got mine."

Samantha looked up from where she had a death grip on the sidecar. "Sometimes life in Dallas is like being caught in a horrible Saturday morning cartoon."

After a few harrowing minutes, they arrived at the foot of a cell phone tower. Another cruiser sat there. A tall, lean, uniformed officer stood over a pile of clothing. He briefly took cover behind his car until the mayor stopped. The cruiser and van pulled up behind them.

The mayor pinched Jeremy's butt as he got off the bike.

Jeremy and Samantha followed the mayor to the foot of the cell tower. A shredded leather jacket with metal studs stood out from a pile of miscellaneous rags and two sneakers.

The sheriff looked over at Samantha. "Hello, Samantha. Sorry, no news about Rub."

He turned a look at the mayor that clearly said he wished her back at the Town Hall. "Hello, Mayor. It's Rita Mackey's clothes all right. She was wearing that jacket when I used to pick her up for truancy. I always told that girl that she'd come to a bad end if she didn't mend her ways."

The mayor shook her head, her mouth in a grim line. "Have you found a body?"

"Not yet. He may have stripped her here and taken her somewhere else to molest her."

"Jesus Christ," Samantha said, looking straight up.

They all lifted their eyes. Atop the cell phone tower hung a mass of foliage.

The mayor and sheriff looked up. "Well, yeah," the sheriff said. "It does kinda look like Jesus if you think of it."

"That's it," Samantha shouted. "That's the thing that Rub was showing me."

"Now, Samantha," the sheriff said wearily. "No more of that, please. We didn't find your plant by Rub's clothes and that was miles from here."

"What's this?" the mayor asked.

"Samantha thinks some plant has something to do with Rub's disappearance."

"Oh, come on, Samantha," the mayor said. "You've been binging old *X-Files* again?"

"I tell you it's the same plant," Samantha yelled, pointing. "Shoot it or something!"

"Samantha," Jeremy said, "let's take a walk and leave these folks to their work."

She gave him a mutinous glare but followed as he led her away.

"No use," he said. "Ordinary people will never believe."

"Get Shadowheart to tell them," she said.

Jeremy shook his head. "She won't. Something about rules and our free will. You're the first person that she's actually manifested for and she only did that 'cause you are already involved."

Samantha looked up. "It's the same damn thing."

Shadowheart appeared next to Samantha. "And things are worse than that. Now it's aware of you."

"What?" Samantha said. "You think it's listening?"

"It's not a natural creature," Shadowheart said with unusual patience. "It's demonic and aware. It heard you without ears. It sees you now without eyes. It may have been here for years. How many times have you seen clothes by the roadside or shoes hung in lines? Ever wonder what happened to those people?"

"Does it know where she lives?" Jeremy asked.

"We have to assume it does," Shadowheart said.

Above their heads, the foliage rippled and moved. There was no wind.

They retreated to Samantha's colonial revival home on the edge of town. The grounds were partly overgrown and wooded, but it was obvious the home was undergoing a loving restoration. A scaffold occupied the front porch. Two dogs greeted them noisily. A beagle introduced as O. Henry and a Corgi called Duke, who was wary of Jeremy.

"Sorry," Samantha said. "He's not too fond of men. I think he was abused before I had him."

"I sense you aren't that fond of men yourself," Jeremy said.

"Not awfully," Samantha admitted. "That give your Christian theology a problem?"

Jeremy laughed, but could not keep bitterness from it. He reached under his coat and pulled out his Templar sword. Duke growled, but Jeremy sat on the arm of an overstuffed chair.

"I'm not a Christian," he said. "I suppose if I am anything, I'm a Taoist. I was born in Normandy into an old Scottish Catholic family."

"I wondered about your accent," Samantha said. "Kind of hard to place."

"My father brought me into the Order as a child. I was a good little

Catholic boy till my early teens and his death. Then came the questions, but never the answers.

"So, I bear a magical sword. They tell me that the ruby in its hilt is red because Joseph of Arimathea dipped it in the blood of Christ. I was teamed with what they tell me is a guardian angel. I know both are supernatural and both are real. But I don't know that I'm any closer to the answers I've always wanted."

Shadowheart appeared, seated on the couch opposite him. Both dogs gave little yips of welcome and scampered over to sit at her feet.

"They see you?" Samantha asked.

"Animals see angels and demons." She looked at Jeremy. "Doubt only plagues humans."

"Where you been?" Jeremy asked.

"Off this plane of existence trying to find out about our enemy. I learned only a little, but it's not good. Ever hear of a green man?" Shadowheart said.

"Yeah," Samantha responded. "I have one on a pot in my garden, kind of a druid sort of thing. It's a man, made of leaves, brings good luck."

"Everything has its equal and opposite." Shadowheart stood, pacing. "This is like a green spirit gone evil. This one seems to have gathered the poisonous plant life of this world and imbued it with additional power. So, it's not just a poison ivy but vastly more deadly. Cut it and the urushiol, the fluid it uses for blood and digestion, will poison you. Burn it and it might poison the whole town."

"How do we fight it?" Jeremy demanded.

Shadowheart shrugged.

"Wait," Samantha said. She dove at a cabinet near the TV. Opening both doors, she began flinging DVDs about, tunneling into the cabinet like a gopher digging a burrow. Jeremy watched in bemusement as she muttered, cursed, and tunneled.

"Aha," she said, jumping out and up and tossing a DVD at him.

He looked down at an old black and white science fiction movie called the *The Thing*.

"And?" Jeremy asked.

"One of my writing buddies loves it and loaned it to me. Scientists attacked in the arctic by a monster carrot or something like that. They killed it with an arc of electricity." She grabbed it out of his hand and started the TV. A quick scan brought them to the stalwart heroes rigging up an electrical boobytrap and zapping a balding spaceman who did not look very carrot like.

"I have a generator," Samantha said, "for when the power goes out in storms. Dad taught me how to do wiring. We block the windows and doors and leave one-way in. The beast comes in and zap."

Jeremy looked out the window at the setting sun. "Let's do it."

A two-hour race with the fading light followed. Jeremy wrestled the generator into the house as Samantha wired and hammered, setting the trap. She hung leads from the metal painting scaffold. They covered the windows with the old house's green wooden shutters. Furniture and more boards secured all doors but the front. Duke and O. Henry were locked in her bedroom out of harm's way.

The sun disappeared as Samantha finished hooking up the generator. Jeremy placed some old rubber stall mats he'd found in the disused barn on the ground to protect them. Samantha stared out beyond the leads and cables of the boobytrap. Then she looked at Shadowheart, who had appeared in a T-shirt and ripped jeans, her hair in twin ponytails. "You're sure it's out there hunting for me?"

Shadowheart nodded. "I sense the presence of evil."

Samantha opened the door and strode out onto the porch facing the open expanse of lawn. "Eeeaaaat meeeeeeee," she yelled. She walked in and grinned at Jeremy. "Always wanted to do that."

Jeremy frowned. "Wonderful."

Samantha, now cheerful and confident, got them both a beer, pausing for a second to look at Shadowheart, who just rolled her eyes. Jeremy gratefully accepted the beer as Samantha sat on the rocker inside the doorway in plain view. From somewhere she'd produced a revolver that lay in her lap like a cannon. "Daddy's old .357," she said, noting his gaze.

"I'm bait for the beast," she added, sipping her beer. "Hope it doesn't prefer virgins."

Jeremy kept circling, checking the windows. He'd left the lights on, but the old house was lousy with blind spots.

"Come on, Jeremy. Stick close," Samantha called. "It will be show-time soon."

Jeremy sat near Samantha, sword resting across his knees.

"Don't believe I thanked you for sticking by me during all this. Friends mean a lot to me," she said. "Won't forget it."

"Can always use more friends," he said.

She smiled. "Sorry that I'm not up for giving the hero the traditional rewards."

"You're forgiven," he said grandly.

"Oh, please." Shadowheart grimaced.

Samantha grinned and punched his arm.

A slamming sound came from beneath him. They leapt to their feet. More noise came from below them.

Shadowheart turned to Samantha. "Does this house have a basement?"

"Yeah. But it's cement."

"Any of it natural dirt?"

"Only by the trapdoor."

Shadowheart shut her eyes as if in pain. "A green man might well tunnel through dirt like you swim. This thing might do the same."

The thumping came louder. Something was coming up the inside stairs.

"It's inside!" Samantha yelled.

The door from the basement bulged.

"Run," Jeremy shouted, shoving her out the front door. Shadowheart blinked out of existence.

"I can't trigger the generator from out here," she protested.

"We'll die in there," he snapped.

The door cracked as they fled into the night. Jeremy had a second to see a mass of rustling green.

They raced out to the yard, then circled, heading for the cars, but the creature followed them out and was too close to rush past. Jeremy fled the pricking of its poison on his skin. An overpowering smell of wet earth and decaying leaves bit at his nose.

A *bang* sounded in his ears. Samantha's .357 cracked again, kicking wildly in her hands. "Get off my land," she shouted.

The bullets tore foliage, but the thing came on untroubled. The prickling on his skin grew worse; all Samantha had done was fill the air with poison.

"Back up," he said. He hefted the sword but knew cutting would only do more harm to them. Only one chance. "Get your car," he shouted as they backed toward the barn and shed where they had parked. He reversed his sword, holding the gem at the level of his eyes and concentrated. Latin poured off his tongue. The gem began to pulse with a blood-red light.

The green man stopped its rush at the edge of the light. It looked like a giant starfish, but the top arm was shorter and held a horrible caricature of a face, with holes for eyes and a maw of twigs and leaves. Two thick, ropy tendrils waved from its shoulders. It tried to sidle to one side or the other as Jeremy kept up his chant, feeling his strength drain bit by bit into the stone.

"Jeremy," he heard Samantha call. "It's done something to the tires. They're all flat."

"Run, Samantha," Jeremy cried, despair striking him. "I'll buy you time." He advanced toward the green man, which gave ground, shaking as if in agitation or pain. If he could trap it against the house, maybe he could destroy it. He ran forward, concentrating on the gem…and tripped on a tree root hidden in a harsh shadow thrown by the porch light. He caught himself as the gem winked out and the green man rustled forward, almost upon him.

Suddenly Samantha leapt in, spraying something from a can in each hand. "Eat Roundup, fucker."

The green man convulsed in evident pain. But the chemicals wouldn't kill even ordinary poison ivy quickly. Tendrils struck out. One knocked the can from her right hand; the other stuck her down like a whip. Samantha screamed and lost the other can.

But Jeremy gained his feet and raised the gem hilt. "*In nomine Patris, et Filii, et Spiritus Sancti,*" he shouted, recklessly pouring out strength. The gem flamed, and the green man retreated, holding up two of its appendages like arms to protect its horrid face.

Samantha scrambled up. They turned and fled down the path. A stiff wind rustled the grass and brush around them.

"Where to?" Samantha called.

"We've got to get out of all this vegetation. It can come at us from any direction."

"There's a fish camp down the road," she said. "Nice big tarmac parking lot."

They jogged on. Jeremy kept the sword ready, but he could not see the beast. Probably it was pacing them in the forest to their right. They had to keep ahead of it.

Samantha and Jeremy slowed. He trained at running, but the encumbrance of sword scabbard and weapons slowed him. Samantha was nursing a knee. "Surgery last year." She grimaced.

"Shadowheart," he called.

With you, her voice sounded in their minds.

"Where is it?"

Near, following in the woods. Run faster.

They jogged down the empty country road hoping to see a car. *Not,* he thought, *that anyone is likely to stop for a young man with a sword.*

A sign ahead said, "South Fork Fish Camp." They ran into the parking lot.

"Duck," Samantha yelled.

Jeremy hit a shoulder roll as a boulder sailed through the space he'd just occupied.

They reached the door. "It's locked," Samantha yelled. Then she pointed, her face frozen in terror. The green man was coming from the tree line, moving as fast as a man.

Jeremy pulled his Walther and shot the lock out of the wooden door. They ran in.

"Brace the door," Samantha shouted.

He shook his head. "Too many windows. The kitchen, quick."

The entrance behind them slammed open as they raced into kitchen.

"Jeremy, I can't run much longer," Samantha said, grabbing her knee.

He looked about desperately. They stood next to the meat locker. Its refrigerator unit hummed, and he could see three big tanks of refrigerant next to it.

The double doors of the kitchen opened, and the green man stood there, as if savoring their helplessness.

Inspiration struck Jeremy. He reversed the sword and concentrated on the gem, producing a wan version of the glow he had invoked before. The creature rustled as if stung, but pressed forward, encouraged by the weakness of the glow.

Shadowheart, he sent mentally, *I don't dare speak aloud. Tell Samantha to get the fire ax on the wall and knock over the liquid nitrogen tank.*

He heard the sound of the tank falling.

Suddenly Jeremy raced forward and to the left, circling the creature. The sword's gem brightened, and the monster stumbled back. "Now, Samantha!"

Samantha slammed the fire ax down on the top of the tank in several desperate strikes. Freezing liquid nitrogen burst forth. A high, keening sound came from the creature as it was forced away from the sacred sword into the cloud of vapor. Jeremy poured his full force into the sword's gem to hold the monster in place. Cracking sounds filled the air.

Samantha wrestled the other tank around. Pointing at the green man, she braced it on a chair and opened the valve, blasting the green man at point-blank range.

Jeremy grabbed Samantha and pulled her past the creature. They retreated from the cloud of icy gas, eyebrows and hair already stiff. In a minute, the tank emptied and the room was freezing. In the middle of it, like a horrible ice statue, stood the green man.

Shadowheart appeared. "It's not over. Jeremy, strike now."

Jeremy leapt forward and brought the heavy Templar sword down in a two-handed blow. The green man shattered into a pile of frozen vegetation.

A sound made Jeremy look down and leap backward with a wild yell.

Something rose from the floor.

"A mandrake demon," Shadowheart snapped.

A two-foot-tall creature that seemed made of roots stood up and hissed at Jeremy. It looked like a gingerbread man gone very, very bad.

The mandrake jumped forward, and Jeremy leapt over it, swiping down with the bloodsword and missing.

"Don't let it get out to open ground," Shadowheart shouted. "It will bury itself and regenerate."

Samantha leapt forward with a wild cry and swing of the ax that would have made any Viking proud. The mandrake rolled under her and grabbed her leg. She shook it loose with a howl. It leapt onto a table, heading for a window. Jeremy lunged forward and slammed the point of the sword into the mandrake, pinning it to the wooden window sash. It screeched and twisted, almost freeing itself.

Samantha's ax thudded into the mandrake, neatly separating its head. The root dropped to the floor, curling and starting to smoke.

Jeremy looked at Samantha and smiled. "Nice work, Viking Princess."

She smiled back at him then staggered over to a chair and collapsed into it, arms wrapped about her. Jeremy's hand shook as he sheathed the bloodsword.

"Well done," Shadowheart said. "You have banished the evil."

"We'd better get out here before the cops arrive," Jeremy said. He looked at his hands. They were swelling and itched. "Please tell me you have calamine lotion and Benadryl at your house?"

Samantha looked up. "I'm a country girl. Calamine lotion and Benadryl are condiments out here." She stood shakily and looked at Shadowheart. "One question. One straight answer."

Shadowheart smiled. "Ask."

"Does God really love me?"

"Hell yes," Shadowheart said and vanished.

The End

3

THE DEVIL AND THE DETAILS

Jeremy walked up the stairs to the Steel Magnolia, one of Charlotte's high-end restaurants in the trendy South End. He'd recently moved to a townhouse in the revitalized area, and the restaurant often featured in his dating plan.

A girl in a crisp white shirt and black pants smiled at him.

"I'm here to meet a Robert Diablesse," he said.

"Ah, you must be Mr. Leclerc."

Jeremy smiled. At twenty-two he didn't usually rate a "mister" from people, but he didn't dine at the Magnolia often either. He followed past the white linen tables to an alcove in the back.

A dark-haired man of about thirty sat there. Behind him, like a bodyguard, stood a tall, redheaded woman with a markedly feline countenance. On the table, rested a bottle of Dom Perignon and two champagne flutes.

Jeremy considered the woman. *Beautiful in an offbeat fashion,* he thought. *I wonder why she's standing.*

"Mr. Diablesse, your party is here," the hostess said.

The man who rose to greet him was handsome, athletic, wearing a superbly cut dark-blue suit and slightly taller than Jeremy's six feet.

He smiled at Jeremy and gave him a brisk handshake. "Mr. Leclerc, a pleasure to meet you. May I call you Jeremy?"

"Of course," Jeremy said.

"Please, call me Bob." He gestured toward a seat.

"Diana," Diablesse said to the server, "please bring us another bottle of Dom. It's a special occasion."

"Yes, sir."

He smiled broadly. "I keep telling you to call me Bob."

The girl giggled. "You're a devil, Mr. Diablesse."

Jeremy gave a curious look at the standing woman. She regarded him with unwinking green eyes, as if he were a dish of Purina.

Bob made an idle gesture. "My associate, Prosperine."

Somehow Jeremy knew not to rise and offer his hand. He settled for a pleasant nod.

"A toast," Bob said, pouring the Dom. "To a new business venture."

They both enjoyed the rare, refined taste of the Perignon.

Bob sighed with pleasure after a deep draught. "You seem rather young for your reputation, Jeremy."

"Well, I started in graphic design when I was twelve—"

"Oh, I didn't mean in the arts," Bob said, leaning back in his chair. "I'm referring to your career as a Knight Templar. You see, Diana is right. I really am a devil."

Jeremy slowly replaced the flute on the table and gathered his feet under him.

Bob waved a placating hand. "Relax, this is a friendly discussion between pros. I just wanted to meet you. You've cut quite a swath through evil in this town for the last year."

Jeremy studied the being opposite him. It looked human, but as he concentrated, Jeremy could tell there was an unusual aura about Diablesse. The image shimmered, and for a second, he could see a horned and tailed silhouette.

"Yep, if evil was a stock, it would be up to its ass in bears—just like Goldilocks," Bob continued. "Please, enjoy the champagne."

After a moment's hesitation, Jeremy nodded and reached for his glass. "You wanted to meet me, Demon. Why?"

Jeremy's tone seemed to anger Prosperine. She stalked forward, to be stilled by a gesture from Bob.

"Down, Prosperine," Bob said. "She's a bit touchy; the mandrake demon you killed last year was an old friend of hers."

The growl that came from Prosperine could not have begun in a human throat.

From the gold and crystal pendant that rested on Jeremy's chest came a single clear note, silver and beautiful. Bob flinched as if the sound were filled with pins. Prosperine whimpered and backed away, her arms coming up as if she feared being struck.

Jeremy reached for his champagne flute again. "I'm less alone than it may appear."

"Of course," Bob said. "And no need to bother your guardian angel. We've heard of Shadowheart and have no desire to provoke a meeting with her."

"Prosperine," he turned to the woman, "wait outside."

She walked away without a backward glance, the pantherish power and grace of her movement catching the attention of all the men and some of the women in the restaurant.

Jeremy pulled his glance back to Bob with an effort.

"Jeremy, what I like about you is that you're smart. So many people on both sides see it all in black and white. You're wise enough to see a need for some gray. Take your...relationship...with Debbie Middleton."

This time it was Jeremy's turn to flinch. The vampiress was his sometime ally and occasional bedmate. He couldn't say lover; Debbie's arrangement with him was more pragmatic, part of a truce between her and humanity. But she remained a vampire and a source of friction with his guardian angel. "Let's leave her out of this."

"Sure. I'm just envious. Anyway, my point is that you see the need for accommodations, for boundaries. After all, there has to be a Yin for your Yang."

"I gather you would like to set some boundaries?" Jeremy replied.

Bob nodded. "Exactly. I'm not saying that you shouldn't fight evil. Let's just say you get around to my evil last, after you clean up everything else. Then if we have to dance, well, we dance."

"What exactly is your particular evil?" Jeremy asked. The waitress returned with menus, and they shelved the discussion until she retreated to a discreet distance.

"Nothing disgusting, I assure you," Bob said. "I do high-end evil. None of this blood and guts stuff. Hell, this is a banking town. I can do all the evil I want financially. I'm the guy that makes sure the developers get everything they want. I arrange for arenas when the voters turn them down. I had light rail put in the wrong place for twice the price.

"Point is, I'm your local evil. I'm invested here. I like the place. Got a comfy home in Ballantyne, membership at the country club. I've got reasons to oppose these out-of-towners kibitzing in with their apocalyptic, kill everyone and make Charlotte a big smoking pit, type of evil."

"What do I get out of this arrangement?"

"For one thing, a truce with me. Not inconsiderable. I've been the death of many a soldier of light. Beyond that, information and assistance in rubbing out selected evil."

Jeremy laughed. "You're going to help me destroy other evildoers?"

"What do they teach you guys these days? We're not organized like your side, with God and angels at the top. Essentially we're all independent contractors, locked in a literally cut-throat competition."

"What about your allegiance to the Dark Lord?"

Bob looked over his shoulder. "Enough with the names already; sometimes they summon things. Look, I pay my dues to the big guy and kiss his ring at the Vegas convention, but other than that, I'm my own demon." Bob picked up a menu. "Shall we order something?"

"How do I know you haven't arranged for me to be poisoned?"

"Let's make a pact. The Magnolia will be totally safe, kind of like holy ground in *Highlander*. I loved that series."

"And what oath of yours would I trust, Demon?"

"Hey," Bob said, with an injured air. "I swear it."

The crystal on Jeremy's chest chimed again, and Bob's pleasant veneer slipped.

"Now you know the power that guarantees your oath," Jeremy

said. He waved the server over and ordered the most expensive items on the menu. Evil would suffer tonight, if only in the pocketbook.

After a few seconds, Bob recovered his good humor and joined him.

"Your offer is intriguing, but I want to see some more tangible benefit than just you're not trying to kill me," Jeremy said, watching as Bob drained more champagne with relish and no evident effect.

"Of course," Bob said. "Witches, my friend, it's witches. A coven of bad-ass wiccans is moving in with lawyers, guns, and money. There are places on the earth where certain unnatural forces occur. These forces wax and wane, and only adepts can use them. There's a pool of magical force collecting in Charlotte at the site of the Coliseum."

"What the locals used to call the Hive, from when the Charlotte Hornets were here?" Jeremy said. "But they blew that up, even though it was only nineteen years old."

"Yeah, my doing. It was kind of an evil twofer. I conned the city into putting it in the wrong place and bankrolling the owner. Millions down the rat hole." Bob grinned rapturously. "You see, I knew a force pool would form there and I finished the con by getting the city to blow it up. It's not a force amenable to demonic control, so I'd set up pentagram to divert the force pool to somewhere out of my territory, but something broke the pentagram. The force pool has only been delayed in forming. And it is calling out to those who could use it, witches and warlocks.

"The Agnesi coven is trying to buy the site so they can have a ritual there. They'll use the pool to boost their power and ascend to a higher realm. It'll leave the launching pad, our fair Queen City, in smoking ruin. They're already setting up Al-Qaeda to take the fall for it. Not that I object to that—fuck those ragheads.

"Since I thought the pool was destroyed, I didn't try to buy the property, and there's no way I could outbid the Agnesi anyway. Fortunately, there isn't a major law firm in this town I don't do business with, so I know the lawyer repping them. In fact, Bob Lanier just won a lawsuit for me. We'll be taking possession of a nice piece of change shortly.

"So, Jeremy, it's going to be up to you to save the town. I can't go up against the Agnesi directly—they know me—but I'll loan you what aid I can, including Prosperine."

Jeremy grimaced. "Lovely, does she like Friskies Buffet and scratches behind the ear?"

"She's a kinky minx and I'll leave you to find out what she likes on your own, if you dare. But she'll be useful against witches. As a familiar, she's resistant to their spells."

"Any ideas on how to stop them?"

"You're a bright boy, Jeremy," Bob said with a grin. "You'll think of something."

Dinner arrived, surf and turf, with glorious side dishes and a fine French Beaujolais.

"Dig in, Templar," Bob said. "This is, after all, what we're both prepared to die to protect."

After an excellent dinner, Jeremy made his slightly unsteady way back to the parking lot, leaving Bob to head into the cigar bar with some cronies, for brandy.

Shadowheart waited for him outside by his red Mini Cooper. She was, he noted with relief, in her more terrestrial form, a small blond girl with cornflower blue eyes dressed in jeans, a peasant blouse, and a denim vest. Her archangel manifestation was a formidable seven feet of black-haired warrior princess, with red and black wings. Neither body was human, merely formed ectoplasm, and sometimes she appeared only as an image.

She looked up at him. "So, it's not enough you're regularly banging a vampiress, now we're working with demons?"

Jeremy sighed. Shadowheart's manifestation seemed to affect her speech and attitude, and the snarkiness of her late teen incarnation was a cross to bear. "Three times is hardly regularly and the first time wasn't my idea."

"She had little trouble persuading you."

"With what Debbie knows about sex and the human body after two hundred years, she could persuade the College of Cardinals. As for the demon, I trust him no more than you do. But he's bound to his oath made in front of you."

"Don't overestimate that," she warned. "You're safe from him and catwoman to the sidewalk over there." She gestured at South Boulevard. "He knows not to strike at you directly; that would free my wings. But his familiar is a creature of space-time like you. My mandate does not allow me to strike the creatures of the Realm of Earth, save under specific violations of the Code of the Balance."

"What a damn shame that eating my innards isn't one of those," Jeremy grumbled.

Shadowheart shrugged. "You're the guys who always go on about free will. Well, Heaven can't interfere while you want to be more than puppets. You ask me, all this free will crap is overrated."

"Did I ask you?" Jeremy said. "Anyway, we need to check out this story of his about Wiccans from Hell nuking my adopted hometown. It would look bad on my annual review if I lost a whole city. What do you know?"

Shadowheart shrugged again, looking cross. "Little. Witches are still live humans, and I cannot see them astrally. Not clearly anyway. More of that damn free will. The Agnesi coven is made up of thirty witches. I doubt that they are all here, but these are powerful creatures, Jeremy, intelligent, ruthless, and subtle. A direct attack is not a good idea."

"Was Diablesse telling the truth about the pool of magical force?"

Shadowheart's lips drew into a grim line. "Yes. I checked in the overworld while you were at dinner. It's there, and it is growing. It should ripen around the witch's holiday of Mabon. If it is not used immediately, it will dissipate."

"September 23rd," Jeremy mused. "Three days, not a lot of time. Diablesse's banking connections have found the Agnesi's office space and he knows their bankers and lawyers. They have a lunch meeting on the deal tomorrow."

"Bon appétit," Shadowheart said. "Just don't end up on the menu."

* * *

For lack of a better plan, Jeremy wanted to see his enemies. Diablesse had told him of the meeting and given him a number to contact Prosperine. She met Jeremy in the underground garage below The Green, Charlotte's downtown park. She was leaning against a silver Porsche almost as powerful and sleek as herself. Jeremy walked up but stopped far enough away to draw the bloodsword from its concealed sheath in his custom-made, black leather longcoat. "So, do you talk or what?"

"My master," she said in throaty Lauren Bacall voice, "orders that I ally with you until his work is done. I don't like it."

Between eye-blinks, Shadowheart appeared between Prosperine and Jeremy. This time she was in archangel mode, her long blue-black hair spilled down her between her shoulders to the belt that held her own sword. Jeremy had a moment to see Prosperine's terrified face before Shadowheart's red and black wings spread, blocking the sight of the familiar. Then Shadowheart was gone as if she were never there. Prosperine stood pressed against her Porsche, rigid with terror.

"My side," Jeremy said mildly, "doesn't like my working with you either."

Prosperine straightened slowly. She had to pull her fingers out of holes in the Porsche's sheet metal. Jeremy made a mental note of the claws.

"Let's see what we are up against," Jeremy said.

"Yes," Prosperine returned, straightening her clothing in an exaggerated display of calm. "Bob says they're meeting at the Ratcliffe."

"Good," Jeremy replied. "We'll get a table nearby. Your side will pick up the tab."

The two took the stairs out of the garage, with Jeremy shedding his black coat. Charlotte was shirtsleeve weather in September.

As they walked through the park, Jeremy studied his companion. He suspected her to be more a panther in the form of a woman, than a woman who could change to a panther, but even his trained senses could pick up little magical about her. Prosperine seemed as comfortable in the bright fall sunshine as he did. Her elegant suit covered a body that was more toned than muscular, but there was an extra power in her walk that attracted the eye. Her skin was pale, and her red hair shone, her eyes were wide and green, betraying her feline origin. A human would have to squint in such full sun.

"Take a picture," she growled.

They crossed the park to the Ratcliffe. It had been a flower shop in the 1920s and retained its beautiful Tiffany stained-glass windows and bright yellow walls. They took a table in the back. The server brought over menus. Jeremy ordered a plate of appetizers, pasta alfredo, and bottle of Pellegrino.

The server, a fresh-faced girl of about nineteen, asked, "And for the lady?"

"Do you have any fresh mice?" Jeremy asked.

The server gave an uncertain laugh.

Prosperine ignored the comment and the laugh. "I'll have the tuna poki and a Chardonnay."

As the server departed, probably wishing she could trade tables, Jeremy turned to Prosperine. "That Bob of yours must have a forgiving expense account."

"He isn't mine," she growled. "And I'm his only under duress. He devoured my last mistress."

"Not happy with your employer?"

"Who's happy being subject to the will of others?" she asked.

"*Se la guerre*," Jeremy said.

Appetizers arrived and forestalled further conversation. By the time the main course was served, Jeremy was beginning to wonder if they had picked the wrong restaurant. The doors opened at that moment and in walked six striking women trailed by a number of more ordinary, if well-dressed, men and women. The servers scrambled to get together the long table to hold the party.

"The coven," Prosperine whispered, delicately poking at her tuna sushi with chopsticks. "The others are the bankers from Worldbank and Lanier and Boswell lawyers. Worldbank is bankrolling the wiccans."

"Wow," Jeremy said, "that has to be the most gorgeous coven of witches in history."

Next to him, Prosperine made a cat-like hiss of disgust. "They invest so much of their power in appearance. Below the glamour they're only ordinary women, even ugly ones."

"So why the glamour?" Jeremy asked.

"To manipulate simple-minded men. You invest beautiful women with all manner of virtues they don't have. You laugh harder at the pretty woman's jokes, praise shallow wit as deep thought, and will do harder tasks for a woman you desire, than one you don't."

"Hard to argue that point," Jeremy said. "I notice you chose an appealing form."

"I didn't choose it. Bob did. I would rather run on all fours and sink my fangs into the skulls of creatures like you. Thank the Dark Lord that Diablesse likes an athletic build and didn't choose to hang big tits off me. Look at the black-haired cow in the middle. Those aren't even real-looking."

"I hadn't noticed," Jeremy replied. "Which one do you think is the leader?"

"The bright blonde must be Agnesi; I sense power dripping off her. I don't think I've seen such a powerful witch in decades. The twin brunettes are the Echol sisters, the cow is Llewellen, the black woman is Saytha, and the Asian is Kitsune."

Jeremy studied the women surreptitiously, memorizing the details of their faces. If they caught him looking, they would put it down to their collective beauty. The blonde had an elegant Germanic look to her. She caught Jeremy's eye and gave a reflexive smile, then her eyes tracked past him to Prosperine, who suddenly busied herself with her food. The smile faded slightly and turned to a frown, then Agnesi was distracted by her companions and said something that set the table laughing.

"Tell me she doesn't know you," Jeremy said, with a forkful of pasta in front of his lips.

"She knew my mistress," Prosperine said, "but not me."

"Wish I could hear what they are saying."

"Easy enough," said Prosperine. "They cast a spell around their table to keep their conversation unintelligible—it won't work on me. Hold my hand."

Jeremy moved his chair closer and took Prosperine's left hand as her right, concealed from the witches by the table, whipped through a series of intricate moves. Suddenly, it was if they were at the same table with the coven.

"The contract price is agreeable," Agnesi said, "and we'll sign the memorandum of understanding now, with the final paperwork to follow. But we want the transfer done by the morning of the 23rd."

A balding man of about fifty frowned at her. "This is all highly unusual. A deal like this normally takes months to set up."

"The inconvenience and our unusual needs are why we're paying the premium we have offered you. Worldbank has our financing. They'll send the money to the Lanier Trust fund and then by wire to the owners in the morning. We are waiving all risk on clouded title or appraisal. We simply need access to the property as quickly as possible."

"Of course," he said, "though I would give anything to know the reason for such haste."

Agnesi smiled at him. "If you are in town on the afternoon of the 23rd you'll learn everything then."

The luncheon continued with details of the transaction being discussed at length. Jeremy scribbled surreptitious notes. A plan began to unfold in his head. When the meeting broke up, Jeremy and Prosperine dallied over desert so the coven could leave ahead of them.

"Get the check," Jeremy said. "Tip extravagantly. We've killed this table for two hours. Then get hold of Bob. He needs to get into Lanier's office as soon as he can and switch the keyboard for Lanier's computer with one I'll give you when you come by my office tonight. I suspect your boss has offshore accounts. I'll need the information on how to transfer some money into one. He'd better be prepared to move the funds instantly to other accounts."

"Could I polish your shoes too?" she said with mock sweetness.

"Hey, be good and there's some catnip in it for you."

"Keep it up with the jokes, human. That's quite a tab you're racking up."

"Tell Bob he'll have to get Lanier out of his office tomorrow night and you hidden up there so you can let me in."

"When?"

"Guess, Kitty, guess."

Prosperine frowned. "Of course, full moon, midnight."

Jeremy smiled at the familiar. "The witching hour."

***

Midnight found Jeremy in his car in the IJL building's parking deck. The thirty-story skyscraper deck was still spotted with cars even at this late hour.

Jeremy's cell vibrated, and he flipped it open.

"It's done," Bob said. "Lanier is passed out on my couch after our victory dinner. Bastard. He takes 45% of the settlement on my case. I mean, who's the client anymore? Anyway, I left Prosperine in a cabinet in his office."

"Big cabinet," Jeremy said.

Bob sighed. "Don't be dim. She's a shapeshifter. She can be a big jaguar or a little kitty. She just weighs the same, conservation of mass. Good luck, Templar. Never thought I would be saying that."

"Roger that, Demon." Jeremy flicked the phone closed, then got out of his Mini Cooper with his briefcase of electronics. An elevator took him to the lobby where he donned a set of heavy, brown-framed glasses before approaching the guard post. A disinterested, balding, heavyset black man in a blue blazer regarded him. "Help you, sir?"

"Yeah, I'm from PCS, got an emergency, a sick PC in Lanier's office at Boswell and Lanier."

The guard consulted his computer. "Don't have you on the roster, young man. Sorry, can't let you up."

"They said his assistant is staying later to work with me. Call the front desk. I'll bet she's there."

The guard grunted and picked up the phone, punching the extension as Jeremy hoped whatever cabinet Bob had left Prosperine in hadn't been locked.

"Yes, this is security. I have a gentleman from…Geek? Well, he's the computer guy, I don't know about geek." Teeth flashed in the dark face. "Okay, ma'am, I'll send him up."

The guard took a picture with a small, egg-shaped camera. Jeremy hoped the glasses would be sufficient disguise, but when he looked at the image printed for the temp badge, he stopped worrying. His mother wouldn't recognize him from the poor-quality image. He waved the badge, which allowed him through what looked like a glass guillotine guarding the elevators, then rode up to the twentieth floor. The doors slid back, and he stepped out into the entrance to the law firm. Prosperine, dressed in a pantsuit suitable for a law office, rose from behind a massive marble desk, a look of relief stealing over her features.

"Trouble?" he asked.

"None. Evidently it's not unusual for someone to be on the switchboard even this late."

They quickly walked down the halls to Lanier's office. In a smaller firm, people would be more curious about strangers. Most of the staff had long since gone home, save for unfortunate associates and paralegals, sweating last-minute assignments from demanding partners. Some of them might have envied Prosperine.

At the door to Lanier's office, it took only seconds for Jeremy to pick the lock. Jeremy turned on the lights and went straight to the computer where Bob and Prosperine had switched the keyboard. "How did you manage to get the keyboard switched?"

Prosperine grimaced. "I was ordered to have sex with him on a table in the next conference room while Bob made the switch. Old fool actually thinks I fancy his middle-aged ass."

"Oh," Jeremy said. "Sorry about that."

"It beat the alternative of denying my master. Trust me in that. Why did we do this anyway?" she said, leaning close to look over his shoulder as he linked up his laptop to Lanier's desktop. The heat of her body beat against him. He remembered Simone Simon in *Curse of the Cat People*, swallowed, and put it out of his mind.

"This one is a keylogger."

"A what?" she asked

"It has a hard drive that recorded every stroke he made on it. I've got access to everything he's worked on and every password. With that," he added triumphantly, "I have access to the firm's trust fund. All I have to do is set it so that the money wired in from Worldbank goes right out the other side to Royal Rose Bank in the Caymans to start its trip through all the shell companies your boss set up."

"Hacking with something other than a sword." Prosperine sniffed. "What is the struggle between good and evil coming to?"

"Excuse me," a delicate Southern voice said. "What are you doing in here?"

Jeremy and Prosperine looked up in alarm. The silver-haired woman leaned in, her expression professional but wary.

"Hi," Jeremy smiled disarmingly, "we're with PCS. Lanier's PC crashed. We had a rush order to fix it. He's got something big on for tomorrow."

"Oh Lord," said the woman. "I'm Barbara, his assistant. He never tells me a damn thing." She hesitated. "Why are you wearing gloves, young man?"

"Anti-static gloves," Jeremy replied. "You touch a motherboard without them, and you've got a fried motherboard."

"Oh," she replied, waiving a hand. "Well, let me know when you are ready to leave." She closed the door.

Jeremy turned to Prosperine. "Can you do something about her?"

Prosperine ran her tongue over her full lips. "Sure. Of course, I can't eat a whole human in one setting. I'll have to hide the rest for later."

"No, you stupid panther. Can't you fuzz her memory or something? You were a witch's familiar."

"Oh, all right," Prosperine snapped, as she slipped out of the room.

Jeremy plunged into the mass of data, cutting through all of Lanier's passwords and setting the wire transfer to immediately retransfer to Diablesse's Cayman account at the Royal Rose. Pope and Land would never see a dime, and the witches would lose the land.

But Jeremy soldiered on. He didn't entirely believe Diablesse's claim that the power pool was of no use to him.

"Time to buy some insurance," he muttered to himself. Fortunately, Templars had once been the bankers of Europe and the skills were still taught. Jeremy linked to a Templar cell overseas. There was always a Templar on duty there. He opened a chat window and gave instructions. The brother in Europe was too well-trained to delay him with questions and quickly fulfilled his request. Jeremy closed the window just as Prosperine returned. Her face seemed strained and looked more cat-like than ever.

"You, okay?" he asked.

She gave him a surprised look, then grimaced. "The subtle stuff uses more energy, and I haven't practiced much since Bob enslaved me into his service. Are you done?"

"Nearly." Jeremy finished the transfer protocol. "Let's get out of here before someone else sees us."

Dawn reddened the sky. Jeremy stretched, glad he had showered and shaved late. He'd parked at the only place that he could safely sleep with Prosperine in the back seat, the parking lot of the Steel Magnolia, the holy ground Diablesse had sworn to honor. Shadowheart would enforce that guarantee, and Prosperine would not risk a second encounter with the angel.

A limo pulled into the parking lot. Diablesse opened the door and waved them over.

"Join me," he said in great good humor. "I got coffee, juice, and muffins. Prosperine, I even have lox and bagel for you. If you are going to face witches, you should do so on a full stomach."

Jeremy slid into the limo and helped himself to coffee and muffins. "You're going to confront the witches?"

"Oh, hell yeah. Come on, Jeremy, the only fun in this game is when you crush your enemy's face into the dirt. There's no substitute for seeing it with your own eyes. Don't you agree?"

"In fact," Jeremy said. "I do."

Prosperine gave him a curious look but said nothing.

The limo pulled to the curb of the Trade Street in front of a nondescript glass box building.

The trio stood in the lobby watching office workers stream to and fro, filling the building around them. Then the coven appeared, all six with Agnesi and Kitsune in the lead. They paused at the entrance to the building and, as one, turned to face Diablesse.

Agnesi came forward. "I smell demon."

"Diablesse's the name, damnation's the game. Can we talk in private?"

Agnesi's eyes roved over Jeremy and Prosperine. "I recognize your minions. They dogged my steps earlier. No matter, it is all too late for you."

"There's a conference room on this floor," Agnesi added. "You can do your begging and pleading there." They walked warily to the room. The witches entered first and lined up at the far end of the table.

"I wanted to talk to you about your plans to blow my home to hell," Diablesse said. "I'm afraid I can't allow it. I have too many investments that haven't paid off yet."

Agnesi laughed and tossed her blond hair like she was in a shampoo commercial. "I care nothing for your plans, Demon, or any threats you make. You're powerful, true, but there are six of us, enough to stand you and your minions off. By morning we will have more power than even a demon can dream of."

"About that," Diablesse said. "I'm afraid you won't be celebrating Mabon at the Coliseum site. Did you have a booking somewhere else?"

"It is ours," Agnesi said. "Tonight we hold the ritual; tomorrow we ascend."

"Ha," Diablesse shouted at the witch-leader. "You're through, Agnesi. The money never made it to Pope and Land. It went overseas into my accounts. It's mine. You're bankrupt."

"What?" Kitsune spat, glaring at them. The other witches shifted, their hair rising and shifting though there was no wind in the room.

"Oh," Diablesse continued, "I've made sure the Pope and Land people got an earful about how you are merely a front for laundering terrorist money. There will be agents at your offices shortly. They'll find something, won't they, Agnesi? After all, you did want it blamed on Al-Qaeda. You had to have some evidence of links. And there are already agents all over the Coliseum grounds, looking for whatever made you so desperate to buy it."

"Ordinary humans," Agnesi said in contempt. "They won't be able to stop us."

"Oh, I don't think you'll be up against just plain humans," Diablesse said.

"Meow," Prosperine added.

"One familiar—" Agnesi snarled.

"Oh, and did I mention I have my very own Templar?" Diablesse waved his hands in a grand gesture toward Jeremy.

The witches' eyes turned toward him, their hate almost tangible but tinged with fear now.

Agnesi turned to face the others, who glared at her. "Wait, we can get the money back. We'll trace it through the transaction history—"

"Oh, what are you going to do, my dear?" Diablesse said. "Go to the SEC? My, my, that would involve explaining the sources of your money: murder, theft, and blackmail at Worldbank. Besides, all transactions were authorized by your counsel. We could be litigating this for years, and I assure you the money moved a dozen times."

"Thirteen," Jeremy said.

Diablesse looked annoyed at Jeremy stepping on his moment of triumph. "I can count, Templar. It was an even dozen."

Jeremy smiled. "Oh, sorry, I made it a baker's dozen. I've always been fond of the number thirteen. I had the money switched one last time. You see, Lanier had all your account information too. You had just received an insurance settlement of $800,000 and it, too, was in the trust fund, along with your information on a certain Cayman bank. As soon as the money hit there, it did go on to many different shell companies. Just not the ones you intended."

Now he had everyone's attention.

"What? Where did it go?" Bob roared.

"You gave it all to the Missionaries of Charity," Jeremy said. "A nice endowment for Mother Theresa's continued works."

Both witch and demon looked at him with horrified expressions. Jeremy caught Prosperine's eye. The familiar stared at him with an enigmatic expression. Then she winked.

"Yep," Jeremy said. "A witch coven and a demon have made the largest contribution in history to the newest saint in the pantheon."

Both witch and demon literally shimmered with rage as they stepped toward Jeremy. From under his coat, Jeremy drew the bloodsword. The red jewel of its hilt glowed with equal fury. In his other hand, he held Shadowheart's pendant. Diablesse and Agnesi halted and glared.

"Hey, it's not all bad," Jeremy said, as he backed toward the door. "It's still tax-deductible."

The End

4

THE DEVIL YOU KNOW

Jeremy rested his lean, tall frame against his Mini Cooper in the parking lot of the Steel Magnolia restaurant and eyed the skyline of Charlotte, North Carolina. It boasted a few interesting skyscrapers. One looked like a spaceship with a crown atop it; another resembled a Wurlitzer.

The sound of expensive shoes tapping down the metal staircase interrupted his consideration of the skyline. Jeremy looked up as a handsome thirty-year-old, brown-haired man bounced lightly down the stairs. The form was an illusion. Bob Diablesse was pure demon, and ran, "all the high-end evil" in Charlotte. For once he was unaccompanied by his jaguar familiar, Prosperine, a striking redhead when she was in human form. Diablesse paused for a second when he spotted Jeremy, then came on.

"Jeremy," the demon said with a smile that didn't reach his eyes. "How's it hanging?"

Jeremy's return smile was equally chilly. "If you're asking about my bloodsword, it's hanging straight down under my left armpit."

"Yeah, nice coat, I can hardly see the blade. But there's no need to wave magic swords around." Bob made an expansive gesture at the beautiful restaurant and its environs. "We're on 'holy ground' here."

"Just wanted to make sure you remembered your pledge to keep this neutral territory."

"As if your guardian angel would let me forget. Besides, I got no real beef with you, Templar. The money you rerouted to Mother Teresa's charity when we scammed the Agnesi witch coven wasn't mine." His voice abruptly deepened. "That would have been a totally different matter. Still, you have made yourself quite a dedicated crew of enemies."

"Just me?" Jeremy said. "The Agnesi ignoring you?"

Bob grimaced. "It's Kitsune's coven now. I'm not sure what happened to Agnesi, but I bet it wasn't pleasant considering how she lost their magical wellspring. No, they're not ignoring me. My own stupidity for showing my face in your company. I've lost a werewolf and two ogres so far. At least you have a guardian angel."

"Less useful against witches than you might suppose," Jeremy answered. "Witches are corrupted humans. She can't strike them the way she could for example…you."

"Yeah," Bob said.

"You have Prosperine," Jeremy said. "Isn't she immune to witches?"

"Resistant, not immune. Familiars are kind of a battery pack for witches. A reward for serving the dark powers. Kitsune would love to get her hands on Prosperine, but she's bound to me."

Bob joined Jeremy in leaning against the Mini. "So, we tangled with a coven, and contrary to our expectations, they didn't leave town after we kicked their butts."

"Worse yet," Jeremy added, "Templar intelligence says more are coming, witches and warlocks both. We don't know where they're getting the money for all this. We're trying to disrupt them, but there are so few of us…"

Bob stroked his chin. "As for money, it turns out that Kitsune is the driving force behind Pink Lady cosmetics."

Jeremy gaped at him. "Those women who drive pink Cadillacs and dress like overage Southern debutantes?"

"Yeah," Bob said, "they scare me too. Turns out that some of their more special cosmetic lines involve human byproducts. Whole villages in Africa and India have disappeared into their vats. So

Kitsune will be able to refill their coffers eventually. There must be some other reason they're flocking here. It's hard to believe it's just to duke it out with us. It seems like once again we may be facing an enemy too powerful for either of us alone."

"Might be worth delaying any reckoning between us till the matter is dealt with," Jeremy said. "Truce?"

"Like Charlton Heston said in *Major Dundee*, 'until the Apache is taken or destroyed.'"

"You're a big movie fan, aren't you Bob?"

"Dude, we own Hollywood."

<hr>

When Jeremy returned to his design studio in nearby South End, he found Shadowheart, his guardian angel, sitting cross-legged on the steps next to the sushi place. She chose to appear as a snub-nosed, blond teenage mallrat, God alone knew why.

"Place safe?" Jeremy asked.

"Yep," she said, idly tossing a hackysack from hand to hand. "No attacks by witches, no demonic booby traps. They know I can't do much to them unless they attack me directly, and they aren't that stupid. How did your meeting with Diablesse go?"

"Truce, and Prosperine's aid," he replied.

Shadowheart's face grew stormy. "I don't like it. But in this situation, the best defense is a good offense. Prosperine can attack witches, where I cannot. Crap, you'd think the Almighty would let me bag a few humans for the greater good."

He looked at her with bemusement. "That's a slippery slope. Trust me, we've been doing it forever."

Shadowheart's enigmatic smile made him wonder how much she was having fun at his expense.

"You coming in?" he asked.

She snorted. "I'm never far, but no, I think I'll stay on guard at least until sunrise."

"Right, you never sleep."

She nodded. "Just like rust."

Jeremy walked into the long hallways of the renovated factory building. Known by the pretentious title of The Lofts at Factory South, its residents just called it the old Lance Cracker factory. He gratefully found his way to the studio door that opened into a high-ceiling room full of cameras and computer equipment. The front was his work area; the back was where he entertained during rare parties. He'd partitioned off a bedroom for late nights.

He'd left his phone there to recharge. When he picked it up, he saw a message.

"This is Barbara McCauley of Harris Hospice at Presbyterian Hospital calling on behalf of your great aunt, Elizabeth Agnesi. Your aunt is not doing well, and she asked me to call and see if you would come to see her. I'm afraid she doesn't have much time left. Our number is…"

Jeremy stood stock still, sleepiness banished. Agnesi, calling for him? What could the witch want and why the pretext? He sighed. There was only one way to find out.

The drive to Presbyterian Hospital was short. McCauley, a kindly fifty-year old with tired eyes, greeted him at the entrance to the ward. She expressed amazement at his great-aunt's finding him. "She said a friend mentioned seeing your work at the Light Factory show and here you are. What a lucky coincidence and just in time."

The miasma of a hospital, a mix of disinfectant and illness, bit at his nose as they walked down the corridor, empty at this late hour. They came up to a private room. Inside were a few flowers, from whom, Jeremy couldn't imagine. "I'd like to go in alone if I may," Jeremy said. "My great-aunt and I have been estranged for a long time."

"Of course," McCauley said. "I'll be in my office at the front if you need me.

Jeremy walked in, alert for any sign of a witchtrap. He looked down at the ancient woman. It was hard to associate the emaciated crone with the gorgeous blonde of mere weeks ago. He fought the urge for pity.

Agnesi's eyes opened and filled with a bright malice. There was still force to the former coven leader.

"You asked for me, Witch."

"Yes, Templar," the voice barely above a whisper. "I have little time left before the dark, the judgment, and the fire."

"Don't repent to me. I'm not a priest." Templar he might be, but he was not sure of Heaven or Hell. In that respect, he was as much a heretic as she.

"You're my enemy by blood and oath," she said. "And it's too late for me to change. I have too much pride. I'll pay my bill."

"But," the voice strengthened, and she rose slightly from her pillow, "first I'll be revenged on my coven, on those who turned on me, who betrayed me to a death I could have held at bay for long ages of the world. I'll tell you how to destroy them, Templar, and perhaps you too will die in the battle, making my revenge complete."

"It's nice to have goals," Jeremy said.

Agnesi glared at him. "The coven is depleted of energy and magic. We invested so much in the ritual for the force pool. All of it was lost when you cheated us and we lost the land where the pool was to manifest. So, Kitsune plans a new ritual. She'll sacrifice to Shu, Egyptian God of the Storms, to summon a Witchwind, a demonic spell that tears the souls from its victims, tumbling them in the night wind for eternity, knowing neither rest nor satisfaction.

"You must turn the Witchwind on them. It's a dangerous wind, Templar, sentient and malicious. It can only be handled from within a pentagram protected by candles made from the fat of children." She smacked her lips together and sighed. "So tender, so juicy, and so delicious."

Jeremy's sword hand twitched. He stilled it. The witch would be dead soon anyway.

"Break the pentagram, Templar."

"How—" Jeremy began.

Agnesi's eyes drifted over Jeremy's shoulder and widened. Her face distorted, her mouth stretching open so far it seemed in must unhinge in a scream that did not come. The utter horror on her countenance froze Jeremy for seconds. Then her eyes were fixed forever.

Jeremy slowly turned and saw Shadowheart, not in her great, grim, archangel form but still as the blond teen. She regarded him with level eyes.

"What did she see?" Jeremy asked.

"The face of the bill collector," Shadowheart said.

"It must be a terrible face," Jeremy said.

"For some," Shadowheart replied softly.

"What happens to her on the other side?" He jerked his head toward the corpse.

"It's not for you to know such a dire thing."

He looked down at the witch, frozen in her agonal pose. "She made candles of children. I can deal with her fate quite easily."

"Oh, no, Jeremy. Oh, no," Shadowheart replied. "I have existed from time out of mind and seen all there is to see, yet even I cannot contemplate her punishment with equanimity. The fate of those who prey on the helpless is infinitely terrible. It would break your mind in seconds."

Jeremy looked down at the witch and nodded. "Good." He turned his back on the dead and walked off.

<hr>

Morning came and with it, Prosperine. Mike, the photographer next door, mistook the familiar for one of his steady stream of gorgeous models and tried to usher her into his studio. Jeremy rescued him before Prosperine turned him into breakfast. Mike offered to photograph her for free, capturing, as he put it, "her wild, cat-like expression." But Prosperine's form was of Bob's choosing, and beautiful as she was in a leggy, slim-busted fashion, she disdained admiration.

"Well," Jeremy said, closing the door, "it will be a while before he forgives me for hauling you away."

Prosperine curled up on his sofa, legs under her, enjoying the coffee she'd helped herself to as Jeremy filled her in. Shadowheart drifted randomly through his apartment. It was easier for her to manifest just as an image, but wherever she drifted, she could still watch the familiar. Prosperine no longer reacted with complete terror to Shadowheart's appearance, at least when she was in mall-rat mode.

Jeremy paced up and down, sipping his own coffee. "How does one break a pentagram?"

"This isn't just any pentagram," Prosperine said. Her voice was low and soft, with a hint of growl. She brushed thick red hair out of her green eyes. "One secured with such candles can't be easily fractured."

"I could do it with my bloodsword." He gestured toward the plain Templar long sword with its crystal, resting in wall hooks. Since the familiar entered his apartment, the magic gem pulsed red, as if it, too, watched her warily.

Shadowheart floated by him, upside down. "The backflows would tear your human body to pieces. I can't hold off a whole coven and protect you from the pentagram's shattering."

"Worried about your skin, Angel?" Prosperine said.

Shadowheart flipped over and glared down at her. "Quiet, Jaguar, or Jeremy's home will have a new rug. I can't be killed, but I can be damaged and driven from space-time."

"Then there's the Witchwind," Jeremy continued, ignoring the squabble. "If we do attack the pentagram, how do we avoid the Witchwind to even reach it?"

A smile flashed over Shadowheart's face. "What if we were to substitute one of the candles?"

Prosperine shook her head. "Witches can smell human essence in these candles and they are surrounded with a magic aura. They could tell an ordinary candle easily."

"What if," Jeremy began slowly, "the candle was made from a human, and imbued with magic, just not one friendly to the coven?"

"Who've you got in mind?" Prosperine growled, putting her feet on the floor.

"Relax," he said. He walked over to the phone and punched in the number. "Ms. McCauley? Jeremy Leclerc here. Sorry I left so abruptly last night. I was upset at my great-aunt's death…yes…thank you. I need to make arrangements to pick up her body…"

The embalmer at McDougal Funeral Home was appalled by Jeremy's request, even though he assured the man that it was Great Aunt Agnesi's last request that she literally light a candle, rather than curse the darkness. Fortunately, $10,000 in unmarked bills provided by a grumbling Bob Diablesse soothed the embalmer's conscience.

"What the hell," the embalmer said. "Ever since Keith Richards snorted his dad's ashes, we've been getting these wacky requests nonstop."

Jeremy rode back to his apartment with a plastic tub of witch-fat in the back, hoping none of Charlotte's lunatic soccer moms or self-important, Lexus driving, cell phone addicts rear-ended him. Shadowheart, refusing to have anything to do with the project, rode silently in the gold and crystal housing he wore for her on his chest.

Prosperine was off buying the material for a candle-making kit. She met them at the door to his building. Very practically, she'd bought both sushi and sake. Prosperine delighted in spending Diablesse's money. There was no love lost between the demon and his enslaved familiar.

"Appreciate the thought," Jeremy said, "but considering what else we are going to be cooking, I don't think I could eat."

"Squeamish," she scoffed, but followed him inside.

Jeremy set up the material for making the candle. Prosperine amused herself on the computer and downed a prodigious quantity of sushi and sake. Finally, he dropped into a chair next to her and reached for the sake. "This still seems impossible," he said. "We have to break into the Pink Lady warehouse, find the candles, photograph one so we can make a duplicate, then break back in to substitute it."

Prosperine gave him an amused look. "The candles are six inches tall, three-inches wide, dyed red with Mandarin Six dye. There's a pentagram carved on one side and with an Ankh opposite. They are capped with a one-inch white metal bell."

He stared at her. "How did you know?"

"While you were futzing around, I logged onto the coven's UK webpage. There's a hidden feature in the Pink Lady webpage, but I belonged to a witch once, so I know all the codes. I got into a chat room, told them I was a journeyman witch trying to start a new coven in New Delhi next to an orphanage. They were happy to help. I sent the photos to your printer." She pointed to where the machine was spitting out photos.

"They just told you?" he marveled.

"You may recall I'm actually a card-carrying member of Evil, Inc."

Shadowheart blinked in, floating through the air in a lotus position. "Well, you did say she'd be useful."

"Time to cook the candle," Prosperine said. "I'll get the dye and cap—"

"Tell you what," Jeremy said. "How about you cook the candle and we get the dye and cap."

Prosperine laughed.

After midnight, they drove to the Pink Lady warehouse out on Steele Creek, in a wilderness of giant one-story box buildings south of Charlotte. A few new neighborhoods of cookie-cutter houses and old, smaller homes dotted the areas in between the giant warehouses and their lakes of asphalt. They found a spot at a nearby diner, dropped the car, and walked to the warehouse. Like most parts of Charlotte, it was blessed with trees and undergrowth. They found a small clearing and some large rocks to rest on near the warehouse and watched the staff file out, lighting cigarettes and calling out goodnights.

"I guess we wait," Jeremy said as he studied the building, looking for entrances and weak points. There were still a lot of high-end cars in the lot. Jeremy supposed they belonged to Kitsune and her inner circle. As the sun sank, a small number of automatic lights gave inadequate illumination, though the main entrance glowed.

"I hate this part," Prosperine said. "I'm bored already."

"I thought cats were patient animals; sit outside a mousehole for hours, that sort of thing."

"I'm not a cat; I just play one on TV."

"Funny," he said.

"We could have sex," she suggested.

"I thought you didn't like me," Jeremy said.

"I don't," she replied with a puzzled air. "What's that got to do with anything?"

"No, thanks. I'm not sure you wouldn't eat me afterward."

"I won't guarantee that I wouldn't eat you during."

"Wow, with pillow talk like that, how could any man turn you down?"

"Ah, well," she said, leaning back against a pillar. "I suspect it would only have killed two or three minutes."

Jeremy laughed. "You demons sure know how to hurt a guy."

"You have no idea, yet."

"My guardian angel will beat your ass like a snare drum," Jeremy warned. The reminder had a salutary effect on Prosperine. She shut up.

To Jeremy's surprise, a dozen pink Cadillacs drove into the lot. Some carried several women, also dressed in pink and with a genetically improbable degree of blondness. They gathered and twittered in high voices.

"There must be some sort of meeting," he said.

Prosperine leaned forward, intent on the group, and Jeremy remembered her superior hearing. "Yes, Kitsune is addressing them. I think this is our best chance to break in."

He nodded. "Around back."

The two quickly moved around to the rear of the building. Prosperine proved as sure-footed in the dark as her original jaguar form. Jeremy stumbled behind her. They flitted from shadow to shadow, reaching a back door. Jeremy checked the security system with his tester. It showed no power. They were in luck. Prosperine blocked the view of Jeremy's penlight as he made short work of the lock.

Then they were in a vast, shadowy space of immense crates and parked warehouse equipment. In the distance, there were lights and voices.

"Shadowheart," he whispered to the crystal housing sitting on his chest. "Do you have us cloaked?"

Yes, she mind-whispered. *I'm suppressing their magic wards. Don't distract me!* The breaking of the connection was like a slap.

"Can you smell the candles?" he turned to Prosperine.

"Yes," she said. "And more. There are guard dogs in here, but they must be locked away because of all the humans over there. Good thing too, or they'd be all over me. I smell witches as well.

"There's a boxed room over there," she said peering into the dark.

"We can reach it by climbing these crates and making our way across the top."

Jeremy spotted the room, one of a number of enclosed plasterboard structures in the building, rooms for computers, phones, or people to work out of the unheated and uncooled space.

Prosperine boosted Jeremy up the twelve-foot-high stacks. Then, with claws and legs stronger than human, she followed on her own. Music started up at the other end, along with the flashing of colored lights. Whatever the Pink Ladies were up to, it sounded like a party and provided cover to their progress across the crate tops.

Soon they were leaping across to the roof of the boxed room. Jeremy pried up the hatch next to the A/C unit for the office space below.

Halt, Shadowheart demanded. *There's a ward below I can't neutralize. Any soldier of light will set it off. I can do nothing about it.*

"What?" Prosperine said.

Jeremy remembered the familiar could not hear Shadowheart and relayed what she'd said.

"Fine," she whispered back. "Give me the candle. I'm evil. I won't set it off."

He handed her the satchel with the Agnesi candle safely packed within. The familiar dropped a distance that would have tasked human knees, then disappeared inside. Jeremy waited in the increasing cold of the warehouse, though sweat trickled down his back. It seemed forever before she reappeared, leapt up, and caught at his arms. Jeremy pulled her out and secured the roof hatch.

"Done," she said handing him the satchel.

"I want to get closer to the action," he said. "Find out what's going on."

Prosperine gave him a look. "Wasn't in the plan, Templar."

He grinned at her. "Bug out if you like, but now who's squeamish?"

"Kiss my…"

He raised a finger. "My angel doesn't like bad words."

Bullshit, Shadowheart whispered in his mind.

They made their way more carefully to the area of light and music.

When they gained sight of the mass of pink-clad women before a dais, Jeremy felt they couldn't risk getting closer.

Kitsune and several other gorgeous witches of the coven entered from behind a curtain to loud applause and cheers. The music cut off.

The gorgeous Asian witch with her three feet of silky black hair and perfect complexion mounted the dais.

"Pink Ladies," Kitsune announced. "Tonight is a special night. Pink Lady Cosmetics announces a new line of ultra-rejuvenating moisturizing creams. The *Bewitching* line of creams firms wrinkles, plumps lips, literally takes years off your body."

The women undulated like a pink tide.

"And you, our loyal staff of Best Sellers, will be the first to receive the benefit. Tonight, at the Sleeping Dragon restaurant, you will be gathered for a special demonstration." She smiled with the benevolence of a saint. "Ladies, if any one of you does not feel and look ages different, I will personally pay you $10,000."

Applause filled the room.

"Fiendish," Jeremy whispered.

"Yes," Prosperine said with a clear note of admiration. "The coven has a stock of willing victims, delivering themselves to the slaughter gladly. The Witchwind will tear their souls free, and Shu will enrich the coven."

"Time to get out of here," Jeremy said. The back door was hundreds of yards away, and he wasn't sure how long Kitsune was going to keep haranguing the crowd.

As they moved back to the door, Jeremy opted for a shorter route. The crate stacks petered out, and they dropped to the floor.

It was a mistake. A ghastly green spotlighted them, and the universe turned into a whirling maelstrom of colors.

"Witchtrap," Prosperine shouted. "We're being transported. Grab onto me."

Jeremy could barely make out Prosperine's silhouette in the clashing colors, but he reached out at something human-shaped and found his hand on her lean waist.

Suddenly the universe stabilized into an unending purple plain of swirling fog. A trio faced them: the buxom Welsh witch, Llewellen, and the beautiful, redheaded Echols twins. The witches seemed both shocked and surprised.

"What?" said Llewellen in a high, breathy voice. "You two!"

Jeremy drew the bloodsword; its red jewel glowed with a sullen anger.

"We have you now," shouted one of the Echols twins, her hair twisting and flailing though there was no wind.

Llewellyn's eyes went wild, and she raised clawed hands. A cloud of fire burst from her fingertips, aimed at Jeremy. Prosperine leapt in front of him, her hands cutting symbols that burned green in the air. The bolt of fire rebounded at a right angle, into the Echols who shrieked and dodged.

Jeremy raced around Prosperine, sword raised. Llewellen glared at him. "Slow," she commanded.

And Jeremy did, into a nightmarish feeling of crawling in slow motion, of running through treacle. Prosperine broke the spell by hauling him backward; her powers as a familiar seemed to disrupt the witch's abilities.

"We're in a witch bubble," Prosperine shouted, "a ball of space-time they made. I can't break it. We're dead if we can't escape. Summon the angel."

"Shadowheart," Jeremy called out, "help us." He'd never had to summon his guardian angel before. She'd always appeared when needed. There was no answer, and Jeremy knew fear. For the first time since they had been joined in Scotland years ago, he was out of touch.

The Echols twins recovered, hair singed and smoldering; they too waved their arms. The air filled with shards of sharpened steel. "Steel Rain!" The Echols cackled, and the barrage of pointed metal flashed toward them.

This time Jeremy thrust Prosperine behind him and whirled the bloodsword in a figure eight. The steel rain fell to the ground as natural water.

Llewellen fired a lightning bolt at them, and the charge fell on the bloodsword, which glowed blue but neither took nor transmitted harm from the bolt.

"A Templar," snarled Echol One, "with a familiar to block our spells. Oh, someone will suffer for this."

"Hold them under fire," Llewellen said. "I'll return with the others." She wrapped a fold of her cloak over her face and disappeared. Bolts flew from the Echols, and Jeremy parried frantically.

Prosperine's hands waved, leaving behind a glowing net in the air. "Use the jewel. I'll protect us." The glowing net enveloped them.

Jeremy knelt and placed the gem to his forehead. *Shadowheart,* he sent, *find me. Find me. Hurry.* There was the sense of shouting into a great distance that did not echo. Then with a snap that dazed him, contact was made. Jeremy felt himself pulled spinning into the sky.

Alone.

Below, still in her net of blue, Prosperine's outraged face turned up to him. Llewellen reappeared with five witches. They surrounded Prosperine, closing in with blasts of fire and smoke, swarming over the familiar.

"Noooooooooooo," he screamed. Then she was lost to sight, and he was in an icy limbo with neither light nor sound.

Suddenly the universe reappeared, and he fell, landing on the side of a forested hill outside the warehouse, near where they had parked. He felt hands that held no human warmth on him and looked up into the eyes of his guardian angel's youthful manifestation.

"Jeremy," she said, her blue eyes wide with shock. "Where were you? How did this happen? It felt like you were on the other side of the universe, I could barely get a trace—"

"Never mind," he cried, leaping up. "You left Prosperine behind. The witches have her."

Shadowheart raised her hands. "She was with you? Jeremy, I could not see her. Even with the stone's help and all my power, I could barely touch you. It was as if you no longer existed."

"Can you send us back?" he demanded.

She shook her head, biting her lip. "No, Jeremy. I have no idea where you were."

"Damn," he said. "God damn it all to hell. She's probably dead by now. And she died thinking I abandoned her. Ran like a gutless coward. Oh, some knight, some Templar I am."

Shadowheart gave him a puzzled look and again put her hand on his shoulder. "Jeremy, remember what Prosperine was, a demon familiar. If she fought by your side, it was because she had no means to flee. She'd have left you behind in an instant if she could and without these pangs of conscience, as she has none."

"We have to see if she's still alive," he demanded.

Shadowheart startled him with a rueful laugh. He looked at her, angry and offended. "Oh Jeremy, and I so doubted your faith. Here you are trying to rescue a familiar because deep down you think there is something worth saving in everyone. Oh, poor child, poor child, I thought you a cynic and you are the most dewy-eyed of innocents. You need a better angel than I to protect you. I've never understood you even a little."

He looked at her face, gone sad and distant. "Well, I don't know about any of that, but I want to see if we can find her."

She nodded. "Tell me everything you saw and heard."

Shadowheart paced as Jeremy filled her in. "Kitsune has her victims nearby. While you were inside," she said, gesturing across the street, "a legion of women in pink showed up at the Sleeping Dragon restaurant."

He rubbed a hand over his face, fighting fatigue. "Right, it's a vegetarian restaurant too. Kitsune must have rented it."

He flipped open his cell phone and called Bob.

"Diablesse," Bob answered.

"Leclerc. The ceremony is tonight, and the bad guys have Prosperine."

"Did you complete the mission?"

"Yes, damn it, but they sprang a witchtrap on us. I got away, but they have your familiar."

"Wow, I'll miss her."

"She may still be alive," Jeremy said.

"Bummer for her," Bob replied. "They'll probably eviscerate her or something."

"Gather your forces and meet us at the Pink Lady Warehouse across from the Sleeping Dragon on Steel Creek."

Bob laughed. "Oh, Jeremy, you kill me. Hey, revel in the fact that you've set the witches up for disaster, saved the town, and reduced the demonic population by one familiar."

Jeremy stared at the phone, then put it back to his ear. "You're going to leave her? Doesn't she have value?"

"Oh, yeah, but not enough to tangle with dozens of powerful witches and warlocks at night on their turf. I renounce her." He hung up.

Jeremy looked at Shadowheart. "Looks like it's up to us."

"Yes," she said softly, "but understand, as witches are humans, my powers against them are limited in the Realm of Earth. We will be in peril of our existence."

Jeremy considered. "I guess it comes down to the question of who we are. How can you tell the good guys from the bad if we act the same? Ends may sometimes justify means, but not always and not tonight."

Shadowheart morphed before his eyes into her tall, black-haired, warrior princess form, black and red wings spread wide. She put her arms around his chest. "Then let us face our doom." She vaulted into the sky with a rustle of great wings.

The ground fell away, and they rose to about five hundred feet, well above any stray beam from the streetlights. The wind whipped Jeremy's hair and coat, and he was grateful for it in the coolness. Shadowheart's black hair streamed out behind her as her wings beat slowly, with surprisingly little sound. But the night was not quiet. Every sound of a human city, traffic, voices, airplanes, reached him. He spied a couple walking a dog and wondered what would happen if they suddenly looked up.

They flew south. The parking lot was filled with pink cars and women walking into the building under pink parasols and hats.

The warehouse remained dark, save for a few small lights near the main entrance. In the parking lot beyond, he saw bobbing blue will-o'-wisps and shadowy figures. Shadowheart dove for the treetops in a motion that made Jeremy gulp and landed in cover of some trees and bushes, just short of the asphalt.

"Closer than this I cannot go, unless we plunge into open battle," she said, her voice strained. "They have many magical safeguards I've circumvented, and I have wrapped us in a magic they cannot see through. I cannot remain undetected closer than this. There are at least thirty powerful witches and warlocks out there."

He looked up at his towering angel. "Only stealth serves us now. We must wait till the Witchwind is summoned and the pentagram breaks. Then I can race in and find Prosperine, if she is still alive. Can you hold the Witchwind off me?"

"Yes. But you must hurry back to me. The range of my defense is only tens of feet if I must battle witches at the same time."

Jeremy nodded and, drawing his bloodsword, circled around the parking lot. A couple of vans were parked back there, and he moved among them. Finally, as close as he dared, Jeremy saw the coven. Witches and warlocks stood in the pentagram, drawn on the parking lot's surface. As he watched, the horrid candles were lit. The witches outlined the shape of the pentagram with their bodies and there, just outside the pentagram, lay Prosperine, nude, bound, and bruised.

Kitsune stood forth, dressed in a white and orange kimono that changed shape and color as they watched. Behind her, the coven began to chant in a low deep voice.

"Shu," Kitsune called. "I invoke the ancient bargain. Souls and life, I offer you, including this traitorous familiar." She glared down at Prosperine, who returned the favor. "Come, sup deep and refill our powers, rejuvenate our bodies and our fortunes."

The trees rustled. The chanting rose. Leaves and paper trash began to whirl about. Prosperine rolled onto her back. A snarl burst from her lips. But the sound was quickly drowned by blasts of wind that struck in the lot, rocking the van near Jeremy. The wind rolled over him, feeling somehow filthy, cold and hungry. Yet it did not bite. Shadowheart held the hungry wind off him, but Jeremy could feel its malicious intelligence questing about, as if it knew something was there, but frustrated, was unable to seize on it.

Jeremy, stand ready, Shadowheart's voice said in his mind. *The Witchwind senses a weakness in the pentagram.*

As if to confirm this, the wind's probing blasts abandoned him. It whipped over Prosperine, who screamed in pain.

And then a candle guttered out.

"No," Kitsune shrieked as the wind invaded the pentagram. It was as if a hurricane had poured into the contained space repressed by the pentagram and its glowing magic candles. Witches and warlocks were tossed like matchsticks. Some fought back, and the resulting bolts of energy sizzled against the interior of the pentagram.

Jeremy plunged out, running for Prosperine. She lay, temporarily safe, outside the pentagram with the Witchwind raging within it. As he closed in, a warlock, his clothes blasted away along with much of his skin, stumbled out over the extinguished candle. He looked at Jeremy with crazed eyes. The warlock's hands flew up, blood spraying off them, and a bolt of radiant force licked at Jeremy. He parried it with the bloodsword, and in the same continuous motion, whipped the sword in a circle and plunged it into the warlock. Then he booted the man off his sword, back into the maelstrom in the pentagram.

Jeremy reached down and hauled an astonished Prosperine to her feet, slicing the bonds off her wrists and feet. "Follow me," he shouted.

They raced back to Shadowheart as the wind howled around them. In seconds, they reached the angel, who cast her great wings around them, shutting out the wind. The battle to keep the wind at bay must have lasted only minutes, but it seemed like hours. In a gap over their heads, Jeremy saw the Witchwind. Saw its prisoners, the thousands of souls blown through the night without rest. Saw Kitsune's face, mouth open in a scream, before her image disappeared into wind and clouds.

Finally, Shadowheart's wings opened. The three turned back to the pentagram and a scene of slaughter. The candles were out, their magic exhausted. A pile of shattered and torn bodies lay in the center.

"Hey," a voice called. "Did I miss the party?"

They turned to see Bob Diablesse emerge from the woods at the head of a company of ogres and goblins. But none of the company approached Shadowheart, closely watching the towering angel with a wary fear.

"Thought you weren't coming?" Jeremy said, fatigue and pain slowing his words. He handed his long leather coat to Prosperine, who slipped it on. The sight of a naked redhead in his black leather coat made him glad he'd survived.

Bob shrugged. "I changed my mind. Figured I would come by with the boys and see how things were going."

"Meaning whether or not we were winning," Jeremy said.

"Umm, yes."

"What are we going to do with all the bodies?" Jeremy wondered.

Bob waved his army of ogres and orcs forward. "Come on, boys, team-building dinner. Everybody finish your plate."

The ogres jogged by, chanting, "Yum, yum, eat em up, eat em up good."

Bob grinned. "They're doing that for your benefit. They're really a lot more sophisticated than they let on."

"Yeah," Jeremy said, carefully not looking at the human smorgasbord. "We're going to go now."

Bob looked at Prosperine, his pointed tail lashing. "You going with them?"

Prosperine looked down her nose at him. "Your power over me was broken when you gave me up for dead."

Bob shrugged. "Hey, if you want to give up a great 401K and a killer benefit package, that's your issue." He joined the shuffling mob, pointed tail standing straight up between his leathery wings. "Hey boys, wait up, save me a leg."

Jeremy, Prosperine, and Shadowheart wasted no time setting off at a brisk pace.

At the rise of the hill Shadowheart was again her teen self, clad in mall-rat clothes.

"I suppose," Prosperine, said to her, "that I must thank you for your help."

"Your thanks would be as uncomfortable for me to receive as for you to give. Thank Jeremy if you must. Anything I did, I did for him."

"What are we going to do with her now?" Jeremy looked from Shadowheart to Prosperine. "I'm not sure I can go for catch and release on a familiar."

"Well," Shadowheart said, "based on your prior track record, I expect you'll sleep with her."

Prosperine grinned. "He won't be sleeping."

Shadowheart's right hand snapped up. There was a flash. Where

Prosperine had stood was now a tiny black kitten. It gave a piteous mew as it sat on Jeremy's coat.

Jeremy sighed. "Shadowheart."

"Oh, all right," Shadowheart said, snapping her fingers again. Prosperine reappeared, made a squalling sound, and, naked again, leapt up into a tree.

"We could call the fire department," Shadowheart said, crossing her arms and tossing her blond hair.

"No," Jeremy said, "but you've given me an idea. Come down, Prosperine. She's not going to hurt you."

"And if I was," Shadowheart murmured, "hiding in a tree wouldn't help."

Prosperine dropped to the ground on the other side of Jeremy and peered around him at the angry angel.

"Your natural form," Jeremy asked, "is a panther. Right?"

"Yes," she said slowly. "I was born a jaguar in South America a thousand years ago. An Aztec priest invoked my demonic essence, and I became a familiar."

"I can't have you hanging around here snacking on the locals. If we let you go, will you return to the wild?"

"Great solution." Shadowheart applauded. "Maybe she can make lunchables out of a few hundred humans as she hikes back to Brazil."

"Oh, I imagine that you could ensorcell her with something special that would make eating people unpalatable."

A smile stole over her snub-nosed face. "Yes. Cramps from hell and explosive diarrhea…"

"Humans taste lousy anyway." Prosperine sniffed.

"Well?" Jeremy said. "It's a long way back to South America where the jaguars lair in trees and drop on peccaries, but you'll make it. It beats a Templar dungeon in Scotland."

Prosperine gave him an enigmatic look. "I'll take your deal, Templar."

Jeremy turned to Shadowheart and nodded. Prosperine stepped clear of Jeremy as Shadowheart's hands came up again and waved through the air, cutting blue lines through the air. Prosperine's form shimmered, and in place of her red-haired slim form was a beautiful, black jaguar.

But only for a moment, the image shifted again, and a smaller, tawny cougar appeared in its place. It looked up at him with golden eyes, and to his surprise, Prosperine's voice sounded in his mind.

I like you, Jeremy, you're interesting. Fun things happen around you. If you find yourself in need of a familiar, head for the mountains near Asheville. Open your mind on the highest hilltop. I'll find you. Something like laughter rippled through his mind, and the cougar made a long leap and vanished into the bushes.

Jeremy picked up his coat, and Shadowheart fell in with him as they walked back to his car. Before they got there, they were surrounded by a horde of women in pink, shrieking and leaping about.

"Look, look," one woman said to the crowd, "all the lines on my face are gone. My arthritis doesn't even hurt."

"The heck with that honey," said a rare brunette. "My breasts are three inches higher and firm as rocks."

The crowd of rejuvenated pink ladies swirled around them. Shadowheart shook her head at Jeremy's bemusement. "The coven was set up to drain the Pink Ladies' life force. I guess when we broke the pentagram, the energy flowed the other way."

"Well," Jeremy said, "looks like there is some justice after all."

The End

5

MEDI-EVIL

An elf is walking into your studio, Shadowheart mindspoke.

Jeremy saved his latest graphic design and pushed back from his flatscreen. "Okay, what's the punch line?"

No punch line. His guardian angel sighed from her home in the crystal and gold housing he wore on his chest. *If you could take you mind off making money for a second, there is an actual elf walking up the stairs.*

Jeremy debated reaching for his bloodsword, hidden under his desk. It was the weapon of the Knights Templar, but the folk of Faerie were not usually evil.

She came in through the door, setting off its electronic chime. Tall and elegant, she had thick blond hair, framing a pale face with sea-gray eyes. Delicate pointed ears poked from the golden hair. As she walked toward him with a balletic grace, she said, "Jeremy Leclerc?" It was pure music; he could have listened to it forever.

Snap out of it, Shadowheart sent.

Jeremy recovered his voice. "Yes."

"Thee are young for a Knight Templar."

He swallowed. "Most people around here know me as graphic

designer, but yes, I'm a Templar. How it is that one of the fair folk walks abroad in Charlotte, North Carolina?"

She laughed like a brook running over clean stones. "You know of the Renaissance Festival in Huntersville?"

"Sure," he began, then stopped. "You're kidding."

She smiled. "Did thee not wonder why the humans would have come up with such longing for what was otherwise a period of hunger, pestilence, and war? The idea was planted by we who still dwell among the humans. Look—" She twirled in her black leather and green velvet. "I can wear the traditional garb of my people and they put down any peculiarity to my being artistic.

"There's a circuit of such events: Shakespeare revivals, Burning Man festivals, Medieval Times restaurants, Las Vegas, Indievision's Halloween party… We get around."

Jeremy shook his head. "What do the fair folk want of me?"

"The festivals have been good to us," she said. "But of late, a shadow has grown. A human has learned that some of us who travel with the festivals truly are of otherworld. He has been…shaking us down."

Jeremy realized his mouth was hanging open. "May I get you something to drink?"

"Pure water," she said.

Jeremy reached for the small refrigerator he kept in his studio and pulled out two bottles of Poland Springs. As he handed one to the elf, he said, "May I know your name?"

She sipped the drink. "Eldárwen Táralóm, but on my 1099, I use Tara Lom."

"Very well, Tara. I sympathize with your problems, and there is no enmity between Templars and Elvenkind, though we have fought others of the Sidhe." He shivered with remembrance of a deadly encounter with a Bain Sidhe near SouthPark Mall last Christmas. "But my charge is to protect humans from supernatural evil. Not the other way around."

"Jeremy," she sang, and his resolution wavered. "We cannot go to the human authorities. If you do not police this matter, then it may draw humans and us into conflict. Word reached us of the existence of a Templar in this unlikely place, and I slipped away to seek you."

"Can't the folk of Faerie dispose of him?"

"We cannot," Tara said. "Orc, witch or goblin, we could deal with. But he has invoked the old magic and raised a Norse goddess to protect him. She of the dark and light countenance, Hel by name and by homeland. Against an Elder God, we are powerless. He gives her worship and," Tara shuddered, "sacrifice. In return she protects him. He calls himself King of the Festival now, but I think he aims for wider dominion. None of the other folk know that I have come to the humans for help. My only ally is Copperfist the dwarf. The others are either taken, under guard, or utterly cowed."

"Who is this human?" Jeremy asked.

"His name is Derek Acre. He is aided by his cousin, Lester Shales."

Shadowheart? he mindspoke, wanting his guardian's advice. *Does she speak the truth?*

To Jeremy's surprise, Shadowheart manifested, something she rarely did. His guardian angel appeared in her usual guise of a small blond girl, more cute than pretty, wearing a simple blue dress.

"An angel walks with you?" Tara said in surprise. She bowed, her hands outstretched, and the pure beautiful speech of the Eldar flew from her lips. Shadowheart spoke the same in return, then turned to him.

"What do you say?" he asked.

"I do not make your moral choices, Jeremy. I am guard and guide only."

"Oh sure," Jeremy said, uncapping his bottle of water. "Now that I want your opinion…"

Tara turned to Shadowheart. "Is he always like this?"

Shadowheart rolled her eyes.

There were no other Templars closer than New York, but a few friends knew of his supernatural mission. Jeremy called Samantha Pelton, with whom he'd fought a Mandrake demon last year.

"You're kidding," she said, upon learning of the details.

"I could use your help," he said.

"Count on it," Samantha said. "Will I get to meet the elf babe, and is she broad-minded?"

"Yes, to the first, and your guess is as good as mine on the second."

His next call was to Sydney Tindall. Jeremy had rescued the Aussie expat from an unfortunate one-sided love affair with a local vampire, Debbie Middleton. Debbie enjoyed a truce with the forces of light, preferring to trade her legendary knowledge of sex for a nonfatal "nip and sip." But Sydney had the soul of a poet and had fallen in love with his demonic one-night stand. To avoid having to kill him for constantly interfering with her dinner plans, Debbie enlisted Jeremy's help. Jeremy consoled the tall Aussie through a three-day bender, and they'd been friends ever since.

"Sounds bonzer, mate," Sydney said. "Will I get to meet the elf-babe?"

<hr>

Jeremy met Sydney and Samantha at the gates of the festival early the next day. Despite the bright sunshine, it was mercifully cool for Halloween in North Carolina. Bagpipers skirled notes up to the blue of the sky. Red dust, stirred by hundreds of feet, hung over them. Revelers, many in Celtic or fantasy dress, wandered about.

Samantha waited in her usual jeans and T-shirt. Gold-rimmed glasses perched on her slender nose, and her auburn-gold hair reached her shoulders. Sam's small frame hid a surprising strength, and she looked a decade younger than her true age.

Sydney—tall, gangly, and blond—stood next to her in khakis, boots, and blue shirt, carrying a leather satchel. He wore sunglasses but still squinted in the sunlight.

"Jeremy, honey," Samantha said and kissed him. For a woman with no interest in men, she kissed well.

"Mate," Syd said, pumping his hand.

"Glad you both could make it" Jeremy smiled. "Last chance to back out."

"Don't be insulting." Samantha slapped his shoulder.

"Besides," Syd said, "who wants to live forever?"

"We do," they all chorused.

"Where's Shadowheart?" Samantha asked.

"Good question," Jeremy answered. "Well, Angel?"

I sense something, came Shadowheart's thought. *There are those here who will detect me if I manifest. For now, I will ride in my crystal.*

"Her feet are sore," Jeremy said aloud. "She wants to ride."

The crystal thumped him on the chest.

Samantha pointed at his cloak, mail, boots, and sword. "Nice get-up."

"One advantage to being a Templar." He grimaced. "I have the stuff, and it fits."

They bought tickets and walked up to the gate. A Charlotte cop gave Jeremy's ruby-hilted longsword a disapproving look.

"It gets peace-tied," the cop said, wrapping a piece of red ribbon about the weapon and scabbard. "No drawing it at the festival."

Jeremy and his friends passed through the ornate faux city wall and left human law on the other side. Once inside the festival, a few girls with daring décolletages that could only yield serious sunburn greeted them. "Welcome, masters and mistress. Enjoy the festival."

Jeremy led them down the main street with its faux medieval buildings, past the harpists, the giant walking tree, and various musicians, jugglers, and warriors. They entered a costume shop slightly back from the main street. Inside, Tara Lom waited for them. Samantha and Sydney needed a few seconds to recover from meeting the elf. Jeremy had to stop Syd from pulling out his journal and penning lines of poetry to her.

"Later," he insisted. "For now, we need to deck these two out in costume so we can move about in the back areas."

"Yes," Tara said. She smiled at Samantha, who looked a little faint. "Come with me. Thee does not seem the delicate type, so no fair maiden. Nor are thee quite tall enough for an elf..." In minutes, Samantha returned clad in green leathers and mail. Over her shoulder was a bow with a quiver of fletched arrows.

"An archer of the Rangers," Tara presented.

"I'm a bit rusty," Samantha said, "but I used to be a good hand with a bow."

"Now for you." She reached for Sydney's arm. A blissful smile lit his face. "I see a gentle soul, not a warrior, save at need, a cleric and scribe perhaps."

"Oh yes," Sydney said. "Perhaps I can even write a sonnet about you."

Samantha sighed. "Has he ever met a woman he hasn't fallen in love with?"

Jeremy shrugged. "At least he doesn't have commitment issues."

Sydney returned clad in a long, flowing cowled robe that he looked down at dubiously.

"Now, it is time for you to seek the dwarf, Degn Copperfist," Tara said. "His shop is down by the taffy store. Get word back to me when you are ready. Those of us that who are free await your word to strike."

It took a while to separate Sydney and Samantha from Tara, but eventually they made their way to dwarf's shop. They passed the haunted dungeon on the way. Jeremy's sharp eyes pierced the shadows, and he saw actual goblins in the dark, safely away from the sun's bright rays. He gritted his teeth at the abomination.

As they entered the dwarf's armory, a thickset fellow with a beard and sharp eyes waved them in. "Greeting, gentles. We take Master Card and Lady Visa both." His thick Scottish accent sounded genuine.

Jeremy answered him in the ancient tongue of his kind.

The dwarf's eyes widened. "So, Tara did find help among the humans."

Jeremy gestured to Syd and Samantha. "I'm armed, but the others need weapons."

The dwarf pointed at the walls, racked with heavy swords and axes.

"Not this tourist crap," Jeremy said. "These things are for actors to bang on each other; they're thick as bricks."

Copperfist roared in laughter and slapped his knee. "So, ye know true weapons. Come to the back." They followed the dwarf past two more of his kind and into a back room. "Lass, you're well equipped with a bow of Tara's people. But you'll need a decent knife. Something light…" He looked about.

Samantha walked over to the nearby anvil, picked up a heavy hammer, and casually flipped it several times.

"Well maybe not so light." Copperfist pulled down a short, broad blade of twenty inches length. "Not elf-pretty, but it will take off an arm."

He looked up at the lanky Aussie. "Do you have any experience with edged steel?"

"I had a Swiss army knife when I was twelve."

The dwarf sighed. He pulled a six-foot, metal-shod staff from the wall and tossed it to Syd, who caught it awkwardly. Then he pulled a small metal war ax from the wall. "Keep it under your cassock in the back," he grumbled. "If there's trouble, hit things in the head with it."

He handed Jeremy a beautiful white-hilted dagger. "I sense the magic in your sword and will ne'er touch that. But your armor leaves a lot to be desired." Ten minutes later, Jeremy stood in a new set of mixed plate and mail. Copperfist did the same for Samantha and Syd.

"Good luck to ye," Copperfist said. "Best you slip out the back."

Once outside, Syd turned to Jeremy. "What's the plan?"

"I'm going to find this King Acre. You two stick together, try and find out what you can. Look for places that are guarded or where they won't let you in. See if you can find where Tara's Faerie friends are being held. Watch out if you go near the torture chamber. There are real goblins there."

"Will you be all right alone?" Samantha asked.

Jeremy put a hand on her shoulder. "I'm never alone. Remember?" He tapped Shadowheart's crystal and gold pendant. "Though I'd better tuck her away." He placed the pendant under his mail. "For god's sake, be careful," he told his two friends.

"Thought you were agnostic, mate?" Syd grinned. "Though what more proof could you want than your own guardian angel?"

Even Doubting Thomas had nothing on you, Shadowheart murmured.

Jeremy grimaced. "Theology later, survival now."

Jeremy wandered the festival, taking in the scene. The fair was large and, at first glance, innocent fun. But to Jeremy's eyes, conditioned to see through both glamour and spell, there was much amiss.

He stopped at one show where a ventriloquist dummy dressed as a pirate insulted the audience. While some howled at the ribald humor, others seemed hurt and slunk off. They had no idea how easily they were escaping. The dummy and his handler were one parasitic demon, siphoning off emotional energy from the victims of his japes.

Finally, Jeremy saw the royal procession. At the head of it strode a florid, red-bearded man with crown, looking like a young Henry VIII. A trail of warriors with practical-looking weapons and armor accompanied him. Jeremy looked for guns but saw none. Not surprising with so many human police just outside the festival gate. The guards looked human though.

Not, Shadowheart whispered in his mind. His vision suddenly sharpened, and he could see that most were not men at all, but goblins, protected from the sun by a spell, though their tongues still lolled in their mouths as they panted, trying to keep to the shadows. One was a true man, dressed as a knight, probably Acre's cousin, Shales.

Behind the warriors were a train of beautiful girls, half in medieval costume and the others dressed as belly dancers. Over them all towered a woman. The right side of her imperious face was golden of skin tone and hair, beautiful if remote. The other side was blue and the hair dark gray, the skin drawn and still like that of a new corpse. Her right hand, bejeweled with rings and bracelets, hung from its sleeve, but the left was covered in a glove of the same Nordic blue as her dress and clutched a delicate, slender scepter. There was an unpleasant suggestion of excessive slenderness in the glove, as if it concealed not skin, but bone.

Hel, Shadowheart mind-whispered.

As if sensing Jeremy's regard, Hel turned toward him. Jeremy dodged behind a troupe of jugglers. The procession continued, and when it was nearly passed, Jeremy joined it. He pulled up the hood of his cloak to discourage conversation. Others followed the royal procession, mostly musicians and guests. A few looked admiringly at Jeremy's gear.

A tattooed biker wearing a Viking helmet and toting a huge mug of beer grunted at him. "Nice sword. Gem's a bit much though. Who made it?"

"Joseph of Arimathea," Jeremy replied.

"Never heard of him," the biker said. "Does he have a webpage?"

The procession wound its way into the huge royal tent near the fair entrance. King Acre's booming laugh filled it. "Welcome all my fine subjects. Here is to you." He swilled wine from a gold goblet. As people sat on bales of hay strewn about the floor, the goblin men took station behind his throne on a raised wooden stage. Shales, the master-at-arms, stood by his king. Hel mounted the dais slowly, being given wide berth by all, and sat on the king's left.

Jeremy looked for a way to get closer without being conspicuous. The tent was large but very open. Something brushed his sleeve, and he looked down to see a tiny woman with chestnut hair and deep brown eyes. She held a wreath of autumn flowers and wore gossamer wings. "A song fairy," he muttered.

She nodded and held up her wreath. He touched it, so she could sing to him. "Follow me," she sang softly, "friend of Tara. In a corner we shall be, unseen through the magic of Faerie."

She placed her small warm hand in his, and they walked around the tent to the back. Jeremy felt like he was out of phase with the world. Colors were more vibrant, and the air seemed to shimmer. People took no notice of them, and they sidestepped Acre's minions. They found a quiet dark spot beside some unused bales.

If Hel was the queen, she was not a jealous one as the king was fondling a particularly well-endowed belly dancer in such a way that a couple with a small child abruptly left the tent, towing their protesting offspring.

"Well," King Acre said, burlesquing offense. "You know what I always say, if they can't take a joke, to Hell with them." He leered upward at his silent queen.

"Good one, Your Majesty." Shales bowed. Acre's minions roared with laughter, but more of the regular guests left. The smell of wine and smoking meat was heavy in the air. The belly dancers started a lascivious dance to the wild Eastern music. One of the nearby guards snuffled, his head turning as if he were hunting for a scent. The song fairy tugged Jeremy's hand urgently. He took the hint, and they slipped out of the tent. Once outside, he smiled at the song fairy and put a twenty in her purse, despite her raised hand. It was always lucky to be generous to the Sidhe, and they had bills too.

He found Sydney and Samantha near a stage where a man dressed as a giant chicken entertained a crowd. Sydney sported a fresh black eye and bruises.

"What happened? Are you all right?"

"No worries, mate," Syd replied, though his voice was shaky. "I found myself tangling with a couple of drongos back by the animal cages. They got a big croc back there. Nasty bugger. I was investigating what looked like a human leg bone there when two of them tried to put the rough on me. I managed to get away." He shook his staff. "Gave one a set of sore nuts."

Jeremy looked at Samantha.

"The captured Fair folk are in the dungeon, all right," she said grimly. "And Jeremy, they don't look good. We have to do something soon."

"Wait here," Jeremy said. He walked apart from his two friends and pulled his mobile. A voice answered on the third ring. "Yes, Barbara. It's Jeremy. I need Cruzar at the Renaissance Festival in Mooresville. Money's no object. Get him on a trailer and get here as soon as you can. Call me on my mobile when you arrive. Right."

He turned back to the others. "Human authorities can't help us here. Either Acre and Shales will fade away, or worse, make a fight of it. Human guns can handle most monsters once they figure what they are, but there is something else here. An elder Norse goddess named Hel, queen of the underworld of Niflheim. There's no telling what she could unleash."

"So, what do we do?"

"Hel is a warrior goddess and answers to Odin," Jeremy said. "And above all other things, Odin demands courage. It gives me an idea…"

Halloween night fell over the festival. Acre had declared a joust would take place at eight that evening and torches glowed around the arena. The stands were full of Halloween revelers, unaware of how close and real evil was. Goth teen and goblin rubbed elbows along with Celtic music fan and elf.

Acre and his entourage filled the balcony. Shales sat uncomfortably on a gray mare, mace in hand, on the tourney field. Behind him, a bored young man dressed as a knight waited for the evening program of the joust to begin. Acre and Hel took to their thrones.

"Lords and ladies," Shale began, "on this Halloween night we have something special in mind for you—"

"More than you know, Shales."

Jeremy urged his horse, Cruzar, forward into the arena, past a group of confused staffers. Samantha and Sydney followed, weapons at the ready. Jeremy was concealed under a black cloak. He bore a shield, but it, too, was covered in fabric.

"What's the meaning of this?" the king demanded. "Where is Sir Randy?"

"Your play knight is gone," Jeremy shouted back. "You face a Knight Templar now."

"Now, now, young fellow," Shales said. "Don't get carried away. Guests aren't allowed to participate in these events."

"Quiet, Shales," Jeremy said. "I am not here to bandy words with a fool or a pretend king. I address myself to you, Lady Hel, goddess of the Underworld."

The crowd murmured, getting caught up in what they thought was a play.

Hel glared down on them, her eyes blazing in the half-and-half face. "Have a care, human. I am not casually named by mortals."

"Nor do I do so," Jeremy replied, trying to keep a quiver out of his voice as ancient evil regarded him. "I bring before you and all these assembled witnesses—a challenge. King Acre is a fool, a thief, and worse. I challenge him to mortal combat, here, now, in this arena. The winner will rule the Festival."

"You must be drunk." Acre laughed. "Who put you up to this? Your stupid stunt is going to get you arrested," his voice went cold, "by my guards." With nightfall, the king's goblin guard had reverted to their natural form. They growled and advanced in a flood from below the king's balcony. A troll followed them out.

"Hold," Hel ordered, and the air itself seemed to freeze. "The challenge is fairly made and lawful." Her voice sounded like a mournful winter wind. "Odin does not care for cowards, King. You must accept wager by battle."

"Very well," King Acre said, "but as a lawful monarch, I am within my rights to name a champion to defend my throne. I name the black knight, your servant, Lady Hel."

Hel inclined her head and the smile she gave Jeremy made his skin crawl. "Let it be so."

"Wager of battle it is then, young Templar," Acre boomed. "You shall face the demon warrior, the black knight, tonight on the eve of Halloween. Or you will depart, never to trouble my kingdom again. The Fair folk will all swear allegiance to me."

"I will accept—" Jeremy said. A blast of jeers from the host of goblins, orcs, and gargoyles drummed out his voice. He raised the bloodsword. The gem in its hilt, touched by Joseph of Arimathea to the blood of a carpenter dead 2,000 years, flashed angrily, cutting off the goblin's coarse voices as if their throats had been slit. "On this condition. If I win, the forces of darkness return to Hel's domain and never trouble the festival again."

"Accepted," Acre said.

"Then you are all bound to this doom," Hel said, rising. "Let the combat begin now, under the light of the moon."

Hucksters on either side got the crowd going with awful puns and lame jokes. Jeremy's "side" was seated on his right. He saw Tara and Copperfist with others of Faerie, watching hopefully from behind the bleachers.

"Tonight, my lords and ladies," Shales called. "We have the wager of arms. Stand forth the challenger!"

"Give them hell," Syd said.

Samantha whipped off her scarf and tied it around his right wrist. "A favor from your lady."

Jeremy smiled down at her and urged Cruzar forward.

Shales gave him an evil grin. "The young knight fancies he has a grievance…"

"I will announce myself." Jeremy's voice again cut across Shales'. He shrugged out of his cloak and shook his shield's covering off, revealing the white surcoat and shield, both bearing the red cross. "I'm Leclerc, Knight Templar. This festival has been suborned by evil. I call your champion to single combat."

"You're cute," some teenage girls called.

"Fundamentalist," someone else shouted.

"Very well, Sir Knight," Shale called back. "You will face the king's champion."

The hucksters on the king's side began to chant, "Cheat to win!"

His own side answered, "Cheaters never prosper." General din and shouting broke out.

Just like a Manchester United match, Jeremy thought. An air of unreality took hold of him, and he felt distanced from the whole scene. *I'd never imagined that all that riding and sword practice would ever mean anything in the 21st Century.* He shook himself. *Concentrate.*

Hel looked down on him, her eyes, set in the dark and light face, seemed to catch and reflect the torchlight.

"I could put an arrow in her," Samantha called.

"It would not help," Jeremy said over his shoulder.

"Let us hope you can match your brave words with deeds," Master Shales said. "I summon the Black Knight."

With a high-pitched scream, a huge, black Hanoverian burst into the far end of the field. The anvil-headed horse stood at least eighteen hands tall and atop it sat the Black Knight. He wore a Teutonic helmet, and no sign of his features could be seen, but Jeremy fancied he saw an evil yellow gleam through the eye-slits. His lance looked like a tree-trunk. A massive sword rode on his saddle. Even allowing for the size of his mount, he sat two feet higher than Jeremy.

Jeremy's sorrel pawed the earth, seeming unimpressed with his giant adversary. "Easy, Cruzar."

The crowd, perhaps finally sensing that something was amiss, fell silent.

"As master-at-arms," Shales announced, "I declare that the first pass shall be with lance."

Sydney brought a gray wooden lance to Jeremy. "Get him, mate."

Samantha, bow strung and arrow nocked, watched the knight's capering goblin minions, as they hurled insults in their uncouth language.

Jeremy. Shadowheart finally spoke.

"At last," he said. "Any advice?"

His lance is ensorcelled with an evil spell and dipped in scorpion ichor. It will cut through any armor. Their attempt to cheat allows me to respond. I will strengthen your shield. Take the blow directly on it. He will not try to get around it, believing his lance will pierce through. I will shiver his weapon.

The crowd began to chant, "Leclerc, Leclerc, Leclerc."

The Black Knight's side remained quiet, despite the urging of the hucksters.

"Enough," King Acre shouted, his facade of joviality cracking. "Let the combat begin."

Jeremy couched his lance, and Cruzar whinnied, accelerating. The knight's beast reared and charged ponderously. Three tons of horse-flesh headed for collision. At the last second, Jeremy urged Cruzar to sidestep, avoiding the worst of the blow. The Black Knight's weapon tracked left and slammed Jeremy's shield at an angle. Jeremy's left arm and shoulder went numb, and he was almost shoved from his horse. But the knight's spear broke with an ear-shattering crack.

Jeremy pirouetted the nimble quarterhorse. Cruzar spun, dashing back toward the knight. Jeremy aimed his lance for his adversary's broad back.

The Black Knight could not spin his huge animal as quickly, but he turned in the saddle. His two-handed sword swept out, and red flames ran down its blade. With an inhuman roar, the knight swung a left-handed blow that drove Jeremy's lance past his back. The lance burst into flame and flew from Jeremy's grip.

Jeremy raced past the knight and drew the bloodsword. The gem of its hilt glowed a fiery red. He spurred toward the knight. The demon switched his flaming sword back to his right hand and steadied his shield on his left.

Cruzar closed on the knight, who used his reach and height to strike first. Jeremy's shield took the blow and, strengthened by Shadowheart, was not cleaved.

"Have some back," Jeremy shouted. He struck with the blood-sword. Light flashed as the blessed sword struck demon steel. The horses backed as both warriors hacked at each other. The crowd roared Jeremy's name.

Jeremy caught a movement out of the corner of his eye. A goblin squire had snuck behind him with a polearm. The knight, seeing Jeremy's attention divided, redoubled his attack. Cruzar stumbled, shouldered by the big Hanoverian. The stumble saved Jeremy's head as the black sword whistled over it. The miss gave Jeremy a bare second to deal with the goblin. He raised his sword, but the goblin was falling backward, an arrow quivering in his chest.

"Got him," Samantha crowed.

Jeremy summoned Cruzar's remaining strength and crashed into the Black Knight, striking furiously in a series of quick cuts. As they locked shields, the rotting meat smell of the demon almost overcame him. Their swords ground together. Neither fighter could get off a strike.

Jeremy, Shadowheart called. *Reverse your blade. Bring the gem down on his helm.*

Jeremy disengaged and struck; the ruby slammed on the heavy iron helm. The gem didn't shatter as he expected but blazed brighter and emitted a loud, crystalline note. The knight tumbled from his mount, which bolted from the arena. The helmet rolled free of the body. There was no head underneath.

A moan went up from the crowd.

"Cool," a child shouted from the sideline. Cheers rang out.

Jeremy swayed in his saddle but stayed grimly upright. Samantha and Syd came up to stand on either side. "Victory is mine. Renounce the throne," Jeremy shouted.

"Kill him," Acre shouted. "Guards, kill him."

The master-at-arms spurred himself at Jeremy. But he was no fighter. Jeremy looked contemptuously at the way he held his weapons and bumped up and down on the mare.

"No, Samantha," he said, as she snapped up her bow. Sydney raised his staff, but Jeremy waved him off. He spurred Cruzar and met the awkward swing of Shale's sword. With a casual twist, he disarmed the so-called master-at-arms, then cracked him several times with the flat of the bloodsword, unhorsing him. Syd ran up to plant the staff on Shale's chest.

From beneath the tower, a company of goblins and orcs joined the troll on the field. The crowd booed. "You suck," someone shouted.

Jeremy swore as Sam nocked an arrow and Sydney fumbled under his cassock, coming up with his ax.

A sudden blast of wind quelled everyone. Shadowheart appeared next to him. She was in her archangel mode, pale, near seven feet tall with black and red wings and long, silky black hair. She stood clad in armor with a sword belted at her waist.

"Isn't that the chick from Salon Bang Bang?" somebody said into the silence.

But the orc and goblins knew what she was, and they cringed, falling backward in terror.

"Come forth, Hel, and put a stop to this." Shadowheart's voice effortlessly filled the space.

Hel, as if under a compulsion, walked to the edge of the balcony.

"What do you do here, Archangel?" she said in her dull monotone. "I have not struck with my powers that you should manifest. All that transpired here came from human choices."

"Do not belabor me with the law." Shadowheart's voice flowed with contempt. "I am come from beyond because the Old Magic was invoked. A bargain made. Wager of battle. All are bound to its outcome."

"True." Hel gave a ghastly smile. "I was only waiting for the king to damn himself further with oath-breaking."

"Destroy her," Acre shouted. "You're a god."

"I am a god of the universe, made inside it and limited by it." Hel frowned. "The angel is from beyond, from the Origin, and has no limits. I cannot withstand her."

"You have lost, King Acre," Hel said, turning her divided face to him. "Follow me to Niflheim. Do not fear. You will find my hall to be a fascinating place."

A fog billowed out around the castle. From all over the festival, orcs, goblins, and other servants of darkness came racing, plunging into the fog. The troll lurched forward and snatched up the body of the Black Knight, then it, too, disappeared.

Hel reached for the king. "No," he screamed. "No, please no." But Hel's cold claw closed on his arm, and she began to drag him. "No," he screamed a last time before the fog closed on him.

Jeremy dismounted and stood over Shales, whose face was waxen in terror. "Mercy, please."

"One condition," Jeremy said. "Or your new zip code is Niflheim 90210."

"Anything," he whimpered.

The folk of Faerie gathered round, Tara and Copperfist in the lead. Dwarf and elf had raided the dungeon while Jeremy and his friends faced Hel.

"You will serve Tara and Copperfist, administering the fair for the benefit of Faerie. You will deal with human matters and protect them from intrusion. They'll work out a fair salary for you—"

"It won't be much," the dwarf interjected.

"Cheat them only once and you are meat for Hel," Jeremy snapped.

"Swear on the gem," Shadowheart ordered. "And know you are bound to it every second of every day."

Shales reached out a shaking hand. "I swear."

The fog dissipated. The crowd went wild. One Goth kid turned to another. "Totally bogus, man. There wasn't even any blood."

The End

6

JEREMY LECLERC AND THE CHICKEN OF DOOM

I t's barbaric!" Samantha Pelton shouted. "And must be stopped."

Jeremy Leclerc raised his hands against her outrage from where he leaned his tall, slim body against the desk. "Look, Sam, I know how you feel, but the Knights Templar defend humans against supernatural evil—"

"Evil is evil," she stated, pushing her glasses back on her nose.

Jeremy made coffee and pulled out some mugs from the Scandinavian-style bookshelf behind his battery of computers. He hadn't expected to see Sam at his design studio this morning, on her day off. But as he'd opened the glass door to his studio in the South End of Charlotte, the short, thirtysomething ran up. He'd put his hand under his jacket to his Walther PPK, staring beyond to see what was chasing her. She'd come in, green eyes ablaze. For a second, he'd thought there'd been trouble between her and her new girlfriend, Marisol. In a way, he'd been right.

"Marisol's brother runs a cockfighting ring!" She fumed, pacing around the small office. Sam, a vegetarian, loved animals. She claimed that if she went back to meat, it would be human, as they were plentiful and annoying. Jeremy, who'd grown up in France and been to

90

bullfights in Languedoc, didn't quite share her American zeal for animal rights.

"Sam," he said gently, "sit down and we'll figure something out. There are police for this sort of thing."

"Police," she said bitterly but sat. He put a mug of steaming coffee in front of her and then placed a hand over hers. After a second, she squeezed it. "I'm sorry. I just hate when people hurt defenseless animals."

"Sure," he said.

Suddenly there was another figure in the room, floating above them. Shadowheart, Jeremy's guardian angel, drifted over in her teen guise. She wore, as usual, the latest fashions—today, torn jeans and sweater. Her blond hair was tied back in a ponytail.

Sam looked up. "Couldn't you make a sound when you pop into existence?"

Shadowheart snapped her bubblegum derisively. Sam sighed.

"That's enough, Shadowheart," Jeremy said. His guardian angel could be snarky at the oddest times. "Sam's upset."

"Again?" Shadowheart rolled her eyes. "What failure of humanity has provoked her now? She's more judgmental than—"

"An angel?" Jeremy shot back, nettled at the criticism of his friend.

"Don't fight with her on my account," Sam said, suddenly subdued.

Shadowheart floated to the top of Jeremy's desk and commandeered his coffee cup. "Don't worry about it. We fight all the time about our own stuff. I have my own Mad Monk right here."

"Hey," Jeremy said, "I never took a vow of chastity."

"Nope," she said, slurping his coffee. "No chastity and no 'shut the hell up and do what you're told by a divine being' either."

"Do you think the divine being could stop showing up at my office dressed as Lolita?" he asked.

"See what I gotta put up with?" Shadowheart asked.

"Everybody's got problems," Sam replied with a shrug.

"And my bet is we are going to hear about yours," Shadowheart said.

"We are," Jeremy said, reclaiming his coffee cup. "And we are going to do it in attentive and respectful silence."

"Oh bother," Shadowheart said, in the voice of Winnie-the-Pooh. "In that case, I am going to be comfortable." There was whooshing sound, and Shadowheart whirled into a pool of light that plunged into the large crystal-and-gold locket he wore on a heavy chain on his chest.

"Jeez," Samantha said, "attitude much?"

"She's just pissed off because her favorite soap opera got cancelled," he said.

The housing on his chest gave a spiteful thump. *I heard that.*

"Tell me your troubles," he said to Sam.

"It's Marisol's family in trouble," Sam said. "Her father is ill. Her idiot brother, Rafael, is managing the restaurant, but mostly he's raiding the till for his own benefit and for the fighting bird ring he's in. He's going to run the restaurant into bankruptcy."

"Sam," he said gently, "isn't there anyone in the family who can handle him?"

Sam moodily moved the coffee cup around in her hands. It was his cup, but her favorite to borrow, with a dragon's claw for a handle. "His mom just lets him do what he thinks best; he's the 'man of the house' now."

"No uncles to…"

"None are any better than Rafael is. Marisol's been the strength in that family. But her brother…" Sam looked at him. "I think she's afraid of him. But with you and me to back her…"

In his heart he knew this was futile and to intrude into a family fight was a poor choice, but he also knew that Sam was trapped too. She'd helped him many times and never asked anything for herself. He also didn't like the idea of the brother getting handsy with Sam, even if she could usually take care of herself.

"All right," he said. "I'll talk to the jerk…"

"Tomorrow maybe?" Sam said. "I was going to help out at the restaurant. They're so shorthanded."

"Tomorrow," he agreed.

Rafael fumed as he sat in his old Saturn in the parking lot of the apartments off South Boulevard. Bad enough that his sister turned out gay, worse that she was dating that Yankee bitch, but now she had the gall to tell him how to handle his family's business! Not that the business was going well lately. He didn't mean the Taco Cabano, that was just a way of gathering money for the cockfighting. That was where a man could make real money without the government taxing it all away. He'd pinned his hopes on his newest acquisition, El Riojo Diablo. The cock was supposed to be his ticket out and away from under his mother's eyes. The damn bird had proved listless and ineffective, putting him further into the hole with people he dared not offend.

That would change now, he thought, as soon as the Nahualli arrived. The Aztec medicine man had come to Charlotte to visit his daughter in the rundown apartments. He was well known in the immigrant community as a man whose curses or blessing carried weight.

A stooped figure shuffled into view with a silver-hilted cane in one hand. Rafael studied the man; his white hair projected from under the narrow brim of his fedora. He wore a fine dark suit over a white shirt with a bolero tie. Gold rings and chains reflected highlights off the streetlights.

Rafael wondered at the display of wealth. It was well after dusk and this was not a good neighborhood. Moments later, it seemed his concerns might be realized. A few toughs, their baggy pants hanging below their asses, hats on sidewise, grins lighting their sharp faces, appeared. Rafael rolled his window down to shout a warning, but it was too late.

The gang surrounded the old man. The Nahualli raised his eyes to them. A smile cut across his face. It was not a friendly smile, but that of a true killer facing pretenders. Rafael could swear the old man's eyes glowed a feral yellow.

The toughs scattered as if the old man had turned into jaguar. They fell back to what they thought was a safe distance, and in the way of such human garbage, the leader yelled obscenities at the Nahualli.

The gang leader has misjudged his safety. The Nahualli raised his cane and chanted something.

"Something bit me," the leader screamed, clutching his leg and falling. "Oh God, I'm bit. It burns." The others closed on their leader, and staring in fear at the old man, they grabbed their fallen member and ran off. His screams faded in the night.

The old man chuckled and shuffled on.

Rafael got out of the Saturn and walked up to the old man slowly, his hands open and level in front of him. "Greeting, Coyotl," he said using the old man's name rather than his title.

The old man looked up at him impassively.

"My name is Rafael Ortiz," he said. "I am a follower of the old ways. I have come to you for help."

The eyes buried in the ancient, seamed face no longer glowed. In the fading light, their color could not be told, and they seemed to lead to unguessable depths.

"I am an old man," Coyotl said. "I wish only to visit with my daughter and her baby. The concerns of this world no longer interest me."

"Ah, Coyotl, but I have brought the traditional gifts, tobacco and the best mescal," Rafael wheedled.

"Hmmm," said the older man. "My daughter does not allow me to smoke in the house with the baby."

"My family has a restaurant there." Rafael pointed at the back of the building. "I have a shed out back. You can use it to smoke when you want."

"Let's go," Coyotl said. "I feel like a drink."

An hour later, Rafael and Coyotl sat in a cloud of blue smoke and the smell of mescal. The old man had put away an immense quantity of the fiery drink with little effect other than obvious enjoyment. He sang to himself and spoke in several languages to beings that Rafael could not see.

"Please," Rafael said, "Coyotl, I need your help."

The old man seemed to focus on him with difficulty. "Yes, young one. You have manners and know and respect the old ways. What is it that you need?"

Rafael staggered to his feet. "Come, come."

The old man rose with a fluid grace that belied age or intoxication and followed him to a covered cage in the back. Rafael pulled back the cover. "El Riojo Diablo."

The old man chuckled. "Ah, a fighting bird. Good."

"Not much fight in him," Rafael said in bitterness.

"Bring me a container for liquid," the old man said, "and the bird's feed."

Rafael made his way on unsteady feet to retrieve a large plastic tub of feed and a mason jar with a lid. The old man took a knife from his back pocket and flaked tobacco into the feed, then from the pockets of his vest, he pulled other herbs and bits of animals. He poured some Mescal over the feed and chanted in an old and dark language. Finally, he reached for the jar and, to Rafael's surprise, urinated into it.

"Ah," he said. "Too much." Then he screwed the cap on the jar.

"Boy," he said. "Pour a quarter of this," he handed Rafael the jar, "into the feed over three days and the Riojo Diablo will earn his name. He will not fear any other cock. Hell, he will kill dogs."

Rafael looked at the jar trying to conceal his distaste at holding the warm jar.

Coyotl nodded, then reached over and picked up the last bottle of Mescal and his cigar and walked out the door, singing softly to himself.

Rafael finished his own bottle of Mescal. Sodden drunk by that point, he fell face down on a cot.

Hours later, the morning sun opened Rafael's eyes like a can opener. He cursed God, devils, and holy men as the hangover gnawed at him. His eyes fell on the jar of dark amber liquid by the bin of feed. He grimaced as bile rose in his throat. Rafael picked up the jar and looked at the feed and the covered cage with Diablo inside it. He opened the jar, and the smell damn near killed him. He quickly upended the contents into the feed and covered it. Rafael masked his face with a hand and pushed the feed bin next to the bird's cage. He'd feed the damn bird later, he promised himself, fleeing the shed and its awful stench before he lost the battle with his stomach.

Just as he left, Diablo poked his head through the bars of his cage, eyeing the feed bin. His head ducked, and he attacked the feed. After a few moments, his eyes began to glow with a dull, furnace red.

Jeremy drove down South Boulevard in his red Mini Cooper, grumbling. "How, Shadowheart, how do I get talked into these things?"

From the crystal and gold pendant on his chest, which served as her home, he heard Shadowheart sigh. "Because when Samantha gives that disappointed, pouty look, you fold like a bad poker hand."

"Well," Jeremy said, with a touch of defensiveness, as he dodged Charlotte's harrowing traffic, "she was pretty upset. You know how she loves animals."

"Yep, I think she sees you as one."

"Very funny. I'd also like to point out in my defense that I want things to work out between her and Marisol. Be nice to see the holes left by the last vixen patched up."

"So," Shadowheart replied, "add all of that the fact that she is your only wholly human confidante, and you have, in the fashion God intends, answered your own questions."

"You know at least in *I Dream of Jeanne* the astronaut had a cork for that bottle."

"*I Dream of Jeanne*," Shadowheart said. "What are you, a hundred years old? You've got to stop watching Me TV."

Further banter about streaming services was cut off by a Hummer ignoring rights-of-way, the traffic lights, and the existence of Jeremy's Mini.

"I'm going to give your license plate to a demon," Jeremy shouted at the Hummer. "Couldn't you inflict a pox of something on him?" he demanded of Shadowheart.

"Her," Shadowheart corrected, darkly, "and she will get hers."

Jeremy spotted the Mexican restaurant and Sam's older, dark-green Land Rover outside it. Sam sat on a bench outside the luridly painted restaurant, with a very pretty and agitated Hispanic woman in her late twenties. Restaurants usually closed between three and five to get ready for the dinner crowd, and they'd arranged to meet him on a break. Sam gave a smile of relief at seeing him pull in. Jeremy stretched as he extracted his lanky frame from the Mini.

Sam stood on the bench, which made it easier for her to kiss him hello. "Hi, handsome, thanks for coming."

"How could I resist?" he replied.

How indeed? Shadowheart sniffed from inside her crystal.

"This is Marisol," Sam said. The Hispanic girl stood, eyeing him uncertainly.

"Hola," Jeremy said, and then continued in Español. "A pleasure to meet you. You're as pretty as Sam said you would be."

Now she smiled. "Your Spanish is excellent, but your accent is not Mexican."

"I'm from France, but my family was often in Languedoc. It's not so different, and I picked it up along with a little Catalan. So, what's going on?"

"My idiot hermano is going on," she said, smile vanishing. "Mi padre is sick, and he thinks that makes him the man of the house."

"The Patriarchy strikes again," Sam growled.

"He's borrowed a lot of money from my mother. She gives him anything he wants. The fool is going to bet it all on a cockfight. He says it is a sure thing, like always."

"But there is more," Sam urged.

"You will think me mad," Marisol said, hesitating.

"Maybe not," Jeremy replied, offering a reassuring smile.

Marisol drew a deep breath. "He says he has powerful magic on his side. My brother is a superstitious fool. He fancies that we are descended from Aztec royalty and says he has the power of an Aztec shaman named Coyotl on his side."

Jeremy frowned. "That name is…"

"Familiar," Shadowheart finished. Marisol jumped as Shadowheart sauntered up in her teenage mall rat guise.

"Where did you come from?" Marisol asked.

"I was napping in the back seat," Shadowheart said and yawned.

"Marisol," Jeremy added, "this is my associate. She goes by Shadowheart."

"Chica," Marisol said, "aren't you a bit young to be—"

"I'm a lot older than I look," Shadowheart interrupted. "Coyotl is the real deal, Jeremy. He's priest, a Nahualli. He has real power."

"For good or for evil?" Jeremy asked.

"More for good, but he will curse as readily as heal. His power is more of nature than of the forces of Light or Darkness."

He motioned Sam over. "Excuse us a second." He shot a thought to Shadowheart to keep Marisol distracted. The angel began asking Marisol about her brother's childhood.

"What have you told her about me?" he asked.

"Little," she replied. "I said that you were versed in the occult and that you liked helping people with unusual troubles. Also mentioned you don't charge for your help. She thinks I brought you down here for a little man-to-man conversation with her brother, who won't listen to anyone without a—"

"Got it. Well, Shadowheart says this Coyotl is the real deal, so I better look into things. I will tell you that I'm more likely to have success with a wandering demon than a witless brother."

"The stakes have gone up since last night," Sam said. She waved to Marisol. She and Shadowheart came over.

"Que?" Marisol asked.

"Tell him what you told me," Sam said.

"Rafael's disappeared. Just this morning—he took all the spare cash, and I think he's raided other accounts. He was wild, kept saying how now is his chance and he is going to show them all. It's crazy.

"I don't think he's coming back today," Marisol continued. "He was talking about his fighting bird. I think he went to get it and go to the fight."

"Do you know where?" Jeremey said.

"No, but I think I can get it out of one of my uncles. It will not be in a nice place. Not safe."

Jeremy nodded. "I'll try and find him after you get the location."

Marisol hesitated. "No police."

Jeremy nodded. "No police."

"And you can't go alone," Sam said.

"Now wait—"

"Oh, come on, you're whiter than white. Worse, you're from France."

"And how is having you with me going to help?"

"I'm a least Southern."

"And small, white, and gay. Not endearing to the sort of folks gathered around a cockfight."

"No pun intended?" Shadowheart said sweetly.

"Shaddup!" the pair said, turning to her as one.

"I must go with you," Marisol said. "With the other men around and with you there, he will not hit me. But neither will he listen to either of you. If I am there, he may be too ashamed to argue in front of the other men and talk to us quietly."

They looked at Shadowheart. She shrugged. "I'll be with you…in spirit." She grinned cheezily and gave them a thumbs up.

A couple of hours of detective work and Marisol's leaning on her uncles produced the location of the cockfight. A decrepit Quonset hut in a run-down section of Gaston County full of junkyards. They rolled out in Sam's Rover, which would be less conspicuous than the Mini in the back woods and better if they needed to get off the road. Unfortunately, the older car had British air-conditioning, which was only barely coping with what had turned into a hot evening. They stayed out of sight near a pile of car wrecks with the lights out. Jeremy was soon glad that he'd left his long duster with the bloodsword lying in the back of the vehicle. His Walther PPK rode on his belt and half his plan was that anyone seeing him would assume he was a cop.

Meanwhile, as the sun faded out of the sky, vehicles of various sorts, from disreputable pickups and beaters to a limo, brought people of all types here, who apparently shared a love of watching poultry fight to the death. The cars parked, and people, some carrying crates, came out. They didn't seem overly worried about police, and while they were not overt, it had none of the security or circumspection of a drug deal.

But they caught no sight of Rafael.

"No choice," Jeremy said, looking at a photo of Rafael on his phone. "I have to go look for him."

Both women started to stir.

"Not a good idea," he said. "You see a lot of women out there?"

Marisol shrugged. "They'll be some. Not a lot of whites either. A gringo on his own…trouble. With two women, maybe a white boy trying to play in the hood. Like I told you, he won't talk to you anyway."

Jeremy didn't like it, but it was hard to fault Marisol's logic, and this was her family and her problem. He was just the top cover. "Alright, but both you stay by me at all times."

"Good, I am glad you left the little chica home, though."

"Oh," Sam said. "We'll see Shadowheart if there is trouble. And trust me, she will be useful in ways you can't imagine."

"Well, I can't," Marisol said, opening the door. "What kinda name is that anyway? Is she in a band or something?"

"It's a long story," Jeremy said.

They walked up to the building drawing dark looks from the men watching the door, who looked him and his gun over. They didn't seem relieved to be addressed in Spanish and just took the money he extended without comment, but with looks at Marisol. They went in. The place was full of plastic chairs and some bleachers that had been scrounged from somewhere. They slipped to an inconspicuous spot between bleachers and toward the back, barely noticed by the crowd of fifty or so around the ring of haybales that seemed to mark the fighting spot. The air quickly grew heavy with the smells of tobacco, pot, and alcohol.

Despite Marisol's warnings, the crowd was diverse, with people of all backgrounds, including a guy who could have been a banker with a pair of well-dressed women.

Good, he thought, *maybe the door guards were more concerned with the gun than the pale skin. Less notice for us.*

"Let's get going?" a man shouted. He was tattooed and muscular and wore a shirt that said "My cock is bigger than yours" with an enraged rooster on it. The ring of men moved up inside the rings made of bales of hay. Several of them held struggling birds in their hands. The buzz of Spanish and English made a steady drone.

"Jeremy," Sam said hotly, "I am not going to let those assholes fight those birds."

"First things first," he whispered, shushing her with his hands. "We're here for Rafael and to save the restaurant. Also, there are guns in that crowd. I break in there and shooting is likely."

We may be too late, Shadowheart whispered in his mind.

Rafael emerged from the shadows at the back, next to the trailer that had been backed in to form the fourth wall of the Quonset. He looked exactly like his picture down to the cowboy hat and mustache.

"Damn," Jeremy swore. "How did he get past us?"

"He must have been in that pickup with the trailer," Sam growled. "Where did he get that, I wonder?"

Rafael looked feverish, his eyes darting about from under his hat, his face slick with sweat. He stood by the panels of the trailer. The other men grew quieter looking at him, though a few called disparaging names.

"I called you here," Rafael said, ignoring jibes, "to finally see some real action. Not the bullshit fights that have been staged before."

Raucous laughter followed, and the announcer waved a derisive hand. "The puppy keeps barking," he mocked. "Go home, puppy. Take your Red Devil and make a chimichanga out of it." Laughter erupted.

"El Riojo Diablo," Rafael shouted, "will fight all your birds at the same time."

"Chickens don't have teams, fool," a bearded man shouted. "They'll attack each other."

"The birds will know who their enemy is," Rafael said. "I got 10K in cash here to back up what I say. El Riojo Diablo will be the only bird alive at the end."

"El Moto Gross is twice your bird," a bald man spat out. "He will tear your bird to pieces by himself."

Rafael flushed. "El Diablo has grown. He is four times the bird he was."

"Idiot," Baldy scoffed. "Full grown birds don't grow. But I do not care what bird you have. Mine will fight him first. There will be nothing left for others. We will cover your 10K," he finished, gesturing at his posse. One man put down a large crate, from inside of which a bird gave a shrieking challenge.

From the trailer came heavy thumps and a sound of something snapping.

As one of his handlers pulled Grosso from his crate, Baldy gave Rafael a glare of contempt. "Fool, you have a friend in there. You think noise will frighten us? Get your bird."

Rafael opened the doors of the trailer and stepped onto the ramp, then froze. A second later, everyone else did too.

El Riojo Diablo stood inside, shaking the remains of his cage off his shoulders. The snapped metal was what they had heard, though the cage could never have gone around the eight-foot-tall horrible cross between a chicken and a dinosaur. It spun the cage off its head and advanced out of the trailer as Rafael stumbled, back raising an arm. The sound that emitted from the massive beak should not have come from a fowl, and the hair on the back of Jeremy's neck raised. Its feathers glittered metallically as if the great bird were armored.

It surveyed the shocked men like Colonel Sanders nightmare of revenge. The short wings, now tipped with wicked spurs, flapped.

"Oh God," Sam said.

"Hermano," Marisol managed, "what have you done?"

"Looks like a velociraptor with a bad hat," a dazed Jeremy added.

And it's pissed off, Shadowheart yelled. *Run!*

Diablo sighted Grosso just as men dropped the squawking birds to run for their lives. Diablo raged a guttural squawk and ploughed directly into the crowd, sending men and birds screaming and flying. In a moment, El Matto Grosso met his end in the monstrous beak of the Chicken of Doom.

Jeremy seized Sam's arm and pushed her and Marisol ahead of him as chaos broke out. Over his shoulder, he saw a man firing a pistol at Diablo, to no effect. The metallic feathers sparked with the hits, but Diablo was no natural animal anymore. They did not penetrate his armor. The ricochets did cut down a screaming man and explode a fleeing bird.

Diablo, enraged, leapt, slamming into the rafters then down on the gunner, who disappeared, crushed under the weight of the bird and its flashing red claw. Jeremy's last sight of Rafael was of a pair of cowboy boots disappearing under a trailer.

Men leapt out of windows and crashed through both the door and a nearby rent in the wall. More shots sounded, and Jeremy felt one zip by him as they ducked and dodged around parked cars.

With a shriek of tearing metal, the side of the Quonset caved out and exploded, metal and wood flying through the air. Something caught Marisol, who fell. Sam dove and caught her before she could hit the ground. Jeremy skidded to a halt and grabbed for his pistol, cursing that he'd left the sword hidden in his leather duster in Rover.

Diablo strode out, red eyes glowing. He seemed to have grown even in the moments since they last saw him, and the sound that emerged from his gore-stained beak was like a steam engine. It leapt into the parking lot, crushing a red pickup and then an old Buick. It was coming right at them. Jeremy dodged as a huge, spurred foot struck the ground in front of them.

He looked up into Diablo's blazing eyes. The bird clearly remembered his ancestors were once dinosaurs. The enormous chicken voiced something like a loathsome chuckle as it glared at Sam holding Marisol and Jeremy standing before them.

The chuckle turned to a scream of outrage. Diablo leapt sidewise to show the teen Shadowheart behind it holding two handfuls of bleeding tailfeathers she'd just yanked out of Diablo's ass.

"Get them to the car and get the bloodsword," she yelled as she took to her sandaled heels, Diablo in pursuit. "Hurry, I don't think I can die in mortal form, but I ain't anxious to find out."

She plunged out of sight faster and more limber than any human, but only a little ahead of the Chicken of Doom.

"Sam," Jeremy demanded, "are you alright?"

"Sure," she said, her mouth in a grim line. "I can fight."

"You have to take care of Marisol," he said. "I'll handle Big Bird." Without waiting for her to argue, he pelted back to her car, used her set of spare keys and got the bloodsword and its duster-sheath coat out of the car, and raced in the direction Shadowheart had fled. He came out on a jogging trail through the woods where a dazed-looking marathoner was yelling into his phone.

"It was a giant chicken," he shouted, "eight feet tall and chasing a girl. We need the Army. No, dammit, this isn't a prank."

Jeremy ran past him without pausing. Since the vegetation off to either side was not crushed, Diablo had stayed on the trail. He wasn't too worried about Shadowheart; while whatever she was made of paid some nominal allegiance to the laws of spacetime, he didn't think the bird could catch her…still he picked up his pace.

He'd run most of a half-mile along the unlit trail when, with a flapping of huge wings, something surged from the bank of magnolias to his left. He whipped the sword up to the *In No Kamae* position for his most powerful strike.

Shadowheart came into the moonlight, all seven feet of her, long, raven hair and with her great black and red wings. "Tell me," she demanded, glaring down at him, "that you didn't just mistake me for a chicken."

His breath came out in a whoosh. "I thought you couldn't turn into your warrior-queen manifestation unless some evildoer broke the rules of engagement?"

She grimaced. "New exception. Divine messengers are not to be disrespected by being pecked to death by chickens. It's bad for the angelic image to be dissed by poultry."

"Good point."

"Unfortunately," she continued, "my activities also broke the rules on involvement in the mortal realm. Without the seal of the law on my intervention, my strength is limited to what this mortal dust can do."

"In the body of a seven-foot-tall Amazon Queen?"

"Exactly."

"Good to have you along anyway."

"Thank you."

"Where did the COD go?"

"COD? Oh," she scoffed, "more of your juvenile humor. "It must be the American influence. Why must you have an acronym for everything? COD, FOL, FOE—just say Chicken of Doom."

"Oh, come now," he teased. "Let's have a little fun."

She sighed and stretched out a long, elegant finger. In the distance he could see what looked like a factory of some kind, showing some lights. She fell in beside him as he walked. Her wings arched over him, almost reaching across the trail, and her feet barely made any impression on the earth.

From ahead came a crashing of metal and a menacing squawk. In the distance the huge beak of their enemy was briefly silhouetted by a light.

They raced forward to where the massive bird had crushed a chain-link fence.

Jeremy squinted at the sign laying partially shredded on the ground below, then looked up at the ramshackle plant facing them.

"That's not… that never is a…" he began.

"Chicken processing plant," Shadowheart said. "What better place to battle him?"

"Oh, I don't know," he replied. "Perhaps somewhere he's not standing in righteous rage over the corpses of a billion fellow chickens. Maybe Bojangles."

She slapped him on the arm. "You people are the apex predators of this planet. You've already extincted most of the other species. Start acting like it."

Their conversation was interrupted when they heard a vehicle bumping over some rutted road toward them. Jeremy, if he had ever prayed, would have prayed then that it not be the police or security. Part of his charge was to keep supernatural events out of the evening news.

Sam's green Land Rover pulled onto the road near them. Jeremy ran up to the window.

"I thought you were taking Marisol home?" he asked, unhappy to see her here again.

Sam did a double-take out the window at Shadowheart and whistled. Then she focused on Jeremy. "I dropped her and her idiot brother at my place. He told me that monster came out of some truly disgusting potion that this Coyotl gave him to feed the bird. Now he's begging for our help. What an asshole."

She killed the light on the Rover and got out. Under her left arm she wore her deceased father's .357 in a shoulder holster. It looked like a bazooka on her small frame. She caught his glance. "Bullets soaked in holy water with crosses cut into them."

"I don't know it that will help," he said.

"Couldn't hurt."

"Don't suppose telling you to stay in the Rover would do any good?" he added.

"Nope, none whatever. I got you into this; I have to stand with you getting out of it."

"She's as reasonable as you are," Shadowheart chipped in unhelpfully.

She gave the angel a look, but mouthy as she could get with Shadowheart's teen manifestation, she was less tempted to verbal jousting with the warrior queen version.

"We've got to get rid of this thing before sunrise," Jeremy said. "This plant, whatever it is—"

"It's Fairmont Fryer," Sam said. "Used to be a local attraction, a chicken processing plant that fried tons of chicken and sold it cheap. Lot of poor folks would get their Sunday dinner here."

"Is it open?" he demanded.

"Shut last week when old man Fairmont died and the grandkids wanted shed of it. There might be some caretaker staff, but that's about all."

"OK. Follow me."

They set off, but Shadowheart moved to the middle, her great wings stretching protectively over them.

"If there are humans about," she said, "they will not see you under my wings."

"Don't suppose you could fix this with a flap of those black beauties?" Sam asked.

"I'm already in trouble for interfering this much," she replied. "Coyotl was a human menace, not a supernatural evil. I'm supposed to be a spiritual guide, not a chicken-hawk. Much more and the geas laid upon me will force me back into the crystal."

"We'll deal with that if and when it happens," Jeremy said.

With the angel's wings hovering above them, they approached the ramshackle collection of industrial buildings.

"This place has been everything from a railway siding to a grain silo," Sam said. They came to an open area near some rusted railway track. The massive bird could not have come this way as the barbed-wire-topped, chain-link fence was undamaged. It went on undamaged as far as they could see. Worse, the barbed wire was set so that it overhung their side.

"Shadowheart," he said, "we don't have time to look for another entrance, and it's dangerous to scale it."

She nodded, reached down to put an arm around each of them, and with a beat of her great black wings, they were airborne. But as she had warned, Shadowheart's powers were limited. She was clearly struggling with their weight, and her wings beat furiously as she gained height. But they cleared the top of the tangle of rusted barbs.

As they settled toward the ground on the other side, Shadowheart dropped them the last couple of feet.

"Crap," she said, and vanished.

Jeremy struggled to his feet, as did Sam.

"What happened?" Sam demanded.

From inside the crystal and gold housing he wore under his shirt, Shadowheart's voice sounded chagrinned. "Ref threw a flag on the play. I'm out. Interference."

"Great," Jeremy said, annoyed by any rules and particularly these.

"We're on our own," Sam said.

"I'm still with you," Shadowheart insisted. "Just not in body."

Jeremy stared at the bulk of the buildings around them, looking for any sign of their enemy. The buildings at least promised cover. He sighted in on the biggest one.

"This way," he said, drawing both sword and pistol. Sam unlimbered her pistol and fell in behind them. The yard around the place was overgrown and marked by discarded equipment and some vehicles such as forklifts and the odd golf-cart. They came up to a locked door, but with the carelessness of a failing business, the window next to it was unlocked, and he boosted Sam through. In moments, they were in a huge open interior space, filled with machinery and banks of tables with rollers laid on them, presumably to slide trays of chicken around.

"What is that?" Sam asked as she wrinkled her small nose.

"Oil," he replied. "A lot of it. You said that they had a huge fryer here. It smells like they didn't drain it."

"Yeah, there," she said, pointing.

"God, they used a huge tank for it."

"Old Man Fairmont made it out of an old fuel oil tank that he cut up and made into a fryer. It was one reason he gave away so much. Anything that didn't make commercial grade was fried up, including some rats probably, but poor folk could always get food here."

"So?" Shadowheart said from her banishment to the crystal.

"It may be useful," he replied. "Bullets don't work on it. Sam, can you see if you can get the burners going on this?"

"Why?" she said. "I'm not a process engineer, you know."

"You're pretty good with heavy machinery."

"Mostly farm machinery and house furnaces, but I'll see what I can manage. What will you be doing?"

"Getting a better look at our enemy, and if the opportunity permits, maybe I can finish him. The bloodsword is most effective against demons and unnatural creatures. Against this earthly creature transformed by a human-originated magic, it may be nothing more than a big knife. It will kill it if I can get close enough and do a lot of damage."

"Jeremy," she said. "It was nine feet tall when we last saw it. Chickens kick."

"I know. It's why we need a Plan B."

Both of them jumped when the monster let out a shriek from somewhere on the grounds. The sound bounced so much, they weren't sure where it originated.

"I'll do what I can," she said and headed for the vat controls.

"Text me if you get it working," he called. "Don't call."

"What are you, a teenage girl?" she cracked.

He gave a quick grin. Height might be safety, so he quietly made his way up a metal staircase through an aluminum-covered walkway. The chicken processing plant smelled terrible and made his eyes water. Wind moaned through the rusted corrugated metal and broken windows and he fancied he heard a rumble of thunder in the distance. Rain would not help.

The few lights did little to illuminate the interior of the plant, which was a jumble of bizarre shapes of machinery, hoists, and hanging chains. It added to the feeling of unreality as he stalked his monster. He came to an opening onto the black tar-topped roof. After sliding the door slowly open and wincing at the unexpected screech as the runner scraped, he moved out, sword in the right hand and pistol in his left.

Now that he was exposed, the wind blew harder and was unexpectedly chilly. He looked up. The quarter-moon was up, but it threw less light than the clouds did, bouncing down the streetlights from Charlotte and Gastonia. He waited for his eyes to better adapt. His sword glittered under the moonlight, but the fist-sized gem wired into the hilt held only a small, sullen flicker. Normally it glowed in the presence of supernatural evil. Shadowheart has said Coyotl's magic originated in neither Heaven nor Hell, and the sword could not quite judge it. The gem, however had not been close to the thousand pounds of berserk poultry.

Thank God there's no staff here tonight, Shadowheart murmured from her housing. *We're supposed to keep the supernatural off the evening news.*

"Not to mention they might be made into birdseed," he returned, crabbing onto the rooftop. As he reached the far edge, a crash made him freeze. Below the rooftop, an old pickup truck left abandoned in the parking lot went tumbling.

The Chicken of Doom strutted into view below.

"It's grown again," he whispered, in shock. "It must be fifteen feet tall."

Jeremy, Shadowheart demanded. *You are not to close with that thing. It will kick us past the orbit of Mars, and not in one piece either.*

Fortunately, the parking lot was down the hillside from them, and he was still well above the chicken. He moved back toward the door. But it seemed the beast had spent enough of its rage. It squatted on the truck as if on a nest and seemed to settle, though its head snapped around suspiciously. He slipped back inside. He felt the phone vibrate against his chest and withdrew it from the inside pocket of the duster.

"Turning and burning," she'd sent.

"Good," he sent back. "Plan B just got moved up."

He returned equally slowly and carefully to Sam, who sat beside her huge and now bubbling cauldron like a happy witch.

"Got them running flat out," she said. "I think he used an old jet engine to heat this damn thing. Never saw so many burners. How long it'll run, I have no idea."

"Time is not our friend," he agreed. He began grabbing at chains and cables and eyeing the machinery tables and conveyors, looking for ones bolted to the floor. His father had been determined that his son needed to hunt and had shown him the art of making snares. He'd spent enough miserable days on the Scottish moors near the Rosslyn Chapel making them, but never on such a scale.

"Too bad you're in timeout," he said to Shadowheart. "We could use the extra arms."

"Your guardian angel is always watching over you," she said, "even when you're playing with yourself. Get to work."

"Sam," he said. "I need your help."

She nodded and grabbed up the chain that he pointed to.

They made a cat's cradle of snares and traps about the bubbling oil. Jeremy went over to the largely glass wall that looked out in the direction of the parking lot. They could see their adversary if he came up the hill. He worried about the time they were taking, but they dared not attract attention before they were ready. Perhaps the bird had gone to sleep.

"I'll provoke it and get it to chase me in here," he said, as they finished. "I can get through this door, it will crash through the glass and hopefully get tangled in enough of these snares to fall into the vat or to where I can get at it with my sword, safely. Then, Kentucky-fried."

"Yuck," she replied. "Where do you want me?" She rested her revolver on her thigh.

"In the safest spot possible. There's a wood-walled office there. The one with the small window. That outer wall is corrugated metal. It's the safest spot."

"And leave you on your own?" she said, outraged.

"I will be running for my life, Sam, and I'll be safer on my own."

"Well," she grumbled, "you do have a ten-inches more leg than I do. I don't like it, though."

"I know, but its best. Now tie off that chain with that cable. I'm going to rig some lines aloft too. Maybe it will clothesline itself."

Twenty minutes later, he headed out of the first-floor section opposite the parking lot. The bird had looked as if it were settling in, likely to sleep. He needed to rouse it to chase him back toward the vat, but from what he had seen, it was easy enough to provoke. Just seeing him ought to do it, and if not, he had his pistol. The sword was still in its sheath to make running easier. He could hear sirens in the distance and wondered if it was related to them. Perhaps someone besides the lone jogger had called for help.

Jeremey reached a hedge of boxwoods over the parking lot, took a deep breath, and straightened up pistol held out.

The crushed pickup lay by itself.

Behind him, he heard a crash of tearing metal and the bang of a revolver. He'd miscalculated. Bored or hungry, the monster must have circled back and was tearing through the metal walls of the factory. It could be after only one thing in there, Sam.

Furious at his mistake, he raced back and up the outside stairs to the elevated passage he'd been in before. Running flat out brought him to the second-floor gallery over the stinking vat and machinery. The monster was shrieking like a steam engine, one leg caught in a snare. It had come in right through the office he'd sent Sam into, possibly sighting her through its high, small window.

"It's gonna eat me," she screamed, revolver empty, as she dodged among the machinery. "I'm a goddamn vegetarian!" The monster pecked alternately at her and the chains holding its leg. Jeremy rapid-fired his entire magazine at the abomination. "Run, Sam!"

The gunfire enraged and confused it long enough for Sam to hit a table of rollers and slide out of range of the monster's beak, but she was pinned in a corner now. Her movement attracted it again. This time its lunge broke the bolts holding the chain-laden table in place. Sam got as far to the other side of the vat as she could. The blue fire of its burners threw a confusing light on the floor, perhaps why it had missed her.

He grabbed one of the lines he'd rigged as an aerial trap, unhooked it from another, and seized the big D-ring at the bottom, large enough for him to hold with both hands. There was no way to swing out and still use the sword. Only in movies were people strong enough to hold onto such a thing with one hand. He leapt out and swung low as the monster dragged its burden of chain and table closer to Sam. The rusty metal he rode on groaned and sparked against the girders as it slid on a ceiling-mounted pulley.

He swung down all in a whirl of lights, sounds, and smell. Only the silhouette of the great head, his target, was clear. As he arched up, both feet connected with the side of Diablo's head. But he'd miscalculated again, and the blow was glancing. Jeremy swept by the bird, over the boiling vat, struck by its furious heat.

"Twist left," Shadowheart shouted from her housing.

Diablo had righted itself from the blow, and its beak flashed out. It hit the duster and the bloodsword's sheath instead of his body. He lost his grip and came flying off, crashing down on a pile of tarps and boxes with a bruising impact that drove all the air from his lungs. He rolled over to fall behind the pile.

Diablo's luck had run out. As it struck at Jeremy, it overbalanced and hit another snare. Legs hopelessly entangled, it fell into the bubbling vat with a shriek like a calliope exploding. A tsunami of hot oil fountained up and out. Sam dodged into her last redoubt, a small closet, and Jeremy was protected by the pile of boxes and tarps, though some struck his duster.

Jeremy struggled to his feet, wondering if any ribs were broken, but pulling his sword. A lesser blade would have surely bent or broken under such abuse, but so long as the stone existed, that fate could never befall it. As for his duster, it would join the long list of such garments that had perished in the battle against evil. He rounded the pile tarps and the nearest machinery.

Diablo's head and legs projected from the vat, and the red eyes were tinged with agony, looking to Jeremy as if in entreaty. For a moment, he felt a stab of pity for the creature, which had not asked for its fate.

With a deep breath to keep his ribs as still as he could, he brought the sword up and swung. The blow cut half-way through the thick neck. The red light faded from its eyes, and Diablo's suffering ended. The body sagged and indeed seemed to be sinking into the vat.

"It's shrinking," Sam said. She'd emerged from her closet to come up behind him.

"Yes," Shadowheart's voice sounded, "it's unnatural powers were only given to it in life."

He peeked over the edge. Inside lay the flash-fried corpse of a normal bird, disappearing into the ooze.

"Can you turn it off?" he said, wearily. "We don't need a fire too."

Sam disappeared to the far side. In moments, the roar of the industrial burners cut out.

"Let's get out of here," he said. "It'll be sunrise soon."

"Yeah," she replied. "We're not too far from my house. Come with me. We'll get you cleaned up and get some breakfast in you."

"Ah," he said with a smile. "What's for breakfast?"

She glared at the vat. "I'm thinking chicken and waffles."

The End

7

THE AUDIT

To The Holy See
From Raoul Esposito SJ *Calificador*,

Your Holiness,
We have heard disturbing reports of irregular activities by the Knight Templar Jeremy Leclerc, assigned to Charlotte, NC, USA. An inquisition has been ordered...

O h my God," Jeremy Leclerc said "I'm being audited!" The tall, lean, twenty-four-year-old leapt up from the screen where the offending e-mail glared at him.

"Oh no," Samantha said, pushing her gold-rimmed glasses back on her small nose and looking up from her laptop. "The IRS?"

"No," Jeremy said, running his hands through his thick brown hair. "Far worse, a *calificador*. He's arriving tomorrow."

"Sounds like a Mexican drink," Samantha observed, hopping off the desk where she'd been sitting cross-legged. Wearing a blue sweater and jeans, she looked thirty but was older.

"You know them better as the Spanish Inquisition," he added.

She grinned. "And no one expects the Spanish Inquisition! Which one are they sending: Cardinal Ximinez, Cardinal Biggles, or Cardinal Fang?"

"This isn't a Monty Python sketch; this is serious," Jeremy said, pacing around the design studio. "With the old Grandmaster on sick leave, the Templars have taken a very conservative turn."

Suddenly another figure blinked into existence. Above them, legs akimbo in a posture that mimicked Sam's, floated a teenage girl, snub-nosed, blond, dressed in mall-rat clothes.

Sam jumped. "Shadowheart! I've asked you to stop materializing like that."

The angel ignored her. "An audit, huh? Knowing your propensity for violating the tenets of the Order, I wouldn't give a fig for your prospects."

He glared up at her. "Some have said that I've cut quite a swath through evil in Charlotte since I arrived."

"That's a nice quote," Shadowheart said. "Pity that it comes from Bob Diablesse, the local demon lord. I doubt the inquisitor will find it much of a recommendation."

"Nonetheless," Sam challenged, her ire doubtless roused by the mention of church orthodoxy, "Jeremy's wiped out demons, monsters and a witch coven."

"And made deals with Diablesse and boinked a vampire," Shadow-heart pointed out.

"It was only one vampire," Jeremy grumbled.

"Multiple times," his guardian angel retorted. "So much for the vow of celibacy."

"Oh, that," Jeremy said dryly.

"Perhaps a little audit would do you some good," Shadowheart mused. "Maybe it will teach you that there's a reason for rules." She gave Jeremy a disturbing grin. "Let me know how it comes out." She disappeared.

"Shadowheart," Jeremy called, "come back here." But no amount of calling could summon the angel.

Jeremy went home to prepare for the inquisitor's arrival. After sunset, Samantha left to make her own preparations. She ended up at The Crossing Apartments at the address she'd lifted from Jeremy's files, nervously fingering her grandmother's golden cross. The sun had faded, and the moon rode over the fashionable complex. "I suppose I should be grateful that she's no longer in the old Montezuma apartments," she muttered.

"Yeah," a voice twanged in her ear, "that was kind of a hole."

Samantha jumped, pulling a vial of holy water from one pocket and a stake from the other. She found herself facing a short, blond, busty woman of about thirty, clad in denim and rhinestones that made her look like a country singer. Debbie Middleton regarded her with steady blue eyes that held an odd glimmer. "You looking for me, honey?"

"Yeah," Sam said, her mouth dry.

"I know you," Debbie said.

Sam nodded. "I had monster issues. You sent me to Jeremy. I work for him now."

"He's cute, isn't he?"

"I guess so, yeah. Sometimes he seems very young."

"Most people do to me."

Samantha shuddered a little. "I came to get your help." Sam quickly explained about the inquisition.

"Sure," Debbie shrugged, generating an impressive jiggle, "but what can a sexy vampire do about it?"

"Help me. I need to get word to Diablesse, from someone he will listen to. Evil needs a vacation, unless it wants to deal with a new Templar and the Inquisition."

Debbie sighed. "I've been through these cycles before. I'll arrange to see Diablesse. I'd hate to break in a new Templar. He might not know how to give a girl her propers." She gave Sam a speculative glance. "Say, honey, that's a lovely neck you have there. What's your blood type?"

Sam backed up. "Restricted."

Debbie's laughter followed Sam all the way back to her car.

Hours later, Debbie Middleton walked into the plush downtown offices of Bob Diablesse, lobbyist and local demon lord. The blond vampire had left behind her usual boots, denim, and rhinestones for a business suit. For all that, her impressive bustline strained the red blazer, drawing looks from men and glares from women. Most of the people around her were actually people, but lesser demons and minions disguised as humans lounged around. There were no other vampires. Debbie didn't tolerate them in Charlotte. It interfered with her ability to trade her favors for a "nip and a sip" and threatened her truce with the forces of light.

She sashayed to Bob's office. A stunning woman sat at a desk before two huge, gold-colored doors guarded by goblins glamoured to look human. The secretary looked up with a professional smile. "Good evening, Ms. Middleton. Mr. Diablesse got your call and is expecting you." The goblins swung open the doors.

"Debbie, sweetheart," Bob boomed as he stood up from an elegant mahogany desk. To those without the sight, he appeared as an athletic, handsome, black-haired man. "How are you doing, baby?" He whisked around the desk and kissed her a bit too enthusiastically on both cheeks, squeezing the melons in the process. She got a whiff of sulfur and brimstone off the demon.

"Bob, you old devil." She smiled with false warmth. "How's it hanging?"

"Straight down and forked as usual. So, what brings your blond bustiness my way this fine evening?"

"We have a mutual friend with some trouble," Debbie said.

"I have a friend?" Bob said, putting a hand to his chest in mock surprise.

Debbie sighed. "Knock it off, Bob. Jeremy Leclerc is being audited by the Inquisition."

Bob grimaced. "Hell, I wouldn't wish that on my worst enemy, which incidentally, he is. But why tell me?"

"Jeremy, as you know, has been…accommodating for a Templar."

"More to you than to me," Bob said, leaning back against his desk.

"I don't kill humans or turn them into vamps."

"You just bang them into a sexual stupor."

"Honey, you say that like it's a bad thing," Debbie returned. "My point is that if Jeremy fails and is replaced, we might draw one of these shave-pated fanatics who don't see shades of gray."

"Who won't make deals," Bob mused, his chin in his hand. "Yes. I see what you mean."

"It might be a good thing," Debbie added, "if evil took a holiday soon."

Bob shrugged. "Makes sense, but I can't do much about the free-lancers and out-of-towners."

"Course you can," Debbie said. "You can decorate lampposts with their innards. Good for our friend and not bad for you either."

"Hey," Bob said brightly, "you've got a point there."

Debbie rose. "Glad we could get together on this."

Bob smiled more broadly. "As long as you're here—why don't we get together on something more fun?"

Debbie gave a neutral smile. "Sorry, Bob, but your blood doesn't appeal to me, and it might take me several weeks to recover from your idea of fun."

"Another time perhaps."

"Perhaps." She backed toward the doors.

Jeremy met Brother Esposito at the baggage level of Charlotte-Douglas airport the next morning. Esposito walked down the stairs, disdaining the ease of the escalator. Clad in brown robes and tonsured, he carried a staff and a small sack over his left shoulder. How he got the staff past security, Jeremy had no idea.

Esposito's face was pale and bony with intense dark eyes over an aquiline nose. Jeremy felt the weight of those eyes across the space. The inquisitor recognized Jeremy with a brief nod and strode over to him. People scattered from the monk's path.

"Brother Leclerc," Esposito said, his voice deep and pleasant.

"I prefer Jeremy, especially as my identity here is a secret."

A chill seemed to roll off the inquisitor. "Would that it were the old days, when a Templar Knight would wear the Lord's cross on his surcoat."

"Would that it were," Jeremy said. "Your bags?"

Esposito lifted the small sack on his shoulder. "All that I need is here."

"Very well. This way." The pair walked across to the parking deck and Jeremy's red and white Mini.

"A sports car?" Esposito said.

Jeremy shrugged. "Costs the same as a Camry and is easier to park."

"You have expansive views on the vow of poverty."

"I have an identity to maintain as a graphic designer. No one hires a guy driving a heap."

As they drove out of the garage, Jeremy began to wish he was facing demons instead what was supposed to be an ally. Esposito remained silent as they cut through traffic, somehow broadcasting disapproval of Jeremy, the car, and perhaps Charlotte itself.

When they arrived in South End, Jeremy led Esposito into his studio, which seemed rather more luxurious today. It held a kitchenette and a small bedroom sectioned off by bookshelves. Sam sat among the battery of screens and computers that made her look like a flight officer on the Starship Enterprise. She gave Esposito the look Kirk reserved for aliens due for a phaser lunch.

"My assistant, Samantha Pelton," Jeremy said.

"Yes," Esposito said, not offering to shake hands. "I read the report on the Mandrake demon incident she was involved in."

"Since she knew about Shadowheart," Jeremy said, "it seemed safe to bring her onto the team."

Esposito looked at him. "Is she Catholic?"

"Hey, Cardinal Fang, you got any questions about me you can ask me directly, and no, I'm not."

"For that matter, I'm not Catholic either," Jeremy said. "I'm a Taoist."

"Yet you claim to be paired with a guardian angel?" Esposito returned with a glare at Sam.

"I'm teamed with a powerful entity who tells me she is an angel," Jeremy responded, sitting on a table next to a fuming Sam. "But you know that."

"Really?" Esposito said.

Jeremy stared at him. "Surely the old Grandmaster told Rome? You've read my reports."

"The Grandmaster said that you were paired with an angel, but neither he nor anyone else ever saw it. As for your reports, many more plausible messengers than you have claimed to speak to or for God."

"I saw her too," Samantha added.

"Her?" Esposito's eyebrows rose.

"Shadowheart appears female," Jeremy said.

"So you say."

"Call her, Jeremy. Show this sanctimonious—"

"Sam," Jeremy interrupted.

"Yes, by all means," Esposito said. "Call the angel."

Jeremy felt a sinking feeling in his gut, but he lowered his head and concentrated.

Shadowheart, he called into the void. Nothing came back. He put his hand over the crystal and gold amulet he wore, which was Shadowheart's ostensible home, but again, there was no response.

"I see," Esposito said.

"She's a bit pissed at me," Jeremy said, "feels I've been bending a few too many rules."

"Then your imaginary friend and I have something in common."

"She's not imaginary," Samantha said.

Esposito ignored her. "Pull your reports and dismiss your assistant. We can get a few hours work done before I head over to St. Peter's and the company of the godly."

A harsh rapping came from the door. Jeremy used it as a distraction. "Sam, would you get that, please?"

By the time Sam got to it, there was no one there. Only an old duffel bag lay outside. She picked it up and set it on a table. "Hey, there's a note." She unzipped the duffel, then leapt back. "Oh, yuck!"

Inside the duffel bag were eight heads, wrapped in plastic. Most were clearly demons or goblins. The human one bore a strange symbol on its forehead.

"The mark of the werewolf," Jeremy said.

Esposito looked at Sam. "Please read the note."

Sam glanced toward Jeremy, he nodded, and she opened the expensive stationery.

"To Jeremy Leclerc," she read. "*Eight Heads in a Duffel Bag* is an underrated movie and one of my favorites. Just a little tribute of our respect and fear of the mighty Templar warrior. Good luck on your audit. Those inquisitors are pricks. Kind regards, Bob."

Jeremy groaned inside.

"What is the meaning of this?" Esposito demanded. "Who is this Bob, and how does he know of my presence and your review?"

"Er," Jeremy said, "Charlotte is kind of a small town. Diablesse is the local demon lord, but he's more of a corporate and financial hazard than a moral one."

"And this?" Esposito gestured at the duffel.

"Bob's kind of a film buff."

"You're on a first-name basis with the demon?" Esposito snapped.

Jeremy felt the leash he'd placed on his temper slip. "With Diablesse's help, I was able to stop a coven of witches from destroying this town. I live here. Because disorganized, blood-sucking, flesh-tearing evil is more of a danger to the common person than organized evil, I make use of Diablesse when I need to."

Esposito shook his head. "You make distinctions that don't exist. There is only good and evil."

"Maybe it seems that way in the Vatican, protected by 2,000 years of ritual and holiness, but out here in the real world, I'm one Templar in a thousand square miles. I don't have such luxury. I have to pick my fights."

Esposito stared coldly at him. "It seems to me that you have too much of both heresy and luxury."

"Hey, Cardinal Fang," Sam interjected. "Didja notice that evil is down eight players just because Jeremy is here."

Esposito looked right through Sam. "Meaningless, doubtless just minions."

Jeremy took Sam's arm, feeling the tension in his friend that told him she wasn't far from throwing a punch. "Come on, Sam. I'll buy you dinner at Phat Burrito—the air is kind of thick in here.

"As for you," Jeremy said, "my reports are on the desk. You can let yourself out, and St. Peter's is within walking distance."

"Your attitude will be mentioned in Rome," the Jesuit said with a thin smile.

"Come on, Sam."

Sam gave Esposito a smoking glare but followed Jeremy out.

When they were outside, she couldn't contain herself any longer. "Where the fuck does he get the nerve to judge you, after all you've done to help people? And when the hell is Shadowheart going to show up and straighten his ass out?"

Jeremy walked alongside her, pensive. "Sam, what if he's right? What if I am making distinctions that aren't real? What if I am trying to stay alive more than trying to do my job?"

He stopped and faced her. "What if I'm compromising too much? Where's the line and what side of it am I on?"

This time she took his arm. "Look youngster, whatever side of the line you're on- is the side I want to be on."

Impulsively, Jeremy hugged Sam. "Good to know."

Debbie Middleton got out of the Lincoln and smiled at the dazed teenager lying in the backseat with a grin on his face. She finished buttoning her blouse. "Thanks for the good time and the blood, honey."

"Huh?" he said. His feet were propped up and a Gatorade was by his head. Two Band-Aids covered the throat wound.

"Never mind," she said, as she walked off, enjoying the last tang of his blood on her lips. She'd enjoyed the rest too, typical teenage boy, hotter and faster than a pistol. Just as well. It gave her the whole evening, and there was a concert at the Triple Door she wanted to catch.

She cut between buildings, heading through an alley toward her pink VW. Human muggers never worried her. They formed that part of her diet that she didn't have to get sexy over. Halfway up the alley, she felt a chill up her spine, unusual for one of the living dead. Her eyes swept the alley, shadowed to humans, but bright as day to her. Nothing, yet the sense of threat persisted. She stood as still as only the dead can and listened. Only the sounds of a city full of humans reached her. Debbie allowed her fangs to slide out.

A whisper of leather on stone warned her. Debbie leapt backward as a heavy body landed on the spot she'd vacated.

Debbie gave a hissing warning and drew herself up, facing the huge hairy figure that rose from its crouch. Yellow eyes glared at her over a face that was a twisted mix of wolf and man. A heavy musky smell wafted from the creature.

"You're the vampire, Debbie Middleton," he growled.

"You're old," Debbie returned. "You can reason after the change, even speak. You still look mostly human. That takes time."

"Yes." The yellow eyes regarded her steadily.

Debbie knew the vampiric shimmer of her own eyes would have no effect on the creature before her. She thought about running, but the wolf would be as fleet of foot as she. As for strength, she could die if he tore her to pieces, and the wolf feared little beyond silver and certain magics.

"I have lived for a long time," the werewolf continued, "too long to suffer insults at the hands of your friend, Diablesse."

"Demons don't have friends," Debbie said, buying time, "and I don't answer to him."

"Lies," he growled. "You were seen there."

"Hell, I didn't say I didn't know him. I said, I don't serve him."

He considered. "I am Bora, from Kosovo. I chose this place for my new home. I journeyed with many and have 'recruited' others. Diablesse has threatened me and mine and killed some. I judge him unworthy to represent evil. He is too accommodating with those of the light, too soft. I intend to kill him. Join me."

"I don't do werewolves."

Bora growled again. "Join me or die."

"You forget the soldiers of light," Debbie threw back.

"What?" The werewolf paused.

"Diablesse leaves me alone because I'm under the protection of a Templar and a guardian angel."

"Angel?" the wolf repeated, stepping back.

"Yes, a bad-ass bitch named Shadowheart, also known as the Witchbane. Lay a claw on me and you'll see an angel, up close, personal, and very briefly." She held up her hand and a white stone glowed softly on her ring finger. Any creature of evil knew there was only one source for the glow, one meaning.

The werewolf watched her, perhaps suspecting she was stretching the truth but unable to chance an encounter with something as impossibly lethal as an angel.

Debbie pressed her advantage to continue in the direction of her car, walking with an assurance she did not feel. Relief flooded her as she gained the streetlight. She kissed off the idea of the Triple Door. The night suddenly had teeth other than hers.

———

After a quiet dinner at the funky burrito place, Jeremy left to deal with a sighting of a werewolf in Southern Charlotte. There'd been rumors of a new evil player moving into Charlotte, and Jeremy was concerned about the increase in were activity.

After he left, Sam made her way back to the studio to close up for the evening. She was almost done when her cell buzzed. "Samantha here."

"Debbie Middleton."

"You have a cell phone?"

"Yes, dammit, and cable and a Jacuzzi. I don't sleep in a coffin either."

"Whoa, blonde and busty, what's with the attitude?"

"Sorry, I got bounced by a werewolf and not in a good way."

"There's a good way?" Sam wondered.

"His name is Bora; he's moving into Charlotte. Diablesse killed some of his minions."

Sam remembered the heads in the duffel. "Yeah."

"I think we may have been a bit responsible."

"We?" Sam's elegant eyebrows rose.

"You asked me to prevail on Diablesse to put evil on hold."

"Yes?"

"That meant putting the fear of Diablesse into all the freelancers," Debbie continued. "I'm afraid they decided to push back."

"Oh great, I ask for help, and you start a Satanic turf war!"

"Now you know what they mean by 'No good deed goes unpunished.'"

"This is going to kill Jeremy," Samantha groaned.

"Honey, it may kill all of us," Debbie said and hung up.

Samantha sighed and finished locking up the studio. Thoughts rolled around her head about how to help Jeremy deal with the inquisitor. She'd been unable to restrain tongue and temper around Esposito. Fundamentalists of any stripe frosted her pumpkin.

Samantha sighed. "Shadowheart, damn you. Where are you? Why aren't you helping Jeremy?"

But the angel refused to manifest and put an end to the reign of terror. Samantha trudged back to her Subaru.

She was thinking so longingly about a quiet evening at home that she didn't sense a shape until it was almost on her. A growl sounded in her ears. Sam jumped and swung her laptop bag. It slammed into the jaws of the creature that sprang at her from between parked cars. Samantha got a quick impression of bulk, hairiness, and teeth along with an overwhelming smell of musk and heat, a physical representation of rage incarnate.

The werewolf staggered for a second. Then the creature spun back to her, yellow eyes glaring. Sam realized she had no second act, no weapon, and no chance of outrunning the creature. When all else fails, she thought, defiance.

"Fuck you," she said to the advancing werewolf.

A blaze of yellow and black fur engulfed the werewolf's head as an explosive snarl froze them both. The jaguar knocked the werewolf flat, almost at Samantha's feet. She leapt backward, cracking her head on the mirror of a Hummer, and fell to the rough asphalt, skinning her hands. Before her, the jaguar had the werewolf by the back of the neck, its fangs buried deep. The wolf convulsed once, then crashed to the ground. The jaguar snarled and bit again, fangs crunching into the skull. The wolf's yellow eyes dimmed as blood poured over them.

Sam, unsure if her situation had improved, stared at the jaguar as it licked blood off its chops. Then both beasts blurred in her vision. When she could see them clearly again, the werewolf was a naked man, pitifully young. The jaguar, also naked, now stood on two legs as a redheaded woman, tall, in her twenties, with a lithe, small-breasted body that Sam might have appreciated under better circumstances.

"Most incautious," the woman said in a husky voice, "for one who befriends a Templar."

"Who are you?" Sam asked, annoyed that her voice sounded so high and shaky.

"Prosperine."

Sam's brain raced. "The witch's familiar. You and Jeremy destroyed that coven. He saved you from being sacrificed."

"Yes, perhaps now I can return the favor."

Sam remembered that Prosperine wasn't a were, but an actual jaguar, ensorcelled by an Aztec priest a thousand years ago to be a human familiar. "I thought you returned to the wilds."

Prosperine grimaced. "Too boring and too many fur-hunters. I preferred to stay by the city lights. Unfortunately, it also led me to be caught up by the new power in town."

"What?"

"Bora, a werewolf and a very old one, far more powerful than this cub." She toed the body at her feet. "He dominates the weres, familiars, and other animal spirits in this area. He is going to destroy Diablesse and Jeremy. Claims Diablesse is too comfortable with the forces of Light."

"Oh no," Sam groaned, "evil fundamentalists too? Just when I thought it couldn't get worse." She looked at Prosperine. "I gather you weren't planning on lunching on me yourself."

"No," Prosperine said with a chilling note of regret. "Shadowheart has cast a geas on me, preventing my eating humans. Otherwise I'd have made a sizeable dent in your homeless problem."

"Oh, so you're a Republican."

Prosperine ignored the jibe. "Listen, Bora plans to ambush Diablesse, then with his own forces added to Diablesse's survivors, he's coming for Jeremy."

"And you're playing monkey-in-the-middle," Sam said.

"If by that you mean I want to get free of Bora and remain free of Diablesse, you are right. Remember, I was made a witch's familiar. I did not choose it and originally was a natural creature. I belong neither to the Light nor the Dark."

"Yeah, you're part of *Mutual of Omaha's Wild Kingdom.* I get it. OK, where is the ambush going down?"

"Diablesse is involved in something he doesn't want known. Tomorrow night at seven, he is going by himself to a function on Brevard Street, downtown. No one knows what it is, and his people aren't talking, but he will not have his usual retinue of guards. Bora plans to destroy him there."

"Okay, I'll let Jeremy know." Sam left Prosperine to dispose of the dead werewolf. She preferred not to think about how.

Jeremy took the news of a Satanic turf war and the return of Prosperine well.

"Holy crap!" he said.

"What do we do?" Samantha said after he ran down.

Jeremy stroked his chin. "I guess the question is whether Charlotte is better off with Diablesse or Bora?"

"Prosperine thought Bora was real bad news," Samantha offered.

"Whereas Bob is the devil we know?" Jeremy said. "Call Debbie. Have her meet us down on Brevard. Let's see if we can find Bob. I wish we could contact Prosperine, but I suspect we may find her down there."

"To the Batcar," Samantha said.

"The hell you say," Jeremy replied. "This is way too dangerous."

"You need the help," Sam insisted, "with Shadowheart out of the picture. You've got the blood sword; give me the Walther with some silver bullets."

Jeremy looked a little shame-faced. "Sam, I don't have any silver bullets. They don't make them at Wal-Mart, you know, and they're inaccurate as hell."

"I don't care," Sam said. "You're not doing this alone. I can drive the car, at least."

Jeremy's expression grew thoughtful. "Silver bullets... That gives me an idea..."

Brevard Street was busy with limousines and couples in fancy dress heading into the Combined Way Charity Headquarters when Sam and Jeremy arrived. What Bob Diablesse would have to do with this, neither of them could guess. They found Debbie hanging out under a streetlamp dressed in, what was for her, a relatively subdued jacket and slacks. Her bright blond hair was piled into a red hat.

She smiled at Jeremy. "Hey, honey."

"Have you seen him?"

"No."

"But I smell him," a new voice came.

"Prosperine," Sam said.

The shapeshifter walked out of the shadows—tall, pale, with blood-red hair flowing over her shoulders. She wore a fine-tailored suit and a pink blouse that showed off her figure.

The vampire and the witch's familiar eyed each other coolly as Jeremy made brief introductions.

"So, you smell him," Debbie said. "Anything more specific?"

"No, but he is in this area and alone. I neither smell nor sense demons, other than her." She gestured with her head toward Debbie.

"That's Chanel *Coco Noir*, you're getting, Kitty," Debbie returned.

"Let's split up," Jeremy said. "Search for Diablesse."

"I'm a little underdressed for black tie and tails," Sam said, gesturing at her jacket and jeans.

"We'll have to make the best of it."

"I'll work the crowd," Debbie said.

"Naturally," Prosperine said.

Debbie's eyes developed a vampiric shimmer.

"What will you do?" Jeremy interjected.

"Switch back to my natural form so I can sense what is going on."

"Run around as a jaguar?" Debbie said. "Better watch out, sweetie. Lot of women might like to wear you around their shoulders."

"A black jaguar," Prosperine said archly. "Human senses are so dull they rarely detect me, until it is too late."

"Sounds good," Jeremy said.

"Come with me," Prosperine said to Sam. "I'll give you my clothes. You can throw them in Jeremy's car." She turned her back and swayed into the darkness.

Sam grinned at Jeremy. "Rooowwrrr," she said and followed.

Debbie winked. "See you later, honey."

With Prosperine's clothes tucked in the car, Jeremy and Sam prowled Brevard Street among the illuminati of Charlotte, looking for Bob Diablesse. They watched women in evening wear and men uncomfortable in tuxes as they went into the building. Jeremy looked about until he found an unguarded side door and picked the lock.

* * *

Debbie found herself distracted by thoughts she'd never expected to have again as she walked the alley behind Combined Way. She'd worked with Jeremy since he'd arrived in Charlotte. True, his original hunt for her ended up with him tied to her bedposts, but their arrangements had been beneficial to both in subsequent adventures. She'd been the one to warn Jeremy against developing any emotional attachment to her, turning aside any attempt to see her, save when they were working together. She was no good for the living, despite the best of intentions, and she was never sure that her intentions were the best. She was a creature of darkness, controlled and benevolent as far as that went, but her motivations were selfish by her very nature. She had no moral compass; the needle simply spun.

That had worked for them both until she learned of Prosperine. The witch's familiar seemed to have a similar arrangement with Jeremy. The familiar was not a human woman but clearly had some interest in the young man and place in his regard. Debbie hadn't minded that Jeremy couldn't be hers, until she realized he might end up being someone else's.

She shook her head. "I'm being stupid. Jaguar can't have any interest in the boy beyond a meal."

Something struck her from behind, slamming her into the pavement with tremendous force. A large hand came down on the vampire's hand, wrenching off her ring with its white stone.

As her consciousness flickered out, she heard a voice growl, "You're right. You were being stupid…"

Prosperine padded down a Charlotte street, moving from shadow to shadow under the streetlights, often close by people who did not sense the lurking black jaguar. As she passed an underground garage, her nose tickled at the scent of wolves. She stalked down the ramp past an oblivious lot attendant, heading for the lower levels.

Crap, she thought, *I've got to get a collar or something I can keep a cell phone on. Be nice to call for backup. But if I change back to human, I'll just be naked.*

As Prosperine came around a large van, the smell of catnip nearly overwhelmed her senses. A plate of it lay there, as alluring as a fresh kill.

The scent was so overpowering that it took her a second to feel the net as it dropped around her. She came off her feet as the net tightened…

Sam and Jeremy walked backstage as the dull roar of hundreds of the well-to-do talking filled the hall. Bad rock music played loudly.

A prim woman stopped them. "Can I help you?" she said, actually meaning, "Who the hell are you?"

Jeremy handed her a business card.

"Tech-support To Go," she read. "You must be here about our internet problems," she said, adjusting her glasses. "About time."

Jeremy nodded, and she wandered off.

They walked up to a second-floor balcony, watching the crowd.

"There he is," Jeremy said, pointing.

Bob Diablesse walked onstage to thunderous applause. Jeremy's jaw hung slack as Diablesse addressed the crowd. "As you know, we have had some difficult times in Combined Way, but the needs of the community have never been greater and no organization is better suited…"

The speech that followed was an amazing mix of platitudes and aphorisms on raising funds for the poor and getting the Combined Way back to its core mission of helping the downtrodden. For the life of him, Jeremy could not figure what the local demon lord was up to. They made their way down the backstage stairs.

Bob came off stage, shaking hands and slapping backs. He turned, hand outstretched, and took Jeremy's before he realized who it was. The smile froze on the demon's face as he looked at them.

"Would you all excuse me?" Bob said to the crowd. "I see some special friends."

The others drifted off. The three of them faced each other.

"Bob?"

"Hello, Jeremy."

"What are you doing here, alone, unarmed at a Combined Way fundraiser?" Jeremy asked.

The demon looked simultaneously embarrassed and defensive. "Hey, Combined Way does a lot of good."

"Precisely."

"Look, you probably heard about the trouble they were in, scandals over compensation and where the money went—"

Jeremy nodded. "It was all over the papers: resignations, investigative committees."

"Some of my less-disciplined colleagues were involved in that, doing a little work on the side. They caused me to lose face, and I arranged to return the favor. There was no way I could turn down the Chamber of Commerce when they asked for help, not and maintain my position in Charlotte. You're not the only one with a cover here. I get a lot more scrutiny than you do.

"But it wouldn't look good for me to be seen doing good. I have a rather traditional bureaucracy to answer to."

"Tell me about it," Jeremy said with feeling. "But you don't think your side will hear about this?"

Bob gave him a scornful look. "You think demons scan the society page or listen to NPR?"

"Guess not," Jeremy said.

"So now you know," Bob growled. "I'm going to trust to your Templar discretion on this."

"I'm not your problem. We need to get out of here. There's an incredibly powerful werewolf named Bora hunting you. He may be more than a match for the two of us, so I brought reinforcements: Prosperine and Debbie. We have to get you out of here and back to a secure location."

Bob stared in disbelief. "You're helping me? Very tender of you and why should I believe so—"

"Diablesse," Jeremy said, wearily. "I think you should burn in the ninth ring of Hell—"

"Thank you," Bob said.

"—but I suspect Bora would be worse. So, I am saving your horned ass."

Bob studied him. "You're serious."

"Yes, the back way. Now."

Bob considered. "Let me say goodnight to a few people."

"Quickly," Jeremy said.

As the demon turned to make his apologies to his guests, Jeremy gestured to Sam. "Call Debbie. We have no way to reach Prosperine, but she'll find us."

Sam fiddled with her phone. "No answer, went to voicemail. Maybe she's out of bars."

"Or maybe," Jeremy replied grimly, "Bora is already here."

The lights suddenly cut out. People gasped. Emergency lights flicked on. For a split second, in the light of one of them, Jeremy saw a distorted shape. Yellow eyes flared in a face caught between man and animal. Then it was gone.

"He's between us and the front door," Diablesse said.

"Only good news is that he appears to be alone," Jeremy said, eyes narrowing.

"We can take him," Sam declared.

They looked at her.

"Can't we?"

"Maybe," Jeremy said. "A werewolf is incredibly durable. If we fight in this crowded hall…"

"Not to mention any survivors would have seen things they shouldn't," Bob added. "Add to that I share one thing in common with your angel, limited powers in the Realm of Earth."

Sam chewed her lip. "Is there a Plan B?"

"Yeah," Diablesse replied. "Run like hell out the back door."

"I'm liking it," Jeremy added.

They shoved their way through the crowd of partygoers, who perhaps through some primal instinct, were increasingly uneasy. In the distance a woman screamed, followed by a man's hoarse shout. Panic gripped the crowd behind them as they raced out a fire door leading to an alley. Jeremy was debating which way to run when something burst through a second-floor window above them and landed with a snarl among some fenced-in power equipment to their left.

"Exit stage right," Bob said, running as if the devil was chasing him, which with Bob's career, had probably happened.

They ran through darkened alleys, over pedestrian walkways and through underground garages. People stared at them and stepped out of their way in suspicion. The werewolf pursuing them was only occasionally visible, and Jeremy got the impression they were being herded.

They emerged at street level opposite St Peter's. Sam made a beeline for the church door. Jeremy followed for lack of any better plan.

Bob had been so intent on their back trail that the demon didn't notice their destination until they were on top of the ornate wooden doors. He skidded to a halt. "Whoa, I can't go in there."

Argument died on Jeremy's lips. The werewolf was emerging from the garage they had just left, loping toward them at an easy pace. It wore no clothes now and looked like an immense wolf balanced on two human-looking legs.

"Sam, get inside," Jeremy grated, drawing the bloodsword from its concealed sheath in the leather longcoat. The red gem in its hilt winked balefully at the oncoming beast.

Sam opened the door but lingered, unwilling to abandon Jeremy. Bob grinned, showing fangs that hadn't been there before. "Let's see if these wolves are as tough as everybody says."

None of them were prepared when Bora pulled up well short of them, reached into the leather pouch strapped over his shoulder, and pulled out a large revolver.

Bob and Jeremy were so shocked they simply stared, but Sam reached forward, grabbed Jeremy's coat, and hauled him backward. A shot cracked the stonework where Jeremy had stood. He fell backward into the church and tried to get his feet under him.

Bob wasn't so lucky; bullets thudded into the demon. Bora tossed the revolver and charged Bob with blinding speed, hurling the demon into Jeremy and Sam. They were all thrown into the church. Jeremy's sword flew from his grip as he struck a pillar before caroming into church pews. Bob flew over Jeremy and crashed into the pews. Sam, protected by both their bodies, slid right up the center aisle.

Bob struggled to his feet, black fluid leaking down the front of his chest. He stared around him in horror. "No, no, not Holy Ground!" then slumped down between the seats, unconscious or dead.

Bora laughed as Jeremy staggered to his feet; the werewolf reached behind to seal the church doors.

Broken bones grated in Jeremy's right arm; pain made his eyes tear. To his shock he saw Prosperine, in jaguar form, bound and netted and lying beside the door. Next to where Diablesse had crashed to the ground lay Debbie, bound by ropes she should have been able to break. The vampire lay utterly still, her face waxy and corpselike. Her eyes were slits, but they glittered; she was still aware but weak.

"Don't look to your vampire friend," Bora said, in a heavy Eastern European accent. "She seems to have misplaced her magic ring. In here, she's nothing but a corpse." He twitched the net bag holding Prosperine. The jaguar snarled explosively, but its helpless rage merely amused the huge werewolf. Bora laughed, a twisted sound of human and wolf. "Even you, Templar, never dreamed I would drive you into a church. Your allies are helpless."

"Why isn't he?" Samantha demanded.

"Werewolves aren't affected by religious weapons of any faith," Jeremy grated.

"Just so," Bora said. "We owe no allegiance to gods or devils, only to the nature of the Wolf."

"Bet you guys love Jack London novels," Sam snapped.

Great, Jeremy thought, *annoy the werewolf.* If only I could reach the bloodsword.

Samantha, as if sensing his thought, locked eyes with him and started moving to the right.

OhmyfuckingGod, Jeremy thought, *she's going to decoy Bora.*

"No, Sam," Jeremy yelled. He raced forward toward Bora. The werewolf dropped the rope to Prosperine's net and spread his arms wide, huge claws out. Jeremy skidded to a halt, just short of the werewolf's grasp. From under the coat, he pulled a large spray can.

"You going to paint me out of existence, Templar?" The werewolf, puzzled by the can, hadn't even bothered to strike.

"Yes," Jeremy grated. "I think silver is your color." He triggered the can. A cloud of silver nitrate spray enveloped Bora from head to toe as Jeremy emptied the can's contents.

Bora gave a howl of utter anguish and leapt away, blue flames enveloping his wolf pelt.

Sam raced around the burning wolf to get the bloodsword. Jeremy chased Bora as the can sputtered out its remaining contents. To his surprise, the blue flames generated no heat, and, rather than burning,

Bora seemed to be diminishing. The huge bulk of muscle evaporated. Teeth and claws disappeared along with the hair and pelt. All that was left was a naked, pot-bellied man with big ears. Still flickering blue and screaming, Bora ran for the front door, falling as his legs tangled in the straps of the leather bag.

Jeremy stood there, torn between terror and relief. "I can't believe that worked."

Samantha handed him the sword. She hadn't struck the fleeing wolfman. "Aren't we going after him?"

Jeremy looked at her. "You want me to chase a naked man down Tryon Street and stick him with a sword? That will look great on YouTube. Besides, I don't think I can catch my breath, much less him. My right arm's broken."

"Siddown, fer Crissake," Sam said. "I'll look for a first aid kit. Don't move until I get back."

As she ran to the back of the church, Jeremy picked up the fallen leather bag. He walked slowly and painfully over to Debbie.

"I feel like I've been eaten by a wolf and shit over a cliff," Debbie whispered.

"I think that was Bora's plan." Jeremy nodded. "This might help." He scooped up the white stone ring out of Bora's bag and placed it on her finger. The effect was immediate. The corpse-like look faded, to be replaced with her usual vivacity.

Bob had no such relief, and he groaned as he crawled up onto the pew. "I can't say that I like being under obligation to a Templar for my life," Bob said, wiping his face. "Yet I owe you a favor. Got anything in mind? Gold, jewels, a date with the girls from Hooters?"

Jeremy looked at the demon and considered for a long moment. "I want Charlotte to get a soccer team. Give me something to do on weekends."

"That's not an easy one, kid," Bob said. "Sunday is for manly sports. OK, done deal and we are square. I'm outta here." He made his shaky path past a returning Sam to the exit.

"Will someone let me out of this net?" a voice came from the floor.

Prosperine, now a naked redhead, looked up hopefully from the floor.

Debbie untangled the shapeshifter as Samantha returned with a first aid kit she'd found and splinted Jeremy's forearm. Prosperine donned his duster, looking as erotic as a sailor's dream in the black leather.

"We won this time," Sam said. "I wonder how long it will take for Bora to recover?"

Prosperine laughed like Lauren Bacall. "If he's smart, he won't stop running until he hits the Canadian border. Whatever you did to him, stripped away hundreds of years of power and strength. There are a lot of creatures here in Charlotte who would be delighted to get claws and teeth into that saggy, white ass."

"What is the meaning of this?" an outraged voice shouted.

The four turned to face Cardinal Esposito, who advanced on them from the rectory door, cross outstretched in one hand and container of Holy Water in the other.

"Crap," Debbie said, and dodged behind Prosperine.

"Nothing much," Sam said wearily. "We just stopped a demonic turf war, saved Combined Way, assorted humans, two demons, a familiar, and perhaps the economic future of the city."

"We're better than Batman," Jeremy said, a little giddy from shock.

"You did all this with a vampire, a witch's familiar, and a lesbian," Esposito said.

"Sounds like a promising series for Apple TV," Debbie replied.

Esposito glared at Jeremy's defenders, though he carefully kept a large crucifix between him and Debbie. "Do you even have any male acquaintances? You seem to associate only with unchaste women."

Samantha gave him a defiant look. "Smile when you say that, Cardinal Fang."

"I'm not a woman; I'm a jaguar," Prosperine said, insulted.

"And I get chased all the time, honey," Debbie added with a false sweetness.

"And I am an angel," came a new voice. A snub-nosed blond girl dressed in jeans suddenly stood among them.

Esposito barked a laugh, but it was cut short as the lines of Shadowheart's body shimmered and changed. In place of the blond teen, stood a raven-haired woman nearly seven feet tall. Emerald eyes blazed from her flawless, pale face. She wore leather and silver mail, and a sword hung at her side. From her shoulders towered wings of black and red feathers.

"Do I still amuse you, Inquisitor?" she said, her voice high and musical, so beautiful that it was hard to concentrate on the words.

"I see your *auto-da-fe* and raise you a *deus ex machina*," Samantha said, her grin nearly as sharp as Debbie's.

"Surely, surely," Esposito sputtered, his face blank with shock. "You cannot be real. Not a true angel. Not serving with this heretic. He has broken every rule—"

"God is not a bureaucrat," Shadowheart said. "These rules you prize come from men, not divinity. Your traditions work on evil because they are sanctified by belief, but your disdain for other beliefs is unfounded. A Buddhist monk is as holy, or more so, than you."

"But there are so many more worthy," Esposito insisted, pointing at Jeremy.

"Do not presume to question me," Shadowheart said. Though she did not raise her voice, the power of it rang off the walls, and everyone froze. Jeremy realized that he had never before seen his guardian angel *angry*.

"I am Jeremy's guardian by appointment and by my will. He is foolish, vain, self-absorbed, and generally all those things young men are. But he is also valiant and prone to defend his friends past the point of reason. He's faced enemies that would break your mind, even turning some of them, if not to good, then away from evil."

She lowered her head, and the full power of her gem-bright eyes smote the Jesuit. He fell to his knees, raising his hands.

"You are," he said, "you're a real angel."

"Yes, Raoul, I am. Why is it that you always found it so easy to believe in demons and devils and so hard to believe in angels and more? You never really believed. Did you?"

"No," he said, tears streaming down his face.

Jeremy, who still harbored doubts about who and what he served, felt a mute sympathy for the priest.

"So, Raoul," Shadowheart continued. "I now elevate you from inquisitor to the level of a simple shepherd. For you have that in common with those who kept watch on the hillside; an angel of the Lord has spoken with you." She spread her black and red wings until they seemed to fill the cathedral. Debbie squeaked and cowered behind a column. Prosperine ducked under a pew.

"What must I do?" Esposito whispered, his eyes burning.

"Do you not already know?"

"Command me," he said.

"Inquisite no more. Heal the sick. Comfort the poor. Defend the helpless."

"So, it shall be," Esposito said. "I swear it."

He turned to Jeremy and to the Templar's embarrassment, bowed his head to the floor. "Forgive me. Forgive my arrogance." The Jesuit rose and backed away, his eyes only for Shadowheart, until he reached the door and vanished.

Shadowheart blurred and transformed back into her mall-rat form. She snapped her bubble gum derisively at Jeremy. "You are a pain in my ass. You break rules just to hear the sound of them cracking."

"Yet you stay with me," he said, his voice low.

Shadowheart scowled. "I must have a 'bad-boy' thing."

To The Holy See

    From Raoul Esposito SJ *Calificador,*

Your Holiness,

    The audit of Jeremy Leclerc has been cancelled. He is beyond the powers of the Realm of Earth to judge.

I submit my resignation as Inquisitor and request reassignment to Sub-Saharan Africa where I may finally begin God's work...

The End

8

—————

PAS DE DEUX

Jeremy almost dropped his latte on the keyboard as he read the headline from the Charlotte Observer website: POLICE SEEK "VAMPIRE" KILLER.

"Dammit," he said. People in the Brown Ground coffee shop stared as the lanky, brown-haired man wiped hot coffee off his wrist. Jeremy ignored them as his eyes devoured the text.

"Twenty-six-year-old Desmond Rovelo was found dead near Park Road Park by teens in the early morning hours. The teens claim to have seen a small, white female fleeing the scene. A witness, Latesha Williams, said that the man had two bite marks on his throat and appeared to have lost much blood."

As if on cue, his cell phone vibrated. He flipped it open.

"It wasn't me." The voice belonged to Debbie Middleton, vampire and sometime ally. "I was in a threesome last night, and other than being a bit anemic, they're fine and can testify I was with them all night."

"Never mind. You may be the evil undead, but you worked too hard to get a truce with the forces of light to throw it away so soon."

"Damn right. But we both have a problem."

"Let's meet. The sun's down, and I'm in the Brown Ground on East Boulevard."

"Yuppie scum. I'm outside. I just wanted to make sure you wouldn't stick a bloodsword in my petite derriere before coming in. You Templars are quick with those things."

"I never stab a lady without warning."

"I ain't a lady now and wasn't when I was alive, but thanks."

The door opened and Debbie stepped in, putting her phone in her purse. Most of the men in the place glanced up from their laptops and electronic toys. Debbie looked a lot like a country singer, small, but with a pile of bright blond hair and a bust that threatened to burst her blue jean jacket.

She dropped into an overstuffed chair in the quiet corner he'd settled in. Jeremy glared at the staring men who went back to their PCs, tablets, and phones.

"Any idea who or what it is?" Jeremy said. He tried to keep his eyes up on Debbie's. The vampire had turned their first hand-to-hand combat into something more erotic and lingering. For two hundred years Debbie had lived a life of sensual decadence. She played the human body like an instrument in return for a "nip and a sip."

"No. The cops think it was a psycho, but it's a vamp."

"Friend of yours?"

"No vamp that knows me would come near. I'd kill them. This town ain't big enough for two of us. Least not the way I want to exist."

Jeremy scanned the story. "Victim was a mugger with a record of robbery and assault. Another vamp with a heart of gold?"

Debbie shrugged, which was fun to watch. "Vamps love criminals. For those few of us bothered by feeding on humans, it's an out. And y'all don't really care if they go missing. They're also the ones out at night in isolated areas. Convenient snacks."

"Yeah."

"Whoever this is has to go," Debbie said. All the coquettishness disappeared, and something old and deadly faced him now. "If this is a new vamp, they need to feed way more than I do, and they aren't that careful. I leave humans alive, tired, and happy. A killer vamp is going to make my hunting and feeding way harder."

"The White Pass protects you." Jeremy winced mentally as he remembered the Templar Master's expression when Jeremy told him how he'd bound the Order to exempt Debbie from being hunted by the forces of light, in return for her aide against a Bain Sidhe haunting SouthPark Mall.

"Not from the police or what would follow if I'm revealed," Debbie countered. "We have to find this new vamp and kill it."

"This sounds like the setup to a bad buddy movie," he said.

Debbie's lips twisted. "Yeah. You, me, and your guardian angel." Her eyes darted around. "Where is she anyway?"

Suddenly, a girl stood next to Debbie, medium height, cute, cornflower blue eyes, and wearing a loose white blouse and jeans. She looked down at Debbie, who'd frozen like a rabbit.

"Shadowheart," Jeremy acknowledged. He hadn't seen his guardian angel manifest in several weeks. Shadowheart had several manifestations to human eyes, this being the least alarming. But Debbie saw her as she actually was, warrior archangel, and as terrifying to her as any monster of darkness to a human. "Debbie is going to help us."

The angel turned her gaze from Debbie, who sank further into her chair. "Templar, you spend too much time with such creatures."

A flash of anger lit Jeremy. "It's hard to meet nice girls doing what I do."

"Uh, Jeremy, honey," Debbie interrupted, "I don't think you should argue—"

"Or what? I'll be condemned to a lonely life of fighting in shadows until I die?" He snapped his laptop closed and rose. "Too late."

Debbie rose and stretched. Shadowheart used the distraction to step into a shadow and vanish. Jeremy felt a weight in the gold and crystal housing that he wore on a chain under his shirt. Shadowheart rode him again.

I feel a disturbance to the south, Shadowheart mindspoke. *Something evil prepares itself. Seek the area of the Greenway.*

Debbie and Jeremy piled into his red Mini Cooper and drove to a side street near a pedestrian entrance to the McMullen Greenway, a bike path and trail of packed dirt and wooden walkways over swampy ground. A few joggers and bikers in brilliant clothing were leaving as the Greenway closed at dusk. When they were safely out of sight, Jeremy and Debbie climbed out of his Mini.

Though the evening was warm, Jeremy carried a black leather duster in his arms. Rolled in it was the bloodsword, a plain Templar blade with a jeweled hilt. No ornamentation that; the jewel was a potent force against evil. Under his loose beach shirt, a Walther PPK rode at the small of Jeremy's back. Debbie and he split off the trail. She went for the swampy areas where the mosquitoes wouldn't trouble her undeadness. He went off to a piece of high ground with a view of the trail, sprayed himself with OFF, and sat with his back to a tree. Time dragged by.

Anything? he finally mindspoke to Shadowheart.

I feel a sense of something, she replied, *a sense of something evil nearby, but it is hard to filter it out from your E-cupped ally.*

Jealous? he said.

Your infantile fascinations with sex are of no interest to me. I am of the same stuff as the stars.

Hot gas, huh?

The gold and crystal pendant he wore that held Shadowheart's essence thumped him on the chest. *Silence, I am searching.* In a second, Shadowheart flicked into existence in her normal mode of the small blond girl. She pointed. "That way."

Jeremy stood and drew the bloodsword, slipping on his leather duster as the evening had cooled. He stumbled over the clinging undergrowth that seemed to be everywhere in the South, finally resorting to a path to make some speed. A sweet, smoky smell from ahead slowed him, and he saw a cigarette glow in the darkness of the woods. He recognized the smell of pot.

Jeremy gained a vantage on a small hillock. On a bench below sat a girl about his age, small and dark-haired, pale and intent. She wore jeans and a black bolero jacket and held a joint. Facing her on the bench was a big-muscled goon, with tattoos, spiky hair, and a small beard.

"That's a little taste, baby," he said, crossing his booted feet. "I got all the good stuff. I can even get you serious drugs. Pills, whatever you need." He smiled at her. "For the right favors, I can even cut the price some. Hey, it's not like I want to suck you dry."

"Funny you should put it that way," she said in a high, sweet voice and leapt at him, eyes glimmering silver, fangs out.

"What the fuck?" he screamed.

Jeremy plunged out of the undergrowth, drawing the Templar bloodsword.

The vampire's head snapped around. She spotted him, then dropped the struggling drugger to race away with inhuman speed. The drugger stumbled off the bench and directly into Jeremy's path. They collided and went sprawling.

"Hey man," the drugger shouted. "What you and the bitch up to?" He pulled a snub-nose pistol out, but before he could aim it, a small, slender hand clamped down on his wrist.

"Now don't be going off prematurely," Debbie purred in the drugger's ear. "I hate that in a man. Wanna party?"

Leaving Debbie to deal with the drugger, Jeremy scrambled up and set out after the female vampire, running flat out. She'd fled down a side trail, one that the locals had made to reach the Greenway from their backyards.

Jeremy spotted her. Foolishly, she'd stopped to see if she was pursued. She saw him at the same instant and took off. They reached a street outside the park, and Jeremy thought of taking a shot at the fleeing girl. The gun would not kill a vamp but would drop her.

As he slowed to pull the pistol, an SUV flashed its brights into his eyes. The yellow vehicle roared from the corner where it had been idling and skidded to a stop. The vampire leapt in, and the Nissan sped off. Jeremy caught sight of the frightened man's face. But his night vision was just returning and he caught part of the license plate as the Nissan screeched around a corner.

Jeremy was left standing, pistol in one hand and sword in the other.

You look like an extra from Pirates of the Caribbean, *Shadowheart said. Head back into the park before someone sees you.*

He found Debbie sitting on the drugger's chest playing with his pistol. The man was naked, gagged, bound with his clothes, and sporting two bandages on his thigh.

"You get her?" Debbie asked. She dumped the bullets from the revolver cylinder on the ground, then bent the cylinder so it wouldn't fit back in the revolver, and threw the weapon into the bushes.

"No."

"Damn."

"Target of opportunity?" he asked, gesturing at the wide-eyed man.

"I figured you wouldn't care about a druggy losing a little blood. He'll lose more than I took to mosquitoes before he works himself loose."

Jeremy glared down at him. "You're right. I don't care. Come on. Let's get before the cops show up."

"Nice eating you," Debbie said to the drugger. "Drink lots and lots of fluids and take extra vitamins, honey."

The next day Jeremy hacked the DMV database. In hours he'd found the information: George Bexley, owner of a 2019, yellow Nissan Pathfinder. Bexley lived in a new development of townhomes south of Charlotte on Johnston Road.

Jeremy rented a white van and threw magnetic signs of the local cable company on both sides. No one would question the presence of a cable van in the neighborhood, though he might run into irate customers.

Jeremy drove down in daylight and staked out the three-story townhomes. Bexley's home was at the end of the block; every shade and curtain was down and drawn.

It made sense in a way. A new neighborhood would usually be made up of transitory people who did not know each other. He studied the building, looking for a way to break in. There were too many people about to try now. A couple walked a dog past his parked van. Some kids rode by on scooters.

Jeremy got out and strolled up to the house, dressed in coveralls and toting a toolbox and satchel. No one paid any attention. Quickly he set up mini-mikes and a camera on the house. Even standing at the windows, he could see nothing inside.

He returned to the van and set up his equipment and settled in, reclining the seat so he could barely be seen. Vampires had to avoid the sun, but it could be active inside the building. Contrary to the Dracula legend, vampires were not unconscious during the day, though they were less active. Jeremy preferred to attack in daylight, but there was no opportunity. Hours passed. The sun drooped behind the massing clouds. Cars returned to garages. People went in for the evening.

The yellow SUV rounded the corner and drove right by his van, not three feet away. Jeremy slunk further in his seat as the Nissan pulled into a driveway. A man, near Jeremy's own height of six feet, got out. George Bexley looked to be thirty, with thinning hair. Bexley picked up the mail and walked up to the door. Since he walked under the setting sun, he was clearly not a vampire.

As the door opened, Jeremy flipped up his binoculars. She stood just inside the door, but the wide smile on her petite face at the sight of Bexley disturbed Jeremy. His distress grew when the man laughed and walked in, sweeping her up in his arms. The door closed, shutting off further view.

Jeremy flicked on his mikes. For a few minutes, all he could hear was indistinct voices and the sound of dishes clattering.

"Sabella, do we have any ranch dressing?" Jeremy assumed the male voice was Bexley. He'd moved into the dining room near the miked window.

An indistinct female voice replied.

"Aw, I hate vinaigrette. What about French?"

"Well, George," came the female voice, "if you absolutely must drown all my tasty vegetables in dressing, here it is."

"Thanks, honey. Quiet day?"

"Yes, I dozed a lot. I am still a bit weak from the chase. I know you hate it, but I must hunt soon."

"Not tonight," he said. "That guy with the sword might be out there. I can give you enough to keep you going."

"Darling, I'm always so afraid that it will make you sick. I can't risk you dying."

"Hey, don't worry. I'm eating all this iron-rich spinach that you got for me."

"I'm so sorry about this, George. So sorry. You should never—"

"Baby, don't do this to yourself. It was either be turned by that monster that bit you, or the cancer would have killed you within weeks.

"We'll hunt another time. Either a bad guy, where it doesn't matter, or somebody strong, and you'll have to get better at controlling yourself. You're making progress. You hunt so much less than you used to."

"Yes, yes it's so hard. I'm always so hungry. My hatred of the living rises like a tide in me. I don't want to but—"

"I love you. Somehow, we will beat this thing. Find a way back, manage it some way until then."

"Poor George, you don't deserve this. I don't want this for you."

"Darling, please don't cry…"

Jeremy turned the mike off so he didn't have to hear the sound of weeping. He felt ill. This was not what he expected. Instead of a merciless vampire and her minion, he had a tragedy on his hands: a human in love, a vampire trying to contain its evil in the hope of living again.

"God," he said, "all I want to do is turn on the car and drive off."

"Thee cannot." Shadowheart appeared in the seat next to him in her teen mall-rat guise.

"You heard," he demanded.

"I did and it grieves me in ways that you cannot begin to know."

"Then find some way for me to help them."

"Help them, Jeremy?" Her face lay shadowed by the harsh streetlights, but her eyes glittered, hard and bright. "There is no help in the Realm of Earth for Sabella. The only release is to pass beyond. As for George, for the best of reasons, love, he is self-chained to one who must destroy. His only salvation comes with repenting of murders he has abetted."

"I don't have to be the one to do this," he said, jaw clenched so hard that the muscles jumped.

"No," Shadowheart said. "If she stays, Debbie will eventually find and kill her and probably George as well. Allow them to move and it will fall to another soldier of light to battle them, over the bodies of all they slay or injure in the interim."

"Go away," he said. "I need to think."

Shadowheart vanished.

Jeremy looked at the door behind which a vampire wept and a man sought to protect his love. He reached for his cell phone and called Debbie.

"Hey, honey," she said. "Found them?

"Yes." He gave the address. "I'm in a white cable van. How soon can you get here?"

"Look for me in twenty minutes."

Jeremy sat in the truck and waited. Finally, a pink VW pulled up behind him, driving without lights. Vamps saw well in the dark. She opened the door and slipped into the shotgun seat. Debbie wore black leather pants with a matching jacket; a kerchief hid some of her bright yellow hair.

"Hey, Templar. Nice job of tracking. So, what's the plan?"

"Listen to this." Jeremy played the digital of George's homecoming.

Thunder rumbled in the distance as the recording stopped. "Ain't that sweet? Can we kill them now?" Debbie said.

"I need to know something, Debbie. Why are you good?"

"I'm not good, honey, I'm just not that bad."

"That's no answer."

"Oh goody, we're going to do *Interview with the Vampire*."

"Debbie, I may need options here that I've never considered."

Debbie shifted, seeming annoyed, then her face smoothed out, becoming as cool and remote as marble. "Jeremy, I live among humans without harming them. You're thinking that's because of regret or guilt. Maybe thinking that it has something to do with atoning for the people I killed when I was a regular vamp. It doesn't. I just don't want to have to dispose of fifty to sixty bodies a year or keep moving on."

"That can't be all," he demanded.

"Can't it? Two hundred years ago I was an ignorant whore in New

Orleans, dying from yellow fever when Ben Carrier made me a vamp. I was twenty-six. That wasn't young in a time when human life averaged forty years. Suddenly I was immortal and amoral. A vampire isn't a human who drinks blood, Jeremy. It's a change in being. I rise with the moon, drink blood, screw like a mink, and party all the time. I'm a Hollywood starlet in warp drive. That life would kill a human in years, from ennui or despair. But I'm not heading for a degree, motherhood or retirement. Every day is Groundhog Day for me."

"Doesn't explain why you stopped killing humans. You're the only one that ever has."

"I'm a time tourist, honey. I've got a practical eternity if I don't screw it up. I've learned to drive a car and use a computer. I've read Jane Austen when it came out and seen first run Charlie Chaplin films. One incredible night, I saw men walk on the moon. Who knows what the future holds? I'll get to see it."

"Unless," she turned to look at him, "a Templar, or some other soldier of light, cuts me down. Hell, half the vamps that get whacked get it from humans who know enough to stake them during daylight. There's one fucker on the West Coast who uses UV lamps and fries us. So, I helped you in return for a White Pass. For my pardon."

"So, it's all about you?"

"You bet, baby. A vampire is all Id and don't you damn well forget it. My moral compass just spins, honey. It doesn't point anywhere. Most of us hate the living and the light. I'm different...for now, Jeremy, for now."

They sat in silence for minutes; it began to rain. A thin drizzle, it obscured the far end of the block.

"We won't kill the man," he said finally.

"I hope not." Debbie shrugged.

He looked at her. "Kill him and I'll kill you. You can kiss your White Pass goodbye no matter what happens. Win or lose."

Tension filled the small space and finally Debbie smiled. "You're learning, boy."

Jeremy opened the van door and unsheathed the bloodsword. Then, before his wavering resolve could fail him, he ran across the street, through the pelting rain, up the driveway, and slammed into the front door. It was the usual cheap builders'-grade lock and snapped. Jeremy rolled up and ran into the dining room. Debbie came in on his heels.

Sabella and George leapt up from their candlelit dinner table as he barged in. Jeremy knew he should have thrown himself at Sabella, cutting her down by surprise. But he slowed, facing the pair across the table.

"Vampire," he said. "I'm Leclerc, Knight Templar. You know why I am here, know what I must do. Bid your man withdraw."

"Sabella," George screamed, "run." He threw a chair at Jeremy.

Jeremy batted the chair away with his arm. Sabella leapt across the table. But she'd reckoned without his trained reflexes. The bloodsword licked out and cut deeply into her left arm and side. She screamed, wounded bitterly by the supernatural weapon. Twisting in the air, she crashed into a wall, bringing down a painting.

Before Jeremy could finish her, George made a clumsy lunge at him. Debbie intercepted the human, slamming him to the floor. Jeremy paused to be certain Debbie hadn't killed him.

The blond vampire glared at Jeremy. "He'll live. Get her."

Sabella had staggered to her feet, leaking stolen blood. With a wild, despairing look at George, she ran out the French doors to the deck.

Jeremy started to chase her when three shots made him turn back. Debbie sank to the ground, the front of her leather jacket torn by exit wounds. Shock and surprise filled her face as she fell forward. George had pulled a pistol from the sideboard. Now he advanced toward Jeremy. Debbie scissored her legs, catching George and making him stumble forward.

Jeremy lunged across the space, seizing George's gun hand with his left. His right hand held the bloodsword, but he could not bring himself to cut George down. He dropped the sword and hit George in the face twice, but the older man hung on doggedly. "Leave her alone," he cried. "It's not her fault."

Sickened by what he was doing, Jeremy slammed an elbow against George's chin, dropping him unconscious.

He knelt down by Debbie.

"Crap," she groaned. "A goddamn .44. Everybody's carrying fucking cannons these days. Oh god, that hurts."

"I'm sorry, I'm sorry," Jeremy stammered. "I didn't—"

"Get her, you dumb shit," she hissed. "I'll just lie here and suffer."

Torn, Jeremy looked at the French doors and at the prone George.

"Don't touch him," Jeremy ordered.

"Bastard," she swore, as she held her hands over her blasted middle.

He dashed into the rain after Sabella. She had not gotten far, staggering into the woods that adjoined the development. She spotted him and redoubled her speed, disappearing into the woods and the gloom.

He managed to follow the vampire's trail for a hundred yards before losing it. He strained his ears for the sound of her but could hear only wind and rain rustling the leaves and foliage.

"Sabella," George yelled from behind Jeremy.

Jeremy spun around, this time drawing his own pistol. How had George gotten past Debbie?

The man stumbled about the woods. From somewhere he produced a flashlight.

George's presence might play to Jeremy's advantage. The blood-sword was very effective against the unliving, and he'd wounded Sabella badly. She might try to return to George.

Jeremy circled back, taking a trail doubtless made by the neighborhood children. It ended at a small clearing. In it stood an amalgam of wood and tarps, a child's hiding place. Sabella knelt by the little tarp shack, her small, pale face contorted. George, sobbing, held her in his arms. He stared as Jeremy walked into the clearing, then jumped as Debbie came in from the other side.

"I shot you," he said, astonished.

"Yeah, you did. Son-of-a-bitch." Jeremy saw that her abused middle was wrapped in a bloodstained sheet. She must have left George to find something to bind herself up with. Fortunately, George's big revolver was stuck in her belt.

Sabella stirred weakly. "You're a vampire too. Like me."

"No," Debbie said. "Not like you. I didn't choose it."

"Leave us alone," George said, tears and rain washing down his face.

"I would trade anything if I could," Jeremy said. He felt cold and numb, empty of emotion, of pain, even of volition. A leaden dread enveloped him as he watched the pair. George embraced Sabella. Her tiny form almost disappeared against him as blood leaked from the vampire's slashed side. She glared back, pale face defiant.

"You win, Templar. You and your vampire whore," she said, a bitter smile twisting her lips. "Go ahead and destroy me."

"No," George shouted and made as if to stand, but she clung to him.

"You can't fight them," she demanded. "You can't. I should have died of the disease when I was meant to, should never have hoped I could have a place in the world. I'll be damned to Hell before I will lose you to a hopeless fight."

"But you are damned already," a voice said.

Jeremy didn't turn. He just wanted it to end. No speech, no drama, but that was too much to hope for.

Shadowheart glided past him in her archangel manifestation. Now far taller than Jeremy, with skin as pale as the vampire's and long hair as dark, she made an eerie counterpoint to Sabella. But for the black and red wings, she might have been kin to the vampire. The mail and leather that Shadowheart wore made no noise and had no scent.

Unfazed by Jeremy and the bloodsword, Sabella gave a frightened squeak at the sight of Shadowheart, pressing back against George, who stared in awe at the towering angel.

"Who are you to damn her?" George finally managed. "Where were you when she was made into this? Where was the merciful God that day?"

"Yes," Jeremy spoke thickly, to everyone's evident surprise. "Where was God when Sabella got sick? Where was he when Sabella's soul was drawn out? Where was God when she fed on her victims? Where is God, Shadowheart? Go on, answer them. Answer me, damn you."

Shadowheart half-turned toward him. "This again, Jeremy? I have no more answers for you than I did the first time you demanded them. God is not answerable to his creations for the outcomes of their lives so long as they have free will. Sabella chose not to die but to exist and take other lives. For that, she too must answer. Or do you forgive her for those she slew simply because it is now her nature?"

He stared at his guardian angel and said nothing.

"To all of creation there is a choice. Go toward God, on a path sometimes perilous and agonizing, or go away into nothingness and meaninglessness," Shadowheart said.

"And what of mercy?" George said. "Since we found each other, she has taken less lives and fed only on the evil and the worthless—"

"Worthless?" Shadowheart said, her clear gray eyes boring in. "No part of God's creation is worth more or less in the eyes of the divine."

"Enough," Sabella whispered. "Take me. Just promise you won't hurt George."

"The hell with that," George growled. "They get you over my dead body."

"No, no, no," she said, tears tracking down the small face. "I could not bear it."

Jeremy, weary and grief-ridden, gestured with the bloodsword. It seemed an immense weight at the end of his arm. "Tell me, Angel. You're supposed to know everything about right and wrong. Do I hack down the demon in front of her lover, or do I kill him first so I can get to her?"

But it was Debbie who answered. "George won't live forever; Sabella will. And without him, she'll lose herself to what she is, undead and taker of life. Let her go now and all she kills after will be on your head."

"You stopped," Jeremy said.

"You said it yourself, I'm the only one who ever has. I control it, for now, night by night. One night maybe I won't stop. Then it will be you or me, Templar."

"It's hopeless," George said to Sabella. "Isn't it?"

She nodded. "I'm afraid so."

"Then take us both," George said. "Just make it quick."

Debbie looked at Jeremy, something like pity on her face. "You don't need to be the one, Jeremy. Wait for me by the van."

"No," Jeremy stated. "I'm a Templar. If it means anything, then it means I protect humans from the supernatural. I won't let you kill George, and he'll die before he'll let you at Sabella. If this has to be done…"

Jeremy stalked toward the pair on feet that felt like they belonged to someone else. He tried to lift the sword. Then tried again.

"The sword," he muttered. "The sword forbids it."

"The sword, Jeremy, or your arm?" Shadowheart asked softly, only barely audible above the rain.

He raised his eyes to the angel, now certain. "Whichever it is, I have no power to do this. Not even if it is right. Not even if it is necessary. These aren't the monsters I trained to destroy. And I won't have Debbie do this. I won't cheat that way."

Shadowheart gave him an enigmatic look, but he refused to turn away. Did some uncertainty enter her regard, he wondered? Some hint of doubt or of sympathy?

"Perhaps," she said. "Perhaps this once, a third way exists."

Sabella and George shifted, trading glances.

"Anything," George said.

"I cannot give Sabella back her human life, nor let her continue as a vampire. But I can give you another existence as creatures of the Earth, not children of Adam or Eve but of the dominion. Will you take this life?"

George looked at Sabella. "It's this or death," he said with a lopsided smile.

"As long as I stay with you," she said, clutching his hand.

He turned back to Shadowheart, who nodded.

"You will," George whispered.

Shadowheart raised her arm, and her wings spread far. A song came from her lips, so gentle and heartbreaking in beauty that it fled the memory.

Sabella and George shimmered with a silver light, and before Jeremy's eyes, their images blurred and shifted.

Standing between Jeremy and Shadowheart were two beautiful, black swans. The swans regarded them both with eyes that held more than an animal awareness. Then gently they entwined their necks for a second. Without a backward glance, the two vaulted into the air, disappearing into the night in a thunder of wings.

Shadowheart, Jeremy, and Debbie remained silent for many minutes. Finally, Debbie asked, "Do they know? Are they still themselves in those shells?"

Shadowheart's wings folded down and around her. "They know that they love and that they belong together. They will have many years of peace to come."

"Then they are the lucky ones," Jeremy said. He turned his back on vampire and angel, walking off into the night, rain stinging his face and covering his own tears.

The End

9

THE TITHE OF HELL

Jeremy Leclerc sighed as National Public Radio began yet another article on American politics. He downshifted his red Mini Cooper, then changed the station. Even a Charlotte traffic report would be useful.

"Hey, Billy," a Southern voice said on the radio, "what's with these reports of little green men being seen in South Charlotte?"

"Well, John-boy," Billy drawled, "we can't even make up a whopper like this. There's been a second report of little green men chasing women near Ballantyne Village."

"I tol ya, Martians is after our women—"

Jeremy shut the radio off.

You don't believe in Martians, a cool, feminine voice sounded in his mind.

"No," he replied aloud, "only werewolves and vampires. Martians? Well, that is crazy-talk.

"What woke you up?" he said, a hand unconsciously touching the gold and crystal pendant he wore under his shirt. It held the essence of his guardian angel, Shadowheart.

A man awaits us at your studio, Shadowheart mindspoke. *"He needs the services of a Knight Templar.*

She faded from his mind, Shadowheart at her most annoying. Jeremy looked at the traffic ahead of him and sighed again.

A half-hour later, he pulled into the garage adjacent to his studio. His cover as a well-off graphic designer irritated the Temple. Templars were supposed to be poor Knights. But Jeremy did no better with celibacy.

The door to his studio stood open, which meant Samantha was inside. She worked for him when things were slow at her pottery store. Small and attractive, she wore gold-rimmed glasses and an expression that said that she was up to something.

Sam sat on the desk, speaking to a gray-bearded man dressed in khakis and a sport-jacket. "Here's Jeremy now."

"Hi, Sam."

She gestured at the man. "This is Mr. Sean Lin. Father Bixby sent him to us."

"This boy is a Knight Templar?" Lin said, giving Jeremy a frank look of disbelief.

"Shadowheart," Samantha called.

His guardian angel manifested in her most impressive form: seven feet tall, flowing black hair, a pale face of heartless beauty and black and red wings that once spread would fill the room.

Lin looked up at her, his mouth hanging open.

Then the archangel was gone, and in her place stood a petite, snub-nosed blonde dressed in jeans and a T-shirt not much different from Sam's.

"Yep," Sam said. "I didn't believe it until I saw her, too."

Lin moved to speak.

"Yes, I'm an angel," Shadowheart said.

He opened his mouth again.

"Yes, there's a God," she added. "No, I am not going to tell you more."

Lin looked at Jeremy.

"Let's stick to what brought you here," Jeremy said.

Lin wiped a shaky hand over his face. "You've heard about the abduction and molestation of women near Ballantyne. The little green men story?"

Jeremy frowned. "I thought that was a joke."

"I wish," Lin said, his face grim. "My daughter Fionna was with a girlfriend when she was ambushed by a group of these little green men, six weeks ago. The friend got away, she didn't.

"The police didn't believe it, of course. Before they'd even call her missing, she showed up again, forty-eight hours later. Only she was pregnant and near delivery. She delivered a baby boy the next day."

"What did she have to say?" Samantha asked.

"My daughter has been very vague and distracted since her return. She claims she met an incredibly handsome young man. She went off with him to a foreign land where she was treated like a queen. She can't remember much beyond she was in love and happy."

"The child?" Shadowheart asked.

Lin looked unnerved at being addressed by the angel. "At first the child was normal, an attractive healthy boy. But something happened one night; I believe it was substituted for a changeling."

"Are you sure the baby is a changeling?" Jeremy asked.

Lin handed him a photo of a dreamy-eyed young woman holding a...well *something* in a diaper.

Samantha whistled. "Wow. Put a pipe in his mouth and he'd be the spitting image of Popeye the Sailor."

"She's named this thing Tam," Lin said. "Until we get the real child back, there'll be no way to substitute it for this changeling."

"Okay," Jeremy said. "I'll see what I can do. Sam, would you see Mr. Lin out?"

"Sure, I have to get going and feed the dogs." Samantha towed a somewhat dazed Mr. Lin to the door.

***

"Shall we go check out the area where she disappeared?" Jeremy said. "Maybe you can sense something?"

"We must start somewhere," Shadowheart answered.

Near sunset, Jeremy parked his car at Ballantyne Commons. The last news report had put the little green men at the nearby intersection.

Shadowheart popped into existence as the blond teen as he got out of the car. Jeremy could tell that this manifestation was merely an image; she'd have to be careful that no one walked through her. He looked at her in shorts and a T-shirt. "Can you possibly update the look?"

"What?"

"I mean you look sixteen. Could you possibly add a few years so I don't get arrested for transporting you across state lines?"

She gave him a raspberry. "Hey, buy me an ice cream at the Creamy Spoon."

"Won't you have to manifest more to enjoy food?"

"For Rocky Road, I'll do it."

"Work first, play later. We're hunting Martians."

For lack of anything better, they walked over to one of the four arches that marked each corner of the intersection. The post and lintel-style arches stood on grassy mounds on each corner of the intersection. Each arch towered over ten meters and was decorated with bas-reliefs.

As they neared the shadow of the archway, Shadowheart gasped and staggered, her image wavering. Jeremy whipped out a Walther PPK from under his jacket, wishing he'd brought his Templar blood-sword from the car.

"Back," Shadowheart managed.

"What is it?" Jeremy demanded.

"Evil," she said, recovering and looking at the arch with narrow eyes. "I do not know how I didn't sense it before. These structures were made by men but usurped by evil. They lead to netherworld dimensions. Jeremy, the child may be in the netherworld."

"So, I go in and get it," Jeremy said, quickly, before his common-sense could assert itself.

"The netherworld is a part of the Realms of Hell. I cannot go with you and you dare not go alone. I can think of only one ally for you," Shadowheart said, her face grim and drawn.

Jeremy studied her. "Wow, go on, this I simply have to hear out loud."

Shadowheart grimaced. "Debbie Middleton."

Unable to resist, he said. "That would be the vampire, Debbie Middleton."

"Yes, her truce with the forces of light makes her a safe ally. *If* you can keep your dick to yourself around her."

Jeremy's eyebrows went up. "If you recall, she used her hundreds of years of sexual practice to seduce me when I first went to destroy her."

"If you recall, you resisted for all of three minutes."

"They didn't teach me about that sort of thing in Templar School," Jeremy replied, "but you're right. The question is, will she help?"

Debbie agreed to meet him right after sunset. He waited in Pasticchio's Bakery watching the four arches.

Jeremy spotted Debbie's hot-pink VW pulling into the lot, and out popped Debbie. The short, busty vampire wore a rhinestone denim jacket and painted-on jeans. She gave Jeremy a casual wave as she strutted up in her high-heeled cowboy boots. A couple of young men were leaving and almost fell over themselves to get the door for her.

"Thank you, boys," she twanged. "Oh, so many good-lookers, makes me want to take a bite out of one of you." They must have been married, as no one took her up on it, though the looks she got spoke volumes.

Jeremy rose and pulled out a chair for her.

"I do so love your old-fashioned manners." Debbie sat at the table with a sigh. "I swear I'm going to get these things reduced after two hundred years of lugging Double D's around. Thank God I'm dead already and don't have to worry about sagging."

Jeremy shook his head. "Too much information."

"Nice to hear from you, sweetie and I see you ordered me key-lime pie and coffee, lovely. So, what's up? Did you decide to join me in an eternity of blood-orgies?"

"Er, no."

"Good," she said. "I like you, boy. If you had, I'd be kicking your ass over the archways there."

"Thanks. Those archways are why I called you."

"Yeah, I read in the paper about the weird goings on around here. Seems some girls been getting their skirts lifted by aliens? So, what do you think is going on?"

Jeremy said, "The local radio hosts seem to think it's Martians."

"Oh, honey," Debbie laughed. "Everybody knows there's no such thing as Martians."

He looked at the vampire silently.

"Okay," she said. "The irony was lost on me for a few seconds. But Jeremy, vampires and demons are of the Realm of Earth. Even the other dimensions are merely shadows of this earth. Like the forms that Plato wrote about, those dimensions only exist as alternatives of this one."

"You read Plato?"

"I got a lot of daylight to avoid, baby."

"Who's to say that this is the only place imbued with life," Jeremy replied. "In all this vastness, how could we be the only world?"

"I don't know," Debbie said around a mouthful of pie. "Your pipeline to God is better than mine. Why don't you ask your foxy little guardian angel?"

"Well, there's an idea."

Debbie dropped her fork. "Don't you go calling her here. She scares the crap out of me. One day she's going to conjure a private sunrise for me. Oh lord, I just know it."

Jeremy grimaced. "Shadowheart's never threatened you."

"She doesn't like me," Debbie finished.

"Well, you are the evil undead."

"Hardly, sweetie. I'm the neutral undead. Remember?"

"A man came to see me today." Jeremy changed the subject. He relayed the tale of Sean Lin. "Shadowheart confirmed there was something mystical about those archways though. She thinks they're gateways to the netherworld. But she could barely function in this area. The longer we were here, the farther she had to get from the archways. So, we're thinking something demonic rather than Martians."

Debbie frowned. "Most of the passages between the netherworld and the Realm of Earth are ancient and ran through Europe. Those archways are only a few years old."

"I need to find a way to the netherworld," Jeremy said. "I have to get that baby back."

"And you want my help? Shadowheart's halo will catch fire."

"Never seen her with a halo," Jeremy said, "and she suggested it."

Debbie whistled.

"The question is will you help and what do you want for your help?"

"Oh, I'll help you, honey. The charge goes to your angel. She owes me a favor. I'll name it when I need to."

Jeremy lowered his head and concentrated. This close to the archways at full dark, Shadowheart's voice came to him muted but tinged with annoyance. *Yes, dammit.*

He looked up at Debbie. "Deal."

They hiked over to the archways around eleven p.m. Traffic still buzzed, and more than the usual number of police cruisers rolled by. The cops might not buy the story, but they knew something was up. Jeremy selected the southeast arch. They could hide in the nearby bushes and trees on a nearby rise and keep watch.

Hours passed along with the occasional fanatical jogger. Traffic thinned and crickets chirped. Around two a.m., Debbie shifted impatiently. "This ain't working. Or if it does, it may be weeks or months."

"Suggestion?" he asked.

"Bait," she said. "These sightings are accompanied by girls disappearing or getting groped. Well, let's give them what they want." Debbie took off her jacket and whipped off her blouse, uncovering a black bra that gave new meaning to "lift and separate." She slipped the jacket back on. "I'm gonna be a stoned floozy passing out in the hollow there."

She waited for some cars to pass and then staggered out, her jacket open and her bra visible. She stumbled around until she reached a spot near the archway. The ground dipped there, and she pretended to fall, then sat up and rolled on her back.

Debbie lay unmoving, something the undead were very good at, for more than an hour before the archway developed a shimmer. It was so faint that a weary Jeremy almost didn't notice it. A pack of figures slipped from between the pillars. Short, mostly naked but for what looked like animal-skin pants, they were bald, green-skinned, with red eyes and leering mouths. The crew of gnomes piled out of the gateway and descended on Debbie.

"Look at the tits on this one," one cackled, slapping his hands together.

"No chasing ass tonight," another said. "This is practically delivery."

As the first lecherous gnomes reached her, Debbie came to life, so to speak, swinging. Gnomes flew.

"Hey, she's awake," one said.

"You got it, Brainiac," she said and decked him.

Jeremy piled out of the bushes, sword in one hand and pistol in the other. But the gnomes were already running for the gate. Debbie jumped on Brainiac as he tried to rise. Jeremy thought of shooting but wasn't sure if any misses would go through the netherworld or across the street. When he reached the gateway, both the shimmer and gnomes were gone, leaving only cold stone.

Jeremy turned back to Debbie, who hauled the struggling gnome upright. It froze when it saw the steel sword; things of faerie hated iron. "Back to the bushes," Jeremy said. "I have questions for our lean, green, leching-machine here."

Debbie dragged the gnome and tossed it to the ground in between the bushes they'd hid in before.

Jeremy was searching his memory for the ancient gnomic tongue when it spoke.

"What's your beef anyway?" the gnome said, its beady eyes looking for an escape.

"I'm a Templar. I hunt supernatural evil."

"Doesn't seem to have stopped you from hanging out with Boobzilla here." The gnome jerked a crooked finger at Debbie. "She ain't no human. Not hitting like that."

"Watch it or I just might let her drain you to the last drop of whatever you use for blood," Jeremy shot back.

"Oh, Jeremy, honey, there ain't enough toothpaste in the whole world for that," Debbie said. "Why don't I just tear off his head and shit down his neck?"

"Okay, okay," the gnome said. "No need to get tough. I see you're serious people. Whaddya want?"

"I want to know what you and your little green brothers have been doing around Ballantyne."

"I want to know why he sounds like he's from New York City," Debbie said.

Jeremy sighed. "Let's stick to the point. You're a gnome."

"Actually, I'm a Martian—"

"My ass, you're gnome. What are you doing here?"

"Hey, come on, Mac-the-Knife, we're just guys like you trying to get lucky with some local broads."

"What?" Jeremy said

"We cast some glamour on some hotties so they see us as gods, some get a quickie, some we whisk off through the portals to the netherworld for a couple of months of slap and tickle. Then we shower em with gold and jewels and return them to your world only twenty-four hours later. No harm done."

"That's disgusting," Jeremy snapped.

"Yeah? You wouldn't think so if you were a three-foot-tall gnome trying to get laid."

Jeremy whapped the flat of the blade down on the gnome's rock-like skull; its skin crackled and sizzled under the touch of iron.

"Ow, ow," it cried, dropping to the ground. "What's the problem? The babes get the big O in the netherworld for months and a wagonload of gold and gems."

"Faerie gold and gems turn to twigs and dust," Jeremy growled. "Not that real gold or jewels would be compensation for months of being ravished by gnomes while deceived under a glamour."

"Hey, Sir Knight, some of these Georgia Peaches have been around the block a time or three. They ain't exactly innocent."

"This ain't Georgia, you ignorant pile of crap," Debbie said.

Jeremy switched to a two-handed grip and raised the sword.

"Okay, okay I'm sorry," it wailed. "Lay off with the cold steel and I'll do anything you and Boobzilla want."

Debbie caught his arm. "Jeremy, we need this one. We can use him to get through the portal and get that human baby."

"See," the gnome said. "That's thinking, baby, despite what they say about blondes."

"First though," Debbie said. "We need to establish some ground rules and a framework for cooperation." She turned to the gnome, smiled, and kicked him square in the nuts. Not a delicate lady-like kick, but rather a kick that any punter in the NFL would have sold his soul to make during the closing seconds of the Superbowl. The ox-like bellow of unadulterated agony was muffled when Debbie picked the gnome up and tossed him through the gates. Its ghostly witchfires glowed and shimmered; the gnome's passing had opened the netherworld.

"Well, honey," Debbie said, dusting off her hands, "come on. We've got a baby to find."

She and Jeremy raced to the gate and into the shimmer. Sensations exploded on Jeremy—smells, sounds, some pleasant, others bitterly not. Then he was through, standing in a cave, wide, high, with a floor carpeted with rushes and pine needles and a few ice-encrusted pools to one side. The cold struck Jeremy, and he was glad for the long leather duster that concealed his bloodsword. The cave wouldn't have been unpleasant, but for the shrieking gnome.

"Oh god, my balls," it bellowed over and over. Apparently agonized screams were not uncommon in the netherworld, as no one came to investigate. Finally, Debbie threatened to hold the gnome's head under water unless he stopped. The gnome cut the noise down to a whimper and found some relief by sitting in a pool of icy water.

Meanwhile, he noticed a change in his other companion. Debbie seemed to glow from within, her eyes were red-tinged with fire, and she moved with an almost explosive energy.

Of course, he thought. *I've taken a vampire closer to Hell. Her powers—*

"—have increased," she finished, plucking the thought from his mind. She smiled a lazy, almost cruel smile. "I feel wonderful. Would you like to feel me, Jeremy?"

"We have work to do," he said carefully, not wanting to offend her and also fighting off a tremendous wave of desire. A vampire was all about dark seduction.

He moved the sword between them, and the red jewel of its hilt glowed. It seemed to break the spell. The desire receded, and Debbie shook her head as if to clear it.

"Jeremy, honey," she said. "Don't stand too close to me and don't turn your back. I ain't quite myself here."

"You better run the bitch through before she sucks you dry," the gnome said from his icy pool.

"That's enough," Jeremy said. From under his coat, he produced a rope of thin nylon and bound the gnome's hands behind its back. It cursed under its breath in its own miserable tongue. Jeremy prodded it with the sword. It yelped and led them out of the cave. Debbie walked to the gnome's other side, and Jeremy was careful to keep her a little ahead.

"How long till dawn?" Jeremy asked.

Surprisingly, it was Debbie who answered. "Never. This is a dimension of Hell. It's always twilight and full moon here. If this wasn't a faire forest, it would die. Thanks for the thought though."

"You got a name?" Debbie said to the gnome. "Little green piece of shit takes too long to say."

"Ganal," he replied.

"Okay, Ganal," Jeremy said, "take us to the baby and you go free. Mislead us and it's a steel enema for you."

As they trooped on through the woods, Jeremy prodded the gnome for information. "How could you imagine that the changeling wouldn't get noticed in this day and age?"

"Are you kidding?" Ganal said. "Have you seen what human kids are like now? It used to be harder. Changelings are loud, hungry, ungrateful, misbehave, and are generally a pain in the ass. People used to kill em. Now the parents insist the kids are special and go berserk when somebody tries to make them be quiet. Used to be spare the rod and spoil the child; now, it's two more Ritalin for little Timmy."

"He's got that right," Debbie said. "Humans can't hardly raise kids anymore. You got Millennials and post-Millennials raising Generation Ain't No Damn Good."

"What the hell would you want with a human baby anyway?" Jeremy said, a little put out by the undead and unholy dissing humanity.

"Funny you should put it that way," Ganal said. "This being the outskirts of Hell, sometimes the big boys pay us a little visit. You know, kinda like taxing the peasants, only they literally take the taxes out of your hide. Hell loves humans for some damn reason. Rather than fork over a dozen dryads and nymphs, we find they're happy with one lousy human."

"The Tithe of Hell!" Jeremy said in shock.

"Yeah, that's the fancy name for it. Anyway, long time ago some yahoo named Tam Lin rode through a faerie forest in Scotland. He fell off his horse, was found and boffed by the Queen of the Fairies. She gave him a good time, and in return, all he hadda do was go to Hell and be devoured. He bugged out on us with the help of some minx named Margaret. Ever since then, Hell's been taxing us heavy. So, if we can ever sacrifice a male member of the Lin family, taxes will go back to one lousy fairy or gnome every seven years. When one of the boys realized he'd knocked up a Lin, King Gazarg decided we'd take the youngling, raise him as one of our own, and turn him over to Hell. Kid gets a free ride till then, room, board, entertainment."

"But isn't the child half-gnomish?" Jeremy asked.

"Species comes from the mother with demons," the gnome said, "just the opposite of the old Greek gods where it came from the father. Jeez, you don't know shit, do ya?"

Minutes later, they came upon a glen full of satyrs, dryads, goblins, nymphs, and gnomes, dancing and feasting around loaded tables and divans. It was a party that Pan would be proud of. Jeremy spotted a boy of about sixteen, dressed in a toga, with laurel leaves in his long hair. He had an indolent, spoiled look to him as he lounged on a divan, a nymph on each arm.

"Who's the brat?" Debbie asked.

The gnome was laughing silently. "Time doesn't track with the Realm of Earth here. That's your baby boy, Tam."

Then before they could react, the gnome plunged to the end of his tether and yelled, "Hey, Rube!"

Jeremy jerked the rope, dropping the gnome, and bashed him on the head with the bloodsword. The red crystal touched the gnome, and he was instantly reduced to ash.

"Crap," Jeremy said. He quickly rolled up the rope.

He and Debbie walked out into the silent clearing, dozens of eyes on them. "Tam Lin," he called. "We've come to rescue you. Return you to your family, to your mother."

Tam stood on his divan. "They're from Earth," he screamed. "Good guys. Kill them."

"Don't you understand?" Jeremy yelled. "You're going to be the Tithe of Hell. Fed to devils when you're thirty."

"Don't you understand?" Tam shouted back. "I'm up to my balls in dryads and nymphs until then! Screw you, Mom, and Earth. I'm living for today. Get em."

"You get the boy," Debbie snapped. "I'll handle the rest."

"Alone?"

But Debbie was already among the charging Fairies. Far stronger and faster than human in the realm of Earth, here she was a true demon. She was a blur, grabbing and biting fairies like potato chips.

Tam fled. Jeremy beat fairies aside with the flat of his blade. After seeing the gnome's fate, his kin fled the baleful red glow of the stone in his sword hilt. Tam fled into the woods. Jeremy slowed to look back at Debbie. He needn't have worried.

Debbie stood atop the feast table. She had her fangs in one satyr's neck, had a dryad under one arm and a nymph caught between her legs. Her eyes glowed red, and she practically radiated power. She threw the satyr aside and bit the dryad on the thigh, then spat her out. "Crap, I'm not a damn vegetarian." She swatted the dryad and seized the screaming nymph. "Smorgasbord," Debbie yelled, "no diet today, yee-hah," and bit the nymph.

Jeremy raced after Tam, but the boy hadn't run far. He'd run into tent nearby and emerged with a golden trident.

"Tam," Jeremy yelled. "Don't be a fool."

"I hate you," the teen screamed and plunged at Jeremy. The tines of the trident glowed an evil green. Jeremy batted the trident aside with his sword and checked his return swing, which would have decapitated the boy. They parried and slashed, circling each other. Jeremy backed against a tree. Tam, thinking him pinned, lunged, but Jeremy blocked left with the sword, and the trident struck the tree, sticking in and causing the wood to smoke.

Jeremy rolled forward counterclockwise and swept the boy's legs. Tam fell. Jeremy jumped on his chest and struck once to the temple. Tam groaned and slumped. Jeremy quickly bound the boy and heaved him up on his shoulders, then headed back to the glade.

Debbie stood in the middle of a glade carpeted with gnomes, satyrs, and the like. At first, he thought they were all dead, but then realized most were moaning, twitching, and nursing bites.

"You got him," Debbie said. The vampire's clothes were torn, but she didn't even have a bruise. Her skin glowed with health. She looked a little taller and younger as well. She caught his gaze. "Nah, I didn't kill any. I was like a bad kid, taking a bite out of every candy bar, not finishing any."

"Let's get out of here before any reinforcements show up."

The denizens of the netherworld had evidently had enough of Super-Vamp and the bloodsword. They were unmolested as they returned to the gate. Only a steady stream of threats, pleading, and cursing by Tam marred the trip. "Don't take me back. I'm evil. I'm beyond redemption." Finally, Debbie gagged him with a bit of torn fabric.

Jeremy went through the gate first. To his relief, exiting the hell dimension didn't require a gnome. He covered Debbie with his long coat and took Tam by the arm and wrestled the boy through the stone gateway.

Once again, smells and colors assaulted his senses. It was still night on the other side. Jeremy yelped and grabbed as Tam almost slipped from his arms. A second before, the spoiled teen had been taller than Debbie. Now he shrank till he was a baby again.

"Well, well, honey," Debbie said to Tam. "Looks like you get a do-over."

Debbie handed Jeremy his coat and took the baby. "From the sky, I'd say we've only been gone a few minutes, plenty of night left. Trust me. I know the night sky."

They rode of over to Sean Lin's house in Jeremy's car, hoping no cops pulled them over for not having a child seat. Debbie exchanged her torn top for a T-shirt, fortunately fresh, from his gym bag. Jeremy tried to keep his eyes on the road as she changed.

The Lin house was off Rea Road on a private drive. They rang the bell at the Tudor-style home. Sean Lin opened the door after only a minute, clad in a robe. He spotted the baby in Debbie's arms. "Is that my grandson?"

"Yes," Debbie said. "He's all boy too. Gonna be a handful."

"Is this your angel friend again?" Sean asked, looking at Debbie. Debbie chortled.

"Not quite," Jeremy said, "but she's a friend. Please invite her in."

"Don't stand on manners, my dear," Lin said. "Come in."

"Let's take care of your changeling problem first," Jeremy said. He didn't need any guidance to the nursery; he just followed the infantile howling. They opened the door and walked in together.

The changeling looked more like a one-year-old than a baby and sat up in the crib. It looked at them and the real Tam Lin.

"Crap," the changeling said. "The jig is up." There was a puff of foul-smelling smoke, and the changeling vanished.

"Daddy?" a voice called sleepily from behind them. "I thought I heard the baby."

"You did, Fionna," Lin said.

A red-haired girl in a robe entered the room. "Who are these people?"

"Oh, this is Jeremy and his...wife...Debbie. Their car broke down. Debbie's a...."

"Pediatrician," Jeremy added.

"I heard the baby crying," Debbie said.

"I asked her to take a look at Tam," her father added.

"Oh look," Fionna said. "He's trying to nurse on you. Isn't that cute?"

"Why you little dickens," Debbie said sweetly, pulling the baby away from her and giving him a mock smack on the butt. "Here, let me give you to Mommy for the next twenty-one long years."

"Well, good luck to you both," Jeremy said. He glanced down at Tam.

The baby looked up at him with eyes that were wise beyond their years and really, really pissed off.

The End

10

THERE'S SOMETHING IN THE WOODS

I think we need a vacation from each other."

"Jeremy, how can you say that? We've been together five years."

"I know, and I feel smothered. We're always with each other, night and day."

They faced each other in his design studio. Jeremy, tall and lanky, stood with his arms crossed, determined not to lose this argument this time. Shadowheart, his guardian angel, floated in midair in her usual guise of a sixteen-year-old, snub-nosed blond, addicted to the latest fashions. He was glad of that at least; her archangel form was that of a winged, raven-haired Amazon, nearly a foot taller than his six feet.

"Honestly," he continued. "I care for you. I really do, but I can't spend every waking hour with you."

"You get into trouble when I am not around."

"And I intend to. I plan to head up to the mountains for the fall color. I plan to drink, smoke questionable substances, and do a variety of extremely naughty things with as many different women as I can talk into it. In short, I am going to try and have fun like a normal twenty-four-year-old."

"You're not normal; you're a Knight Templar. Besides, Templars are supposed to be chaste."

"Perhaps that's why there are so few of us."

"I think it has more to do with legions of slavering evil," she said, floating inverted with her legs crossed, as she sometimes did when she was trying to make him laugh.

"Why don't you do something as well? You must need a break too."

She righted herself and stared at him. "What?"

"Come on, even angels must have some form of recreation."

"The life of an angel is beyond your limited understanding."

"Smile when you say that. Seriously, what do you do when you see other angels?"

"We get together at the local pub and complain about our feckless and unappreciative wards."

Despite himself, Jeremy smiled. "Great. With me for a charge, you must be the star of the bar."

Shadowheart sighed theatrically. "Very well, you're human and I never was. There are things about you that I don't understand and I'm not sure that I wish to. Perhaps some time apart will be helpful. There are some things I have put off doing in the Overworld that I could attend to. Don't expect me to answer your phone or email."

"It's just for a week. We'll be back slaying the forces of evil before you know it."

Shadowheart yawned and drifted down on a nearby couch. "Okay. Whatever. Hey, what's your Netflix password?"

A day later, Jeremy stood before the immense stone pile of the Grove Park Inn in Asheville, NC, a cross between a castle and a hunting lodge. He walked into the interior wooden hall, checked in, and ditched his bags. Next stop, the veranda, with its beautiful view of the mountains and valley below. The air was brisk, but an attractive waitress brought him a hot spiced cider. He took a rocker and contemplated the setting sun as the sky flamed with banners of color and clouds of purple and blue with a blissful feeling of solitude. The gold and crystal housing that Shadowheart rode in, when not corporeal, lay on his dresser at home. The angel's absence was almost palpable. While he'd spoken the truth about liking his supernatural companion, when it came to fun, she was the ultimate buzz kill.

He switched to a cabernet when another waitress, this time a cute Hispanic girl, came by. Her smile at him hinted of possibilities, and Jeremy returned it with his best. She giggled and blushed, and Jeremy remembered that, while it hadn't been relevant in a while, he was considered good-looking and American girls loved his European accent. How long had it been since life had been simple for him? Had it ever been?

He shook off the thought. *I'm on vacation. With any luck I'll meet a nice girl and have some fun, maybe forget what I know crawls the dark places for a while.*

He whiled away some time with a swim, dinner was on his own, and then he spent some time at the bar. Unfortunately, the men wanted to discuss sports, politics, or, as was not uncommon in the South, religion. The women were either in couples, or seemed stand-offish. Most people were talking about the disappearance of five local college students in the mountains.

He enjoyed some off-color jokes with a lesbian lawyer from California, but she was leaving in the morning and declined his offer of hiking around the mountains.

The end of the evening found him in a melancholy state as he sat by the vast fireplace, his feet propped up facing the fire. *Oh well,* he thought in drowsy contemplation. *Here I am again, on my own.*

Samantha, his closest friend, had a new girlfriend. While Jeremy was happy for her, it meant she had little time for him. Sydney, his Australian mate, had moved north for a computer job and to escape the rapidly contracting pond that was Charlotte in the bad economic times.

What did that leave him for friends? Debbie Middleton, a sexually carnivorous vampiress, who occasionally helped him, and Shadowheart. Some of the people he'd helped remained in touch, but many wanted to forget their encounters with the supernatural. Everyone he met was also another chance to blow his cover. The work of the Knights Templar was secret from the rational world.

Tomorrow, he planned a hike in the mountains, then maybe he'd hit some clubs in town.

Jeremy slept in, then dropped in for a massage at the spa. Hours later, he parked his car at a scenic overlook and started up the mountains on a well-marked trail. Compass in hand, he struck off down a side trail. He'd walked for fifteen minutes when a familiar sickly odor hit his nose. Something was dead nearby. He heard the sound of something sizeable moving through the woods.

"Probably a deer," he muttered to himself and walked on. The odor grew worse—blood, a lot of it, recently spilled. Remembering there were black bears and the occasional cougar in this country, he reached under the light jacket he wore and pulled out his Walther PPK. He jacked a round into the chamber, wincing at the loudness of the slide. He found himself wishing he'd brought his bloodsword, but the Walther PPK felt solid and reassuringly lethal. He stalked forward, keeping close to the tree trunks in case he had to put one between him and…whatever the hell was out there.

The wood was alive with natural sound, which he blotted out of his conscious mind, listening for evidence of a large body moving. If there was a hunter here, he was inhumanly patient.

Jeremy waited for a few more minutes, but the sun was westering and the mountains would shut off the light soon. Time to be bold. He moved forward, stepping around leaves and sticks, aiming for rock and dirt, slipping through bushes.

A clearing opened before him, and it held two sights that made him freeze. One was a human body, so mauled he couldn't even tell the gender. The second was a naked redheaded woman with a flawless, lithe body. She sensed him in the same moment and his eyes locked and met in a shock of recognition.

Prosperine, the witch-familiar, leapt away, morphing into her original form as a huge black jaguar and fled into the bush. Startled and hesitant, Jeremy didn't get a shot off, but ran forward looking into the bushes where she'd disappeared. But she was gone, and the idea of hunting the shapeshifter in the fading light with a handgun was clearly suicidal.

Why had she fled instead of attacking? He didn't even know if the pistol would harm her. She'd originally been a jaguar in South America, ensorcelled by an Aztec priest ages ago. She'd become a familiar to one witch after another until he liberated her from the demon, Bob Diablesse. They'd fought side by side against a coven in Charlotte until she'd left for the mountains. They weren't friends, but he no longer thought of her as an enemy, until now.

He turned back to the body; he wondered if it might be one of the missing teens. The upper part of the body was mostly gone. Jeremy wondered how she'd done it. Even in her jaguar shape, gnawing at the body shouldn't do such damage. He was no forensic scientist but the body was recent, dead only a day or so.

"Prosperine," he shouted. "Did you do this? Why? Show yourself."

Silence answered him.

He walked around, stepping where she'd been, up to the area where she'd hit the ground as a jaguar. With her animal skill coupled with human intelligence, she'd left few tracks. Jeremy headed back to his car, keeping the pistol in front of him.

I'll call the police when I get back to the car, he thought, *then lead them to the spot.* It was too much to hope they wouldn't find some trace of Prosperine, but for now he wanted to keep her presence under wraps. She was the obvious suspect, except for a geas that Shadowheart had placed on her to prevent her feeding on humans. Could the geas had broken or somehow been circumvented? What he did know was that the shapeshifting familiar was too dangerous for the police. If she had returned to her old ways, then it was a job for a Templar.

Overhead, a fine rain began to fall, which suited his purposes. Jeremy sighed as he exited the tree line heading for the Mini. *This is turning into a busman's holiday.*

The police showed up quickly and in force, enormous Suburbans with state troopers and Crown Victorias. They were better equipped than some armies. A grim and business-like uniformed lieutenant, named Dietrich, was in charge. He looked like he could run a marathon and still kick someone's ass.

Jeremy told him his story; Dietrich's face betrayed little. "Hiking by yourself?" he finally said.

"Been trying to find someone to go with." He shrugged. "I love the woods."

Jeremy showed Dietrich the license for the Walther and told him the weapon was in the trunk. Dietrich checked the weapon and held onto it. Then Jeremy led them back to the body, making sure to get lost once or twice in the fading light to disguise his woodcraft and let the rain further conceal Prosperine's presence.

The troopers murmured in alarm at the destroyed body. One young officer got sick. Dietrich posted men around, shooting questions at Jeremy as he did. "You walked all over this ground," he said after examining the ground. "Why?"

Jeremy gave him a sheepish look. "I wasn't sure what I was looking at, if this was a joke or something and, well hell, I don't do this every day. I guess I was scared, couldn't stay in one place. I looked around to see if there was somebody that needed help or if there was more of… of whoever that is. Then my brain started working again and I walked back to my car where I'd left my phone and called you."

Dietrich gave him a steady look. "You didn't do bad for a civilian, son. Surprised you didn't barf here like Rogers."

"Too scared to puke," he replied.

Dietrich gave a wolf-like grin. "Been there." He looked up at the lowering sky.

"Jerry," he called, "send for lights and dogs. Fat chance of getting some scent with this rain but we have to try. Call the forensics guys and get them out here."

"Yes, sir."

"You plan to be here for a couple of days?" Dietrich said.

"All week at the Grove Park."

"Fancy," he said. "Rogers will take your statement. We can do it now, back at the car, or at the station."

"Now's fine. I wasn't figuring on getting any sleep tonight."

"Yeah, me neither."

"So, Lieutenant? What the hell happened? Who was this?"

"Forensics will have to confirm it, but he was one of the missing college kids. As for what got him? Bear maybe. We got wolves out this way, but I never heard of them attacking a man. Coyotes might, if there were a lot of them. Can't say I ever saw a body damaged this way."

"Will I get my Walther back soon? You're welcome to Paraffin test it, or even to fire a bullet for ballistics."

"Know a lot about police procedure?" Dietrich said.

Whoops, Jeremy thought. "I watch *Bones* on TV."

Dietrich snorted. "Our forensics guy ain't as pretty as her." He pulled the Walther out, ejected the magazine, then jacked the round out of the barrel, catching it in midair. "I'm pretty sure yours hasn't been fired, but we'll run the weapon. 'Course if I find a 9mm hole in that body, your stay at the Grove Park will get shortened. You'll get it back tomorrow otherwise."

"Okay. Good luck."

Dietrich nodded and then walked toward the bushes, flashlight in hand, water dripping off his gray-brimmed hat.

Jeremy sat with Rogers for an hour, answering questions and dreading a return by Dietrich, but evidently the lean cop found nothing in the gathering downpour. Men with lights on poles and others with dogs arrived and trekked into the woods. Reporters also began to appear.

"Can I get out of here?" Jeremy said. "I like reporters about as much as you cops do."

Rogers eyed him with more friendliness. "Sure. We'll give them your Charlotte address; it should throw them off you for a day or so, but I think your vacation is over. This story with the missing kids is all over the media. I think the fall color season is going to fold up."

"No sign of the other kids?"

Rogers closed his laptop. "You better get going if you want to avoid the press."

Jeremy nodded and slipped out of the Suburban, making it to the Mini unmolested and drove back to the Grove.

Jeremy surprised himself later by finding an appetite. He avoided the bar this time; the place was abuzz with talk of the body. The reporters had wasted little time.

"Crap," he overheard one server say, "first the recession now this. So much for tourists, we're getting cancellations all over."

Jeremy tucked into dinner, his mind running furiously. He'd made Shadowheart promise to stay out of his brain for the entire week. It never occurred to him to wonder how to get hold of her if he changed his mind. She didn't have a cell phone. Usually he could touch her housing and summon her, but it was back in Charlotte. To retreat to Charlotte, when he knew so little seemed wrong, an admission that he was helpless without her.

Jeremy raised a glass of cabernet to his lips. As his head tilted back, he saw a woman in a killer miniskirt. His eyes roved up over her fantastic legs, up the taut body to the green eyes and red— He spit his drink across the table.

"Hello," Prosperine said, in her husky dark voice. "Don't shoot or stab me."

The waiter came over, looking nervously at both of them. "Was there something wrong with the wine, sir?"

He coughed. "No, sorry, went down the wrong pipe."

"Will the lady be joining you?"

He looked at her. "I'm hoping you haven't eaten today."

She shrugged. "A squirrel for lunch."

The waiter laughed uncertainly. Jeremy gestured at the chair opposite him. Prosperine folded into it. The waiter changed the tablecloth, brought a menu and another glass, and poured for both of them. Prosperine handed the menu back. "Veal steak, no vegetables."

After the waiter slipped away, Jeremy stared at Prosperine. Her makeup was perfect, as was her hair. The dress was designer and fit like a second skin. "Well, you haven't been living in a cave."

"Nor eating hikers. I keep a room with a widow who asks no questions. I'd made some provisions moneywise for becoming masterless. Most of the time, I'm out living a natural existence in the woods—"

"Hence the yummy squirrel."

"—but I keep a foot in the human world as well."

She leaned forward. "I didn't do it. You know I'm not good, but you also know I'm under a geas from your angel, no human snackage. I was out hunting when I smelled blood and something...else. I found the body only a bit before you. I switched to human shape to check the corpse for pockets. Then I saw you with the gun. You're good in the woods, human, you surprised me. Wasn't sure you'd give me time to talk. I didn't think you'd shoot me in the Grove Park."

He sipped the wine and forked some pasta. "I believe you, mostly because of the geas."

"Thanks."

"So, what the hell is going on? You said you smelled something."

"Yes. Hard to explain to a human, but I felt and smelt a nonhuman presence, something magical. Large, but I found no sign of anything on the ground. In fact, I think the body was dropped there. I found this by the corpse." She placed a piece of turquoise jewelry on the table. It was a small and cunningly wrought turtle. A scrap of leather thong ran through its mouth; the yellow gem eyes seemed to regard Jeremy with malice.

"What is it?" Jeremy said.

"An object of power," she said. "A dark power I'm unfamiliar with."

"I didn't see you with it."

"I had it in my hand. I put it into my mouth before I morphed. Jaguars have no pockets."

"Neither do naked redheads."

Her dinner arrived, which she attacked with an animal single-mindedness. Jeremy finished his and they worked on the wine. Jeremy signaled the waiter for another bottle.

Her meal finished, Prosperine turned her attention back to him. "I've been in these mountains since I left you. Life has been good until recently, when these kids disappeared. I had to move more into the human world to avoid all these trackers and police. It's causing me to run through my money, so you're paying for dinner.

"I checked with the local evil after the first three bodies—" she continued.

"Three? I thought this was the first."

"Humans haven't found them. One male and one female, they're the missing kids from what I can tell. They are all pretty well destroyed, partially eaten by something that doesn't eat like a natural beast, unless you know of any Tyrannosaurs wandering around. I know animal bites; these bodies were bitten to pieces."

"Were you able to find out anything?"

"Only that the local evil has had more casualties than the human world. Stands to reason, most of what evil is up here, lives in the mountains. The area's empty. I found one boggle in the woods. It told me it was tunneling down to the netherworld for a couple of years to avoid whatever's moved into these woods. Whatever it is out there, it may only have turned on humans because it exhausted the supernaturals."

She looked around. "Speaking of supernaturals, where is your tall, dark, and menacing archangel?"

"We're taking a bit of a vacation from each other."

She stared at him.

"I told her I wanted a week by myself. I can't even get back in touch with her unless I return to Charlotte."

She leaned back in her seat. "Can't say I'm sorry."

"I want to see what I can do about this on my own," he replied. "We can always turn tail and head for Charlotte later."

He eyed her. "You in?"

She yawned, a surprisingly animal-like gesture. "Yes. But it will cost. I need money to keep up my human guise. Ten thousand dollars and you've hired yourself a fearsome werebeast of extraordinary intelligence and beauty."

Jeremy signaled the waiter for the check. "The Knights Templar is a poor order."

She drained her glass. "Bullshit. All these religious orders have tons of golden treasure, land, and artwork."

Jeremy signed the tab. "Yeah. Okay. You have a deal."

"Good," she said. "Let's go up to your room and have some violent sex."

"Huh?"

She took his arm. "I'm evil. I like it rough, and it will be rougher on you than me. Don't worry, you'll still love it."

"And if I am not in the mood?"

"You're a twenty-four-year-old human male. Plus, I can smell you're in the mood. I'm in heat, and I'll be a lot easier to deal with after you satisfy me."

"I thought that was perfume. Guess I'd better satisfy you then."

"Yes, you had. We'll go looking for trouble tomorrow. Tonight, we eat well, have sex, and sleep deeply."

"I like to watch TV after."

"Shut up," she growled.

Prosperine proved to be a handful in bed, two handfuls, with a delightful if demanding directness. Jeremy did keep flashing back to the movie *Cat People"* but fortunately, however much Prosperine growled and yowled, she did not lose control of her human form. She was not big on cuddling afterward, preferring a solitary couch to the wreck of the bed.

If it wasn't for the mutilated teens, he thought before plunging into sleep, *this would be the best vacation ever.*

Morning arrived too quickly. After showers and breakfast, they pulled Jeremy's Mini out of the garage and headed into the mountains.

"Any idea where to look?" Jeremy asked.

Prosperine stretched sinuously. "I've been over the areas to the north and east. While I sensed disturbances in nature, they were transitory."

"The kids were last seen near Bat Cave, NC, about twenty minutes south of here. Maybe we can get a lead from that turtle object."

They spent the morning driving around the area around Bat Cave. Checking at small towns, camp sites, low rent hotels. Some people had seen the kids in the area, all had told the police what they knew.

They stopped in a few jewelry stores and souvenir shops, showing off the turquoise turtle. They hit pay dirt with a local artisan. "Yeah," said the man, an aging hippie in a tie-dye shirt. "That looks like it might be old Adahy's work. He makes Cherokee handicrafts, ceremonial objects, knives, pipes. Has a general store north of town on Old Bat Drive."

"Is there anything out that way?"

"Not much, some places that don't even qualify as towns, a lot of hills where people go hunting."

"I'll buy it from you," the man offered.

"Thanks, I think I will hang onto it."

The man grinned. "Present for the hot babe?"

"Something like that."

Jeremy collected Prosperine, who was examining some stuffed animals with too much interest. They took the road to where it went from asphalt to tar and chip. At one scenic overlook, Jeremy parked the car; they ate the lunch he'd bought in the last town. Prosperine was quiet but good company.

Good, he thought, *because I'm not sure how to make light conversation with a thousand-year-old jaguar wearing a girl costume.*

He pulled the car over. "This Adahy's place should be around this hill according to the map. Let's approach on foot." They hiked up the ridgeline, looking into valleys that no one beyond the occasional hunter might have seen in hundreds of years. At the crest, Prosperine pulled up short.

"What is it?" Jeremy asked.

"Power," she said. "Old power, not familiar but not good either."

"Can you tell where it is?"

"Can try." She stalked forward. Even in the loose-fitting hiking clothes she wore, there was an explosive tautness in her movements. She unzipped her jacket despite the cool autumn air. "Don't want to get tangled in clothes if I need to jag on short notice."

They trekked through the pines until they found themselves on a hillside over a back road. A one-story building with a tin roof sat off the roadway with its back to the hillside. Some sheds and smaller buildings filled a fenced yard behind it. Jeremy took out a small set of binoculars. Animal skins were stretched out on frames. Small skulls dotted poles. The building had a foreboding look to it with its dark wood siding. There were windows on the sides, but they were papered over.

"Bad place" Prosperine sniffed. "Dead animals and something more."

They worked their way down the hillside so they could come out on the road as if they were hiking alongside it. A sign over the covered porch read, "Adahy's General Goods." The front of the store was less foreboding. Dreamcatchers vied for space with a Coke poster of a girl in a bikini. Some sturdy rockers sat in invitation next to a checkers set on a barrel. The windows were uncovered but filled with pottery and other Cherokee handicrafts. The door was covered with glyphs and symbols he didn't recognize.

Prosperine shrugged when he looked at her. "Do we go in?"

The decision was made for them as the door opened. An old man in jeans and a beaded jacket looked up at them. He was slightly stooped and wore his long gray hair in a braid with a feather hanging hanging in it. Black eyes looked out of a seamed and leathery face.

"Morning folks," he said in a deep voice. "Can I help you?"

"We were just out for a hike," Jeremy said, juicing up his own French accent. "We saw your store and thought we'd drop in."

"Sure," the old man said. "Come on in and look around. I got pottery, woodwork from the Cherokee and Natchez tribes, even some Iroquois stuff. Not that crap like you get from the 'Souvenir Cherokees' down in the big towns. I got the genuine article. Make some myself and I'm genuine." He gave a dry chuckle.

"We prefer the authentic," Jeremy said.

Prosperine was staring at the old man until Jeremy nudged her. "Let's see if we can find a present for your dad."

"What? Oh yes."

"Is that a European accent, young man?"

"Yes."

"French, I'd say but I also hear a hint of Scotland in it."

"Very perceptive," Jeremy replied.

He chuckled again, but the sound was devoid of humor. "It pays for an Indian to know about Europeans. Our problem is we learned too slow. Look around. I gotta go get the mail and the paper."

They walked through the store past shelves of canned goods, tools, and pottery. Jeremy paused by the stacks of refrigerators full of drinks and some wrapped sandwiches.

"We should buy something so it doesn't look suspicious."

She eyed him. "You're a fool if you take food or drink from this place."

"Where is he?" Jeremy said. "I want to get into the back rooms."

She looked out the window. "Coming back."

"Damn." Jeremy walked over to the display cases. In one lay a variety of turquoise animal pendants and bracelets. In the other were ranks of knives. The blades showed they were handmade. He opened the case and picked out one. The knife was finely made and balanced.

The owner walked back in with a paper and some envelopes in hand. "You know your knives."

"I collect them," Jeremy said.

"Those are tribal-made blades, I finish them out myself. That's one of my best," he said as he walked past Jeremy to the counter, dropping the mail next to the cash register.

"How much?" Jeremy asked.

"I modeled it on the old Puma White Hunter. Sharp enough to cut through a bad dream. Couldn't let it go for less than two-hundred dollars. Sheath comes with it."

"You take plastic?"

Again, the dry chuckle. "Yep, no wampum for me. Me heap big modern injun." He pulled out a small credit card unit.

"You have a sale," Jeremy said, not reacting to Adahy's mocking tone. He handed the knife to the old man, careful not to touch flesh with him. Jeremy noticed the pictures of the missing teens on the wall. The one of Hans had a neat "X" drawn through it. "Shame about those kids."

Adahy looked up. "Oh, them, yeah."

"They find the others?"

"No. Ain't gonna either. There's more in these mountains than white people believe."

"Such as?" Jeremy asked.

"Nothing you would credit, young man. No offense. Anyway, I haven't heard anything about them finding the kids. You know, they were in here."

"Really?"

"Yeah, bunch of punk kids, all dressed in leather, chains, with crap hanging out of their eyes, ears, and noses. Two boys and three girls, real trash-talkers, all of them."

"They give you trouble?" Jeremy asked.

"Ah, the usual stuff: stupid war-whoops, bad jokes. At least they bought some stuff but even that… Well, they got no respect. They just thought there might be some black magic or bad medicine in the objects. The dead one, they found, he fancied himself some sort of adept in the occult. The others just lapped that up.

"You ask me, he's the one that was trouble. I bet he killed the others. One of those murder-suicide things all these Goth kids are into."

Adahy handed him back his credit card and a slip that Jeremy signed. Then he wrapped the knife in plastic and handed it to Jeremy. "You folks take care," he said, with a smile that did not reach his eyes.

"We'll do that."

Jeremy felt relief wash over him along with the sunlight as they stepped out of the gloomy store. Prosperine was on his heels as if she, too, had no desire to linger. They walked quickly down the road until they were out of sight of the store then cut into the woods.

"What did you sense?" he asked, as they made their way back toward the car.

"Hard to say," she replied. "There's a scent of evil on him, but it's hard to say if it is more than old bitterness and hate—he does not like your kind—or something more. He does not feel like a witch, yet somehow there is something familiar… He reminds me a little of my first master, an Aztec priest. As if his power came from an old and different source than the European witches I served."

Jeremy frowned. "A shaman? Templar records show those mostly to be myths. If these Native American myths held any real power, the European absorption of the Americas would have been slowed or stopped."

She shrugged in response. "Compared to what? Technology trumps most magics. A 20mm chain gun will kill all the witches and warlocks you want. Magic can move mountains, but it does so subtly. How do you know shamans didn't slow it up? Anyway, this Adahy bears watching."

"Yes," Jeremy replied. "There was a certain satisfaction in how neatly and carefully that 'X' was drawn on Han's photo. Like a guy keeping score."

"What now?"

"I think back to the Inn, then back here around midnight, we'll check out those backrooms. See if he is up to something supernatural. He is not a right guy."

"You're feeding me, right?"

"Yeah, you're still on expense account."

As they walked into the Grove Park Inn, Jeremy spotted Dietrich at the front desk.

"Trouble?" Prosperine asked, following his gaze.

"Maybe. Make yourself comfortable by the fire." He walked over to the desk. Dietrich turned well before Jeremy reached him, maybe picking him out of a reflection or the corner of his eyes.

"Oh, there he is," chirped the girl behind the counter.

"Looking for me?" Jeremy asked.

"Yeah. I have something of yours." He gestured at some nearby seats. Jeremy followed him. Dietrich sat, stretching out his long legs. Jeremy sat opposite him. The lean state-trooper reached into his overcoat and pulled out a package and some paperwork. "One Walther PPK in 9mm, seven rounds all unclipped and loose, one magazine. Said Walther is empty, with the slide locked back and the safety on." He slid the pen and paperwork over to Jeremy.

"Safety first," Jeremy said, as he signed and handed the material back. Jeremy took the envelope, but laid it aside without opening it. Cops didn't like guns in civilian hands, not even unloaded ones. Dietrich's lips quirked, as if he had somehow divined the thought in Jeremy's mind. "Any luck on the case?"

"Identified the body, as I suspected from the size, it was Hans Ulrud, eighteen-year-old German exchange student at UNC Asheville."

Jeremy shook his head. "Young, hardly more than a child."

"You're kinda young yourself to think so."

"Perhaps it's the miles, Officer, not the years."

"It is sometimes. Lots of hard miles in the graphic design trade?"

"You might be surprised."

"Oh, you surprise me in a couple of ways. Not too many graphic designers have a concealed carry permit."

"Well, studio space is often cheapest in the poor neighborhoods."

"Your address in South End is pretty trendy these days."

"Don't cross the light rail tracks; it gets less trendy quickly."

Dietrich leaned back, studying Jeremy with his cool, denim cop-eyes. "I got a friend in Charlotte PD named Detoma. She says you sometimes show up around, let's say, unusual events in the company of equally unusual people."

Jeremy's ears pricked, had he heard a slight stress on "people"?

"Wow, she must be in the Charlotte PD's Vagueness Section."

"She says you can be useful to people in unusual trouble. She's heard good things about you from people she trusts."

"Nice to hear."

"You staying in the area?"

"Yep, still got plenty of vacation."

"Plan on hiking with your lady friend? She looks like the outdoorsy type."

Damn, Jeremy thought, *this guy misses nothing. He must have spotted us coming in.*

"The hills are beautiful this time of year," he replied, aware that Dietrich was trying to rattle him, though unclear as to why. Perhaps he just did it to everyone.

Dietrich leaned forward and handed him a card.

"It's got my cell number on it. My instincts tell me you may be a right guy. They also tell me you're not what you say you are and you might turn up stuff I need to know about."

Jeremy pocketed the card.

"Try not to get the pretty lady killed while hiking," Dietrich said as he stood. "That would be a sin."

"No worries. She can take care of herself. She's a bit of a wildcat."

Dietrich flashed him a grin. "Lucky you."

Armed with bloodsword and pistol, Jeremy and Prosperine pulled out of the Inn at about 10 p.m. The drive to Adahy's shop wasn't a long one. They made their way by the same trail they'd used earlier that day. As they crested a hill, Prosperine touched him on the shoulder. "We're being followed. Behind us. One man. I smell gun oil."

Jeremy nodded. "At the opposite side of the clearing."

He drew both the pistol and the bloodsword from its concealed sheath in his black leather duster. They stepped behind trees and waited. After thirty seconds, a man stepped out of concealment. He was tall and lean in a gray uniform and carried an M-14. Dietrich. The lean officer hesitated, then took a knee, sensing something.

"Lieutenant Dietrich," Jeremy called. "Why don't we all step into the open carefully."

"You're good, Leclerc," Dietrich called. "Yeah, how about you and the lovely lady step out slowly."

Jeremy stepped out, his pistol pointed at the ground, sword resting casually on his shoulder. From nearly alongside Dietrich, Prosperine stepped out. Dietrich gave a low whistle.

"I'm good in the woods too," she said with a toothy smile.

"Quite a cleaver you got there," Dietrich said. "You want to tell me what's going on here?" His M-14 remained poised between Prosperine and Jeremy.

"We're working on a lead on the missing kids," Jeremy said.

"Wow. Did they hire you for some graphics work?"

"Officer, I can't tell you much, but I'm not quite what I seem. You've guessed as much. There's a man here who doesn't feel right to Prosperine or me. We've come to check it out." Jeremy omitted the turquoise turtle. Dietrich wouldn't thank him for withholding evidence.

He eyed Prosperine. "You a graphic designer too?"

"I'm into wildlife."

"Who are you checking out?"

"Adahy. He owns a general store. The kids were in it before they disappeared."

Dietrich frowned. "The old Cherokee? He's had some brushes with the law when he was young. Nothing recent. Local folks say he's kind of an old-style medicine man. He ain't too friendly. Most of his own folks seem afraid of him. But why would he harm these college kids and how? You saw that body."

"That's what we hope to find—"

A horrible croaking sound came from above them. The moonlight was blotted out by a huge shape that passed over the treetops. They all crouched, weapons up, save for Prosperine who gave such a growl that Dietrich gave her a double take.

Jeremy looked at the officer. "Follow me if you dare. But understand this. You are crossing over into my world now. It's not the rational place you've inhabited. You follow my lead, fight when I say fight. Run when I say run."

He stared. "Who are you? Rod Serling?"

"Prosperine," Jeremy said.

The familiar started to strip out of her clothes.

"Not that I mind the view," he said, "but what the hell?"

Jeremy holstered his pistol and leaned the sword on a tree. "Safe your rifle."

Dietrich gave him a dubious look, but Jeremy heard the click. He returned to contemplating the naked Prosperine. "Rocking hot body you have there."

"Yes," she replied, "both of them." With no more than a shimmer, she transformed into a hundred-thirty-pound black jaguar and sat down.

"Don't shoot," Jeremy barked.

Dietrich stared over his weapon, clearly shaken. Prosperine sat up and was again the gorgeous naked redhead.

"So," Dietrich swallowed, "you weren't joking about her being a wildcat."

Prosperine stood, brushing dirt off her butt. "I was going to get naked anyway. It's difficult to unzip with claws."

"What we are after here may be as much out of your experience as she is. So, if you come, you follow my orders. Agreed?"

"Yeah, but remember. I'm an officer of the law. If I say stop, you stop."

"Then follow," Jeremy said, picking up his sword and drawing his pistol.

The three of them walked close, eyes searching the darkness alongside and above.

"Did you get a look at...whatever that was?" Jeremy asked, knowing she had the best night vision of any of them.

"No. I was concentrating on Dietrich and the trees blocked my view. But it was big and not of this earth. Adahy is our man."

They reached the section over the general store and started down to the large fenced yard.

"This gate wasn't unlocked before," Jeremy said.

Suddenly a chanting began. Across the yard, Adahy stood in the center of a star shape of glowing lines.

"Pentagram," Prosperine spat.

The chanting paused, and the old Cherokee looked at them with a mirthless smile. "You folks looking for me?"

"Yes, we are, Shaman," Jeremy replied. "Something's been unleashed in these woods. I think you know what it is."

"I get the cop, and the sword tells me what you are. Who's the naked chick?"

"Never mind," Jeremy huffed. "What do you know about those missing college kids?"

"Lousy white kids, they were good for fodder. Punks thought they knew magic. I showed them magic. I introduced them to HIM!" Adahy threw back his head and voiced a chant. From over their heads came the awful croak they'd heard before and the rush of huge wings.

Jeremy looked up to see the face of lunacy in the sky above them. Bodiless, the giant head was easily ten feet across. Basketball-sized eyes glared down at him over a huge mouth of massive teeth. Where ears should have been, massive wings spread.

Prosperine's scream of challenge snapped them out of it. The M-14 and Walther blazed. The huge head banked away with a scream of its own. While the weapons had clearly stung, they did not bring down the giant creature.

"Let me introduce you to my friend," Adahy called. "Ko-rea-ram-neh-neh. Fancy Iroquois name for the Flying Head. You see, some young warriors wanted to abandon the ancestral land due to a famine, but the old chiefs wouldn't let them. So, they murdered the elders, sank their heads in a lake. The gods weren't happy with that. No sireee. Sent Ko-rea-ram-neh-neh back to punish them."

"How did you invoke it?" Jeremy said.

"I told you. Me modern injun, study a lot on the computer. Found a lot out about the legends. But I'm also a shaman. I knew some spells, minor stuff. Then along came those punk kids, giving me a lot of lip. Well, me and Ko-rea-ram-neh-neh both dislike young punks. I told the kids I would show them some real magic. None of this Goth bull-shit. I set up the pentagrams. One for me and one for them. Dumb shit Hans thought he knew about pentagrams. I summoned the ancient demon and well, you have to give them something when they show up. I broke their pentagram."

"You gave it the kids," Dietrich raged.

"Yeah. I kept one of the girls for myself for a week or so. It ate the other two. Chased the boys into the forest for fun, I guess. I gave it the other girl when it came back later in the week."

"Bastard," Dietrich swore. "You're under arrest."

"No white man's law up here, mister. Just my law. That law says you gonna die." He raised his head and arms and began to sing.

"He's summoning," Prosperine said.

Dietrich's M-14 came up in a smooth motion and he fired. A spark appeared in the heat shimmer around Adahy. He didn't stop his chanting.

"The pentagram puts him in a different space than ours," Jeremy said. "Bullets can't penetrate it." As he stepped forward a shadow fell over him.

"Down, Jeremy," Prosperine shouted. She knocked Dietrich to the side. Jeremy dropped and swung upward with the sword, scoring on the huge shape swooping over him. A horrid croaking sounded in his ears, and the weapon was nearly jarred from his hands. He heard Dietrich's M-14 rattle out rounds as the reek of the monster swept over them. It bounded back into the sky

"Should have stayed out of the mountains, white man," Adahy taunted. "Guns and science won't do you no good. Ko-rea-ram-neh-neh must eat. He likes souls, but he'll chew a body up good too."

Jeremy stared at the twenty-meter bat-winged shape. The blood-sword has scored the cheek of the monstrous head. Its foul tongue slapped out to ease the wound. But it showed no sign of serious injury. Quickly, he reversed the bloodsword, bringing the huge gem in its hilt level with his eyes and concentrated. The stone quickened to life, its blood-red radiance filling the clearing with a soft glow.

Adahy cursed and chanted the monster to attack. Ko-rea-ram-neh-neh swooped on them, but pulled up with a screech when the red light fell on its skin, which puckered and bubbled. But the sweep of its wings sent them all to their knees. Jeremy's concentration broke for a second and the stone pulsed weaker. The slavering mouth opened above him, but Dietrich's flung M-14 filled it. The teeth clamped on the weapon. Jeremy concentrated on the stone and the glow brightened. Ko-rea-ram-neh-neh backed away with a croak.

"How long can you hold it off?" Dietrich shouted.

"Dammit," Prosperine interjected, "I can't change with that damn stone glowing. I can't use my powers!"

Ko-rea-ram-neh-neh hesitated, wary of the stone. Adahy's chant grew louder, a note of anger in it.

"He's trying to force it to attack despite the pain," Prosperine shouted.

As the Cherokee's voice reached a fever pitch, the shimmer of the pentagram grew, and his image wavered. Above, Ko-rea-ram-neh-neh croaked its protests but seemed dragged toward them by some great force.

Jeremy raised the stone, but its spiritual power was limited by his own, and exhaustion was setting in the young Templar's chest.

"Jeremy, fling the sword at him," Prosperine demanded. "It's the only object that can get through the barrier!"

"I can't," he grated. "It'll be on us the instant I stop focusing on the jewel."

Suddenly Jeremy was clawing under his duster with his right hand. From the back of his belt, he drew the White Hunter knife. He flipped it in his hand until he held it blade first.

"Adahy!" he shouted.

The shaman's eyes flicked to his, though he did not pause in his song.

"Take back your own, Shaman, made by you and of you." Jeremy flung the knife. The weapon, imbued by the shaman's own spirit, flew through the barrier and lodged in his chest. Adahy staggered and yelled, blood staining his shirt.

"A hit," Jeremy exulted.

"Not fatal," Dietrich snapped.

"Oh, yes, it is," Prosperine said.

The shimmer of the pentagram vanished; the lines on the ground went dead. Adahy screamed and started chanting, pulling out the knife.

"Fool," Prosperine shouted. "Your own blood is spilled; the pentagram is destroyed."

"Wait, wait," Adahy shouted as Ko-rea-ram-neh-neh turned toward him. The shaman turned to run.

The monster settled to the ground just behind Adahy; its wings corralled him, pulling the shrieking man toward its hideous face. Adahy screamed and begged, but Ko-rea-ram-neh-neh gave a low obscene chuckle in imitation of the shaman's. Then the wings pulled and the screams became agonized.

"For God's sake," Dietrich said, horror distorting his face. "Do something."

"Not if I could," Jeremy returned. "Or do you forget that he sowed this fate for those kids? Let him reap the full measure of it."

"He's lasting a while," Prosperine observed, over the screams and wet slobbering sounds. "Maybe it likes to play with its food."

The head rolled about to face them. Adahy hung half out of its mouth, his face distorted in mind-shattering terror.

Even Jeremy felt ill at the sight as Ko-rea-ram-neh-neh's cheeks sank as it sucked on what was left of the shaman, who gave a last despairing scream as he was pulled inside.

Ko-rea-ram-neh-neh stared at them, and Jeremy felt his blood chill and his will weaken under those horrid eyes, portals to some place that humanity had no business in. Next to him, Dietrich staggered and fell.

Prosperine squalled and struck him with her nails. He shook himself and raised the bloodstone, concentrating what was left of his power. The stone brightened. Dietrich seized a large rock and stood. Prosperine hunched, human hands held like claws.

Ko-rea-ram-neh-neh gave that horrid chuckle again, dark fluid running from the corners of its obscene mouth. It humped away from them, then launched itself into the air. It rose on its giant wings, impossibly quickly and steeply. In seconds, it had disappeared into the night sky.

"It's gone," Dietrich murmured as if afraid to believe it.

"From this plane of existence, yes," Jeremy said, his voice dull with fatigue.

Prosperine walked over to Jeremy, who sagged against her taut, powerful naked form. "Unnatural demons like that," she said, "find our world painful. They aren't grateful to be summoned, and no magic creature loves those with power over its existence. Once it had its revenge over what forced it into our universe, it wasn't interested in us."

"Thank God for that," Dietrich murmured. "Though I suppose I really should be thanking the two of you."

"You can thank me," Jeremy said, "with a damn good bottle of red back at the Grove."

Dietrich looked at Prosperine. "And you?"

"You can turn a blind eye to the occasional loss of cattle and goats," Prosperine said.

Jeremy looked at her. "You coming back with us?"

"No," she said. "I've had enough of the human world for a while. I want to run wild on my own. But I'll be here, Jeremy. As I said last time, life around you is fun. Find me next time you need a familiar." She leaned forward and kissed him hard on the mouth. Then she stepped back and the panther was there. With an explosive snarl that made both men flinch, she leapt into the darkness of the woods.

Jeremy pulled up to his apartment, shouldered his bag, and turned the key to let himself in. Inside Shadowheart lay on the couch, surrounded by junk food wrappers, watching TV. He recognized *Heaven Can Wait*. She raised an eyebrow at him and gave an elaborate yawn. "Oh well, look who's back."

He grinned at her. "Miss me?"

"Were you gone long?"

"Long enough," he said.

"Well, now that you're through slacking, maybe we can take care of some evil."

He dropped on to the couch next to her and put one arm over her shoulders and grabbed up a Moon Pie with the other. "After the movie."

The End

11

———

LET'S GO TO HELL

Jeremy Leclerc, Knight Templar, rocked back on his office chair and stared at his guardian angel. "You want me to do what now?"

"Go to Hell," Shadowheart said. As usual, his guardian angel had appeared in her guise of a fashion-conscious, snub-nosed, blond teen.

"You want me to go to Hell?" he repeated.

"Well, I'll go with you," she said pensively. "It's clandestine, even though it *is* a rescue mission."

The world, he thought, *is off its axis today.* He saved his latest design project on his computer, then turned back to Shadowheart. Only the angel was no longer alone. A tall, slim man in a fine suit stood next to her, but for the white-feathered wings towering over his shoulders, he looked like any lawyer or banker one might see stalking downtown Charlotte, North Carolina.

"Who is this?" Jeremy asked.

Shadowheart gave the other angel an ambiguous look. "His name is Velos of the Cherubim; he runs the Embassy in Hell."

"There's an Embassy in Hell?" Jeremy said.

"It's temporary duty," Velos hastened to add, "more or less a community service."

Jeremy turned back to Shadowheart. "How come he has white wings and yours are red and black?"

Shadowheart grinned. An instant later, she stood in her other manifestation, nearly seven feet tall, an Amazon clad in leather and mail, girt with a sword, with black hair falling to her waist and blazing green eyes. "He's cherub; I'm so much more."

"Ah," Jeremy replied. "So, about my going to Hell, if this is about that little three-way at the Old Edward Resort, both the girls were over twenty-one and quite satisfied with the whole matter."

Velos looked at Shadowheart. "You don't have it easy, do you?"

She sighed. "This is a good day."

"You're sure he's a Templar?"

"Don't get impertinent, Cherub. If it wasn't for your own weakness in the matter of succubi, you wouldn't have had your tour of duty in Hell extended."

"Yes, yes." Velos raised a placating hand. "No need to get your back up. Anyway, back to the matter at hand. I find myself in need of help of a specialized sort. Have you heard of split personalities?"

"Yes," Jeremy said. He stood and walked over to the kitchenette in his suburban studio. He quickly poured iced teas, the lifeblood of the American South. Velos declined with a polite shake of the head. Shadowheart, once again the mall rat, took hers. She occasionally manifested enough to take part in earthly pleasures, usually involving sweets.

"In extreme cases," Velos continued, "it's not only the mind that splits, but the soul."

Jeremy shrugged. "What does this have to do with a Knight Templar? My therapies are usually administered with the edge of a magical sword, or the occasional shot from my Walther."

"This has need of a warrior," Velos said, his wings rustling slightly in annoyance, "as it will involve a journey into Hell."

Jeremy looked at Shadowheart.

"He shits you not," she said.

"Wouldn't that involve like…death?" Jeremy asked.

"Normally. I can arrange for you to venture into Hell, temporarily, to retrieve souls that ended up there by mischance."

"How does that happen?"

Pain drifted across Velos' perfect features. "By cruelty and narrow-mindedness, which happens when angels forget that they are not perfect, that they are not God. We are of the forces of law and of order, but both those, when carried to the extreme, are as brutal as any tyranny born of evil. This miscarriage was realized, and I am tasked with redeeming it."

He paced about the floor. "Her name was Camille. She was fifteen when she killed herself. Her father was abusing her; it had gone on for a long time. To cope with this misery, she developed an imaginary friend, a heroine to defend her. She chose Joan d'Arc. Joan became more and more real to her over time. One night the drunken beast came for Camille. She hid in her mind, which freed Joan to possess Camille's body. Like the Maid of Orleans that she was named for, Joan seized steel and flew upon the oppressor. Joan loves Camille as well as any sister could. In the purity of her love and valor, Joan became real, she developed a soul.

"But when the deed was done, the personality that is Joan was dispelled and faded. Camille was there all alone with the slain molester. She fled into the night, knowing the police would soon be there and it would all come out. More than Camille wanted anything," the angel's voice sank, and his face turned ashen, "she did not want people to know of her abuse. There was a bridge and a river below…"

"And she was sent to Hell?" Jeremy demanded, his voice quivering with rage.

"Jeremy," Shadowheart said, pain in her face as well.

"No," Velos said, "let him rail as he wishes. It's merited. Shadowheart has told me of your doubts: about God, the meaning of it all, even whether Shadowheart and I are what we say we are. Today your doubts are justified.

"An angel looked on this and saw but a suicide and a murderer, one body with two souls. Camille who chose death over discovery, and Joan, who would not leave Camille even for fear of Hell, condemning herself for her sister's—for I will call her that—for her sister's suicide. Neither would defend themselves. Both believed they deserved Hell for what was done by them."

"Where was God then?" Jeremy said.

Both angels stared at the floor. Finally, Shadowheart sighed and said, "What would you have me tell you that I have not said before? The Realm of Earth is the dominion of Man, and for better or for worse, you must have your free will, else you are but puppets. More than that is not given to us to explain to living man."

"Why don't you just get her out?" Jeremy asked.

"Angels are powerful," Velos said, "but not all-powerful. The universe is balanced so that good and evil have their places, rules and limits, or The End would be upon us now. In Hell, an angel's power is restrained. It is the enemy's place—the enemy's rules. To petition for their release would be both fruitless and damaging through all the Realms in ways you cannot comprehend. Beyond that, there is this truth: these souls, conjoined as they are, believe that they deserve their punishment. They must be persuaded otherwise, or they cannot escape Hell. Only another human can do this.

"Will you risk a journey to Hell to save these innocents? Before you agree, I must tell you that if you, or Shadowheart, are killed in Hell, you will never emerge from it, having traveled to that land of your own free will."

Jeremy shuddered. Only once before had he ventured beyond the dimension of Earth into a Faerie otherworld to rescue a human exchanged for a changeling. That suburb of Hell had proved dangerous enough.

"I have no ally I could take with me. When Debbie Middleton came to the Faerie realm, the proximity to Hell almost overcame her."

"Debbie Middleton?" Velos said.

Shadowheart rolled her eyes. "Vampiress, big boobs, sharp teeth, bangs humans for blood but doesn't kill them. We have arrangements."

"Wow," Velos said. "You really don't have it easy."

"Don't get me started. You should hear about the panther woman."

Velos looked intrigued. "Really?"

"Excuse me," interrupted Jeremy, "back on task. We couldn't trust Debbie, or Prosperine…the…er, panther woman."

"As I said," Shadowheart began, "I'm the one going with you."

"Shadowheart, you couldn't even manage Faerie."

"Faerie is antithetical to angels. It was less that I couldn't go than that I'd be damn near helpless. As for Hell, didja forget about fallen angels? I can't go as I am, but in disguise, yes."

"You'd make a delightful succubus," Velos said.

"Smile when you say that, Cherub."

"Seriously, it would be an excellent cover—freedom of movement, hellish access everywhere. People notice succubi, but they don't take them seriously."

Shadowheart looked at her teenage self. "Well, clearly this won't do. My angelic form would get us attacked…" Her brows knit in concentration, and she wavered like a heat mirage for most of a minute. When it stabilized Shadowheart stood as a voluptuous young woman, with blood red hair and ruby eyes, and she stood on par with Jeremy's six feet.

"Excellent," Velos said.

"You're butt-naked," Jeremy added, disturbed as he hadn't been since being joined with his guardian angel.

"Yes, ah, which reveals a small omission," Velos said, tugging at his collar. "Succubi have tails, slender, black, with a heart-shaped tip that some consider their most attractive—"

"We get the idea," Jeremy interrupted. He reached into a closet and tossed Shadowheart a long black leather duster.

"I'll have to work on the tail later," Shadowheart said, her voice sultry. "It's not easy for me to assume another form, quite a strain actually."

"When do we begin?" Jeremy asked. "How do we get to Hell?"

"You're certain?" Velos asked. "There will be no turning back once we begin."

"There's a fifteen-year-old girl suffering in Hell right now because of divine bureaucrats," Jeremy said. "We're getting her out."

Velos handed him a passport folder and a suitcase. "I have arranged for you to appear as an agent of the Collectors, returning from harvesting damned souls. They wear a black suit and a tie from their training center. You would be one, a human soul but so long established in Hell as to be essentially a trustee. Shadowheart will be your succubus."

"Oh, I am never going to live this one down," she said. "You tell Debbie this and I will kick your butt over the Bank of America Tower."

"Midnight is the easiest transit time to Hell," Velos said. "There's an express elevator down."

"Elevator?" Jeremy said.

"That's how you would perceive it."

"Where?"

"Well, any bank building with an elevator will do. Bankers have a special relationship with Hell. Wait till midnight; you'll see the floor appear since you have a pass."

"That gives us about eight hours," Jeremy said.

"Good, we need to go to the mall," Shadowheart replied.

"What?"

"Lingerie store. I have nothing to wear."

"Got it."

Velos stepped back. "See you in Hell." He disappeared.

Shadowheart buttoned the duster. "Wardrobe first, then dinner. Get your gun and sword."

Jeremy grimaced. "Hi ho, hi ho, it's off to Hell we go."

Midnight found Jeremy outside of the Stoneheart Bank Building, doubting his sanity. While Shadowheart could pop into the building, he had to phone the Templar on watch in Roslyn for help hacking his way through security into the building itself. Shadowheart did make herself useful by glamouring a drowsy guard into a deeper sleep. Fifteen minutes later, they stood in the too quiet and too brightly lit lobby before the elevators.

"Time to change," Shadowheart said. An instant later, she reappeared as the red-haired, busty vixen, in an outfit to make a Vegas showgirl blush: corset, stockings, and leather panties. This time she'd gone the whole way and her tail drifted behind her, ending in a heart-shaped tip. Jeremy's heart skipped a couple of beats—and he began to understand Velos' fascination with tails. Fortunately, the elevator dinged for his attention. He checked his watch: 11:59.

They walked in, and Jeremy stared at the panel as the seconds ticked off. At 12:00, a button appeared. It said, "Down baby, really down."

He pressed it. A momentary disorientation made him sway. When it cleared, he was still in the elevator, but it had changed. It stretched hundreds of feet in all directions and was filled with humanity—well, mostly humanity. Many stood in chains, some in cages, their faces and bodies marked with wounds. These were the recently damned, the scum of humanity whose acts of vileness merited Hell. Moans and cries stirred whip-bearing guards, some human-appearing, others clearly demonic with wings and hooves, into brutal action.

Some trustees and demons who could pass for humans also stood there, casually chatting among themselves. A nattily dressed pair stood close by, male and female. "Well, I can't say I'll miss New Jersey. Honestly, I have no idea what you see in that dump."

"You have to develop an appreciation for the outré, my dear. New Jersey is an acquired taste, I'll admit. As a happy hunting ground for the damned, it's hard to beat."

Jeremy realized the male demon might be from the Collection Agency; he didn't need awkward questions from a "colleague." He and Shadowheart slowly moved away. As they did, he noticed that she'd wrapped her tail around him and that one silk-clad breast rested on his arm. He gave her a curious glance.

"I'm supposed to be a succubus," she whispered.

"This is too weird."

They passed a young boy, dressed in a gray cloak with a curious hat that looked like a European policeman's cap. He stood with a blue wooden staff in hand. His eyes were golden and seemed focused on infinity. Jeremy saw a leather satchel under the cloak. He raised his eyebrows at Shadowheart.

"A Grey Messenger," she said, "one of the souls that are not quite human. Sometimes they end up as messengers moving around the afterlife and in between the Realms. Think of them as freelance diplomatic couriers."

Jeremy muttered, "What Can Grey Do For You?"

The falling sensation of the elevator continued, and Jeremy grew conscious of another sound. "Of course, it would be a feature of Hell."

"What?" Shadowheart asked, rubbing herself against him. Her body was warm and soft in a way it had never been. Normally Shadowheart was merely a form of ectoplasm.

"Elevator music," he said, trying to distract himself from his partner's newfound sexuality by imagining an eternity of bland music. "God—"

"Don't say that name," she hissed, glancing around.

"Sorry."

The elevator slowed. "You are now arriving in Hell," came a pleasant female voice with an upper-class English accent, "where you will begin suffering your punishment for the prescribed period, or until the appropriate level of remorse is reached. Those of you permanently sentenced here, please follow the green-clad demons with silver pitchforks to your left for orientation and torture.

"Hell may be perceived differently according to your religious beliefs. Many of you will experience Hell as a series of rings. Please have your damnation papers ready or expect immediate evisceration. Have a nice day."

The front of the enormous elevator was suddenly gone. Other voices came on and droned additional information through the air, as the damned wept and shouted. Whips cracked and gleeful demons prodded with pitchforks. Jeremy looked at Shadowheart, her eyes on par with his own in this incarnation, expecting to see horror or anger, but there was nothing but a cool lustfulness; either she was an excellent actress, or Hell was having an effect on her as Faerie had on Debbie Middleton. He wondered if it was having one on him as well.

Jeremy walked forward, gripped by the feeling of unreality that had haunted him since Velos' visit. They weaved through the damned, some of whom reached out toward them, as they headed for a large archway labeled, *Staff and Visitors*. They hung back as the Grey Messenger passed. The demon that greeted him and inspected his papers was handsome, almost a caricature of a perfectly developed bodybuilder but with red eyes and black horns. He inspected Shadowheart with interest until Jeremy sharply demanded they move on. Velos had been right about the succubus. The guard demon had scarcely looked at their papers. Likely there weren't that many people trying to break *into* Hell.

The staff hallway provided a blessed relief from the wretched sounds of the dead. Jeremy fought the feeling of sympathy welling up in him. He could not understand the very concept of Hell; there were some that surely deserved an eternity of torment: Hitler, Stalin, Mao, and Pol Pot. It was too easy to populate such a list, but Jeremy's sense of fairness rebelled at the thought of an eternity of punishment for most sins.

"One more bone to pick with God, when I meet him."

Shadowheart nipped his ear, warning or what, but it reminded him to watch his mouth about God. A passing demon leered at her and squeezed her bottom as they went by. Jeremy expected her to lash out, but she merely wiggled her tail.

They exited the massive structure onto a shockingly ordinary street, lined with what looked like East German Communist architecture under a leaden sky. A line of cabs with fat, greasy cabbies awaited them. Jeremy didn't like the look of the cabbies, or cabs, some of which appeared ready to burst into flame.

They were saved by a demon in a chauffer's uniform, with a handwritten sign that said, "Jeremy." They walked over to the homely demon.

"Boss is in the limo waiting for you." He gestured with his head toward a black stretch Cadillac, bearing a license plate with a halo on it. The chauffeur opened the door and Velos waved them in. He paused for a moment to goggle at Shadowheart, who slid over and sat on Jeremy's lap.

"Get us out of here, Scruff," Velos said to the driver. The limo roared with a sound that was not an engine. They lunged into traffic that made Naples look rational. Scruff began spewing insults and gestures at the other vehicles as Velos hit a control that raised a divider between them and the peripatetic driver.

"Somehow," Jeremy said, "I expected something more medieval."

"Hell is wide and deep," Velos said. "Dante had a useful device in seeing Hell as ringed and within each major ring are further rings. This is Pandemonium, the administrative ring of Hell. Usually it's not much worse than LA, and of course it also depends some on why you are here. We get so many government bureaucrats and Wall Street types that they've recreated where they were in life."

Shadowheart pressed her lips against Jeremy's throat.

"Cut that out," he said.

She giggled.

"I'm afraid that this place or her new body are having an effect on Shadowheart," Jeremy said.

"Definitely," she said, "for the first time in my existence, I'm turned on." She looked at Jeremy. "Is this how you are all the time? It's amazing you get anything done." She slid off his lap, fetching up against the window.

"I was afraid of that," Velos said. "Since she came here illegally, she's not protected as I am. She'll have to manage on willpower."

"Great," she muttered.

"I'll help you," Jeremy said.

"With your track record for resisting temptation? We're doomed."

"Back on task," Velos said. He handed Jeremy a computer tablet. "GPS built in along with apps for transportation and lodging."

"Are the girls here?"

"No, both are down on the Seventh Ring, but far from each other, Joan killed—"

"In self-defense," Jeremy said.

"She is not here for slaying the beast, who himself is in the lowest ring reserved for those who betray those they should protect. Joan is here because she felt her act of violence killed Camille. She feels she murdered her 'sister.'"

"And Camille?" Jeremy asked.

"In the same ring, but in the section for those who take their life in despair when they are healthy. She might have escaped Hell entirely with a more sympathetic judge, but she feels Joan killed her father because she was too weak to stop the abuse. Because Camille did not act, Joan had to."

"This is f'd up beyond my powers of description," Jeremy muttered, passing the tablet to Shadowheart.

"Let's hope that it is not beyond your powers of persuasion," Velos said. "I need you to bring them up to this ring. If you can, then I will do what I can to get them out of here. Irony is that as the Representative for the Heaven down here, I'm usually denying requests for rendition or asylum."

"It will not be easy. Joan especially may fight you."

"That's a problem," Shadowheart said. "If I have to manifest in my true form, it would bring all Hell down on us."

Velos shook his head. "Down here you're a succubus. You'll have to fight as a succubus. Your angelic vitality remains, but not your powers."

"So, what, I beat things to death with my breasts?"

Velos smiled. "Looks like you could win with those."

"How'd you like this tablet shoved up—"

"Shadowheart, please," Jeremy said.

She grumbled, but put the tablet down.

"More practically," Velos continued as if he had not just been threatened with an electronic enema, "I have some weapons in the trunk, supplied by Scruff. Jeremy, your bloodsword, with its enchanted gem, will work here. Be careful of its use. Its power is based in goodness. Its effect will be felt far, once drawn. Your pistol will work on most things down here that are mere base matter, but demons are stronger than men and can take much more damage."

The divider rolled down. "Boss," Scruff said. "I think we're being followed."

Velos turned in his seat. "Who?"

"I got a decent look at the last red light. I actually stopped for it and she didn't expect it. I'm pretty sure it's Isolde."

"I would curse," Velos said, "but it will just get my time here extended."

"Who's Isolde?" Jeremy asked, peering through the back window. A red car about four lengths back slowed and ducked behind a Hummer.

"An actual succubus," Velos said. "She works for my opposite number, Screwtape, Head of the Collectors. He likes to keep tabs on, me and she's quite good at it."

"Major Hot Babe," Scruff agreed. "She could give Liberace an erection."

"Lose her," Velos ordered.

If the driving to this point had been Neapolitan, what followed next would have made a NY cabbie buy a horse. They were thrown from side to side as Scruff handled the Caddy like a fighter jet, taking off-ramps, underground garages, and traffic circles at frightening speed. A coup of Squeegee-men tried to slow them as they exited one underpass. Scruff bounced them off the hood. There was a squeal of tires and a crunching sound behind them.

"That'll slow her down," Scruff said with satisfaction. "Screwtape will probably take the repair bills out of her hide."

"Let's hope not," Velos said. "It's such nice hide."

Jeremy noticed the buildings around them were getting shorter and traffic thinning.

"We're getting close to the bullet train station on the edge of Pandemonium. It will take you to Dis. From there you will have to search for Joan. I don't see how you can get Camille unless you get Joan first."

Jeremy flicked on the tablet and tooled through the apps. He whistled when he looked the maps of the Seventh ring. "How do we find them in all that?"

"I also added a file on all their known movements," Velos said.

They pulled up to a building that looked like it was the subject of a fight between Frank Lloyd Wright and Gaudi. Scruff opened the door.

"Good luck," Velos said.

Scruff popped the trunk. He handed Jeremy a case labeled "Heckler and Koch." Jeremy admired the MPN submachine gun within. For Shadowheart, he drew out a black tined pitchfork straight out of legend. It had more in common with a gladiator's trident than a farm implement. She stood there, tail swishing, holding it.

"It's you." Jeremy nodded.

They both received back packs with clothes, a variety of lesser weapons, and money and gems for bribes. Scruff looked them over and grunted approval.

"Hell is bad for the damned," he growled. "For us who work here, not so bad. But there is little good or kindness here. Be prepared to kill at any time. It doesn't end the damned, but sends them back to the lowest place in Hell they've ever been."

He pulled an envelope from his jacket. "Tickets for the *tre gran velocitas.* The staff are mostly French, which makes it hellish. Kill 'em if you feel like it. They kind of expect it."

As the limo sped off, Jeremy and Shadowheart shouldered their packs and weapons and made for the train. A crowd was gathered about. From what Velos said, it seemed transportation in Hell was more for the operators of Hell than the damned. In the distance, Jeremy saw a hooded man with a scythe leading a group of people in a *danse macabre* across the fields beyond. Their faces were twisted in despair, and he quickly looked away.

They boarded the train without incident, carrying their own bags, which seemed to annoy the porters. Velos had booked them a private room, a good investment in their cover. They slipped into the compartment with its pull-down bed, bathroom, and small table.

"Very cozy," Shadowheart purred.

"Uh, yes," he said. "Perhaps we should go get dinner."

"Yes, having a body is very demanding."

They made their way to the dining car. Demons, humans, and things he couldn't identify passed them. They passed the same two porters they'd refused to let handle their bags. The man-shaped one had the face of a Doberman pinscher; the other resembled a pig. He assumed they were some form of lesser demon. Both watched them with unfriendly eyes.

The dining car was straight out of the Orient Express, with small alcoves lit by ornate oriental lanterns. They headed for a quiet corner, cutting through the buzz of conversation and bodies.

A waiter greeted them. "Monsieur and Madame?" He looked at them as if they'd come in stuck on his shoes. Remembering what

Scruff had said about the staff, Jeremy addressed the waiter in French. The waiter, far from being charmed, seemed even more disdainful. Jeremy's tone became sharp as he ordered for them. The waiter, a supercilious smile on his face, wandered off.

"Not pleased to meet one of your countrymen?" Shadowheart asked.

"I'm only half-French and that half is Norman. That swine is Parisian. Even the French hate them."

The waiter returned quickly, dropping the food on their table with a clatter of plates. The meal was stunningly good. Jeremy couldn't figure why there was good food in Hell, but he was grateful for the break. A fine quiche and white wine soothed his nerves. Shadowheart had the same thing and, if anything, seemed to enjoy it even more. Physical sensations seemed to be overwhelming her usual nature.

They ate in silence while Jeremy studied the tablet, trying to find out about the environment they were in. Hell seemed almost like an alien world, rather than what he expected. A great civilization had grown up in Hell. Bizarre, since time did not seem completely linear. All times seemed to link in Hell, a Spartan Similar and a Nazi occupied the same contiguous patch of Hell. One could face attack with anything from a Schmeissier to a scimitar. Maglev trains and mule trains moved goods and people.

Well, he thought, *isn't that true of my own world?* You can take an Airbus to the Mideast and a camel caravan over the Silk Road. Still, Hell was confounding.

Two women sat down at a small table next to them. They looked so skeletal that Jeremy wasn't sure if they were members of the damned, demons passing for people, or something else. The Parisian waiter approached them. "Ladies, what may I get you?"

"Perrier, with a twist for both of us."

"Oh, and I think we'll split a salad."

"Perrier and salad?" the waiter repeated with a faint air of disbelief. "The TGV boasts the best food in Hell. Our chef trained at the Sorbonne."

"Oh, and have the chef put the dressing on the side," said one. "I hate it when they drown a salad. Don't you, Gladys?"

"On the side? On the side? Don't you think our chef knows how to use dressing? You...you, Americans!" the waiter shrieked. He snatched up a cleaver from a nearby cart and raised it high. Both women shrieked and raised their too-thin arms to ward off the berserk waiter.

Jeremy's Walther cleared his holder before he even considered whether he should interfere. He fired one round, hitting the maddened waiter between the eyes. He dropped as the women fled. Jeremy stood. Shadowheart had left her pitchfork in the cabin, but she held a large dagger in her hand. For some reason, the angel had always abhorred firearms.

The maître d', a heavy-set man with red eyes and wearing a fez, approached them. "Forgive us," he said, in an oily voice. "Pierre is rather high-strung. Perhaps the long journey back from the lower session of Hell he came into will help him with his customer relations skills."

More staff came in, including Dogface.

"Poor Pierre," Dogface said. "Just couldn't take the hags."

"Clean this up," Fez ordered.

"Nothing to worry about," Fez said to the car at large. "A round of drinks on the house."

Dogface glanced at Jeremy. "What did you have to go and kill poor Pierre for? Nobody would have missed those anorexic bitches. Interfering busybodies don't do well in Hell."

"Then take your own advice," Jeremy snapped. "Get your snout out of mine."

Jeremy turned to Fez. "I think we'll skip dessert."

Shadowheart sidled up to him. "I can think of something better for dessert."

I hope she's just playing in character, he mused. "Come on."

Shadowheart followed on his heels. They quickly exited the car and made their way back to their compartment. Outside the window, the world whizzed by at high speed, indistinct in the fading light. Jeremy quickly pulled down the shades, darkening the room further.

"I think we're safe for the moment," he said. As he turned, he bumped into Shadowheart, and found his hands on the waist of her silk and leather bodice. "Uh, sorry. Are you all right?"

"Yes," she said slowly, as if struggling to concentrate. "This body... this body...is strange..."

Jeremy felt his head swimming and knew he should let go of her, but couldn't seem to remove his hands. Her ruby eyes drew him in. Her body, pressed against his, was fever-hot and lush, soft as it had never been before. In her teen incarnation, Shadowheart normally felt light and insubstantial. As an angel, her body had been strong but lifeless. Now she was all sex and heat; the scent of her was delicious, overwhelming. He felt his body awakening to hers.

He tried to think, but arousal drove reason away. Her mouth came to his, sweet and intoxicating like Amaretto. Her tail slid up between his legs. The angel was gone, and the succubus was irresistible. He shrugged off his duster as his hands discovered her body. She gave a low, wild laugh. He threw her on the table, out of control with a woman in a way he had never been before. Shadowheart, too, was out of control; her red eyes gleamed, the lips shone, her tail slapped his back in encouragement as they tore off each other's clothes.

She reached for him and pulled him into her.

"Now, now," she laughed. He buried his face between her breasts, alternately tonguing each nipple. The universe narrowed to her mouth, her body, her long, strong legs. The climax struck them both at the same instant in a roar and scream of satisfaction. Jeremy thought he might pass out, and it felt as though his entire body was one huge pulse. They collapsed on the table, gasping for breath. Despite having one of the biggest orgasms of his life, Jeremy realized he was still hard as a rock inside her.

Again, a laugh he'd never imagined as hers sounded in his ear. "You're mine. I can make you do anything. I can make you do more." They made love again, building to an apex as strong as the first.

"Oh God," they both screamed at the same moment.

The door slammed open. The two demonic porters glared at them. "I knew there was something wrong with them," Dogface growled. "They called on God. You're spies for the other side."

"Get em," shouted Pigface. They drew extendible batons from under their coats, snapping them to full length.

Jeremy surged off Shadowheart. He grabbed his duster from the floor, pulling the sword from its hidden sheath. There was no time to go for the gun. He flung the leather duster over Pigface's head and blocked Dogface's swing. They slashed and parried. Jeremy found fighting with a raging hard-on threw off his balance. However, it seemed to bother Dogface too. He saw Shadowheart crash into the other porter. Soft and supple as her body was, it still held more strength than any human's. She slammed Pigface into a compartment wall, causing a fold-out bed to come down on his head.

Then he was too busy with his own opponent. He nicked the lesser demon. It yelped in anguish at the bite of the enchanted blade, then struck back heavily with the baton. In the confined space, the long sword was a disadvantage, hard to swing and he was afraid to hit Shadowheart. It rang and belled with the demon's blows. Jeremy heard a body fall but couldn't turn to check. An instant later a heart-shaped tail snapped around the demon's upraised weapon arm, jerking him off balance. Jeremy ran Dogface through. He fell soundlessly, dead the instant the bloodsword pierced his insides.

He turned to Shadowheart to see the other demon dead under the bed, its neck obviously snapped. She stood, red lips parted, magnificent body bruised but radiant. She stepped forward and hoisted herself on to him. "We won," she said, sliding her legs behind his and locking them. "Satisfy me. Now." She rocked her hips back and forth, again driving reason from his mind. He kissed her frantically as she roped him to her with her tail. "Come quietly this time," she ordered.

After the sexual frenzy, he lay on the floor of the compartment with no idea of whether he'd followed her orders. Shadowheart still straddled him. He was still hard inside her for all that he barely had energy to breathe.

What if this is it? he thought. *What if it's never this good again? How could it ever be? She's a succubus, sensual beyond human powers. No wonder men damned themselves for them.*

Her own breathing slowed. "That was...that certainly was... I have never felt such things before. This body—it has powers that cannot—that challenge me. We will have to be careful."

"Yes," he managed, "we wouldn't want anything to happen. Would we?"

She looked down and gave him a rueful smile. Then she stood, sliding off him. "Well, at least now I can think clearly again. I haven't been able to do that since we arrived here."

Jeremy's nerves still thrummed. Most of his muscles, no longer distracted by Shadowheart's new-found erotic power, began to protest his making love standing up for as long as he had. *Hope there's some ibuprofen in the med kit,* he thought.

He looked up at her. She stood in perfection over him, her tail wrapped around her own leg. She ran her hands over her new body as if inspecting it for the first time. Then she stretched languorously. He felt his body stir in response.

"Stop that," she said. "We have work to do."

"You're causing it," he said. "Unless you think I normally rip my clothes off in public places and have maniacal sex on a pile of dead demons."

"We weren't on them," she replied. "That would have been disgusting. Besides, I don't think two dead demons constitute a pile." She reached over and drew a bed sheet off the fold-out bed that had slammed down on Pigface. "We have to get rid of these two. Can you get up? By which I mean, off the floor."

Jeremy struggled to his feet.

"Come on," she said. "Let's get them out the window."

"At this speed?" he marveled. "I don't think the windows will open."

"Hah," she replied, "this is Hell, not America. No one cares about safety."

Jeremy stared at his guardian angel, if he could still call her that. "You know, maybe we should talk about what just happened."

Shadowheart pulled open the window, and air blasted into the room. "Can't hear you."

Wrestling dead demons out the window finally did for his erection, which was a relief. He needed the blood supply for other uses.

It took both of them to shut the window against the force of the wind.

"Look," he began. "I just want to make sure we're okay. I think we need to discuss this."

"Later," she said, giving his rear a playful slap with her tail. "I find myself curiously sticky. I want a shower." She disappeared into the coffin-sized showerette and pulled the door. Water ran immediately.

"I hope it's cold," he muttered.

"Ouch!" she said. "Brrrrrrr... I heard that."

"Your hearing," he added, gathering up their clothes, "is curiously selective."

He sat on the downturned bed, and sleep struck him down in an instant.

The smell of coffee and food woke him hours later. The rust red sky was bright again, daytime. A platter sat beside him with a note from Shadowheart. "I figured you deserved a big breakfast. I'm out hunting for information."

He devoured the food, suspecting that Shadowheart's absence had more to do with a desire not to talk, rather than any valid need for intelligence.

"Greetings, passengers," a voice announced. "We will be entering Old Dis station in one hour."

Jeremy finished the coffee and juice, then headed for a badly needed shower.

When he came out, Shadowheart was there, with her face buried in the *New York Times, Hell Edition,* and was distinctly uncommunicative. He decided to let matters lie for now. The maglev train slowed.

"Entering Old Dis station," the announcer called. "Prepare to disembark. Due to the unexpected disappearance of two of our porters, there will be some delay in offloading luggage."

Shadowheart looked directly at him for the first time that day, over the top of the paper. She gave a somewhat hesitant wink. He smiled back. Without discussion, Shadowheart shouldered her formidable trident. Jeremy pulled a submachine gun from the duffel—an MPN that used the same 9mm ammo as his pistol. In place of the normal H&K logo was the leering face of a devil.

"Local make," he muttered. He jacked the slide and hung the MPN under his leather duster. They shouldered their packs and hastened to the exit as the train pulled into a station that looked like it came straight out of the Swiss Alps. Jeremy and Shadowheart exited the train. Above them loomed black mountains; a castle crowned one of them.

"That looks familiar." He consulted his tablet. "I don't believe this."

"What?" Shadowheart said.

"Houska Castle."

"The one near Prague?" Shadowheart said. "Its chapel sits over a chasm that can lead directly to Hell."

"According to the tablet, this is the other side of the chasm. The castle is duplicated on this side. It doesn't look like a regular castle, though."

"Its strength was never in battlements or archers," Shadowheart said. "More powerful forces guarded it."

A wailing howl made them look into the valley below. In it sat a ringed, medieval looking city, though trucks could be seen on the roads outside of it. From their vantage, they could see over the walls into narrow, winding streets. The wailing howl repeated, and something winged launched from a minaret near the outer walls.

Shadowheart shuddered. "A Fury. We must avoid them."

"No argument."

They rented a Land Rover at the station. The sour-looking clerk put a literally ungodly amount on the credit card Velos had given them. They threw their gear in the back. Jeremy offered Shadowheart the keys.

She stared at him. "I can't drive."

Jeremy couldn't hold back the laughter. When he was done, he had a very cross succubus glaring at him.

"I teleport," she growled, "I fly, on occasions I have been known to walk. Driving never came up."

He tried to keep a straight face. "I'll have to teach you sometime. Hop in."

Shadowheart slid in, the leather of her panties squeaking on the leather of the seat. "Velos said Joan was ordered to this area. He had no information on where. The tablet just says that her punishment was to 'assault the heights, as did Sisyphus.'"

"Wasn't he condemned to push a rock up a hill?"

She nodded. "There was very little other information. We have to remember this isn't the real Joan. In Hell she is just another damned soul, for all that she did not come to exist in the normal way."

"Perhaps we should look for her on the greatest height?"

"I don't think so," Shadowheart said. "Hell tailors the punishment to fit the crime and the personality of the damned. Though this is not the real Joan, she doubtless sees herself like unto Joan who was the Messenger of God, freeing France from tyranny. She who took fortification after fortification in battle—"

"Castles," he said, "on heights." He looked at the looming pile over them. "And here we have a castle guarding an express route to Hell, atop a mountain."

"She was sent to Dis recently," Shadowheart said. "Maybe she didn't get far."

He shrugged. "It's a place to start." He headed the Land Rover up the steep roads toward Houska. It took longer than he figured. The roads were terrible, with neither guardrails nor signs. Despite the GPS, they had to backtrack twice, but eventually they began to close on the castle.

"I don't remember there being a tower in the center of it," Jeremy said.

"There wasn't on our side," Shadowheart replied, looking up. "Nor does it match the rest of the building. I think it's something new."

"Better and better," he replied.

They pulled up to a gate in the low wall that surrounded the castle, which, at close range, looked more like a chateau than a fort, except for the incongruous tower projecting up from its center. They stepped out of the Land Rover, weapons in hand; the air was crisp but not very cold. The sky was as light as Hell seemed to get.

A shrill yell split the air, and a huge bat-winged form lunged over the wall almost over their heads.

"Dragon!" Shadowheart shouted.

Jeremy pulled the MPN from under his duster. But they were not the dragon's target. It banked like a fighter and emitted a thin jet of flame at something on the other side of the wall.

A young girl's voice shrilled. "Pour Francaise y Deo!"

"We've found her!" Jeremy said, rushing forward.

They shouldered their way through the gate onto a lawn of charred grass. A girl stood there. The grass next to her was burning, as was the fountain behind her. She bore sword and shield, and looked up at the dragon wheeling above her with hopeless eyes. It roared and hovered. Jeremy went to one knee and brought up the MPN. It stuttered its death song all the way through its magazine. The dragon pulled up short and screeched in agony. It again spat the liquid stream of fire that ignited in mid-air. Jeremy threw himself behind a column and flinched as the flames washed by. Shadowheart flung her pitchfork, but the weapon simply glanced off the dragon's armor.

The distraction gave Jeremy a chance to snap in another clip. He stepped out and aimed at the wing joint. He held down the trigger. *To hell with controlled bursts of three.* The volley destroyed the joint, and the monster fell to the ground. Before it could recover itself, the slender girl leapt in, her sword held high, hacking at the outstretched neck. The dragon gave a screech and fell. She hacked again and the head came off.

"I won. I actually won this time. I will not have to go back!" she shouted to the sky.

Shadowheart and Jeremy walked over slowly. He let the MPN fall back under his duster. Shadowheart picked up her pitchfork, but shouldered it. The girl looked at them with a mix of gratitude and wariness.

Jeremy looked over the slender girl with her short, light-brown hair. She wore a blue surcoat emblazoned with gold *fleur-de-lis*, and held a workmanlike arming-sword in one hand and a triangular shield on the other. On the shield, two more *fleurs-de-lis* flanked a vertical sword holding up a crown. Chain mail hung under the surcoat. Her chest heaved as she looked at the dead dragon.

"Thank you, Sir Knight," she said with a pronounced French accent that Jeremy could not place. Her voice was light, high, and childlike. This was not the Joan of trial and burning, but a younger version; she looked about sixteen.

Jeremy spoke to her in French, but Joan raised a hand. "I am sorry. I am…not the real Jeanne d'Arc, but rather the creation of a lonely girl. I know only the few words of French that she did."

"I am Jeremy Leclerc, Knight Templar."

"A Knight with a machine gun? Wearing black leather?"

"I am from the same time as Camille. The Knights Templar still live and still fight evil in the shadows."

"How did you die and end up in Hell, poor Knight?"

"I am not dead."

"What!?"

"This is Shadowheart; she's an angel—"

"And looks less like an angel than you do a Knight."

"Revealing my true form," Shadowheart said with a forced patience, "would bring all Hell down on us. Jeremy speaks the truth; he is a living Templar, and I am an angel. We have come to get you and Camille out of Hell."

"I am," Joan said, her face twisted in pain, "where I belong. She imagined me, you know. I was her best friend, her only confidante, the sister she never had. I failed her."

"You saved her from being raped," Jeremy said.

"She had survived that before. When I killed her father, I ripped the shroud off all she had concealed, all she lived in dread of having revealed. She was ashamed of what had happened to her. More than anything else, she wanted it kept secret. By striking down the evil, I brought upon her all she feared most. Then she answered by taking her own life—brought to death and shame by me, her creation, the sister of her mind and soul.

"I did not contest my sentence. Indeed, I called it upon myself. Camille is condemned to Hell; I must embrace it."

Jeremy shook his head. "You are doomed for no reason other than a misplaced sense of guilt."

Joan shook her head. "I failed her."

"How? You struck down a child-molester. You did not make him one. Nor did you prevent Camille from going to the police, her school, her doctor. What choice did she leave you? Stand by while she was violated, or fight?"

Joan sighed. "Yet by fighting I doomed her."

Jeremy's heart went out to her. Camille had dreamt of Joan, the woman—warrior, someone decisive, capable of meeting evil head-on with blade in hand. How could this Joan be other than what Camille had imagined for her?

"So, I am sent here to fight on in a hopeless battle. In the tower above us is a demon. He controls the people of this castle, humans all and condemned souls like me. They see me as a monster and resist my efforts to reach the demon atop the tower. If I can slay that demon, I can release the people of the tower and the prisoners tortured in the dungeons below. As I reach each level of the tower, I am attacked by more powerful opponents. I am driven back or…" she shuddered, "I am slain and flung back to where I came to Hell to begin the long weary journey again."

Jeremy gestured at the dead dragon. "That was never a human."

"This last time I steeled myself to my ultimate effort, I nearly gained the summit before being beaten back. My demonic opponent has upped the ante by bringing supernatural beasts against me. I would rather that anyway. Against those that were never human, I need not stay my hand."

"What manner of forces are inside?" Jeremy looked up at the tower.

"Men of various types, some women."

"How armed?"

"Swords, axes… ah, no guns. At least not before this."

"Then perhaps," he said, slapping a new magazine in his MPN, "we, too, can up the ante."

Shadowheart nodded. "Stay behind me when we attack. This body is not as delicate as it appears."

Joan smiled sadly. "It is not for you to forgive or to aid me in my doleful fate. I am here for punishment."

"Then we will take you to the one person who can forgive you: Camille."

Joan blanched. "I dare not face her."

"Is the Maid of Orleans afraid?" Jeremy said.

"Yes."

"Be brave, Joan, this time you are not forsaken," Shadowheart said.

Joan stared at her.

"Yes, Joan. Look at me, see me. See what I actually am. Trust in Jeremy."

Joan turned to Jeremy.

"I believe there is a reason for hope," he said. "I believe you're guiltless, certainly of anything I would not have done in your place. Don't you want to see Camille?"

"More than anything," Joan said, "but I fear she hates me."

"You must face it as your namesake would have," Jeremy said.

She smiled sadly. "I guess—pitiful simulacrum that I am—I owe it to her to be the best Joan of Arc I can be. Very well."

A horn sounded above them in the tower.

"This will not get easier," Jeremy said, leveling the MPN and making sure his sword was loose in its sheath in the duster. Shadowheart's tail stood erect behind her, now resembling a scorpion's sting.

"Have fun storming the castle," Jeremy muttered.

"Charge," Joan cried.

They raced across the grounds, heading for the gaping door. From above, spears, arrows, and rocks rained down. Jeremy fired a burst to back off the unseen enemies above. A shaft stuck in Joan's shield, till she hacked it off with her sword. Then they were in the building facing a winding stairway. At the foot of it stood a unit of Spartans, their round shields overlapping, their spears glinting. Jeremy fired on the run, telling himself that they were all dead and damned. Shooting them down like mad dogs wasn't evil. Living Spartans might have broken, but these knew what a gun was. The surviving Spartans scattered and flung a shower of spears, charging with their kopis out.

Shadowheart snapped spears out of the air with the tines of her pitchfork faster than a human eye could see. She brought the heavy trident down on one Spartan's helm, crushing it. Joan did good work with her shield as Jeremy fired from between them. Evidently Camille had imagined her Joan as far more powerful than an ordinary girl. She smashed shields with a Spartan, and it was the Spartan who was flung back. A spear thudded into Jeremy's leather duster, but the Kevlar panels spread the impact and kept it from penetrating. Still, the blow made him hiss in pain.

"Upward," Joan called. They raced up the stair straight into Cardinal Richelieu's musketeers charging down, rapiers drawn. Jeremy dropped the first wave, but the MPN clicked empty. There was no time to even draw the Walther. He dropped the MPN, which saved his life as a rapier rammed into it and splintered. The MPN bumped on his chest, held by the lanyard. Jeremy pulled his blood-sword and blocked another rapier.

A tail, with the heart-shaped tip held rigid, impaled the musketeer through the throat, and bright blood splashed as he fell. Shadowheart, her wardrobe in tatters, crashed into the musketeers, flinging them off the stairs onto the pavement below.

Jeremy pulled his Walther and shot musketeers farther up, who were leveling their muskets. Only one managed to fire, the ball knocking chips off the wall behind him. As they reached another landing, a man in an SS uniform stepped out of an alcove, raising a Colonial Luger. His shot scored across Shadowheart's back. She staggered and screamed. Jeremy gave him back a round between the eyes. As the SS trooper fell, Jeremy snatched up his weapon. Another SS trooper stepped out, and into Shadowheart's pitchfork and was flung into the air like a bale of hay.

"I thought they didn't have guns," Jeremy shouted.

Joan shrugged. "They didn't before."

Joan fought as if she were the true Messenger of God. Shadowheart, her wounds closed up, was equally deadly. A musketeer stabbed Jeremy and looked on in shock when the coat stopped the blade. Joan downed the man with a backhand cut.

On the next level, samurai attacked. It was sword versus sword and trident. Joan was knocked down and would have lost her head but for Shadowheart's stabbing tail. Joan nodded gratefully as Shadowheart pulled her to her feet. Jeremy fired the last rounds in the Luger and Walther at two archers who appeared on the top landing.

Shadowheart flung her pitchfork and impaled a charging Japanese soldier. Jeremy grabbed up the bayoneted Arisaka and picked off a

Japanese officer. He worked the bolt, looking for more enemies. "What next?" he gasped. "Trolls?"

They mounted the final landing.

"This is too easy," Joan said, looking about. "The last time I made it this far, this area was full of Teutonic Knights."

"Easy!" Jeremy said. He looked at Shadowheart, clad now only in leather panties and rags. "Are you all right?"

"I can use my powers to heal this body," she said. "It's inefficient but manageable. On the other hand, we won't be able to return anything to Victoria's Secret."

They walked into the round turret to face an old man—dignified, white-robed, and bearded. He sat on a simple wooden throne as the very image of a kindly king.

"You are the demon of the tower?" Joan demanded.

"Or you are," he said in a resonant voice.

"I am Joan of Arc."

"You are a lonely girl's dream. The real Joan of Arc never came to Hell."

Joan flushed; her hand tightened on her sword.

His eyes fell to it. "I hear you are good at solving problems with steel. Come, Pretender Joan, strike me down and take my place. You will, I think, make a good demon of the tower."

Joan stepped forward.

"No, Joan," Jeremy said.

"Silence," the old king thundered. "This is Joan's test. Not yours. Speak but one more word and she forfeits." He stared at Jeremy then at Shadowheart. "Who are you? What are you doing here? Succubus and Collector, this is not your place."

"But it is mine," Joan said. "Keep your eyes to me, old trickster. I am your opponent here."

"Very well, Pretender. Why do you hesitate? Am I not evil? Destroy me without thinking. Deal with problems as you have— plunge in and cut. There is only good and only evil. What is it that stops you?"

Joan stared at Jeremy as if she could will some information out of him, but it was Shadowheart who spoke. "Old Trickster, she called you and you are. You want to play a game without telling her the rules or the stakes."

He glared at her. "Shouldn't you be on your knees somewhere? What does a succubus know of the wider Hell? Your province is the world of lust between the legs. Stay out of mine."

Shadowheart looked at Joan. "You must judge for yourself how it is that you will fight."

Joan walked forward, and the old king smiled at her as she came. Two paces from the throne, she let her arms hang down, sword and shield resting on the ground. "If I let you live, old codger, is the game mine?"

"Oh, not so easily," the old king said. "Weakness in striking evil can be as evil as striking too hard."

"How then shall we contest without bloodshed? Why should I withhold my hand in the presence of evil?"

"I can answer only the first question. You must search in yourself for any answer to the second. We shall do battle by a question. Answer well and win. Answer poorly and you begin your battle for the tower anew from its lowest depth."

He turned to Jeremy and Shadowheart and frowned. "You two are not right, but I will deal with you after I dispose of this childish simulacrum of Joan."

"I *am* Joan," she shouted. "At least I am as much Joan as Camille could dream me. I will *be* Joan!"

The old king laughed. "We shall see. I will put a question to you that was once put to her. Let us see if you are Joan or not."

He drew himself up. "Joan, who styles herself, Jeanne d'Arc, Messenger of God, do you stand in God's grace?"

Joan's face clouded. Jeremy's heart went out to the slender, pale girl, blood-stained and tormented.

"Who am I to speak for God?" Joan said. "I do not even know if he envisioned me in his universe. It was Camille who gave birth to me. Yet, did she not come from God? Am I not—however tiny, however insignificant—some part of his plan for existence?" She hung her shield by a strap from her shoulder then took a cloth out from under her surcoat and wiped her blade before sheathing it. "I can only hope that I am in God's grace now; and if I am not, that he embraces me in it when he chooses."

The old king jerked upright with a great cry. His arms flew up. Joan sprang back, raising her shield and placing a hand to her sword. Shadowheart and Jeremy leapt forward too, weapons raised. But there was no need. The old king's façade faded; in his place was a Minotaur. It gave an ox-like bellow of agony then seemed to implode into black sand that fell to the floor with a hiss. A wind swept into the chamber and dispelled the reek of the place, if only for a few blessed moments.

Joan stared at them in confusion. Shadowheart put up her pitchfork. "Well answered, Joan. Much as your namesake did at her trial. 'If I am not, may God put me there; and if I am, may God so keep me.' It was a trap. If you claimed you knew God's mind, you would be a heretic; if not, then you would be condemned for claiming to be a messenger of God."

"Well done," Jeremy said.

Joan looked at him and blushed furiously. "Thank you, Sir Knight. It seems that part of my task here was to learn that there are other ways to solve conflict than with the edge of a blade."

"Sometimes there are," Jeremy said, "and sometimes nothing else will do. Sometimes our enemies are the blackest evil. Yet you were sent here by a white that could see no gray. That was no less cruel and unjust."

Her eyes shone as she looked at him. Jeremy felt a blush too. *Here I am standing between a succubus and a child,* he thought. *The world remains out of joint.*

"I think we are free of this place," he said, gruffly. "We must find Camille."

"Let us go," Joan agreed.

They walked cautiously down the tower steps, but the tormented dead who'd battled them so savagely were nowhere to be seen. No bodies, no blood, no sign that the tower had ever held anyone.

They exited the tower through the lower gate; a stern cold wind greeted them. Jeremy kicked down a guard room door and returned with three heavy red cloaks such as the Spartans wore. Joan and he gratefully wrapped themselves in them.

"I'm hot all the time," Shadowheart said.

"Young eyes," he said.

"She's a girl," Shadowheart replied.

"But I'm not. Me, boy. You naked succubus…young eyes. Work it out."

"Oh, right." She wrapped the cloak around her. "I have a change of clothes in the car."

Joan lived in a small room in a nearby village. They collected Joan's pitiful few things. The landlady demanded a lease-breaking fee and refused to return Joan's deposit until Shadowheart tapped her on the shoulder with the pitchfork. The terms moderated quickly.

They piled into the Land Rover. Jeremy noted that, for all Joan identified with Jeanne d'Arc, their Joan knew how to use a seatbelt. Well, she had come from Camille's subconscious. Her active personality was that of a heroine, but under that lay the same basic knowledge that Camille had.

"What do we do now, Sir Templar?" she asked.

"You can call me Jeremy and her Shadowheart. Now, we look for Camille. If only we had some idea of where to look."

"I do," Joan said, leaning forward in excitement, "or at least I know the name of the place. When I was killed the first time and the Collector who brought me to Hell," she shuddered, "he thought it amusing to tell me that she was sent to Plandome, only a few days march from my tower. He seemed to think it a fine punishment that we would be near yet unable to reunite. As I was bound to my tower, Camille is bound to this Plandome."

Shadowheart, again attired in the finest lingerie, though still, at Jeremy's insistence, wearing the cloak, consulted the tablet. "Dis had a special section for suicides. This Plandome seems to be one. There are no interstates—at least not in this ring. But there is a route. It winds about. I make it around 150 miles. We could drive through the night and make it."

Jeremy looked at Joan. "Can you drive?"

Joan looked embarrassed. "I'm sorry. Camille didn't have a permit. She was supposed to start in the fall. I don't know anything about life that she didn't."

He turned to Shadowheart.

"No, I haven't learned in five hours. Man-up and drive. I'll set the tablet for GPS."

They drove for hours through the pitch-black night, gradually coming out of the mountains, to Jeremy's intense relief. After sunrise they entered a small, cheerless hamlet. There was a gas station. Jeremy pulled in. To his surprise, out came a Neanderthal. The hairy, powerful man walked up and looked them over.

"We're looking to fill up and for some breakfast," Jeremy said. Shadowheart and Joan stepped out and were stretching.

"Got Satans?" he grunted.

Jeremy shook his head "I've got credit cards."

"No good. Gold or Silver Satans. Or maybe something else." He looked over Shadowheart. "Nice succubus."

"She's not on the menu."

"Okay, how about the young one—"

He froze as Jeremy rested the ultra-long barrel of the Colonial Luger on the bridge of his nose. "I've wanted to try this one out again," Jeremy said in a conversational tone, "and if you don't shut your filthy mouth and get on with filling the car up, I'll drop you and burn your shithole station to the ground."

"Damn Collectors," he muttered, backing off.

"I've changed my mind," Jeremy said. "You just became self-service. Get out of my sight." The Neanderthal fled back into his station.

Jeremy filled the Land Rover, and they drove over to a Waffle House. It wasn't half bad. They were back on the road in half an hour.

"Next stop, Plandome," he said.

***

"I don't know what I expected," Shadowheart said, "but this surely wasn't it."

"It's like Hello Kitty designed a town and pink vomited itself all over it," Jeremy added.

Plandome stretched in all its hideousness across the valley ahead of them. It was a child's drawing of a town, with houses in pink and blue, trees in pink and blue. The Mad Hatter had never dreamed of something this bad. People walked about in the distance and clunky pink and blue cars wandered about the landscape.

"It reminds me of the Polly Pockets and Barbie things that Camille liked when she was younger," Joan offered.

"What do we do?" Shadowheart asked. "Go knock on doors?"

"I think," Joan said suddenly, "I think I *feel* her." She pointed to the center of the hideous community, where a particularly gruesome house sat on a small hill, covered with pink and blue Christmas trees.

Jeremy drove on. Joan acted as a compass, directing them through the winding streets. They finally pulled up to a Tudor house set in a perfect lawn, which would have been cute but for the colors.

"Yes, yes," Joan said in a mix of excitement and fear. "She's here. I know it!"

Jeremy looked around. "No obvious threats, except to one's sense of good taste."

Shadowheart nodded. "This entire town clashes with my outfit."

"Yeah, I guess leather and lace is more New Orleans than Levit-town. Let's go prepared. You want my spare pistol?"

"I'll stick with my pitchfork."

"I have my shield and sword," Joan added. "I know what guns are, but not how to use one."

"Yeah, and none of these are beginner's weapons." He jacked the slides on all three and stepped out. Despite the mild temperature, he kept his duster with his armor and sword on. They walked up to the door and rang the bell.

The door opened. Two ordinary-looking people stood there: a man of his late forties, with a receding hairline, and a woman around the same age, slender, with a mouth that looked as if it supped on lemons. But the eyes told the story; they were black from lid to lid.

"Yes?" said the man.

"We're here to see Camille," Jeremy said.

"Why would you want to see her?" the woman said. "She's a very dirty girl."

"Yes," said the man, "a temptress. A very bad girl."

"Please go away," the woman added. "Camille is ours. We're her new mother and father, and she has to stay here with us to become a good girl."

Jeremy poked the MPN out from under his coat. "Back up."

"You can't do this," the man said in outrage.

Jeremy shoved the man. Shadowheart and Joan filed in behind him.

"Camille," Joan shouted. "Where are you? It's me, Joan."

Footsteps sounded, and a girl appeared on the stairway opposite. She bore a superficial resemblance to Joan, though her hair was longer and darker. She wore dull black robes that covered her from head to toe. Disbelief warred in her face with…hope? "Joan, is it you? Could it be you? You're in Hell, too?"

"Another dirty girl," Fakemother said in disgust.

"Go back upstairs," Fakefather ordered. "Stop displaying your body."

"Silence," Jeremy growled, raising the MPN.

"A dirty girl with dirty friends," said Fakemother.

"No, Jeremy," Shadowheart said. "The battle is again joined. We must leave it to Joan and Camille to break free of this torment."

Joan walked over, and Camille came down the stairs, staring at the literal sister of her soul. "You came for me?"

"I'm the reason you're in Hell," she said.

"She's in Hell because she's a whore," Fakemother said. "She tempts men."

"It's not my fault," Camille whispered. "I didn't want that. I didn't!"

"Yes, you did," Fakefather said, "always showing your body. The way you stand, the way you move. You tempted him."

"Your poor father," Fakemother said. "You killed him."

"I didn't," Camille said tearfully.

"You're a bad girl," Fakemother insisted.

"Camille," Joan said. "You must deny them. Stand up for yourself!"

"Or what," Camille demanded, "will you kill them too?"

"Do you wish me to kill them for you?" She put her hand to her sword. "Isn't that the reason you conjured me into existence?"

"I was lonely, afraid," Camille said.

"I know," Joan replied. "I tried to protect you in the only way I knew how. Bid me slay them and we will be free of this place. Jeremy and Shadowheart are friends. They've come to get us out of Hell. I will make an end of these demons and we will be on our way."

"No," Camille cried. "No more killing."

"They're the dead and the damned already, if they were ever real in the first place."

"I don't want anyone else killed," Camille insisted.

"Camille," Joan shouted, "you must stand up for yourself."

"Not that way."

"Then what way?"

Camille looked at her fakeparents.

"You know you need to stay with us," Fakemother said. "You'll never be clean without us. You'll never be a good girl. You killed your father."

"That wasn't me," shrilled Camille.

"We all know that's a lie." Fakefather laughed. "There is no 'Joan,' she's just a part of you. You can't hide behind her."

"I have no memory of it," Camille said. "I didn't want him to die. I wanted him to stop."

"You liked it," Fakefather said. "We're very disappointed in you, Camille."

"You need to stay here," the mother said. "You'll never be any good if you leave. You have so much to atone for."

Camille stood, her shoulders hunched, hands under her chin. "No," she shouted. "No, my sins were only against myself. I didn't hurt anyone else. I don't deserve this. I don't!"

Joan came up behind her. "Yes, Camille."

"No, Joan. Don't help me. For once, I must do something myself."

She turned to the fake family. "I am leaving. I deny you power over me. I refuse your expectations and demands. I'm leaving."

"You were never any good," Fakemother said.

"Such a disappointment," Fakefather added. "How sharper than a serpent's tooth it is to have an ungrateful child."

Camille backed away from them as if wading through mud. Joan, silent, her hands away from her weapons backed with her. They reached the door, and with a sob, Camille burst through, Joan on her heels.

Fakemother and Fakefather stepped forward.

Jeremy leveled the MPN. "I don't care whose torment this is," he said quietly, but with a conviction that had often eluded him on Earth. "I don't care about the rules. I don't care what will follow. You take one more step, and I'll cut you both in half."

"That was an oath," Shadowheart said, her pointed tail rising scorpion-like behind her. "Count on it being fulfilled."

Jeremy and Shadowheart also backed to the door. Fakemother and Fakefather stared at them with their hideous eyes.

They walked out, and the horrible pink town was gone. When they turned around, the house they'd walked out of had disappeared too. They were on a darkling plain by themselves.

Camille lay in the dirt weeping. Joan stood over her.

"You did it," Joan said, almost as if she didn't believe it herself.

"Finally," Camille said, "I finally stood up for myself. Too late of course, but at least once."

Shadowheart handed Jeremy her trident. She walked over and put her hands on Camille's shoulders. "You're free, Camille. You have broken your torment."

The girl laughed with a wild bitterness. "Oh, not hardly. I carry my torment with me."

"We have another chance, Camille," Joan said. "Jeremy and Shadowheart were sent by the powers to rescue us. We'll be together again."

"I hate you," Camille screamed. "You ruined my life. Everything I wanted to hide, you pulled out for the whole world to see. Why couldn't you wait?"

"Wait," Joan said, anger reddening her cheeks. "For how long? Wait for what obscenity to happen before you acted?"

"I'd have gotten stronger. I'd have put an end to it."

Joan shook her head in sorrow. "You have no strength, Camille. You were always the victim."

"Is that the real reason?" Camille said, anger cutting through her own tears. "Or is that you felt you could live my life better than I could? You wanted to be the real one."

Joan looked stricken and fell back from Camille. "No," she muttered, "that's not true."

"It is," Camille shouted. "You wanted the same things I did: to go out to the movies, to go on vacation, to make Christmas cookies, to have a date with a boy. You wanted our body and my life."

Joan staggered to lean against the Land Rover. "Could this be true? Is this more of my sin? I deemed you weak, worthless, pushed you out of the way to better deal with it all? Was this about my pride?"

"It's *my* life," Camille said. "Well, it was. For better or likely for worse, I lived it as I did."

Joan looked at her, her face drawn tight. "I could not stand by and allow such evil to go unchecked. It was you, Camille, who imagined me into what I am. How else did you expect me to act?

"You wanted to make Christmas cookies, to travel, to date? At least there was some chance that you could have these things. What would I have beyond the moments of being alive when you dreamt of me? What was there for Joan?"

"You're not real," Camille insisted.

"Am I not here in Hell? Do I not suffer? Here I am real."

"You're not," Camille sobbed.

"If she is part of you," Jeremy said softly, "a part of your soul, then you must take her back to be whole."

Camille shook her head.

"Do you hate me so?" Joan whispered.

"Hate you? Yes, but far less than I despise myself. I hate that you're so much better than me. Pure, where I'm...I'm pathetic, Joan. If we were still alive, I would probably have welcomed your replacing me. I'd have been happy to let you live and to become the real one. But that's not even the reason. If I take you back, I'll acquire your memories, the memories of killing my father with a knife. I can't have those memories. I'd go mad."

"If I cannot go back to you," Joan said, "where do I go? Is my only existence to be in Hell?"

"No," Jeremy said. "It's not. I don't understand this. It requires someone better than me to fix what has come before." He looked at Shadowheart, but the succubus' ruby eyes merely gazed steadily back. "What I do know is that neither of you deserves this place. We are getting you out."

"Who are you to overturn the judgment on me?" Camille said.

"We're the ones who were sent to get you."

Camille shook her head. "Take Joan. She's right. She deserves a chance. Me, I'm here because of what I was. It was my fault. I was weak. I could have told my teacher, my doctor, a policeman. Instead, I stayed quiet because I'm a coward. I nursed my hate until it became Joan."

"Joan is not from hate," Jeremy said. "She's from love. She loves you, Camille, as if she were your big sister."

Camille turned away, weariness in every line of her body. "I know. She wanted to protect me. She was the strong one. But because she was strong, I never had a chance to be. When the crisis came, she took over.

"I wanted…I wanted Dad to stop, but I didn't want him to die. He'd been a good father before Mom ran off. I thought he could find his way back. To be like he should—"

"Camille," Jeremy said slowly, feeling hopelessly out of his depth. "I don't know that when a man goes *that* wrong, that he can ever find his way back."

"We'll never know. My father came to abuse me. I went into that little dark place in my mind where I hid. That left Joan there. Joan, my lovely Joan, the creature of heroic charges and noble defeats, to whom right was right and wrong was wrong, took up a knife and ended all my troubles."

"You were a child, an abused child," Jeremy said. "None of this is your fault—not the abuse, not your father's death, not even your own."

"Wrong," she said. "Suicide was the one hard decision I ever made for myself."

"No," he said. "You were there with a weapon in your hands, blood on the blade and your father's body at your feet. You knew you would be blamed for a death you did not cause. It was more than your poor mind could handle. No one your age should ever have been asked to face such a thing."

Camille's eyes remained downcast.

"I am sorry," Joan said. "I destroyed you. I should be here alone to pay for my sin of pride."

Shadowheart walked over to the Land Rover and pulled out the tablet. "Jeremy, there's an airport fifty miles from here."

"Come on girls," Jeremy said. "We have a plane to catch."

Camille sat in the back with Shadowheart, her head on the succubus/angel's shoulder. Joan sat up front, staring at the endless landscape, responding only in monosyllables when addressed.

They reached the airport on the edge of Tartaros. Jeremy dropped the Land Rover at the rental desk, paying a horrific drop-off fee. With the silent girls, they pushed their way through a crowd of the damned. Jeremy saw a room labeled "Pilot's Lounge." He walked in. A man in a leather uniform with a white scarf gave him a look before returning to his paper.

Another man displayed more interest. "Can I help you?"

"You a pilot?"

"Wrong Way Corrigan," the man said. There was a mad cheerfulness in his eyes and voice.

"I've heard of you," Jeremy said. "You're the fellow who claimed he flew to Ireland in the thirties because he misread his compass."

"Yeah, 1938."

"What are you doing in Hell?"

"I was trying to get to Heaven."

Jeremy sighed. "Why did I ask?"

"Can you get us to the admin ring of Hell, Pandemonium Airport?" Shadowheart interjected.

"Sure, babe. You fly up front with me?"

"No, she won't," Jeremy said.

"Territorial, aren't you?" Shadowheart said.

"You'll thank me later."

"You two and the kids, huh?" Corrigan said. "Well, there isn't much going on just now, and I do have some cargo. Okay, four thousand Satans for the whole kit and caboodle."

"What are you flying?" Jeremy asked.

"Tupolev 134."

"Crap," Jeremy said.

"Hey," Corrigan said. "They're not that bad. Problem is all the third-world pilots who kept hitting the planet with them."

"Three thousand Satans," Jeremy said, just to keep Corrigan from being suspicious.

"Thirty-five hundred, I'll throw in snacks. We leave in an hour."

"Deal. You do know how to get there…"

"Sure." Corrigan laughed. "I just head for the ninth ring of Hell and we should end up in the first." He roared at his own joke and walked off toward the hanger.

The was no security at the airport; they simply walked up to the Tu-134, passing a brace of JU-87s and up the gangway—swords, shields, guns, and trident notwithstanding. The Tu-134 had seen better days and not recently. There was a goat pen in the back, and cargo was tied down along the deck. The front section still held seats, so they buckled themselves in—– tightly. Corrigan leaned out of the control cabin. "Make yourselves comfortable folks. It's a long flight, and the transiting barriers can be a bit bouncy." Corrigan's female copilot was working through her checklist.

"There are no airwitches on this flight," Corrigan said. "We aren't Pan Slam Airlines." He tossed them each a bag with sandwiches and drinks. "If you want milk for coffee, though, you'll have to milk one of the goats in the back."

"Just get us there intact and in this lifetime," Jeremy said.

"You bet," Corrigan said. He closed the hatch, and the crew outside rolled back the gangway. Engines whined. "Come on, Amelia. Let's go flying."

"Is this safe?" Camille whispered to him. "He can't navigate, and she never made it back."

Jeremy gave her what he hoped was a reassuring smile. "I guess we have to put our trust in a higher power."

"Never thought I'd hear him say that," Shadowheart muttered.

He looked at his voluptuous guardian angel. "The trip has been full of firsts. Some of which we should talk about."

Shadowheart looked scandalized. "Please, Jeremy, not in front of the children."

He turned to look at Camille, but the young girl was already asleep, exhaustion having claimed her.

The jet started to roll.

As promised, the flight to Pandemonium was long and full of bumps. Jeremy tried to talk to the girls, but Camille wouldn't speak to him. Joan remained sunk in despair as well. They ate Corrigan's snacks and rested.

"Coming into Pandemonium," Corrigan finally announced. "Thank you for flying Wrong Way Airlines. You can get your frequent flyer applications on exiting the aircraft."

The Tu-134 came up to the gate, and a ground crew rolled the gangway against the plane.

The four of them stepped into the brisk wind. At the foot of the gangway stood Velos, beaming up at them. "Wonderful," he called as they walked down. "You got them. It's a miracle."

"Actually," a deep voice called from behind him, "a miracle is what you are going to need." From inside the terminal, a tall, handsome, red-skinned demon in an impeccable suit walked out. A gorgeous succubus stood next to him, and a horde of Minotaurs and other demons trailed along with some SS troopers.

"Screwtape," Velos groaned.

"Yep," said the demon, "in the red-skinned, black-horned flesh."

Velos and Screwtape faced each other. The horde of Minotaurs and lesser demons behind Screwtape rustled their weapons and looked on hungrily. The succubus standing next to Screwtape gave Velos a pout. "That stunt with the squeegee men cost me eight thousand Satans. I thought you loved me."

"Well, I err…" Velos stammered.

"Honey," Screwtape said, "personal stuff later. We got business now."

She pouted more.

"I don't look like that. Do I?" Shadowheart said.

"No," Jeremy reassured her.

"Got a rendition order for these two?" Screwtape asked.

"You know I don't," Velos returned.

The demon shrugged. "Had to ask. Unlike some, I prefer that we do things legally."

Velos smiled. "Do you? Excellent, then shall we look into the legalities?" He pointed at the two girls. "What do you see there?"

"The damned, of course; a suicide and a murderer. I know their story. Your asking around about this case brought it to my attention. Why ask me anyway? You're the Legate; your side sent them here for punishment. You're supposed to be preventing me from getting them un-damned. Instead, I find you staging a breakout. I can barely contain my disappointment."

"Merely correcting a mistake by an overzealous magistrate," Velos said. "They offered no defense and in fact condemned themselves. Joan blames herself for Camille's death. Camille blames herself for her father's death and for not having the strength to put an end to the abuse in some other way. They do not belong here."

Again, Screwtape shrugged. "Who does? But they're the condemned."

"You and I are going to reopen the matter."

"Velos, you know I like you, but come on, this is crazy. There are no grounds for rendition or asylum here."

"Untrue. You see before you something of a miracle: Camille Aldane, who suffered for years alone and in silence until Joan came to be, and Joan, whose love for her creator-sister was so profound that it gave her actual birth into reality."

"Very touching," Screwtape said, "but what does it have to do with anything?"

"Camille," Velos asked gently. "Did you kill your father?"

Camille turned her wan face toward the angel.

"Velos," Screwtape interrupted, "it's all over Hell on the telly. She stabbed her unarmed father to death with a kitchen knife. The SOB is down on Level Nine. You can ask him yourself."

"No!" Joan stepped in front of Camille. "It was I who slew the beast. True, I used Camille's hands and body, but I am Joan, and it was I who struck."

"The Estate of Heaven," Velos intoned, "withdraws the sin of murder on Camille."

"Doesn't get Camille off the suicide," Screwtape said, pinching his chin between clawed fingers. "Sin of despair, you know."

"Exemption," Velos said. "She was not in her right mind."

"On what proof?" Screwtape demanded. The Minotaurs behind him snorted and pawed. He raised a hand to quell them.

"I am the proof," Joan said. "How can you say she was in her right mind when I was in there in place of her? When my task was done, I was dispelled, and poor Camille was left to face the wreck I had made of her life." Tears rolled down Joan's face, and her voice quivered. "I left her alone, with no support. Oh, that I did not want, but I was swept away by the violence and emotion. By the time I could find my way back to her…" Sobs overtook Joan, and she covered her face with her hands.

Camille looked on, made a tentative motion toward Joan, then stopped.

"Not a bad argument, Legate. Maybe I could even see it your way on Camille, but you will leave Joan in Hell."

"She is not real," Velos said. "A tormented girl made up an imaginary friend, a heroine and protector to give hope to her terrible world. Yet Joan is a fragment, a splinter of Camille's soul. You cannot hold part of a soul in Hell. For Camille to go free, that part of her which is Joan must accompany her to be reintegrated. The soul is whole and indivisible"

"Yeah, with liberty and justice for all. Sorry, no sale, Velos. Souls are my specialty. I can smell them, hell I can practically taste them. However she started, however she came to be, Joan is no longer Camille. That," he pointed at Joan, "is a separate and unique soul now. You can take Camille, but you'll leave Joan to her damnation. She killed the father and drove Camille to suicide."

A feeling of unreality gripped Jeremy. Had they come so far to fail now? No. Almost without volition, the bloodsword whispered into his hands. The gem winked balefully, disturbing and roiling the atmosphere, causing Screwtape to flinch.

"Lady Joan," Jeremy said. "You will not be abandoned."

"You're over your head, kid," Screwtape said.

"Jeremy, put up your blade," Velos said, his face heavy in defeat. "We have won all we can."

Shadowheart screamed, a shocking sound that rent the very air. But it was not a cry of frustration or defeat, rather the war cry of a bird of prey. She shook herself violently, and great red and black wings burst from her back. She stood straight as the clothes of the succubus melted off her body, her hair flowed long and black, and the black armor covered her breasts where a moment before a bustier had been. She leveled the tined pitchfork as she stood tall then taller. She shot past her normal seven feet in height until she towered thirty feet into the sky, the great wings spreading over them like a canopy. The Minotaurs and demons shuffled back in horror, confronted by an angry archangel. Most fled outright.

Screwtape and Velos looked up at her with identical expressions of horror.

"Are you out of your mind?" Screwtape shouted. "Are you trying to start an Apocalypse?"

"Shadowheart, you know the powers here," Velos pled. "You can destroy a legion of Minotaurs, but you know what will happen when your fallen brethren come. Even if you could defeat them, HE will come. You're not Michael. Even he could not stand against that force in contravention of the law, in its own place!"

Deep rolling bongs sounded as if from the depths of the sea.

"Hell Bells," Screwtape gasped. "Oh no. Velos, we gotta do something."

"We have not endured Hell," Shadowheart's voice rolled out, "to be stopped now."

"We will not leave Joan," Jeremy shouted, raising his sword over his head. The magic gem in its hilt flamed brighter.

Joan grabbed his arm. "No, Jeremy, you must take Camille and leave. I am not worth it. My sister is all that matters."

Suddenly Camille was between them, throwing her arms around Joan. "No. I won't leave you. I was weak before because I had you to fight for me. I was wrong. I love you, Joan. I won't abandon you. We'll face Hell together."

The bells droned louder. The sky grew dark as the wind began to whip at them alternately with stinging sand and freezing sleet.

"Release them both." Shadowheart glared down at Screwtape.

"I can't," Screwtape said. "There's provision in the treaties. The Powers will never accept it."

"Wait," Velos said. "If it wasn't pure self-defense, Joan still killed to protect an innocent. She was in Camille's body, protecting it from violation."

Hope dawned on the demon's face. "Wait, you said she wasn't real, not a born human anyway."

"That's Heaven's position."

"Maybe we can deal with her under the law for animal spirits."

"She's not a man-eating tiger!"

"Work with me, Velos, or the universe ends today," Screwtape howled. "Legate for Hell stipulates that Joan is non-human but sentient, incapable of moral guilt as she acted as she was made to act, without free will."

"Heaven agrees," Velos shouted over the rising wind and hellish bells.

"Camille goes heavenward, degree to be determined by the Estate of Heaven," Screwtape shouted. "Joan will be assigned to the Grey Messenger service, twenty-year service with a probationary review at the end."

The light began to fade. On the horizon, something the size of a mountain could barely be seen unfurling vast wings. The wind whipped like flails; Screwtape's remaining followers broke and fled in disorder. Camille and Joan sank to their knees holding each other. Joan raised her shield over Camille. Jeremy shielded his eyes. The gem was now the only light, a pool of sanctuary moderating the wind and showing Shadowheart above them, her telephone pole-sized pitchfork leveled at the horizon where eyes red and large as volcanoes turned a soul-destroying gaze their way.

"Lady Joan?" Jeremy shouted above the din.

"We agree," Camille and Joan screamed in unison.

"You are all deported," Velos and Screwtape shouted, running toward each other and clapping hands on the bargain. Both spun toward Shadowheart, their hands glowing white for Velos and red for Screwtape.

"Get the hell out of here," they shouted.

Over Shadowheart's head, a golden circle appeared, its light warm and beneficent in the hellish scene. Shadowheart flung the pitchfork away, stooped down, and gathered Jeremy in one hand and the girls in the other. She vaulted into the sky, through the golden ring and away from the universal nightmare stretching out its mighty hand toward them.

A golden glow surrounded them, calmed them, soothing their cuts and abrasions from the whipping wind. Green grass appeared under-foot, stretching out to an infinite horizon of low rolling hills. The golden glow became the sun of a cool spring day. The sky turned a cornflower blue, with rags of white cloud generously painted on it.

They stood in a circle, facing each other. Shadowheart was again the blond teen of her usual appearance, scarcely older than Joan and Camille.

"We're out," Camille said in wonder.

"You are out, my sister," Joan said, "which is all that matters to me."

"I'm sorry that I could not take you back," Camille said shyly. "I would never learn to be strong if you were within me. I knew that I would fade eventually and you would end up in me, alone. And the memories… I could not endure those."

"I understand, my sister. Do not let it grieve you. For me, too, there was no turning back. I wish to know and be and to become…Joan."

"You will have duties in the Overworld," Shadowheart said. "The Grey Messengers are sent many places in the worlds of the dead. Some are dangerous."

Joan lifted her head in a defiant gesture. "I am Joan. I fear no man, beast, or demon, while Camille is safe."

"Will Joan and I meet again?" Camille asked, holding her imaginary friend's hand.

"I cannot say," Shadowheart replied. "I am a disobedient and reckless angel, not much in Heaven's favor at the moment. Yet I cannot imagine that two such sisters would be forever sundered."

"Camille is bound for Heaven?" Jeremy demanded.

"She goes on the path upward. How far is for others to say, and they will not speak to those who cannot follow."

The two girls followed Shadowheart's gaze. At the top of a low hillock to the west stood an angel in white, its face indistinct. Shadowheart pointed the other way, and they saw a messenger in a gray cloak and blue hat standing on another hill, staff in hand.

"Time for you girls to go," Shadowheart said softly.

Jeremy realized that he still held his sword in hand. He sheathed it in the black leather duster as Camille and Joan embraced and wept.

"You must be brave for us both," Joan said, separating from Camille. "We shall meet again, beloved sister. I, Joan, Maid of Orleans, swear this." She turned to Shadowheart and bowed deeply, then to Jeremy. A mischievous smile broke over her face, and she stood on tiptoe to kiss him quickly. "Au revoir, mes amie."

"Bon voyage, milady. I will remember you."

Joan strode toward the messenger, head high, back straight, without looking back.

Camille came up to Shadowheart, impulsively embraced her. The angel whispered something in the girl's ear. Camille turned to Jeremy. She too kissed him, but on the cheek, a fleeting touch like a butterfly's wing. Then she ran to the waiting angel.

Shadowheart and Jeremy were alone in the endless dell.

"Can we get back?" he asked.

"I think so," she said, as she walked over and stretched out on a mossy stone, half-buried in the ground. "However, I suspect it would be appreciated in the Realms of Heaven, Earth, and Hell if you and I bided for a time in this place between the Realms, out of sight and perhaps out of mind. Don't worry, not much time will pass in the Realm of Earth, and in this place you will neither hunger nor thirst."

Shadowheart gazed up at him, her eyes direct and untroubled. She stretched out arms over her head. The denim jacket and white shirt she wore rode up, showing her flat stomach.

"Look, I think we have to talk about what happened," he said, awkward and tense. "I mean when we… when you and I…"

She looked at him, clear blue eyes over a snub nose. "Why?"

"Because we have to and…I can't have this conversation when you look like you're sixteen."

Suddenly Shadowheart lay there in her succubus mode: long red hair, stockings and garters, her waist cinched in a corset.

"Jeremy," she said, her ruby eyes lighting on him. "What happens in Hell…stays in Hell."

The End

This section is devoted to other works of fantasy I have done. As some of you know, I am the editor of and a co-author in the six Sha'Daa horror anthologies. Well, it seemed like a good idea to let one of my characters take a wander into that world. She came back with an interesting tale in "Debbie Does New Orleans."

"Death in Venice" was published in the anthology *Cities of Death* and deals with one of my favorite cities on Earth.

Finally, we have "In the Mourning," a lonely ghost tale I conceived while under the tutelage of Orson Scott Card in his Intergalactic Medicine Show. I hope you enjoy these bonus tales.

12

DEBBIE DOES NEW ORLEANS

I t's not like I'm a mean drunk," Debbie Middleton said, downing her fourth Hurricane and leaning her impressive rack on the dark wood and gold trim of the bar.

"I'm sure that's right," the bartender replied, wiping down a glass with his bar towel. The moon beamed in through the street-level windows, reflecting off his black eyes and the short dark horns that curved from his forehead. Despite the late hour, he and Debbie had *The French Casket* to themselves. The other night denizens had fled into the shadowed streets when Debbie wandered in, her helmet of bright blond hair shining, rhinestones on her denim jacket, and wearing thousand-dollar cowboy boots. She'd looked more like a country singer slumming than a vampire on a bender.

"Yep. Most people like me, goddamn it. I give them the night of their lives in exchange for some blood. All they need is a day or two of Gatorade and vitamins afterward. Haven't killed a lousy human in eighty years. Well, unless they were trying to kill me." She tipped back her drink, almost falling off the barstool. "Another."

"Careful now," he said, starting to fix another Hurricane. "It's a long way to the floor even for a short gal."

"Who you calling short?"

"Now, now, no offense meant."

"See this ring?" Debbie said, showing a gold ring mounted with a milky white crystal.

The bartender, a minor demon, raised a hand to ward her off. "Yep, keep that back, honey child. Not good for me to touch that there. Didn't think it would be good for you either."

"Like I was saying, I'm special," she slurred. "I'm so damn popular that a Knight Templar gave me this ring, a White Pass. He's pretty, the boy that gave me this. Pretty, young, and naïve. Damn." Debbie sniffled.

"Sounds like boyfriend trouble," the demon said, sliding the drink in front of her.

"Hell yes. I'm a two-hundred-year-old monster that used to kill people. He wants to go on dates. So, I'm here trying to shake him out of my blood. Well, whoever's blood I got in me." She raised her glass as if in a toast. "Damn you, Jeremy Leclerc."

The bartender scratched his chin. "Heard of him. He's bad news to our side."

"I'm a vamp," she said, "got no side but my own. Anyway, quit interrupting. Here I am, broken-hearted, just trying to have a couple of drinks and this witchy-woman tries to drive me out of New Orleans on my first vacation in years. Taint fair, I tell you."

"Still," he said. "It would have been better if you hadn't killed her. She was Baron Samedi's woman."

"Too bad, so sad. Would have been better if she hadn't driven pins into that doll she made of me. She'd have lived if she hadn't driven that one pin… Well, let's just say in a very delicate spot."

The bartender shook his head. "The Baron's going to be pissed. *The French Casket* is neutral ground. Everybody can come here. Once you leave, you're on your own."

Debbie picked up the Hurricane and drained most of it. "Honey, I been on my own since I was born in a Charlestown whorehouse."

"One hears many sad tales here," the bartender intoned.

Debbie laughed and finished her drink. She slid off the stool, hanging up the heel of her cowboy boot on the stool and nearly pitching over on her nose. As soon as she caught her balance, she gathered her remaining dignity and turned to the bartender. "What do I owe you?"

"Tonight is on the house," he said with a shrug and a toothy grin. "*The French Casket* will remember your visit. You'd best be heading underground soon. Sun comes up early in these parts."

Debbie nodded her thanks and staggered out the door into the warmth of the June evening. The streets were still full of revelers wandering about the never-ending party of the French Quarter. She reflexively eyed some of them but felt no need for new blood. She was still full of the life force of Rascatal, Witch Queen of New Orleans, and likely wouldn't need to feed for a week. But as she scanned the crowd, she noticed a tall, lean man standing just beyond the pool of light cast by an ornate streetlamp, watching her.

Her eyes glimmered a warning as she met his stare, but this merely drew a sardonic smile in which a gold tooth winked at her. Despite the heat, he wore a dark trench coat and a fedora that cast his eyes in shadow.

Debbie squared her shoulders and marched right up to the gaunt stranger, who watched her approach with no sign of concern. She stopped a pace away looking up at him; he overtopped her five foot-two inches by a foot and more.

"Hello, little girl," he said in a deep, resonant voice. Then, eyeing her, he added, "Well, maybe not so little."

"Who you with?" she demanded. "Baron Samedi?"

He chuckled and something about that made the hair on her head stiffen and rise. "No, I know him though, the Death Loa of Haiti. He considers himself among the bad and the dangerous."

"Isn't he?" she said, cocking her head.

"Not so much," he replied.

"Oh. Are you bad and dangerous?" she asked coyly.

His eyes widened into huge inky pools, and the gold tooth shone with a light of its own. As if a veil had been ripped away, Debbie now saw what he was: ancient, powerful, and infinitely deadly. She froze. Then the veil dropped and he was just a tall man on a city street. She tried to slow her breathing and thought about running.

"You're a young lady with a problem," he said, the sardonic grin fixed on his face. "You're in love."

"Am not," she returned, startled into speech.

"Are too," he returned and laughed. The laugh seemed to clear the street around them as if it had a physical force of its own. "Worse yet, he's young living human, a Knight Templar you've been helping fight the forces of darkness. Is that a sensible thing for a vampire to do?"

"How the hell do you know all that?" she shot back, too angry to be wise. "And who the hell are you?"

"I'm just Johnny the Salesman," he replied.

Debbie's face couldn't turn any paler, which was good, but the last remnants of her drunk fled in terror. "No. You're…you're a myth, a boogeyman to frighten little imps and demons."

"Hee-hee," Johnny said, and danced a soft-shoe move in front of her. "Here's Johnny! But enough about me—we were talking about you."

"What do you want?" she asked softly, knowing escape and defense were both futile.

"What do I always want?" he returned, mischief and madness in the dark eyes. "To trade and to play the Great Game of the Sha'Daa, the opening act of the Apocalypse."

"It's coming?"

"Oh, darling, it's already here. It's going to be a busy forty-eight hours."

"Jeremy," she snapped. "Jeremy Leclerc—"

"You were about to ask me if he is safe?"

"Yes, dammit!"

The sardonic smile relented some. "Oh dear, you have it worse than I thought. Well, he's young, strong, and not as dumb as you fear. The Sha'Daa will be worse in some places than in others; in some, it won't even be noticed. Who can say?"

"Damn," she swore. "Ain't you got better things to do with your time than chat up a little old country girl?"

"Time, time, time, never ask what's become of it," he quoted. "Yes, I and Santa Claus whip through little holes in time, in the pauses that refresh. But for all of that, I have time for you, Debbie Middleton. You have something I need."

"What?" she asked trying not to shiver.

"Your pretty white-stoned ring, a gift from your boyfriend to the vampire with a heart of gold. The White Pass has greater virtues than those who gave it to you know."

"Can't say I like the thought of giving it up. A woman my age doesn't get that many offers with a ring. Those old bastards Jeremy forced into it weren't that happy, even though I'd helped destroy a Bain Sidhe terrorizing rich bitches at the mall. I might not get another."

"Well, the Sha'Daa will be breaking out here in a number of particularly New Orleans ways, but I understand Baron Samedi has put all his plans on hold till he deals with the insult you did him, draining his current main squeeze dry."

"I'm entitled to defend myself, even from humans, under the White Pass."

"Which may cut some ice with the Templars but will do nothing for you with the Baron. What I have to offer may allow you to see another moonrise." He snapped his fingers, and a card appeared in them. It held the picture of a girl. Her face was covered with a tattoo of a human skull and she wore a top hat. Dark hair and eyes completed the picture. The effect of it all was equal parts horrible and beautiful.

"This is Haumea; she runs a very special tattoo parlor called *Mom's Bane.* It appears various places, various times, and time is various when you are in it. This card entitles you to her services."

"A tattoo on my lily-white skin? I don't think so. Tattoos are a long-term commitment for a vamp."

"Might make the difference between seeing the future or not. You fancy yourself a time-tourist. Be sad if the future happened without you there to see it. Then there's your beau, Jeremy. You could get back in time to help him. If you're alive."

Debbie considered. "So where do I find this tattoo-vixen?"

"The card will take you there," he said. "Just follow where it points."

She looked at the card, and the image on it looked back at her and winked. It raised a hand to give a cheery wave.

"Dammit," Debbie said, slipping the ring off her finger and handing it to him. "I know I'm going to regret this."

"That's optimistic," Johnny said. "After all, only the living have regrets." His smile widened as his image became blurry and indistinct. Finally, there was only the smile hanging in the air with its gold tooth winking. Then it, too, was gone. Debbie caught the card as it fluttered in the air.

"Goddamn Cheshire Cat," she muttered. Then, looking down at the card, she said, "Okay, Haumea, which way are we going?"

The skull-faced girl on the card gave a wicked grin and pointed left. Debbie walked on for fifteen minutes following the card's finger, like a demonic Siri, down the back alleys of the French Quarter. The very air rippled for a moment, and a short wave of nausea washed through Debbie. Instinctively, she realized she'd crossed through some kind of portal, but to where, she was not sure. Debbie finally stepped into a particularly disreputable-looking alleyway where a red light glowed in the window of a sagging, two-story building.

She looked down at the card, and the figure on it gave her a cheesy grin and a theatrical double thumbs up.

Debbie marched forward. Muggers and rapists didn't concern her except as occasional snacks, and her preternatural senses disclosed no other threat. She walked up to the door next to the window with its fringed red lamp and knocked. The door swung open, though by what means she could not tell.

Debbie entered a foyer that could have been to a well-maintained Victorian home. It had red damask wallpaper, dark wood accents, and drapery everywhere. Old paintings hung in dim alcoves with long-gone faces gazing down on her. A few well-upholstered chairs and loveseats dotted the floor. At the far end, and somewhat incongruously, was a large counter at waist-height, holding an old-style cash register.

The curtain behind the counter stirred, and the young woman from the card appeared. She was prettier in person and with a greater dignity. She towered over Debbie, and the top hat accentuated this.

Her dark shirt and jeans showed off her petite figure. She smelled and felt wrong to Debbie's senses; this was something that had once been human, but was no longer so.

"Welcome to *Mom's Bane*," she said in a voice that held the rich green tones of the far Pacific.

"I'm Debbie Middleton. Johnny sent me."

"I'm Haumea. That Johnny has been keeping me busy. Lucky for all that time takes strange turns in *Mom's Bane*. Come with me." She turned and raised the brocaded curtain. Debbie entered, and Haumea took her arm and guided her to a room to the right. This room held a bed and a chair, along with some machinery she assumed was for tattooing.

"So, you going to show me some work?" Debbie said, looking around. Surprisingly, there were no tattoo designs on the walls.

Haumea smiled. "No. Every tattoo here is unique, and I know what you will need."

Debbie arched an eyebrow. "That's a little presumptuous isn't it, missy? I think I'd like some input into something so permanent."

Haumea didn't look offended. "I'm the greatest tattoo artist in the history of the world. What I do is more than art, more than beauty— it's necessity. Or did you think Johnny sent you here for a tramp stamp? Now, please take off all your clothes. I need to see what I'm working with."

Debbie grumbled but slid out of her clothes to stand naked before the other woman, her pale body shining in the unnatural perfection of the undead. Haumea walked around her and then began running her hands over Debbie's body.

"Well, plenty to work with here."

"Yeah," Debbie said. "I'm kinda over-upholstered, especially up top. I've always envied a small, lithe figure."

Haumea nodded and placed her hands on Debbie's breasts, lifting and examining each one.

After a few seconds, Debbie raised an eyebrow. "Well, either pop one in your mouth or turn loose of them."

"Yes, yes," Haumea said. "These will do nicely."

"So thousands of men and hundreds of women have said," Debbie shot back, miffed at the casual fondling.

"But not both," Haumea said. "I think the left one. And even better, you'll heal instantly, so no time in the quick rooms." The skull-tattooed woman pointed to a wall where two framed tattoos adorned the wall. Debbie knew they hadn't been there a minute ago. On one plaque shone a Crusader cross on a shield, a symbol of the Knights Templar. The other held a stylized storm cloud, but it was not a dull gray; it rippled as if with inner lightening.

Debbie shot Haumea a dirty look. "Honey, you tattoo a Templar cross on me and I will burn."

"No," Haumea said with complete confidence, "if *I* do it, you will not burn."

"So, what then," Debbie asked, "one on each boob?"

"No. The cloud will cover the Templar Cross."

"What the hell sense does that make?" Debbie demanded.

Haumea smiled. "Perhaps it only makes sense in Hell, or the Sha'-Daa, but it was for this you were sent here."

Debbie crossed her arms, glaring at the cross and shield. "Damnation, I came to New Orleans to forget about Templars and all their crap. Now I'm going to be tattooed with the mark of one?"

"Seems to me that one has a left a mark on you already," Haumea said. "I force this on no one. But I have much to do. You must decide now."

Debbie sighed, knowing she had chanced on the battlefield of powers far greater than a vampire. She wanted to get back to Jeremy in Charlotte, but would Samedi let her slink off if she wanted to? She could hope the Sha'Daa wouldn't strike with full fury in Charlotte, a town so dull that Sherman hadn't bothered to burn it, but it was too much to hope for.

"Okay, Spooky-girl. My boobs are in your hands...again."

Debbie slipped out of *Mom's Bane* and retraced her route. Long habit made her check the sky in her first few steps away from the shop, and she froze in her tracks. The moon was exactly where she left it when she entered. There were still hours to dawn.

For lack of a better plan, she headed back toward her hotel. Her pink VW with its tinted UV-resistant glass was there. With it, she could dare running through the daylight to get home. There were no buses this early, and she simply jogged. Debbie might not be built like a marathoner, but she simply didn't tire. She stuck to shadows and reluctantly slowed if she saw people in the street. A busty woman running in cowboy boots attracted attention, even in New Orleans.

The motel she'd picked had ironically been named Knight's Rest, but it backed up to woods, which made for easy entry and exit for a woman unfazed by mosquitoes, snakes, or spiders. She'd gained a position only a dozen yards from her pink VW, when an impact from behind threw her to the ground. A hood that smelled of garlic and other herbs noxious to vampires slipped over her head. She clawed and struck and sent bodies flying, but her senses swam and faded as she was borne to the ground by still more enemies.

Debbie came to in a damp-smelling basement, her hands and feet tied and the hood still on her head, though it was pulled off a moment later. She lay in a large room with a huge pot boiling in its center over a propane stove. Around the room stood a rank of zombies, not the ravening ghouls of TV, but the revived dead, servants of the death Loa. They stared emptily at whatever they were facing.

Baron Samedi sat on a chair made of bones and glared down at her. He wore a tuxedo and top hat and a similar tattoo to Haumea, the skull over the face; maybe it was a New Orleans thing. Glasses without lenses perched on his nose, and he clutched a glass of rum in one hand and a thick cigar in the other. While he appeared to be a black male, she knew the thing before her had never been human. Two lesser and skinnier versions of himself tittered obscenely and stirred the large pot.

"I do not like you," Baron Samedi said, in a high, nasal voice, "and I like most women. But you, you come to my town. You kill my woman.

Drink her dry without so much as a by your leave. You disgrace me in front of the other demons. All my plans are on hold, as no one will follow me. No, de Baron does not like you."

His assistants shouted encouragement. Debbie remembered that they were Baron La Croix and Baron Cemitiere, both of whom might just be manifestations of Samedi himself.

"How does Maman Brigette feel about it?" she shot back.

Samedi cringed and looked around at the mention of his wife. "Nary you mind that girl. You should be thinking about your ownself."

"So, what can I do to make it up to you?" she said mock-sweetly.

Now he smiled. "Ah yes, we come to it. You will bargain with me, yes?"

"I might."

"Oh, I think you will." His gaze drifted to the boiling pot.

"Or what? I go in the pot? Wouldn't that be a waste of a truly magnificent pair?"

The Baron laughed. "Sorry, no. Breasts are for babies. De Baron likes de booty."

"So sorry I ain't a Kardashian."

"The pot isn't for soup, vampire. It's a special solution that can shrink anything to the size I want." He jingled a necklace made of tiny human and demon skulls. "Wouldn't affect your kind anyways."

"But as to you. Too many have heard of how you have disgraced me. You, who work with the Templars to thwart our own kind. Many know of you. Having you serve me will give me great face," he said, spreading his big hands. "So, you will swear an unholy oath to me, slave your will to mine, just as these do." He gestured with his cigar at the cordon of zombies. "Then you will kill the Templar, Jeremy Leclerc, and bring me his head. I will shrink it and wear it for a pendant."

Debbie expressively and exhaustively told Samedi where he could insert his own head in a location that it would be forever safe from daylight. He listened, visibly impressed. "Now dat is some fine cursing," he said, sipping his rum. "But enough of your sass, girl. You join my crew or you burn, vampire."

"Go to hell," she said.

"Been there," he replied. He looked at his lesser incarnations. "Okay boys, take her outside." Zombies lurched into motion behind the lesser barons. Debbie kicked and struck as best she could with her limbs bound; the ropes were bespelled or she would have snapped them. But despite her struggles, she was borne out, mercifully still in full darkness and down to the shoreline. There she was chained between metal poles and spread-eagled on the ground.

"Ah," the Baron said, "so much to do this night. Can't even take time to enjoy a woman. The Sha'Daa is a harsh mistress. But you will not have long to wait. The sun rises soon. Come, boys, we have potions to brew and invocations to make before we leave for the front."

He drew a deep lungful of cigar smoke and blew it out. "Last chance to reconsider."

Debbie ignored him. He shrugged and gestured to his followers. "Have fun working on your tan. It gonna be a cloudless day."

The Baron and his followers, little fonder of the sun then most night creatures, headed back to the cellar they'd emerged from.

Debbie threw herself at the chains, but they were heavy and sound. She might wrench the poles out of the ground in time, but already the sky was growing pink. The rosy-fingered child of Dawn reached over the horizon with a hand that would take her out of this existence. She sighed as the rim of the sun appeared. "Well, well, so this is the end. Two hundred and seven years. Not a bad run. Some loving, some hating, seen a lot of life and too much of death."

Hot tears spilled down her face, surprising her. "I didn't think," she said to herself, "it would hurt this much to go. It ain't the pain, though that will be bad enough. It's all that future I ain't gonna get to see."

The first rays of the sun struck her, with the warning of the agony to come. Suddenly she felt something a stirring in her body, almost sexual in nature. The tattoo on her breast was glowing; its gray lit more each second from within. Then it was gone. In its place was the shining whiteness of the shield with its red Templar cross.

Debbie wondered how she was seeing anything and then realized that she lay in the shade. Above her was a thick cloud, not covering the horizon but throwing a deep shade in every direction for a thousand yards. Beyond it, the sun slanted down its golden rays into the world.

"Well, I'll be damned." She looked back down at her breast and the Templar shield was also gone. Then she realized that the shield was lying next to her, on the chain that held her right arm. The chain was softening, glowing as if under great heat. She pulled her arm free as the chain melted. This shifted the shield to reveal a sword under it, similar to the one Jeremy bore, but without its magic gem in the hilt. She placed the shield on the other chain and in minutes was free.

Debbie stood in the shade of her own personal cloud and hefted sword and shield. Step by booted step, she stalked toward Samedi's cellar.

Maman Brigette rose from her rocker and opened the door to her big old house in the swamp to an imperious knock. She looked down at the small, busty woman with her bright blond hair, who held a rum cask under one arm. Her aura was that of the undead.

"What is a vampire doing in daylight on my porch?" she demanded, then glanced up at the sky. "Where has the sun gone?"

"You Maman Brigette, wife of Baron Samedi?" the blonde asked.

"Wife," she replied bitterly. "Yes, of that no good, womanizing, cheating, damn…" She went on for a minute.

"Yes," the woman said, "that's the one. Well, good or bad news, depending on how you feel about it. I'm Debbie Middleton, vampire, sometime good girl. I drank his mistress dry; he came after me. That put me in a pickle." She offered the cask to Maman. "So anyway, I dumped him in a vat of head-shrinking super potion and then pickled him. He's too hard to kill, but he's out of it for now."

From inside the cask, a tinny voice cursed furiously. Debbie shook the cask and it subsided.

Maman stared at Debbie. "How did you find me?"

"I gave his two minions a choice of death or a ten second head start. It worked out for one of them."

"Which one?"

"Damned if I could tell them apart."

"I like you, little girl," Maman said. She tucked the cask under one beefy arm. The high-pitched voice began again. She struck the top of it with a resounding thump. "You shush now."

Maman turned back to Debbie. "How about you come in for some nice iced tea?"

"Sorry," Debbie said. "I have a hot date in Charlotte, North Carolina."

"You be safe then. Roads not good just now." She looked back up at the one vast cloud on the otherwise sunny day. "Damnedest thing."

"Ain't that the truth," Debbie said, with a bright smile as she turned for her little pink VW.

The End

13

DEATH IN VENICE

Death walked up to the maître d' at the entrance to Il Marinaio, a small restaurant off the Rio De Trasti, but well known in certain circles. The restaurant backed up to the canal, embracing it in a series of terraces. The man stood frozen in place as the tall, shrouded figure advanced on him, soundlessly sweeping up the broad, flat stairwell, a scythe on one shoulder. Despite the heat of an unusually warm September evening, the maître d' was pallid and sweating.

"Do not worry," Death said in his whispery voice. "I'm not here for you."

"Grazzi, Mio Signore," the maître d' managed. "Mille grazzi."

"Enough of that," Death ordered. "Groveling does nothing for me. I'm here tonight to meet an old acquaintance, one who has sought to escape this meeting for 177 years. Pauline Altiera has a reservation for one for nine o'clock at the little table in the alcove over the canal?"

"Si, Mio Signore," the maître d' said. "As she has every year."

"A regular habit, unusual and unfortunate. Seat me there. I will wait for her."

"Si, Mio Signore, but the other customers, won't they—"

"No one shall see me, or if they do, they shall see only a handsome man sitting with what appears to be a pretty lady. I appear to you only as a courtesy as I do not wish to be disturbed."

"All shall be as you wish," the maître d' stated, trying to still the shaking in his knees and wondering if he had already departed the land of reason and science for the country of madness and death.

***

At ten minutes to nine, a tall red-haired woman in a fashionable black dress appeared on the bridge leading to IL Marinaio. She walked up to the maître d' and nodded without actually looking at him. The maître d' led her past other couples with their candles, delicate glasses of wine, and tinkling laughter to the small, isolated table on the terrace that jutted over the canal. If she noticed that the maître d' was taciturn and that his hands shook as he pulled out her chair, she said nothing.

It wasn't necessary for her to see a wine list; every year the bottle was the same, a Bardolino from a small village in the hills. The maître d' had opened it and placed it on her table, waiting for her. He poured it as the elegant woman brushed the dark red hair out of her eyes. He lit the candle with still shaking hands as she lifted her glass and drank from it. She settled back into her chair with a sigh, her eyes only for the canal outside as he slipped away. A gondola slid by; a pair of young lovers embraced in its seats. The gondolier sang softly as he poled.

Suddenly a man stood at her table. He was tall, blond, and good-looking, wearing a formal suit that was an excellent complement to her dress. He pulled back the chair opposite her. "May I join you, Paul?"

Perhaps her hand trembled the tiniest bit as she put the glass down and raised her eyes to Death's more pleasant incarnation. But she knew him as Death, as do all humans who see the Lord of Darkness. With the air of someone long resigned to face something, she said, "I am sorry, Signore, but my name is Pauline."

"Is it?" Death said, sliding into the chair.

"I usually dine alone on this night," she added.

"Because this is your birthday, Paul," Death said, "your private celebration of having outfoxed me for another year. And you have been a sly old fox, haven't you?"

"Vixen," she corrected.

"How long is it since you were born in the Navajo country of New Mexico, Paul? Is it 177 years? How long since your mother made that deal with the last of the true medicine men? The deal that let you run, unseen by me, so that so long as you left no mark, no record, so long as I, operating in the world of men and bound by its rules, could not find you, that you would live?"

"Fascinating story," Pauline said. "Do you write in your spare time?"

The maître d' appeared with a second glass, which he placed in front of Death. Pauline did not spare him a glance, nor a harsh word for his betrayal.

Death reached for the bottle, but she waved him off and took the bottle in one elegant hand. "It's bad luck to pour your own."

"A Japanese custom," Death said with a smile. "You were Japanese for quite a while, hiding out in another race."

"Don't be ridiculous," she said, replacing the bottle. "I'm five foot-ten, red-haired, and green-eyed. How could I be Japanese?"

"Oh, Paul, you are so malleable. You've learned every trick of disguise and artifice. You are brave, too, all those horrible surgeries to make you taller or shorter. It helped that you were part Mexican and with minor work could pass for Japanese, especially with contact lenses.

"But year after year, country after country, name change after name change, you felt me closing in. Didn't you?"

"What nonsense," she sighed. "Death finds all men wherever they are."

"Not always. Shall I tell you why?"

"Well, if you must, you must, but you are ruining my birthday. So, tell me, why would I be an exception if I was were this Paul?"

"Even Death needs a challenge once in a while," Death said, raising his glass in salute. "A reason to get out of the crypt in the evening. Sometimes a bit of magic left over from the beginning times manifests and a human is given special powers to defy me."

"I can see what's in it for the huntsman, but what does the vixen get out of all of this?"

"Oh, there must be a prize; otherwise this would simply be too cruel. My quarry ages very slowly while the chase is on. Not only am I limited to the tools and devices of men in searching for you…for Paul Altiera, but if I place my hand on the wrong person believing it to be Paul, he escapes my dominion forever. Immortal."

"Are you prepared to put your hand on me and claim that I am this Paul Altiera?" Her eyes glittered. Looking at them closely, Death could see the fine wrinkles of age, cunningly masked, the work of the best surgeons making Pauline look younger. The body, too, had been worked on; no middle-aged woman had breasts that firm and high.

"Not just yet," Death said. "Tell me Paul…well, Pauline for now. It was brilliant this last time, hiding in a different gender. But tell me, was it worth it? All these surgeries, the pain, the mutilations? How much of the original you is even left? You've never married, never had a child, never stayed with any woman or man long enough. Was it worth it, just to avoid me?"

"My father used to say that *in life there is pain and suffering but in death there is nothing.*"

"That would be your father, James."

Pauline smiled and drained her glass. "I lied. I never knew my father." She gestured at Death for a refill, and he poured for her.

"You know I almost had you in Bergen-Belsen."

"Horrible place." She shuddered. "Nazis."

"You remember it then."

"I watch *The History Channel* on American TV."

"Shall we order?" Death asked.

Pauline shook her head. "I'm sorry, but as I've said, on this night I always dine alone. Do not think me rude, but I am a woman of regular habits, and I have kept this ritual for a long time."

"Yes," Death replied. "A very regular habit and it was the only way that I found you. I have agents, oh countless agents, that it has taken me time to assemble, who are looking through the world for signs of you. Then they told me of a woman who always came to this one place on Paul's birthday. This solitary dinner is your undoing."

She shrugged. "Much of my life has been solitary, would that it wasn't so."

"It need not have been," Death said sadly, "had you been satisfied with a merely human life. I am the way out of time and space. The door to other places, perhaps better than this one. You were a fool to have squandered your whole life for this game."

Death stood. Now he was shrouded and the hand that projected from the sleeve was bony. The scythe rested in his other hand. Pauline sat frozen, staring at Death revealed. His bony hand came to rest on her shoulder. "I name you and I claim you, Paul Altiera."

A cold wind whipped up the canal. Gondoliers cried out as a skein of ice formed on the waters. Lights flickered and candles guttered. The other patrons and waiting staff fled Il Marinaio from the outside terraces.

Only Death, Pauline, and the maître d' remained. Death with his bony hand on Pauline, who was frozen, clutching her shawl about her shoulders, the candle from the table in her other hand.

It was the maître d' who broke the tableau with a maniacal laugh.

"Free," he shouted. "Free, free at last. Thank God Almighty, I am free at last." Every word he said came out in a different language but flowed from his mouth in one easy sentence. Paul Altiera had been speaking for a long time and thought in many languages.

Death stared at him aghast.

"Don't take it so hard, poor dear," Pauline said.

"But how?" Death said. "I traced you from Bosnia, found all the accounts, traced the money for the surgeries—"

The maître d' stared at him and giggled. "Pauline is my greatest creation," Paul said. "I found her in a Bosnian concentration camp. I rescued the surviving part of her family on the condition that she become my stalking horse, that she be prepared to face Death in my stead. I pinned the few scraps of my identity to her, knowing that eventually one of your agents would come across them. We faked her death, not even her children knew.

"She and I had every surgery together, only I had the one to reverse it. She became taller, I stayed short. I changed genders and back. I knew that someone celebrating my birthday, every year, in the same place would draw you to this day…you would come and…I…would be FREE!"

Death raised his scythe in wrath. All through Venice people felt sickened and weak, but only for a moment.

Defeated, Death sat back at the table, again in his guise as the handsome man. Pauline replaced the candle on the table. The temperature rose to normal, and the skein of ice began to crack. People still shouted in confusion, but their voices faded. Somehow, they knew that this part of Venice belonged to dark forces tonight.

Paul glared at Death as if daring him to break the covenant.

"Go, Paul," Death said in a mild tone. "Live free of me. Just remember should you wish to invite me back, as the long years mount up to millennia, stand in the dark of the moon and call for me. I will hear you."

"Never," Paul screamed. "Never. I am free." His eyes rolled back in his head. He began to laugh wildly and tear at his clothes. He fled the restaurant, racing into the darkness of the Venetian night.

Death looked at Pauline. "You suffered much to protect Paul."

"He got my daughters out of the Bosnian camps before they were raped. One is a doctor now. The others are married with children of their own. Every year on this day, money arrives at their homes and will for as long as they live."

"Interesting. Of course, you realize I must punish you. I am Lord Death; I cannot be made sport of."

"You were not," she replied. "This was a desperate battle, right up to the end. But I do not plead with you. I lost my husband and son in the camps. Paul did not find me in time to save me from the Commandant's men." Pauline sighed. "Poor frightened Paul, so very afraid of you. He was a good little man. Maybe someday he will be sane again."

"To fear me too much or too little is the same sin," Death said.

She smiled at him. "I'm sure you are right. Well, before you take me—shall we at least finish our wine? Though its flavor will not be better for the chill you threw into everything."

Death laughed a huge rolling laugh. All the cats of Venice fled, dogs quaked under their master's beds, men cursed, and women prayed that this strange night might end.

"You know," Death said. "Perhaps I should take a holiday occasionally. Venice is lovely this time of year. Will you relent in your reluctance to have a dinner companion?"

"Yes," Pauline replied, but she bit her lip. "It would not be very lordly of you to toy with me. On the matter of my punishment…"

"Oh that," Death said. "Well, it does even the best chess player some good to lose occasionally. Reintroduces zest into the game. Really it was quite well played, particularly by you. I admire sang-froid.

"So, shall we say that you shall live for so long as you do not leave Venice? Rise or fall, your fortunes will mirror that of the city."

"Well, it could be worse," she agreed. "You could have confined me to New York."

"Even Death has some scruples, my dear."

The owner of the Il Marinaio peeked out from the interior, apparently astonished at the sight of the tall handsome man and the elegant lady still at the table high in the back. He looked for his maître d' but did not see him. Finally, he grabbed two menus and walked up the small stairs to the terrace.

In the distance, as if in defiance of all dark things, a gondolier began to sing.

The End

14

IN THE MOURNING

ohn Townsend walked through his new condo, picking up beer and soda bottles and the rounding up the last of the pizza to stick in the fridge. He was alone again. His friends had come over, as they often did on a Saturday night, to watch an old SF movie, talk, and play some cards. He knew he should count himself very lucky. Many people treat death like it's contagious, fleeing the proximity because they don't know what to say, or they're simply afraid. Since Elizabeth's death, John lived in a twilight world where he no longer had to be anywhere or do anything particular.

God, I miss her, he thought. Their friends, well-meaning and kind, had wanted him move on. It'd been over a year. He'd quickly found that he couldn't stand to be in the home they'd made for so long. So, he moved into the condo, in downtown Charlotte, a place that didn't require a woman's love of her yard, didn't require anything from him.

"You've got life left in you, John," Sam had told him last night. "You look young for your age; you've got money. Elizabeth wanted you to live as best you could. Be as happy as you could be. She told you that. She told all of us that."

"Did she tell you how?" he'd demanded.

Good old Sam's face fell.

"Thanks, Sam," John had said, punching him lightly on the shoulder. "I may be only fifty-eight, but I spent thirty-five years married to Elizabeth. Don't know how I could get used to anyone else."

John put the pizza in the fridge then looked at a picture of him and Elizabeth on the fridge. She wore jeans and T-shirt. He was in fatigues. He hadn't reenlisted; they'd gotten tired of bouncing from base to base. Now, he couldn't remember where the photo had been shot.

John walked back into the living room to face the glowing screen of his laptop. The words of his latest story glowed at him with an unfulfilled promise. He'd looked forward to writing, now that he'd made his money and gotten out of the rat-race. But words weren't coming tonight.

Email was empty, so he idly flipped to a folder full of digital pictures, some of the last they'd taken before Lizzie got sick. He'd gotten out of the habit of getting photos printed. They just piled up on the hard drive and now he was in terror of losing any of them. So, he'd begun backing them up and filling albums.

As he opened a folder from their last vacation, an image jumped out at him. The photo showed a slim girl in a floral dress, not quite grown into the prettiness of the woman she'd be, standing on the stairway in the Music Room at Old Beech, the girl's school Elizabeth had graduated from before they'd met. The original photo had been small and the color poor, but she'd cleaned it up so he could see the tousle of blond hair, the slightly crooked nose, the nervous smile. She'd always hated being photographed. But this was an Elizabeth he hadn't known.

One of the few disappointments in her life had been in music. She was good, had talent on the flute, but she'd started late. Her parents thought it a silly thing for a girl to study at school. Old Beech taught her how to play, not how to make a living at it. She'd always kept her hand in, playing in the local symphony, but he knew that that untraveled road always beckoned in her mind.

"What the heck?" he muttered. He checked the detail screen to discover she'd added it the day after they went to the doctor to learn that it was cancer and not a cold making her cough.

Why was she looking at this one? he wondered. She hadn't mentioned it. Elizabeth rarely bothered with computers. Usually she asked him to do anything she needed. Yet she'd taken the time to find this image and clean it up without his help.

It meant something. But hours of staring at it put him no closer to a solution. He fell asleep by that laptop.

Morning brought back pain and a plan.

John packed and began making arrangements. The first thing was a call to Sam.

"John? Why are you up with the chickens?"

"Hey, Sam. I've decided to leave town for a couple of weeks."

"What gives? Everything okay?"

"Yeah. I have a hankering to see some of the places Lizzie and I lived. Some of the places we went. You know after a while, it's…well it's hard to see them as clear as you'd like in your memory. I can't remember what that street in Ocracoke looked like. Remember the little shop that Tammy and Elizabeth found? The one that sold pastries?"

"I do. Those were good times. But hey, buddy, should you be doing this by yourself?"

"Ah, I'll be fine. Can you look in on my place, take in the mail?"

"Of course. Check in by phone or email every few days."

"Sure."

"I mean it," he said. "You let me know how you're doing, or by God, I'll get Tammy and we'll come after your ass."

"Well, you I could handle," John said, " but wouldn't want Tammy mad at me. I'll do it."

With that taken care of, John raced around, getting ready for his trip. Pulling out of his day-to-day life took frighteningly little effort. Three hours later, he was down in the van heading out.

John made his way out of town, stopping first at their old house in Raleigh; the next day he drove to Fayetteville, a home from his Army days. He found the old pastry shop/art store in Ocracoke on the Outer Banks the day after that.

Being in those places had brought him a measure of peace that had eluded him since cancer took Elizabeth. It had been only four weeks from diagnosis to the pneumonia that had stopped her heart. A mercy in a small way as there was no treatment and she hadn't suffered the way many did. The last two weeks had been in a coma.

Walking down the streets they'd walked, seeing a house they'd lived in, left him with ineffable sadness, but he no longer felt like he wanted to kill someone, something, anything.

After Ocracoke, he turned north; it was time to tackle Old Beech in the mountains of Virginia. Time to find that Elizabeth, the one he'd never known, in the place he'd never been.

John finally turned onto Route 60 and traveled the few short miles up to the school. The afternoon was waning as he turned up the hill, under immense trees. Elizabeth would have known what they were. They were just trees to him. John pulled up in front of a rambling, red-painted Victorian building. It seemed to go on forever on both sides. A couple of college kids wandered about. The school was co-ed now. God, how young they looked to him.

Mr. Pelton, an assistant dean, listened to his story with interest and sympathy. John made sure to shave close and wear a suit today. *So long as you're in a suit, you don't scare people,* he thought. After Pelton photocopied John's driver's license and credit card, he let him stroll around.

John wandered over to what had been the stables. Elizabeth had ridden there, but the stables were gone. It was a sports arena now, so there was no peace, no feeling of connection there.

He headed over to the music hall. It was the same old building and fortunately still open. John walked in to a wide echoing room with a piano, stands, and chairs. At the far end was a staircase with a wide, dark, heavily-carved banister. John held up the photo. He'd found the place.

Slowly he walked over, his footfalls echoing in the space. He was glad no one else was around to see the hot tears roll down his face. He stood there in the very same spot she'd stood so many years ago.

"Ah, Lizzie," he said. "How I miss you. The colors don't seem right anymore. The air sometimes seems filled with knives."

"Who are you?" a soft voice said behind him. "Men aren't allowed here, alone."

John whirled around and stared at her, and his heart almost failed him.

She stood on the stairs above him. Her blond hair fell to her shoulders as it had when he'd first met her. She wore the same floral dress from the photo, held her flute clutched to her chest in an uncertain gesture he remembered so well. Her blues eyes gazed at him with concern, maybe trepidation.

He could see through her body to the stairs beyond.

John fought against sinking to his knees, fought to breathe. *Is this how it is when we're taken? Does God send someone we know to collect us?*

She backed up a step as if frightened. "Are you okay? Should I get someone?" The voice was airy, light, lacking substance and timbre, but hers.

John drew a deep shuddering breath. "Don't be afraid." The lunacy of asking a specter not to be afraid struck him. Maybe that's why he didn't just die then.

"Are you sure you're okay?" Elizabeth said, biting her lip.

"Elizabeth," he managed. "Don't you know me? It's me, John, your husband."

"What?" she said, offended. "Sir, you're confused. Maybe ill. You stay here. I'll go get help." She took a step and vanished.

"No!" It was too late. He sank to the floor, his back to the landing. He lost track of time. Eventually a light caught his eye. A man was walking into the next building, locking up. Quickly, John rose and slipped out of the music hall. He didn't dare get caught. If they thought there was something wrong with him, he wouldn't be allowed back.

He made it to the car. It took five minutes for him to start it. His hands shook—hell, his whole body shook.

"John," he growled, "get it together, soldier. Get it together. There's something wrong here. You gotta get back here and you gotta keep yourself under control. Something's wrong. You gotta help, Elizabeth. She shouldn't be here, not like this."

Gotta help, Elizabeth. It raced around his mind like a swooping falcon. His hands steadied, then his breath. *Gotta help, Elizabeth. Get it together, soldier.*

He started the van, driving slowly. There had to be a motel or something nearby.

In the morning at the Motel 8, it all seemed like a dream, a lonely man's brokenhearted dream. Maybe what he needed was a shrink, John thought. He also thought about finding a bar last night but didn't dare introduce alcohol into the equation. His grip on the world was too weak to trust it.

John thought about stopping into a church, but he'd never believed God answered prayers. He thought God was there, but he'd never felt God intervened in the space-time. What was God, a plumber who couldn't do the job properly the first time? Did he have to run around fixing leaks with miracles? No, if God answered prayers, he'd have saved Anne Frank.

He couldn't turn to God. John was still in a rage at him over losing Elizabeth anyway. Maybe God didn't answer prayers, but John hoped he heard curses.

Yet for all the doubts, John knew he couldn't leave. He hadn't dreamed it. At the very least, he needed to return to the hall. But first John needed to know more.

Elizabeth's school records were all on file, though it took a while to pull them up. John insisted on paying for the time and the help. He needed the school on his side. They even gave him a little room to work in after he told them he was thinking of writing a coffee table book on the school. He had a few publication credits; it made for a decent cover. Left to himself, John pored over the records, searching.

Then it hit him. Her last semester before graduating, she'd had a music class Monday, Tuesday, and Wednesday from five to seven. He racked his brain. Yes, it had been near sunset, near seven p.m. when he'd seen her. He looked at the desk clock, it said four p.m. Tuesday. John had forgotten the day. To a retired man like him, one was the same as another.

John gathered his material and said goodbye to the staff. Food was impossible and a drink out of the question and he died right along with the hours till seven p.m., when he walked into the old music hall. A couple of students smiled at him as they walked out. Thank God this wasn't an inner-city school up to its ass in security. No one stopped him.

He stood by the stair and waited. Oddly, he wasn't afraid. He thought of Hamlet and whether the ghost was true. Thought of a frightening Japanese movie called *Kwaidan*. A husband had faced his wife's ghost there and it had ended badly. But John wasn't afraid. This was Elizabeth, and while pain held terror for him yet, Death no longer did. The Reaper had already done his worst to John.

An image wavered and there she stood.

"Mister, are you still here?" she said. "You'll get in trouble."

He had to fight tears from my eyes. *Get it together, solider.*

"Hello," he said. "I'm sorry if I frightened you yesterday."

"You did a little. I went to get help..." Her voice trailed off. "I don't...I don't seem to remember—"

"Please don't worry about it. My name is John Townsend."

She smiled shyly, with that mistrustful look in her eyes he remembered from their first few dates. The look that said, "Are you real? Are you good? Can I trust you?" Elizabeth had little good opinion of men. She'd always told John that he was an exception.

"Are you Elizabeth Lapine?"

"You know my name?" The face clouded over.

"Your teacher, Mrs. Milton, told me."

"Oh." The clouds dispelled. He'd forgotten how Elizabeth's every thought was painted on her face.

"Are you all right?" he asked.

She hesitated. "I don't… I can't seem to remember being anywhere but here."

John sat on the landing again and opened a folder. "Would you please sit, Elizabeth? I have some things to talk about with you. I want to ask you not to be upset, or frightened, and I can stop anytime. But I think I can help you. It will require you at some point to trust me."

Elizabeth sank to the stairs, smoothing her dress over her knees. "All right."

"Do you know what year it is?"

"What? Of course. It's 1972. What kind of question is that? I mean are you sure you are not confused? Yesterday, you thought I was your wife."

"Elizabeth, please listen carefully, but don't be upset. God, I guess that's a stupid thing to say. You say you don't remember any place but here. Do you remember meeting or talking to anyone but me?"

She hesitated. "No."

"Let me tell you a few things about a woman I knew, named Elizabeth. You see, I met her in 1974. We fell in love very quickly and married soon thereafter. We lived together for thirty-five years, until my Elizabeth passed away."

She stared at him.

John slid a picture across to her. She reached for it, but it would not come off the floor. She bent down.

"That's you on this very stairwell, isn't it?"

"How did you get this?" she demanded.

"These are you later, at graduation." He carefully laid them next to her, moving slowly so she wouldn't bolt. "This is you and I when we first met, our first date at the Palms in Lexington." He laid out photos of their life, their wedding, their friends, the trips abroad.

The ghostly image wavered, then seemed to come into clearer focus. "This can't. This can't be true," she whispered.

John reached into the small blue satchel he'd brought everything in and drew it out, a flute, a Varbelli 17-hole silver flute.

"This is yours, Elizabeth. It's the one you're holding. Your initials are on it. See? You even had a pet name for it. *Silversong,* you called it. You kept it with you, always."

She drew breath in a gasp. "No…I'm…I'm dead? No! How? Why?"

"Elizabeth," he said, his heart twisting in my chest. "Why are you here, honey? How? Did I fail you somehow? What's wrong? Why aren't you in Heaven where you belong?"

He was speaking to the empty air.

Sam had called. John shot him a quick text saying he was okay, that reception was too poor to call. If he'd spoken to him, Sam would have been in his car minutes later, coming with a net. John couldn't talk to any of them, or his hold would break and he'd be done. *Gotta hold it together, soldier.*

John brought a camera with him to keep up the fiction of the book and shot enough digital for his cover until he could see Elizabeth again. The hours, Virginia Woolf, you had no idea. None.

But they passed. The sun went westerly and he slipped into the music hall, smiling at the teacher and waving his camera as she left.

He took his station at the stair. Somehow he knew the crisis was on them. Tonight would end it. John had resolved that if his death was part of it, or necessary, then that was okay too.

She appeared at the moment he expected her. Again, his heart twisted. If the damn thing worked again after tonight, it would be a miracle. He saw her face was puffy from crying. Elizabeth cried rarely, but there was no stopping her when she did.

They stared at each other in silence for a few seconds.

"You were right," she said finally. "I am dead. Oh, I can't believe it. I never got to do anything!"

"Yes, you did, baby. Yes, you did. We had those years, oh those wonderful years together. Never enough of them. There would never be enough quiet nights holding you. Never be enough time to listen to *Silversong.*

"But we did so much together. I thought you were happy. You always told me you were."

"I can't remember those things. I'm sorry, mister—"

"John, Elizabeth, call me John. I'm your husband."

"But I don't remember you. You said I lived a long time?"

"Not long enough" His throat threatened to close up. *Keep it together, soldier.* "You lived to be fifty-six."

"Why don't I remember?" she wailed.

"Lizzie."

"I don't use nicknames."

A laugh burst out of him. "Yeah, you used to hate it, but after we were married, you told me I could call you that. You said it had grown on you."

"I did?"

He nodded.

"Lizzie, what did I do? How did I fail you?"

She stared at him for a minute, then, to his surprise, smiled a little. "You seem like a nice man. Better than my mother told me I'd marry. She said I was too bossy and always wanted my own way."

"Well, you were strong-willed."

"Did we have children?"

"No, we always joked that we had hobbies, not kids. You never wanted them, and I didn't care."

"I suppose I took your name."

"No, you always kept yours. You were bossy and wanted your own way."

This time it was her turn. She laughed, and the knot in his chest eased.

"I wonder why I don't remember you. I'm not...not the ghost of your wife. I'm not—"

"You're not all of her." It hit him with a shock. "The rest of her has moved on. You're...you're a fragment of her soul. An unfulfilled wish, a regret perhaps."

She stood slowly, as did he, in an agony that she might disappear.

"I want," she said. "I want to be a musician. I want to tour the world, all the great cities. I want people to hear *Silversong* and listen as if their hearts would break."

She looked him directly in the eyes, and a chill washed over him.

"Did I give that dream up for you?" she demanded. Her image wavered.

"I suppose you kind of did," he said. "I never made you stop. But when we were first married, we had nothing. We struggled for years. There wasn't the money for you to really pursue it. After I got out of the Army, we wanted a house, a place of our own. You played on in a small way, at parties, small symphonies. Maybe if you hadn't been diverted into a life with me…maybe if you had thrown your all into it, you could have made it. I don't know, Lizzie.

"Maybe I didn't support you enough in it. Maybe I was always so goddamn practical that I never encouraged you to jump. Maybe I wasn't there enough for you."

The image was stable, staring at him with a pensive face.

"Lizzie, was I not there enough for you? Should I have done something more? Something else? Please, tell me."

She looked down at her flute.

"There's nothing I wouldn't do for you, living or dead. If my life can—"

"No," she interrupted. "Don't say things like that. I know…I seem to know…that those are dangerous things to say."

"Don't care."

"I do care. Or the Elizabeth I was to become, did become, oh, this is so confusing, did care. Or will care. But I care now."

"Do you remember me, now?"

Her image seemed softer now, a little more indistinct. "Did your Elizabeth have a special song for you?"

He swallowed. "She…you used to play 'Scarborough Faire' for me."

Elizabeth raised *Silversong* to her lips, and notes trilled out from it. He moved to sit next to her, their shoulders almost touching. If only hers were physically present to be touched. The song played and wrapped around them, sad, but sweet and so familiar. They sat safe inside of it while it played.

The last note hung in the air as if calling something. When it faded, John was looking at his love, his Elizabeth, as she had been before that last year.

"Darling John, you found something I forgot when I left, a little piece of unfinished wishing. I am so sorry. So sorry it caused you pain." Her hand reached for his cheek, and he felt the lightest touch, as if spider silk drifted across his face. "I am so sorry, my love."

"No need to be sorry," he said. Perhaps he was in a place beyond shock, surprise, or even pain. His voice sounded so calm and rational to him. "Are you all right, darling? Did I somehow fail you?"

"No, John. Never. There are things that we wish to be and to do. Sometimes we don't get to do them. Sometimes we get other better things instead, or sometimes just different things.

"This was something I wanted with all my heart and soul when I was here. I felt that I could have done it, if a few more things had broken my way. Or perhaps, if I'd had the courage to just throw myself at it, to the exclusion of all else."

"I'm sorry."

"For what? John, darling, this was about me. Not about anything you did, or didn't do. It was about something that I felt I left undone, and I guess it bothered me in a way I didn't understand."

His wife's image was clearer, still pale but he could no longer see through her.

"John, don't think I would have traded my life, our life, for *Silversong*. She was my flute and I loved her. I just loved you more."

"I miss you, Lizzie. Now that you've picked up this fragment of you, what happens?"

"I go on, John."

"I'll go with you. Nothing for me here now."

She shook her head gently. "No, my love. No long speeches, but that is not the way. There's life yet to be lived. I've gone on ahead. That's all. I can't say more. I don't know why, but I can't."

"Will you be far ahead," he asked, "when I get to come after?"

"Not far enough for you to worry, my love."

He put my hand to her face but could feel nothing to hold or to kiss. "I love you. Now and forever."

John was alone.

"Did you finish your book?" Mr. Pelton asked.

John looked over at Pelton as he closed the rear doors on the van. "Yes, I think I got everything I need for now."

"What's in the bag?" he asked.

John opened the thin blue bag and drew out *Silversong*.

"Oh, do you play?"

He smiled. "Not yet."

The End

ALSO BY EDWARD MCKEOWN

The Maauro Chronicles

My Outcast State

Against That Time

The Lost

All The Difference

When Fighting Monsters

The Shasti and Fenaday Chronicles

Was Once A Hero

Fearful Symmetry

Points of Departure

Hidden Stars

Sha'Daa Series

Tales of the Apocalypse

Toys

Inked

Pawns

Last Call

Facets

The Lair of the Lesbian Love Goddess Files

On the Case

Other Works

Knight in Charlotte

www.ingramcontent.com/pod-product-compliance
Lightning Source LLC
Chambersburg PA
CBHW060247100726
47907CB00003B/790